Savage Desire . . .

Jennifer had never known anyone like Savage. His brooding, intense manner . . . the flashes of charming boyishness that sometimes surfaced through his ruthless masculinity . . . all these things struck an emotional chord in her. She felt a powerful feeling of deep desire for him. But she felt anger, too, at the way he refused to give any sign of feeling toward her.

Did he have any deeper feelings for her at all, she wondered. Yesterday, she had caught him in an unguarded moment, gazing at her with a look of strong affection and caring. As she was remembering this now, Jennifer suddenly heard a loud crashing sound. She jerked upright in bed, her body tense. Seeing a hint of movement at her doorway, she gasped and jerked the blanket up to her chin.

Savage stood in the doorway, illuminated by the yellow glow from the fireplace. His lean, powerful body was stark naked. He stood rigidly with his legs braced apart, hands down at his sides closed into fists. His handsome face now looked gauntly masculine and menacing, his cheeks sunken, lips pressed together in a hard, unyielding line. It was the face of a jungle animal that only knew one law: the urgency of its own need.

PASSION'S PROUD CAPTIVE

by Melissa Hepburne

PINNACLE BOOKS • LOS ANGELES

PASSION'S PROUD CAPTIVE

An original Pinnacle Books edition, published for the first time anywhere.

First printing, July 1978

ISBN: 0-523-40329-1

Cover illustration by Bill Maughn

Printed in the United States of America

PINNACLE BOOKS, INC.
2029 Century Park East
Los Angeles, California 90067

To that dashing, ne'er-do-well rogue,
my one true love: Howard Broude

Chapter 1

Jennifer struggled wildly to break free from the grip of the two sweating, smelly sailors as they dragged her down the ship's narrow passageway toward the ladder to the upper deck. She did manage for a moment to break away, after kicking the bearded one in the shin. But there was nowhere to escape to. Desperately she ran back down the passageway a few paces, but then they had her again and the bearded one twisted her arm viciously behind her back, sneering, "You filthy Colonial slut," as he marched her forward.

He would have beaten her mercilessly, Jennifer thought through her agony and despair, but for the fact that the ship's captain was still standing at the far end of the passageway, stern-faced, hands at his hips, supervising her transport to the upper deck. The punishment she would suffer, she knew, would be at the Captain's pleasure, not that of a lowly seaman.

As the sailors forced her up the ladder, her eyes were stunned by the brightness of the midday sky, and her nostrils assailed by the sharp salty tang of the sea air. She had gone too far this time, she was sure. She should never have slapped the Captain. But what else could she have done? The long-faced, rough-skinned mariner had come into her tiny cabin, and this time had not stopped at the lewd verbal overtures he had made toward her before, but had become physical. He had come up to her and without any warning put his cupped hands to her breasts, over her clothes, and squeezed them tightly.

1

She had slapped him stingingly, instinctively without thinking, and that was when he had yelled for the two sailors to come into the room. "To the deck with her!" he ordered in a rage. "Bind her to the mast!" And now, as she was thrown to the wooden decking of the ship's topside, scratching her cheek on the rough surface, he came up the passageway ladder behind her and stood over her, gazing down at her with malicious, evil-eyed fury.

"Too good for an officer of His Majesty's fleet, eh tart?" he snarled. "We'll see." He yelled to his First Mate at the bridge. "Mr. Cleef, the ship's company assembled, if you please. And I believe we'll have use for your excellent right arm on a cat-o'-nines."

"Aye, Sir!" answered the First Mate, who then began shouting instructions to the seamen on the deck.

"Now, to the mizzenmast," the Captain ordered the sailors who had dragged Jennifer topside.

She continued struggling violently, small gasps escaping her lips, as the sailors pushed her back against the mast and forced her arms above her head and then behind, lashing her wrists to the far side of the thick mast that thrust painfully against her shoulder blades. Her ankles were lashed together behind the mast also, so that she seemed to straddle the mast from behind, with her body arched humiliatingly forward in front of it, her wrists and ankles tied behind it. She found herself panting and involuntarily moaning from the pain and exertion and fear of what would happen next.

The sailors, having finished their task, went to join the ranks of the ship's company, now fully assembled on the deck, staring at her in vulgar, hungry fixation. The eyes of the crew were on her voluptuous, firm, full-breasted figure, which clearly reflected her Norse ancestry. The centuries-old Viking influence was also obvious in her fair, light skinned face, with its thick pink sensuous lips, shapely brows, and overly large pale blue eyes. Her hair hung almost down to her waist in richly colored, honey-brown locks that were wildly untamed—wavy and curly both.

Several of the crewmen, Jennifer could see, were actually salivating at the sight of such beauty bound in such a degrading, mortifying way. A bloodcurdling thought crept into Jennifer's mind, terrifying her: What if they were to be let loose on her?

Captain H. C. Trevor strode up to the bridge of the *Rubiyat,* clasped his hands behind him, and braced his long legs apart. His face was seamed and craggy from decades at sea, his eyes were thin slits.

"Some of you have seen this young woman," he said, speaking loudly so the seamen he was addressing could hear him above the tumult of the sea and the wind. "She came aboard in Yorktown with her grandfather, who as you know is the Colonial traitor now gracing our humble brig. She could have stayed back, but she refused to be separated from him and insisted on coming, out of loyalty to her loved one." He smirked. "It seems she could not bear the thought of the poor elder gentleman being left alone to endure whatever 'unspeakable cruelties' she expects him to suffer in London, at the hands of us *beastly* English."

The ship's company laughed merrily at the sarcasm. They were having a fine time, being treated to such rare entertainment: a lovely, full-bodied young girl lashed straining at the mast, and the Captain breaking with his usually adamantly stern behavior to share a bit of humor with them.

"We graciously consented to bring her along," Captain Trevor continued, shouting above the sound of the wind. "Far be it from us to separate a young girl from her feeble grandfather who needs her in attendance." He began striding down from the bridge now, toward Jennifer. "But it behooves us to wonder, does it not, is this *really* a beautiful young girl, as she seems? . . ." He gave a look of mock wonderment to his appreciative audience as he continued striding forward. "Or is

3

it perhaps a Colonial soldier-spy, merely disguised in woman's clothing?"

The ship's crew broke up in wild laughter. They held their bellies and slapped one another merrily.

"It is our patriotic duty to country and crown, gentlemen, to investigate the matter fully. Do you agree?"

The air was shattered with shouts of "Aye!", "Yea!", "Investigate, investigate!" and wild, frenetic laughter. The dirty, stubble-bearded faces of the crew were animated in expectant, feverish lust.

Captain Trevor stopped directly in front of Jennifer, who had to crane her neck back painfully against the mast to see him. A tense hush fell over the ship as the Captain reached down with a crop he was carrying in his hand to the hem of her frilly, high-necked brown dress. Slowly he raised the hem of her dress and the petticoats beneath, up to above her knees. A sharp exhaling of breath and an appreciative murmur emanated from the crowd, along with several low whistles. The seamen's eyes were wide, their attention rapt.

The Captain, looking at his audience, grinned sardonically. He stuck his hand in under the hem of the dress and then let it fall back down into place, so that his hand was inside her dress, hidden from view.

All eyes were on Jennifer's wide-eyed, agonizingly expectant face now. The Captain's hand had not touched anywhere yet, it was clear. The touch would register on the girl's face when it came. Her face was taut with horrified apprehension, as she anticipated the touch, not knowing when it would come or where.

For a long moment there was no movement, no sound, no change in Jennifer's expression. Then suddenly she let out all her breath and yelped in horrified surprise, her mouth remaining wide open. The Captain's hand was still invisible from view.

Another moment of silence and stillness passed. Then: "Ohh!" she moaned, twisting helplessly to escape the hand, *Stop, please stop, ahhh!"*

"Shall we show the good seamen of the Royal Navy?" Captain Trevor asked.

"Stop it, stop it!" Jennifer screamed, squirming and twisting more wildly than ever at the hand's activity. "Not that, not that, nnooo!"

By now the ship's company had dissolved into shouting, lust-crazed animals, screaming to see, to have the girl's dress raised. The Captain obliged. With his hand that was holding the crop he raised the hem of the brown dress, and the petticoats, up to Jennifer's waist. Her gray drawers were visible, having been pulled down around her knees. The Captain's scaly hand was between the girl's slim, fair-skinned legs.

The sight lasted but a fraction of a second, and then the hem of the dress was quickly dropped and his hand removed. Jennifer was panting for breath and sobbing unrestrainedly, in burning shame and humiliation. She had never been touched by any man before. She had never been exposed to a man's eyes. And now, to be laid bare and abused like *this*, before a horde of filthy, drooling beasts!

"I believe, Mr. Cleef," Captain Trevor remarked dryly, "that she is indeed a young woman, and not a disguised soldier-spy after all."

"Aye aye, Cap'n," laughed the First Mate heartily. "Or if'n it be a soldier under disguise, then it be one *hell* of a fine disguise!"

Jennifer looked out through her tears at the assembled seamen and wondered: Was there no escape from this? The faces staring at her were grimy, sweaty, disfigured in maniacal lust. Not all of them, though. Toward the rear of the assemblage she saw the tall, black-haired man again, the one with the scar on his cheek. There was hatred in his eyes, rather than lust. Next to him stood the strong-featured, long-blond-haired man whom she had once heard speaking with a thick accent. His expression was one of disgust.

During the few times she had been allowed to leave her cabin these past days, she had been met with scorn

5

by all the sailors she passed, except these two. These two had given her strange, secret looks that she could not understand. She had not spoken to them, of course; they were British seamen, the oppressors of the Colonies, the captors of her grandfather Silas.

Her attention was quickly diverted to the Captain, who now moved directly in front of her, just inches away. He spoke in a low whisper that only she could hear: "Favor me in your cabin later, and I'll set you free."

She turned her head away.

Captain Trevor began trembling with rage, his face growing crimson. His voice was like cold, cutting steel as he turned to his First Mate and commanded, "Get her on her knees. I want her mouth yea high." He indicated the level of his belt. "And stand ye ready with your cat-o'-nines if she refuse me."

As Jennifer's arms were freed from the mast, and she was forced now into a new position, she closed her eyes tightly. There was no escape now, she knew, nothing she could do to avoid what was coming. Could she have avoided it earlier? she wondered. Could she have done anything differently during the past days and events that led up to this?

She remembered the start of it, waking in the dark of her room to the thunder of galloping hooves rending the night, coming near. This was not one rider or two, but many. She jerked on her robe and rushed into her grandfather's room. He was already up, his half-spectacles on, struggling to get a fire blazing in the living room fireplace. But there was not time enough to burn the pamphlets. There had been no warning, and now the Redcoat troops from the nearby garrison were at their door, hammering at it, demanding to be let in.

"Shall I get the gun?" Jennifer asked her grandfather, frightened.

He looked at her, sadly, and then even through his own fear and understanding of what lay in store for him, he managed to show a warm look of loving

6

kindness for her. "It's of no avail now," he said. "There be too many of them."

She knew even as he said it that his own preference was to take the musket and fight, even though it meant certain death. But the fact of her presence, and his desire not to endanger her, prevented this. Ever since her parents had died in a catastrophic fire a year ago, he had protected her and loved her and cared for her as his own daughter.

The door crashed in as the Redcoats smashed through the lock. The troops marched into the room in their heavy leather boots, bringing caked mud onto the wooden floor, looking over the place quickly, arrogantly. The leader—a thin, ugly man with a pointed nose—glared at Jennifer's grandfather, and then at her. Then he ignored them completely. "Search the cabin," he ordered his men.

There were eight troopers, and by the time they finished gleefully ripping the house apart, it was an utter shambles. They found the pamphlets which were hidden in a space behind a loose stone in the fireplace.

"Silas VanDerLind," the Redcoat officer said to him formally, "you are charged with printing and writing material that is seditious to the Crown, and being a member of the outlaw band, the Sons of Liberty, which has the purpose of inciting revolution against His Majesty King George."

Her grandfather had smiled sadly at the troop leader, and then, as old and feeble as he was, had uttered in a defiantly mocking tone, "Very majestic, is he, your King George? With that quite majestic French disease?"

The officer regarded him coldly. Jennifer thought he was about to strike her grandfather, and she rushed between them shouting no, spreading her arms to protect him.

But the pointed-nosed officer merely said, "Your reply will be noted," and then ordered his soldiers to take Silas VanDerLind away.

When the Sons of Liberty, meeting in secret, learned of Silas's arrest, they were outraged and planned a daring attack to free him from the English garrison prison, where he was being kept pending his transport to England to stand trial. But it was Silas himself, through an undercover member, who sent word back prohibiting the attack. It would cost the lives of too many good men, he stated, who would be more valuable remaining alive for the coming revolution. To sacrifice their lives just to save him would be wasteful.

Jennifer had never actually been to a meeting of the group before, though her grandfather was a founding member. It was felt that if she could not identify the members, she would be in less personal danger. Now that she was at a meeting, she was amazed at how bold these patriotic men were, speaking of an attack that would mean certain death for many of them. It was only due to her grandfather's absolute prohibition against it that the attack was called off.

Many of the men groused about the decision not to attack, but acceded to it. Dr. Kirby, though, upset at himself and his colleagues, had made the comment, "Aye, we'll be willing to turn our bellies up and not respond, if Silas wills it. But I know one man who will not abide the decision! He certainly will not belly up so easily to the maggot Redcoats!" He did not speak the man's name, but others in the group agreed. If the man had not been at that very moment off on a dangerous mission, he would have made it clear himself that he would not abide by the passive approach.

The meeting ended with the question of how young Jennifer, not yet twenty, was to be cared for, now that Silas was taken away and her parents dead. Jennifer resolved the problem by announcing to the group that she would not be around to be worried over, for she was intending to sail on the ship taking her grandfather to England, so that she could be by his side and care for him—as much as they would allow her—during his trial.

This suggestion had met with violent resistance from the men of the group, but Jennifer had always had a will of her own. And even though Silas VanDerLind himself forbade her from doing so, she still presented herself at the dock on the day he was boarded, with papers from the local commandant which she had had forged, ordering the ship's captain to take her aboard.

And now here she was, being tied on her hands and knees to the *Rubiyat*'s deck, with a powder cask being positioned under her belly to keep her torso raised high, and Captain Trevor gesturing at her position while addressing his men.

"This," he declared to the ship's company, "is a political demonstration I've arranged for you. As you know, the Colonies of late have been making noises about such things as independence and revolution. The question now is whether America will submit to the will of England." He walked around so that he was behind Jennifer, and with his crop raised her dress up to the small of her back, exposing her naked, perfectly formed derriere. Jennifer twisted at her bonds helplessly.

"We are going to demonstrate," the Captain continued, "that in cases where the question is whether the Colonials will submit to the English, the answer is that they very definitely *will* submit. Though persuasion may be necessary in some instances . . . may it not, Mr. Cleef?"

Jennifer felt strips of leather against her skin, as the First Mate placed his cat-o'-nine-tails above her naked white backside, letting the strips of raw leather dangle down so that they touched her in intimate places.

The Captain came around in front of her and moved forward quickly, so that the crotch of his britches brushed against Jennifer's lips before she could jerk her head away. There was a hard, roll-shaped swelling behind the britches. He squatted down to face her at eye level and said with sneering superiority, "Does

9

the representative of the Colonies care to submit now . . . or later?"

Jennifer looked at the mob of lusting seamen, staring feverishly at her degradation and nakedness. No, she thought through her terror and agony and humiliation, she could have done nothing differently. She had done what she had to do. And now she would take what Providence had in store for her. She hawked up all the saliva in her parched throat and spit it into the Captain's face.

"Aaarrr!" he roared, reeling backward, jerking his sleeve up to wipe his face. "Flail the bitch!" he shrieked. "Whip her skinless!"

A shout of approval rose from the seamen. The First Mate raised his whip high, the leather straps swishing up in the air, and then, laughing maniacally, he jerked it violently downward.

But the whip leathers did not slash forward. They seemed to be caught on something. The First Mate turned in startled puzzlement and saw that a strong-featured, blond-haired man had come up behind him and grasped hold of the whip lashes. A look of utter disbelief registered on the Mate's face as the blond man smashed the heel of the drawn sword he was holding in his other hand into the center of the Mate's forehead, knocking him down unconscious.

An angry roar went up from the surprised seamen, and they surged forward. But instantly a black-haired man with a scar on his cheek sprang forward with a dagger that he jerked against the Captain's throat. "Have them hold!" he ordered.

"Hold! Hold!" Captain Trevor shouted to the sailors, who stopped in their tracks only inches from the two insurgents.

"Back them away!" ordered the black-haired man.

The Captain hesitated.

The black-haired man slid the blade of his dagger sharply along the man's throat, drawing blood though not cutting deeply.

10

"Back, back!" shrieked the Captain, "yield back, you morons!"

The mob of sailors drew away from them. A few of the sailors, however, remained forward and began drawing their knives. Captain Trevor's eyes bulged. "Back, I command! Yield, halt! Sheath your blades, you vermin, you'll have me gutted!"

"Richards, Benj, Harlan," the black-haired man said familiarly to three of the knife-drawing sailors, "disarm the others. Have them up against the railing."

The Captain watched in amazement as three of the men he had thought were simply ordinary mercenary seamen, who had signed on for the voyage in port as so many mercenary seamen did these days, began carrying out the black-haired man's orders.

"Graves," the black-haired man said to another of the group, "down to the brig. Set Silas free."

"You'll be hanged for this, you pirate!" the Captain yelled at the black-haired man.

At this, the blond man, who was just finishing cutting the lashes from Jennifer and helping her to her feet, said in a heavy French accent, "Excuse me, *mon Capitaine*, but if you please, thees eez no pirate. He eez Lancelot Savage, a captain in ze American Navy."

"American Navy," scoffed Captain Trevor. "There's no 'American Navy', just a band of brigand pirates calling themselves sailors!"

"Again you make weeth ze 'pirates'," exclaimed the Frenchman, D'Arcy Calhoun. "*Non, Non.* Many years have I known Lancelot, and I say weeth sureness zat while pirates rum and carouse and wench, *mon ami* Lancelot, he eez straight like ze arrow. No fun at all. How many times do I say to heem, I say, 'Lancelot, you must relax, you must learn to drink ze wine, love ze women' . . . but does he listen? He nevair listen! Straight as ze arr—"

"Shut up!" ordered the Captain disgustedly.

The blond man sighed and shrugged. "Zeez

11

Briteesh," he said to Savage, "zay have no courtesy, no . . . how you say? . . . no sense of ze 'grace'."

Lancelot Savage stepped away from the Captain, who was now disarmed and being watched by D'Arcy Calhoun. He surveyed the scene on the deck, where his small band had disarmed the English seamen and forced them against the railings, and were now holding them there by waving about the cocked, loaded pistols they had just captured. Savage turned to Jennifer. "Are you all right?"

His voice was deep and low, and as Jennifer looked in his intense, dark eyes and at his face, which was un-believably handsome at this close distance, all she could think was that he had seen her unclothed and with the Captain's hand on her that way. She blushed hotly and turned her head away, wishing she could shrivel up and fade out of sight.

D'Arcy Calhoun laughed. "Lancelot, ze lady she eez modest. She cannot speak to you, she has not had ze formal introduction."

Jennifer had adjusted her clothing the instant she was freed and was now fully dressed . . . yet she found herself suddenly shivering violently. She crossed her arms and hugged herself to still the quaking.

Savage said to the Captain, "Take off your coat."

"I will not!" declared the Captain indignantly.

D'Arcy lowered the tip of his drawn sword to the Captain's groin. *"Monsieur le Capitaine,"* he said pleasantly, smiling, "my good friend Lancelot says you do somezeeng, you do eet. Lestwise you might lose more zan only your coat, *n'est ce pas?"*

Captain Trevor's jaw quivered with rage, but he did as he was told. Savage took the heavy blue naval officer's coat and placed it around Jennifer's shoulders. She was surprised at the gentleness with which he did it. She turned her face to glance at him a moment when he was very near, and was surprised at how much like a young Roman god he looked. He had prominent cheekbones and a fine strong nose and jaw.

12

The ledge of his brow jutted slightly forward above his slate gray eyes, making the eyes seem very intense, like lights burning within deep caverns. He had insolent straight lips, perfect for transforming into a mocking grin. The saber scar at the side of his gaunt face, near the mouth, seemed necessary somehow; without a blemish of some sort, his face would not be believable. His hair was very thick and curly and black as midnight.

"You Colonial scum," the Captain declared suddenly. "So you expect to succeed in your little venture, eh? You have my ship, yes you do, for the moment. With your four-man band of brigands, who could never run a full-rigged frigate like this if their lives depended on it! So here you are, *Capitaine*"—he spit the word out contemptuously—"in the midst of the Atlantic, with my escort vessel just knots away. You think you can outrun her, even if you *could* man the ship?" He laughed derisively and nodded to the British man-o'-war miles away on the northern horizon, which had been sailing a parallel course to them ever since they left port. "That's the *Serapis*, you fool! A triple-tier first-rater! You try to run, she'll be on top of you in minutes!

"And what if you don't run? What if you act as though nothing has happened, to fool them? Why, when they come in close for telescope contact before dusk, they'll see all's not well, and your game will be up then, pirate!" The Captain's face seethed with malice and gloating mockery. "If you plan to bring off your 'revolution' with *this* kind of patch-pocket planning, you'll be drinking English tea in the Colonies in the year 2000!"

Savage had listened patiently. Now he responded to the Captain's words by calling to one of his men. "Richards!"

"Yo!" the man answered.

"The signal."

Jennifer watched as the seaman readied the siege

13

rocket that had been brought up from the magazine, lit its fuse, and then stood far back, his face turned away as the rocket ignited and shot into the sky. It burst high up in a puff of bright orange flame, sending burning pieces drifting slowly back down to the sea.

Soon, a ship appeared on the southward horizon, sailing at full speed toward them. It was Savage's ship, the *Liberty,* responding to the prearranged signal.

"You had this planned," whispered the Captain in astonishment.

So this is the one, Jennifer thought, looking at Savage. The one Dr. Kirby said would not stand idly by and let them take Grandfather away to England.

"But you didn't plan on my forcing your hand early, did you?" needled Captain Trevor, regaining his gloating expression. "You planned on waiting until we were near Portsmouth, I'll wager, when our escort, the *Serapis*, would veer away for a new course. Then you could take my ship as a prize. But I forced your hand, didn't I, pirate, and now look what it's going to cost you." He pointed gleefully at the British man-o'-war on the northern horizon, which alerted by the sight of the rocket flare was heading at them full bore.

Jennifer wondered what Savage would do now, but her attention was distracted by the sight of her grandfather, appearing in the passageway hatch and being helped up the ladder by one of Savage's men. The old man was wearing a gray flannel nightshirt tucked into his baggy breeches. He seemed more feeble and shaken than usual as he came onto the deck.

Jennifer rushed forward and embraced him tightly, crying "Oh, Grandfather!" The old man patted her gently and said, "Now, now, Jennifer. I'm all right, I'm all right." One of his spectacle lenses was cracked, a sign that the imprisonment in the brig had not been pleasant or without incident.

When the old man saw Savage, a warm look of fondness crossed his features, but he quickly disguised it, and when he spoke his voice was scolding. "Blast it to hell, Lancelot, can't you obey an old man's simple wishes! I send word I want no rescue attempt and here you are rescuing me! Risking your men and your ship—God knows our navy is small enough—and for what? For *what*? To save the life of one old man who is on his deathbed anyway!"

Savage was grinning broadly. "You old goat, you've been on your deathbed for nigh twenty years now. You'll outlive us all."

"Very simple instructions I sent," VanDerLind scolded, his spectacles falling lower on his nose so that he had to push them up again with an index finger. "No attempt I said, to . . . to . . ."

Jennifer could tell from the tone of the old man's voice even as he ranted in mock anger that he felt warmly toward the young Colonial captain.

"—And you, Jennifer!" he continued, shifting the focus of his attack. "Can't you respect your elder's wishes when he tells you to remain at home? I tell you very specifically, 'Remain at home.' I say very clearly, 'Don't come aboard ship.' and here you are! What's this younger generation coming to?"

Jennifer could not help but laugh at her grandfather's crotchety ways. She was so overcome with joy at seeing him again, free of the brig, that her eyes began tearing.

"Oh, now, now," said the old man kindly, "let's not get femalish on me."

"Lancelot!" yelled D'Arcy urgently from the helm, where he had gone to bring the ship on a bearing that would head it toward a rendezvous with the *Liberty*. He nodded at the British *Serapis*. "She's closing fast."

Savage watched the prize British man-o'-war as it raced menacingly toward them, slicing forward through the turbulent sea. The wind was on the side of his own ship, the *Liberty*. Savage had made certain of this before ordering the signal flare. But still, even though his ship would reach them first, the English vessel was gaining on them far too quickly.

Savage turned to the English seamen being held against the railings. "I'm going to give you men a choice," he shouted to them. "You can jump overboard . . ."

The seamen, who minutes ago had looked cocksure and bold as they watched Jennifer being disgraced by their captain, now stood craven and fearful as they listened to Savage give his ultimatum. They waited in ear-pricked suspense for the second part of the ultimatum. But Savage added nothing to his statement. Spray from the waves breaking against the ship's hull splashed up on the deck as the sailors waited, tensely.

"W . . . w . . . well," stuttered one of the seamen finally, "what's the *or?* You haven't give us the *or.*"

Savage took a pistol from one of his men and leveled it. "Or you can be shot by me at the count of ten."

"That's no choice!" exclaimed a frightened, pockfaced seaman. "That's—"

"One!" said Savage.

"These here be shark waters!" exclaimed another seaman, his eyes wide with fear. The others in the group murmured nervous assent, their faces disfigured in expressions of anguish.

"Two," counted Savage. "Three."

"We'll be eaten alive! Or we'll drown!"

"Four."

"Oh, you Engleesh, you Engleesh," exclaimed D'Arcy in good-natured mockery. "You really theenk ze sharks have no standards, zat zay would want to taste salty Engleesh meat? You insult ze noble sea creatures!"

"Five."

"Anyway, ze sharks will have time for no more zan a nibble, before your Engleesh sheep stops to pick you out of ze water."

The seamen were frantic now. Several had leapt up to the railings, preparatory to jumping, but had not yet made up their minds. Others were eyeing Savage's men, deciding whether to risk lunging at them in an attempt to wrest away their leveled pistols. Panic was thick in the air.

"Six!" said Savage.

Several of the seamen jumped. Others milled around looking fearful and confused.

"Seven!"

The last of the seamen jumped up to the railing and then dived quickly overboard.

"You scum," the Captain sneered at Savage, "you'll pay for this."

"Lancelot," D'Arcy said, "I can't help but notees zat ze Captain, he ees steel here."

Captain Trevor looked surprised as Savage turned to face him. "Oh, surely you didn't mean me too?" he said.

"Eight," said Savage.

"You don't expect *me* to jump overboard? It's my ship! Why, that's unheard of, a captain abandoning his own—"

"Nine."

"But!"

"Ten." Savage leveled his pistol and fired at the Captain, hitting him in the shoulder, spinning him around with the force of the blast.

The Captain's mouth dropped wide as he clutched his shoulder, turning back to face Savage.

Savage put down his empty pistol and held out his hand to D'Arcy, who tossed Savage his own loaded pistol. Savage caught it and aimed it at the Captain. The Captain rushed headlong for the railing and without pausing leapt up on it and dived over the side.

"That'll slow them down, you think?" said Silas VanDerLind, squinting against the spray of the waves to peer at the British ship that was rapidly gaining on them. "Your idea is to make them stop to pick up the survivors, I gather."

"That's the idea, Silas. I don't believe, though, that they'll oblige." Savage turned away and began shouting orders to his men. "Richards, Harlan, prepare to lower

17

away the boat! Graves, set me a short fuse to the magazine!"

"Ze short fuse, Lancelot?" D'Arcy said, not looking at him. There was a hint of concern in his voice.

"They're closing too fast," Savage explained. "A long fuse, and they might reach it in time to snuff it out."

Savage left the forward section to go supervise the preparations.

"What does it mean," Jennifer asked D'Arcy, "using a short fuse?"

"It means someone must stay aboard ze ship, to light eet at ze very last minute." The powerful, barrel-chested blond Frenchman was unable to keep the look of concern from his strong features as he spoke.

When the Liberty was close by, Savage ordered everyone into a longboat and had them row away from the ship, while he remained aboard. They were a safe distance away when Jennifer, watching with a worried, furled brow, saw Savage sprint desperately down the ship's gangway and dive headlong off the deck in a wild plunge to the water below. He was suspended halfway above the water when the *Rubiyat*'s magazine exploded, sending shards of wood and flaming debris slicing like shrapnel through the air, accompanied by thickly billowing smoke that engulfed Savage and hid him from their sight.

No one said anything as D'Arcy and the lead seaman rowed at top speed back toward the flaming ship and the obscuring cloud of gray-black smoke. They passed planks and broken bulkheads that were still burning on the surface of the water as they came in closer. Tension and fear was almost palpable as all eyes scanned the water for sight of Savage.

"We can't be goin' in much closer, Mr. Calhoun, Sir," one of the seamen remarked nervously. "She'll go under any time now, and us with her if we're in her suction."

"Keep rowing," said D'Arcy.

Then, just as the gutted hulk of the ship began sinking into the bubbling, steaming sea surrounding it, Jennifer caught sight of him through the cloud of billowing smoke, swimming in quick, sure strokes toward them.

"There!" she exclaimed, pointing. "There, there!" They rowed to meet him, and D'Arcy helped pull him aboard. He was gasping and choking and coughing up water and they stretched him out in the boat as D'Arcy returned to his oars, shouting "Pull, man, pull!" to the forward seaman. They were safely out of the suction vortex when the British frigate keeled over to her starboard side and sank fully under the sea.

The *Liberty* reached them now and took them aboard. Cannon shells from the *Serapis* were already being fired, though falling short. Savage rushed up to the bridge, still coughing and choking, and began shouting orders to prepare the ship for battle. The *Serapis* had thrown a longboat to the English seamen Savage had ordered overboard, rather than interrupting its attack to pick the sailors out of the sea. It was charging toward the *Liberty* as fast as its billowing sails would take it.

The first shell from the *Serapis* to bridge the distance crashed now into the *Liberty* amidships, bringing down a cannon station and killing two sailors. The fire was returned. The battle had begun.

Jennifer and her grandfather were ordered below deck. They stood in the galley, listening to the thundering roar of the cannons and feeling the rocking of the ship as the noise and motion intensified more and more, and soon engulfed them totally. The incoming shots crashed on the deck above them, seemingly without letup. Shouted voices rended the air, along with the shrill screams of the wounded and dying. The ship's wooden bulkheads groaned loudly as the *Liberty* heaved to and fro. Jennifer and her grandfather had to brace themselves between two beams, standing with arms firmly out to prevent them from falling and sliding all over the galley floor with the violent pitching.

19

Suddenly her grandfather shouted to her above the din of the battle, "I'm going above to help! They need every man now! You stay here."

"Don't go, Grandfather!"

"They need me."

"I'll go too then, to take care of you, to—"

"*Stay!*" His voice and expression were absolutely unyielding, permitting no argument or appeal. Jennifer remained braced against the vertical beams and watched him as he made his way abovedecks. But then, minutes later, she started after him. He was an old man. She had to take care of him. He was all she had.

She arrived on deck in the midst of the violent tumult of the battle, with flame and crashing timber, and running, shouting men everywhere. Torn canvas sails drooped down from overhead and the sharp stench of fired gunpowder stung her nostrils. The blasting of the cannons was so loud it hurt her eardrums and made her head ring.

To her left was D'Arcy, straining with his powerful muscles and now thickly corded neck to upright a toppled cannon, his back almost being singed by a fire nearby. To her right at the bridge was Lancelot Savage, his face smudged with sweat and black powder, shouting fiercely to his forward battle station, and gesturing wildly. And looking now, Jennifer saw—at the forward battle station, helping to feed powder into the mouth of the cannon—her grandfather, his lined, old face set in hard determination.

She could make out Savage's words now, during a lull in the cannons' fusillade. "Out of there, Silas!" he was screaming. "Get the blasted hell out of there!"

Then with mind-snapping suddenness came a shattering crash and roar, the forward cannon turned into twisted, tortured metal, and the standing figures of Silas and the two other cannoneers became broken, supine forms, strewn over splintered wooden sidings.

"Grandfather!" screamed Jennifer, rushing forward.

Savage had seen the incident, but could not spare a second of his attention now. He remained on the bridge, his face locked in concentrated intensity, shouting instructions to his helmsman and his cannoneers, directing the course of the battle.

Jennifer flung herself upon the broken, bleeding form of her grandfather and wept hysterically, her arms around his waist, hugging him. "Don't leave me," she sobbed hysterically, "I love you, Grandfather, don't leave me!" There was a tiny flicker of life still in him, for his hand which lay bent near her elbow, closed upon her elbow and squeezed it softly. Then the flicker died and the hand fell away. Jennifer screamed; the sound was swallowed up and drowned in the clamor of the battle.

The *Liberty* was being decimated, suffering from an inferiority force of forty-nine cannons, compared to the *Serapis*'s hundred. She could not outrun the *Serapis*, either, being only a mid-class three-masted vessel. But during the fiercest part of the battle, one of her shells struck the British man-o'-war at the highest point above the waterline where the stern was joined to the rudder, temporarily disabling the rudder. The *Liberty* was able to sail off out of cannon range and then to head back in the direction of the Colonies.

Repairs were made, to the extent that they could be, during the voyage back, and the wounded were treated. Speed was essential, since it would be only a short time before the *Serapis* fixed its rudder and came in pursuit. Silas VanDerLind and the other dead were buried at sea, with very little ceremony.

Savage did not speak to Jennifer during the voyage back, even though she was distraught and would have benefitted by his attention. Several times when they passed in a corridor belowdecks he did not even look at her, and once on deck when they were about to pass he changed his direction to avoid having to come near her.

Was it possible, she wondered, that he blamed her

21

for . . . no, it wasn't fair! But, could it be that he blamed *her* for the battle and for Silas's death, and for the near destruction of his ship? If she had not forced him to spring his rescue attempt earlier than planned. . . .

When finally they reached the waters off Yorktown and a longboat was readied to take her ashore, Savage did not even appear on deck to watch her depart. She thanked the crew for risking their lives to rescue her grandfather. She looked again for Savage before stepping into the longboat, desperately wanting to see him one last time. He was nowhere in sight.

D'Arcy came over and said a few kind words to her and even squeezed her hand as a friend would. His brow was tightly knit and he seemed to be debating with himself whether to tell her something and possibly break a confidence. Finally, before the boat was lowered away, he leaned over to her and said quietly, "It is ze guilt. He blames heemself."

An expression of protest registered on her face, but before she could say anything, the boat was lowered and she was being rowed away from the ship to be deposited on the shoreline.

When she was several yards away from the *Liberty*, she looked up quickly on an impulse. There, standing alone at the railing, was Lancelot Savage, his face stern and emotionless, looking directly at her. When she looked back at him, he turned and disappeared from sight.

Chapter 2

In the months that followed, she wondered if she would ever see him again. Rumors drifted in from various places, telling that he had been killed during a raid on an English seaport. A traveling merchant from Massachusetts claimed to have seen his grapeshot-riddled body. A sailor just into port brought word that he had talked to an English participant in the battle and that the man assured him he had seen the *Liberty* blasted apart and sunk, going down with all hands. Other rumors claimed that he had fallen into an English trap while collecting provisions in New York and had been hanged a day after his capture.

Then, one hot day in July, the town assembly bell had rung and she had left her grandfather's cabin on the outskirts of town, where she now lived alone, to go to the assembly.

British troops from the garrison stationed in Haverston were there when she arrived, banging on the doors of the local businesses, rousting everyone who had not yet come out, commanding them to attend the meeting. The townspeople milled around in resentful curiosity, waiting for the Tory Governor of the province, who occupied a central position on the raised platform, to begin speaking. British troops stood at the front of the assembly and a few were circulating throughout the crowd, looking people over. The sun parched dirt of the square had been kicked up as the townspeople came together, creating billows of dry dust that now got into everyone's clothing and hair.

The town crier had been conscripted into service for the occasion to begin the gathering. "Hear ye, hear ye," he announced, the tone of his usually high, resonant voice reflecting his displeasure at having to lend his services to a real, if not yet formally declared, enemy. "The Lord High Governor of His Majesty's province has an announcement. All pay heed."

The Governor stepped forward as the crier quickly and with great relief left the platform. The Governor was a stout, beefy-faced man, who wore brocaded clothing and a powdered white wig. He would have been hooted and booed by the townspeople, but for the British troops that were present.

"I have good news," he began in a ponderous, dry tone. "A pirate ship calling itself the *Liberty*—a ship of the so-called 'Colonial Navy'—was discovered off the coast near New York several nights ago and engaged by our forces. She was well nigh destroyed, but managed to limp away. She's in hiding somewhere in one of the coves along the coast."

He's alive! Jennifer thought exultantly. He's alive, after all!

"Never fear, good people," continued the Governor, "for she will be ferreted out, it's only a matter of time. Meanwhile, however, some of her crew of brigands are on the loose. Most were killed in the battle, and several have been captured since in various townships along the coast. We're quite certain that the captain of the pirates has been killed, you'll be happy to know. A fusillade was seen to totally destroy the bridge during the height of battle."

A soldier walked by in front of Jennifer, slowly looking at the people he passed. He paused a moment to look at Jennifer, his attention attracted because her jaw was quivering and her facial composure seemed about to crumble. When she ignored him, he moved on.

"So this meeting is to warn you," the Governor continued, "that there may soon be fugitive pirates coming into this province. Be on the lookout. If you see an unfamiliar, suspicious face, alert the garrison duty officer. A sizable reward, I might add, will be rendered anyone who helps us apprehend these vicious renegade criminals."

He paused, and when he spoke again his voice was lower and more menacing. "Likewise, of course, a suitable punishment will be meted out to anyone foolish enough to be caught harboring any of the fugitives."

The Governor's voice droned on, speaking now about how grateful the town should be to have the protection of the British garrison so nearby. Jennifer had to turn her eyes away, look to the left, the right . . . anywhere. If she did not distract herself with new sights, her eyes might tear, she knew, and she did not want that. She was past crying, she told herself, past weakness. She had to be strong now, there was no one to look after her anymore, no one but herself.

So to prevent herself from becoming emotional, she turned her eyes away, and looking off toward the fringes of the crowd saw Lancelot Savage, standing in a stooped pose, a pained and barely conscious look on his face. Shock, joy, fear for his safety overwhelmed her at once. She stared at him, barely able to believe that it was really him. But there was no doubt, even though his perfectly handsome face was caked in dirt and the curls of his jet black hair were buried beneath a common villager's cap. He wore an old woolen coat and pants, which fit him badly. Jennifer noticed that he was not standing unsupported, but was bracing himself back against a porch beam. His eyes were cast down and his posture made it clear that he would probably faint at any moment.

What was worse, Jennifer saw with a chill of terror, was that she was not the only one who had noticed his strange posture. A Redcoat corporal who was circulating through the crowd had caught sight of him, and was now advancing in his direction.

25

Immediately Jennifer pushed her way through the crowd, toward Savage. Murmurs of protest greeted her from people she roughly shoved aside, but she paid no heed. The corporal had reached Savage already and had stopped a few feet in front of him. His hands were on his hips and he was looking at Savage closely. Savage's face was still cast down and it occurred to Jennifer that he was probably unconscious even now, as he leaned back propped against the porch beam. Otherwise he would have realized how suspicious it seemed for him to let the corporal block his view of the Governor, without at least raising his head to show he was aware he was being looked at.

The corporal stepped right up to Savage, just as Jennifer reached him, inserting her arm under Savage's to steady him, jarring him to full consciousness. Savage came to with a start, a grunt escaping his lips.

"Oh, Alfred," Jennifer scolded loudly, "a fine brother you are! You've been nipping the rum again, just look at you! What a sight you are! Wait till father hears of this."

Jennifer glanced up at the corporal and smiled at him knowingly, as if to say "Oh, you men and your liquor!" The corporal was still clearly suspicious, though. He narrowed an eye and regarded Savage carefully.

Savage raised his head now, looking into the eyes of the corporal for the first time. He opened his mouth to speak . . . *Please God,* Jennifer thought, *don't let him be too woozy to see the matter for what it is; don't let him ruin it!* . . . but instead of speaking, he let out a loud belch. Then he began to sing in a slurred, off-key voice, the words of a local drinking song.

"Ay, me bonny she be callin', ay, me bonny craves me home." He grinned foolishly at the corporal, and waved a finger to accent his slurred rhythm. *"Serve another round here, innkeep, for me ale's a lost its foam."*

The Governor had finished speaking and the assembly started to disband. As Savage began singing an-

26

other chorus, Jennifer interrupted him, saying, "Alfred, please! You stop now. There's plowing yet to be done and here you are in this condition!" She smiled at the corporal again, giving him her most endearing innocent-young-girl smile, as she put her arm under Savage's shoulder and around his back—it was clear that he could not support himself any longer—and, taking an enormous risk, began to walk him away.

There was a terrifying instant when she thought they would not make it. The corporal's hand closed over her shoulder. She stopped and turned her head back to look at him. His voice was harsh when he spoke, but what he said was, "A brew of strong tea with lemon, I'd advise. Works miracles, it does."

Jennifer smiled her thanks for the sage advice and began forward again.

"Ay, me bonny be a callin' . . ." sang out Savage as Jennifer led him away, using all her strength to support him as he limped and staggered along. Then he began coughing and drooling great streams of blood. But fortunately the British were at his back by then and could not see. When they were farther down the road, she felt his head and saw that he was feverish. She decided to take off his coarse woolen coat. When she unbuttoned it, though, and the flap came open, she saw a giant splotch of blood soaking through his shirt at the left front side. She rebuttoned the coat quickly and continued walking him down the road.

When they reached the cabin, Savage collapsed into unconsciousness on the floor before she could get him to the bed. She did not dare try to tug him up onto the bed, because his stomach wound might then split even wider than it already was. She rolled him onto his back and put a goosedown pillow under his head. She wet a cloth and laid it on his forehead, which was now burning up with fever. Then she drew all the curtains so that no one could see into the room and left to summon Dr. Kirby.

It was over an hour later when she and the doctor

rendezvoused outside her cabin after taking separate routes to avoid arousing suspicions. The doctor immediately rushed up the steps and went into the cabin. Jennifer found herself walking very slowly after the doctor and then stopping just outside the door. She could not make herself go in. What if he were. . . . His forehead might now be stone cold rather than inflamed with fever, his body could be nigh more than a hunk of dead meat.

"Jennifer, for God's sake," bellowed the doctor after a minute. "Will you get the blasted hell in here! I need you!"

She rushed into the room.

"Grab his feet," said Dr. Kirby, who now had hold of Savage under the arms and was preparing to raise him onto the bed. Jennifer put her hands under Savage's boots, lifted when the doctor told her to, and helped transfer him onto the bed. Savage coughed in his unconsciousness, spewing more blood down his chin. The doctor turned his head to the side so that he would not choke.

"Boil some water," ordered Dr. Kirby, unbuttoning Savage's coat and shirt. "Then take a clean sheet and cut it into strips."

Jennifer started away to do as she was told, but turned back for an instant. "Dr. Kirby, will he . . . live?"

He looked at her somberly. "Probably not, child."

A week later he was still alive, though he had not regained full consciousness even once. Several times he had begun babbling incoherently, and once in delirium he had tried to get up out of the bed and she had had to lay herself full on top of him and exert all her strength to hold him down. There had been a few periods when he was semiconscious enough for her to get him to swallow the broth she spooned into his mouth, though even during these he had still been delirious.

Dr. Kirby had stopped by only one time since that

28

first day she brought Savage to the cabin. He was certain the British were watching him, and he could not deliberately risk foiling their surveillance of him again. It would certainly alert them to the fact that a wounded man was in the area.

The last time he came, he had told Jennifer, "There's nothing more I can do for him. I've cleaned out his wound and sewn him up. Now it's in God's hands. Be sure to feed him broth every time he's conscious enough to swallow, and put the powder I gave you into the broth. Also, you're to bathe him every day in cool water, keep him very clean." He looked at Jennifer sternly, when a blush came to her cheeks. "This isn't a time for squeamishness, Jenny. This brave man's life depends on you."

She raised her chin petulantly. "I'm not squeamish."

"I wish I could send someone over to help you with him," the doctor said, getting up to leave, "but the group's been infiltrated, you know that. There's a Tory amongst us. And those we're certain can be trusted are under suspicion by the British, and unable to move freely. It's up to you now."

That had been days ago. Now Jennifer soaked the cloth in the cool water she had drawn from the well, and put her hand at the top of the quilt blanket that covered Lancelot Savage. She hesitated, even though she had done this several times already; she had hesitated each time then, also. It was such a strange sensation to her, laying bare the naked body of a beautiful man. Even though she told herself that she felt nothing at all, that this was purely a medical necessity and she was as impersonal about it as a physician . . . she could not help feeling a tingling surge of excitement that swept all through her.

She had never seen a naked male body before bathing Savage, though she often fantasized about what one would look like. When she saw Savage nude for the first time, the sight startled her. But more than that, it frightened her, with the *power* his maleness seemed to

.29

hold over her. It made her skin feel as if it were being pricked by needles, and she felt hot all over. And there was a quivering feeling deep in her loins. The violence of her reaction to his maleness amazed her. All this, she thought, at just the *sight* of it!

She felt guilty about the way she responded and tried to deny it, to pretend she didn't really feel these things at all. But now, as she squeezed the excess water from the cloth into the bucket, preparing to bathe him again, the tingling excitement surged through her once more, accompanied by an ache of raw sensuality that pricked her loins. She pulled the blanket down to the base of the bed in a quick, abrupt motion.

Lancelot Savage lay on his back before her, naked from his head to his toes. His tanned body was lean and masculine, with strongly muscled shoulders and arms. She washed his arms with the cool, moist cloth, then his broad shoulders and his chest. She washed him down his lean flanks, taking care to apply very little pressure when passing the cloth over the stitched-up wound on the left of his flat, hard stomach.

She tried to keep her eyes averted when washing him down lower, but it was impossible to do a good job that way. So she made herself look at his sex as she washed him there. It was long and thick and clean-looking, surrounded by a jungle of softly curling hairs. Her chin was raised up high as she washed him, as proof to herself that she was divorced from the situation, was simply doing what must be done. The quivering in her loins intensified.

When she finished, she swung out the cloth and put it on the edge of the bucket, grasped the top of the blanket and pulled it up to his chin. It was then she saw that his eyes were open and that he was looking at her. She jumped back in consternation, a short yelp of surprise escaping her lips.

Savage grinned.

Jennifer found her voice. "I . . . I hope you don't think I was . . ."

30

He grinned more broadly.

She was flushed and burning with embarrassment "Really! I was just—"

"How long have I been here?" he asked, his voice soft and low and manly.

"This is the . . . uh . . . seventh day."

"Have any of my men escaped the British?"

"Some have, they said. I . . . I don't know how many."

Savage tried to push himself into a sitting position and winced against the bolt of pain that greeted his efforts.

"Careful!" Jennifer exclaimed, coming forward automatically, then stopping herself and stepping back a pace.

Savage continued wincing, but finally he managed to sit up, his back braced against the bed's strong oaken headboard. The sheet had fallen down to his navel. Jennifer turned her eyes away. Savage seemed sensitive to her feeling of embarrassment, not at seeing his stomach now, but at his knowledge that she had seen much more than that. He made no joke or reference to the fact that she had been bathing him. Instead, he said, "Thank you. I'd be dead now if not for you."

Jennifer stood about fidgeting. She felt very nervous, now that she was alone with him in his fully conscious presence. She went to the fireplace and began fetching a bowl of broth from the hanging pot. "How do you feel?" she asked him over her shoulder.

"I wouldn't care to wrestle a grizzly bear just yet."

"Your fever broke last night," she said, bringing the bowl. "You'll be getting better now." She sat down on the chair next to the bed and, out of habit, prepared to spoon the warm bouillon into his mouth. Then she realized what she was about to do and handed him the bowl and spoon instead.

"What's this?" he asked.

"Venison broth."

"There's no venison in it."

"You've been sick," she said, flustered.

"Yes, but still there's no venison in my venison broth."

"Well . . . well, you've been sick!"

"Meat and potatoes," he said. "That's more to my liking."

She sputtered for a moment not knowing what to say, feeling very flustered and then finally exclaiming, "What gall!" She stood up from her chair. "You couldn't hardly swallow! I had to . . . to pry open your mouth and *spoon* in the broth! To wipe your chin when it all came dribbling down! I didn't know from minute to minute if you would live or die . . . each morning I'd wake and be afraid to look at you for fear you might have turned . . . turned stiff and . . . and now you have the *audacity* to criticize my broth, just because there's no . . . because . . ."

She saw that he was grinning again and she stopped short. She began pacing about the room, stomping almost. She should never have started this, she knew, it was too hard to hold back once started. To show that it was all right, that everything was really all right, she tried grinning too . . . but the grin turned sour on her face and suddenly her eyes were watering.

This was the first crack in the wall of unfeelingness that she had forced on herself all these past days. The crack widened and suddenly she was shuddering and weeping uncontrollably, as all the anguish and misery and loneliness of the past days of not knowing if he would live or die, and the past months without Silas, poured out through her for the first time, racking her body in violent shudders and an unstoppable torrent of tears.

"Come here," Savage said gently.

She remained standing in the center of the room, weeping violently.

"If you don't come here, I'm going to go to you," he said.

She put up her hands to wave him away, to make

him stay back, and she made no movement to go to him. How could she go to him? How could she let herself break down in front of this man who really was a stranger to her? She had to be strong, she had to be proper. What would he think of her? She had to show him that in spite of her bathing him, in spite of what he had seen of her naked body on the ship (Oh, God!) in spite of how he had seen her degraded on the ship (Oh God, oh God!) . . . in spite of all that, she was still proper, she was not some *slut*, some *hussy*, she had to show him she was not some brazen . . . some . . .

He was getting up out of bed, his face reddening with the great strain. Instinctively, she rushed to him to force him back, to stop him from bursting his stitches. And he grabbed her as he fell back against the headboard, pulling her to him. She tried to jerk away, but even in his weak condition he was too strong for her. "I'm not like that!" she cried, trying to pull away. "I'm not like you think!"

But he did not try to kiss her or anything of that nature. He seemed to understand, to comprehend her feelings of shame and embarrassment, and he wanted to let her know that it was all right, he did understand.

He put his arm across her back and pulled her so her head was against his chest and his arm around her. And he held her there, though she tried to back away from him, and he said, in his soft, manly, gentle voice, "Jennifer . . ." That's all he said, nothing more. He said "Jennifer" as she cried and tried to break free, and he stroked her long brown hair, and he held her. And after a while she stopped struggling to break away and she let herself be held, feeling his strong arm across her back, his hand gently stroking her hair.

"Jennifer," he was saying, as she cried brokenly, shudderingly, her face against his chest. As she let the months of pain and misery and loneliness pour out of her. "Jennifer, Jennifer, Jennifer . . ."

33

Chapter 3

Because of the tender way Savage treated her the day he came out of his coma, Jennifer expected feelings of closeness and caring to blossom between them. She soon saw that she was to be disappointed. Though at first he was gentle with her and treated her with growing affection, as the days wore on an uneasy sense of tension developed between them.

It began with Savage's eyes. They were always watching her—with a dark, brooding intensity. She would wake in the morning, dress, and go into the room that had been Silas's, and there he would be, leafing restlessly through Silas's printed books or simply scowling at the torture of his inactivity. He would brighten at the sight of her and demand that she sit down and talk to him.

But then, when she did so, she would find that his eyes inevitably began wandering down to her bosom and hips. He would stare at her with cold, keen absorption. Jennifer always turned her eyes away when he looked at her this way. And she always felt a strangely thrilling sensation, knowing his eyes were on her.

Once he became able to leave his bed and move around, Jennifer began to feel threatened. In his every movement and action, she sensed a smoldering intensity that ran through him, a throbbing violence which lay just beneath the surface, ready to burst forth at any moment. Their being cooped up together in such close physical proximity only made the situation more explosive.

Jennifer made a point of always being fully dressed when she was in his presence, never in a robe or nightgown. And now that Savage was well enough, she insisted that he too be properly attired whenever he left his room. Savage respected her wishes, but at the same time he took pleasure in mocking her insistence on prim, proper behavior. As he had done this evening.

He was passing through the kitchen doorway after dinner, just as Jennifer was about to go through in the opposite direction. Instead of stepping aside, he flattened himself against the side of the doorway and grinned tauntingly at her.

She could have simply waited him out, but that would have given too much significance to the situation. It would have been an open admission that she was fearful of the way her physical closeness was affecting him. So she turned sideways and went through the narrow doorway, the bodice of her blue, high-collared dress unavoidably pressing tightly against his chest as she passed.

She turned her eyes away demurely, so she would not have to see his taunting expression. But when she glanced back, she saw that instead of a taunting grin, his expression was one of tense, agonized frustration. His face was sweating and his eyes were on fire. His attempt to laughingly flaunt her concern at their physical closeness had backfired on him; he was being tormented by the very closeness he set out to flaunt.

His tense look of agonized frustration lasted all the rest of the evening and Jennifer sensed from it that he was on the brink of losing control. This frightened her. Finally she went to bed early to get away from him, to remove her body from his sight so that she would not torment him further—or tempt him. Savage went to bed soon afterward.

Now, as she lay in her chilly, dark bedroom, the only illumination coming from the yellow glow of the living room hearth, she found herself tossing and turn-

35

ing, unable to get him out of her mind. She listened to the crackling of the fireplace logs, thinking about Savage lying only a few feet away in Silas's room. There were no closed doors between them. The doors were kept open all night to allow the banked logs from the hearth to make a feeble attempt at warming the chilly rooms.

The memory of how she had brushed against Savage in the doorway earlier was still vivid in her mind. She tried to fight down part of the memory, but it was impossible to deny it; her nipples had gone hard the instant her breasts came into contact with his chest, their bodies separated only by the thin layers of their clothing.

Jennifer had never known anyone like Savage. His brooding, intense manner . . . the flashes of charming boyishness that sometimes surfaced through his ruthless masculinity . . . the dashing, heroic way he had rescued her . . . all these things struck an emotional chord in her. She felt a powerful feeling of deep affection for him. But she felt anger, too, at the way he refused to give any sign of feeling similarly toward her.

Did he have any deeper feelings for her at all, she wondered. Yesterday she had caught him in an unguarded moment, gazing at her with a look of strong affection and caring. But when he saw her noticing the look, he quickly smothered it. Then when she casually asked what plans he had for his future now that his wound was almost healed, he answered in an unexpectedly harsh, stern voice. "My future involves my men and my ship, and a war, and a *damn* good chance of getting killed. Let's not pretend it's otherwise. I wouldn't be fair to y—" He broke off the sentence, unfinished.

As she was remembering this now, Jennifer suddenly heard a loud crashing sound. She jerked upright in the bed, her body tense. Something heavy had been thrown against the wall in Silas's room, as if in frustration. She heard footsteps upon the wooden floor. She saw a hint of movement at her doorway, and looking there, she gasped and jerked the blanket up to her chin.

Savage stood in the doorway, illuminated by the yellow glow from the fireplace. His lean, powerful body was stark naked. He stood rigidly with his legs braced apart, hands down at his sides closed into fists. His handsome face, which at times could look so boyish, now looked gauntly masculine and menacing, his cheeks sunken, lips pressed together in a hard, unyielding line. It was the face of a jungle animal that knew only one law: the urgency of its own need.

As she watched in pin-pricking tension, he advanced toward her, coming forward with the heavy deliberateness of a panther stalking its prey. She saw his hard, flat stomach moving in and out with his rapid breathing. And looking lower, she saw his sex—it was rigid, angled upward, thick and long and hard. As he advanced toward her, she could not take her eyes off it. It was like some fearsome weapon, holding a terrifying fascination for her, paralyzing her into frozen speechlessness.

He came up to her and ripped the blanket away from her. It was when he grasped her white nightgown at the neck and jerked it down that she came out of her paralyzed shock and screamed, "Get out of here!" She heard the material ripping, then saw the full swell of her breasts nakedly exposed in the firelight.

She tried to scramble away from him, but as she rushed off the bed past his side, his arm reached out and encircled her waist from behind, then he lifted her up with his strong arm around her waist.

"Let me go!" she cried, beating on his back with her fists. Her entire body tensed as she felt the hem of her long white nightgown being grasped at her ankles and pulled up to her knees. Then she felt the coolness of the chilly air on her buttocks and loins as the hem was hiked all the way up to her captive waist, exposing her nakedly to his gaze.

She kicked wildly and beat at his rock-hard lower back and at his buttocks. "Stop it!" she screamed in frenzied horror. "Don't you dare touch me, don't you—"

He threw her back down on the bed, forced her onto her back, and came down perpendicularly across her. He hooked one of his legs over her slim, shapely leg, pulling her leg back and locking it between his knees. Then with his hand he grasped her other leg at the ankle and pulled it back too, so that her legs were widely spread apart.

Suddenly he became still and motionless. She knew what sight he was beholding now. He was staring down at the mound of her womanhood with a feverish intensity she could almost *feel*, shamelessly violating her with his eyes. She blushed hotly in degradation. Without warning, his hand pressed down full upon her sex. She gasped loudly. Her entire body went rigid. His hand lay pressing against her, not moving, just remaining there. Jennifer's eyes were wide with fear and excitement. "Don't," she breathed pleadingly, "Please? . . ."

His palm and fingers began vibrating slowly, then more rapidly, as they pressed down on her. She could not stop herself from moaning loudly as a sensation of startling pleasure shot through her, making her feel as if she were melting inside. She tried to resist the wicked sensation, to fight it down. She began writhing and twisting frenziedly, desperate to escape the damnable fingers that slipped up and down her, causing wave after wave of excruciating ecstasy that made her cry out in a long, loud moan. "Stop it," she moaned, "oh, God, *no!*" She thought it would never end, that the intensity of the sensation would rip her apart and drive her insane.

Finally Savage shifted his position. His legs were between hers now. She felt the very tip of his sex touching against her womanhood. She looked down the space between their two bodies and saw it jutting out long and thick, the end disappearing between her legs.

38

She threw her head back, her eyes opened wide in terror. "No," she moaned, rolling her head from side to side. He pressed harder and harder against her, until finally she screamed in pain as he burst through. His mouth covered hers, muffling the scream. She bit him sharply on the lips, drawing blood, tasting the salty tang of it on her tongue.

He moved about inside her, steadily, relentlessly. The sensation was unbearable: intense pain and pleasure together, both at once, overwhelming her with wave after wave of unending sensation, as if her nerve endings had all been abraded raw and could now be sparked alive by each new thrust. The sensual pleasure in her loins became more intense and *more* intense, until she seemed to burst apart inside with wave after wave of violent, searing ecstasy.

At the same time, Savage culminated a series of rapid thrusts into her with a final lunge that made his body go rigid and tense. After what seemed like an eternity, his body went slack, and he began breathing again, gaspingly. His sweat-soaked forehead pressed down on her shoulder. He released her wrists. He rolled off her and stood up from the bed.

Jennifer was crying uncontrollably, trying to curse him through her tears and sobs. She clutched the rumpled blanket from the base of the bed and pulled it over her, her legs curled up to her chin as she lay on her side. "You bastard," she sobbed, "oh, you *bastard!*"

He said nothing. His expression was that of a man who has done what he set out to do, but was not at all happy about it. He turned and left the room.

She lay awake all the rest of the night, huddled in her bed with the blanket wrapped tightly around her, still trembling from the violent sensations that had wracked her body. The sensations had been unlike anything she had ever experienced. She had not known such feelings were possible.

Her mind wanted to dwell on the feelings, to recall

in intimate detail the things that lean, muscular animal had done to her body to make her feel this way . . . but she forced herself to turn away from such thoughts. At the back of her mind she knew there was grave danger in admitting to herself the way she felt. It went against all she had been raised to think of as right and proper. She would fight the memory of what tonight's brutal, degrading rape had made her feel. Even so, she knew that the true way she felt about it would always be with her, at the back of her mind, threatening to come out. Something powerful had been awakened within her and she would always have to be on guard against it. A frightening thought crossed her mind: how would it make her behave, she wondered, if she let her real feelings loose?

No! She would not think of this! She would resist the feelings with all her might, hold them down in the deep recesses of her soul, no matter what it took!

In desperation she turned her mind to another subject: Savage. How could he have *turned* on her this way? He must have no feelings for her at *all*, to do such a despicable thing. But . . . what could she do now? Force him to leave? No. Even though he was obviously regaining his strength and health, he still had stitches in him. And he was still being fiercely hunted by the British, with no place else to hide.

She worried over the problem all night, without finding an answer. In the morning, she dressed and left early, before he was up. She spent the early part of the day gathering the materials she needed for the sewing and weaving she did for the women of the Colony. When she returned to the cabin, she found him standing in the living room, looking at her with a resolute expression that held no hint of apology. She quickly walked through the room into her bedroom, saying nothing to him. She shut the door, and for the next several hours she did her weaving in her room, not coming out for any reason.

She planned to stay in her room all day and night, if

need be, to avoid him completely. But in the late afternoon there was the sudden sound of hoofbeats outside, and when the horses were reined to a halt Jennifer rushed out fearfully into the living room. Who were the riders? British troops? Had they discovered Savage's whereabouts and come to take him in?

She glanced at Savage with desperate eyes as a sharp rapping came to the cabin door. Savage pulled down the loaded musket from the mantel. He motioned for her to answer the door with a nod of his head and then he disappeared into Silas's room and closed the door halfway after himself.

Every fiber in Jennifer's body was taut. "Who is it?" she called out, trying to keep the fear from her voice.

" 'Tis I, Jenny," came the reply through the door, "Thaddeus Kirby."

"Dr. Kirby!" she exclaimed, the sense of relief filling her voice. She flung the door open.

Savage came back into the room and lowered the musket.

Instead of entering, though, Dr. Kirby stepped back several paces from the doorway, his expression very somber. "Well, you've succeeded," he said in a bitter voice to someone standing out of sight at the side of the doorway. "You've forced me to betray him to you and now I've done it. Here he is, I've led you right to him!"

Jennifer's eyes went wide with shock. Savage jerked the musket back up to his shoulder, squinted his eye as he aimed at the doorway. His face was grim and purposeful.

The figure at the side of the doorway came into view now. He was a big, powerful, long-blond-haired man, wearing fringed buckskin and beaming a huge smile. He looked at Savage holding the leveled rifle and laughed, "*Mon ami,* you weesh to use poor D'Arcy for ze target practees? *Mon dieu!* Who weel tell you ze funny stories if you fill ze great lover and raconteur full of buckshot, eh?"

41

Savage held the musket steady, not lowering it even a hair. "You mean if I shoot you, I don't have to listen to those ridiculous stories anymore? You take your life in your hands with that ultimatum, Frenchman."

D'Arcy laughed and strode forward. Savage lowered the musket, grinning, and was immediately embraced in a huge bear hug, until Dr. Kirby ordered with concern in his voice, "Ease off there, man! This is a sick person!"

"So you are steel alive after all," D'Arcy said, relaxing his grip and stepping back, though keeping his hands on Savage's arms. "Two months now I am searching for you, theenking surely you must be dead."

"I would be dead," Savage said, "if not for . . Jennifer." He looked at her as he spoke her name.

D'Arcy looked too, smiling. His gaze took in her face, and the way her hair fell in natural curls down to her shoulders, where it was loosely gathered together in back by a pink ribbon. He looked at the way she filled out her copper-toned dress, which fit her bustline and waist quite snugly before billowing out into a full skirt with buff-colored apron. "No wonder you take such a long time to heal," he said to Savage. "Weeth such a nurse to care for you, only ze crazyman would hurry ze time of heez departure."

Jennifer was not paying attention to the compliment, though. She was glaring at Dr. Kirby.

Becoming nervous at her stony stare, Dr. Kirby said to her, "You thought I didn't have a sense of humor, eh Jenny?" He forced a guilty smile at the practical joke he played when introducing D'Arcy.

"You don't!" Jennifer exclaimed, her eyes flashing. "You have no sense of humor at *all*, it's . . . it's *awful!*" Jennifer turned away from him, infuriated. Her anger was not directed only at Dr. Kirby, as he probably thought it was. She was angry at the whole room, the whole situation. For a moment she wanted to shout to Dr. Kirby that she had been raped, held down and raped by the man he thought of as so noble and valiant.

42

But she held her tongue. She went to the hearth instead and began brewing tea.

Dr. Kirby went up to Savage. "I've been wanting to get back to you for a long time, Lancelot. Those stitches should have been out weeks ago. It's only today, though, that fortune has afforded me this chance to come see you."

"Fortune, ha!" laughed D'Arcy. "Eet eez D'Arcy zat makes ze chance, not fortune!" He said to Savage: "Ze Redcoats zat stand outside heez office, watching for when he leaves so zay can follow heem . . . I go up to zem and yell 'Ze pirate eez een ze tavern! Ze blackguard and villain, ze notorious D'Arcy Calhoun! In ze tavern!' And when zay run away to ze tavern, Dr. Kirby and I we leave."

Savage laughed.

"Here, lie down on the bed," Dr. Kirby said to Savage, guiding him into Silas's room. "Let me have a look at you."

"I'm healthy as a bear. I'll do a jig to prove it, if you like."

"You just lie down like I tell you, that's what I like. There you go." He told Savage to take off his blouse, but instead Savage just opened the front of it, not wanting to expose the fresh scratches on his back. He lay on the bed with his arms behind his neck as Dr. Kirby began inspecting the healed wound, poking and probing in various places.

"Let me tell you about ze men," D'Arcy said. "Many are not yet captured . . ." As D'Arcy talked animatedly and Dr. Kirby wore an expression of serious concentration as he inspected the wound, Jennifer stood in the living room, looking in through the doorway. She felt isolated, left out. And looking at Savage, who was clearly excited by the visit, she felt anger and—surprisingly—a strong sense of loss. Even though just moments before she had been so upset about the problem of his continuing to live with her, now that she was facing the fact that he would *not* be living with

43

her much longer, she became even more upset. Deep in her soul she knew the truth. She did not want him to leave.

But he, Savage, *he* didn't seem to care at all. Look at him, Jennifer thought to herself angrily. Smiling. Joking. Having a grand time. Hasn't it sunk in yet what this visit means . . . that Dr. Kirby will tell him he's well, that there's nothing to keep him here? He must know, he's not stupid! So . . . he really *doesn't* care about me, not at all.

She had not wanted to believe this, despite all the evidence of it. But now there was no way of avoiding the fact. She felt sad and hurt.

The tea was ready. She took a quilted potholder and poured the steaming brew into ceramic mugs, then set them at the table. "Tea's ready," she called out.

No one took any notice of her. Dr. Kirby had just removed Savage's stitches and was now rubbing his finger along the seam of the wound, frowning. D'Arcy continued bringing Savage up to date on the recent events that had taken place. "Seex men zay have been captured since we leave ze *Liberty*. Nine more zay are killed by ze Redcoats. Ze rest are still free."

"And you're in touch with fifteen of them, you say?" said Savage.

"*Oui.* Like me zay hide in ze villages, or on ze outskirts. Taking jobs under ze false names, being hidden by patriot families. Me, I am ze tanner at ze trading post outside Chamberville. Ze Breeteesh, so far zay not find me."

Fifteen men," said Savage thoughtfully, putting a fist to his lips. "Seventeen counting you and me. It's enough. We could sail with that crew, picking up new recruits as we go along. *Ow!*" He turned to Dr. Kirby, who had just pricked him with a metal instrument. "What the hell are you doing to me? I'm a sick man remember!"

"You'll be even sicker if you curse your doctor once more," said Dr. Kirby.

44

"Sorry," Savage apologized, then turning his attention back to D'Arcy asked, "The *Liberty*. The British have found her by now?"

D'Arcy laughed delightedly. "Zay find her, but *mon ami,* you know what zay do weeth her? Zay make repairs! Zay feex her up so nice." He threw his head back and laughed gaily. "Zees Engleesh, zay are true gentlemen, feexing our sheep so we can steal her back and sail weeth her. But of course, zay have ze idea zat she will sail as *their* sheep, in ze Royal Navy."

"Selfish of them," said Savage. "We'll have to teach them the virtue of sharing."

"Anyway," remarked D'Arcy indignantly, "zay cannot just take our sheep and say zat now she eez theirs. Zat is piracy! Don't zay know piracy eez against ze law?"

Jennifer was watching the mists of steam rising from the cups of tea. When the mists vanished as the tea began losing its warmth she said, "The *tea* is ready!" She said it more sharply than she had intended. Everyone looked at her.

Savage started to get up.

"Cough for me just one more time," Dr. Kirby said.

"I'm tired of coughing. I've coughed for you too much already. You'll have me turning into a consumptive!" He buttoned his blouse as they walked toward the living room table. "You've seen enough to tell me if I'm well or not, haven't you?"

The three men sat down at the table. Jennifer sat also.

"I have, yes," said Dr. Kirby. "And here's my diagnosis. I'd like to keep you inactive for a bit longer. At least a month, two would be better. That's my personal feeling. But, on purely medical grounds, I have to tell you that you'll be ready to end your convalescence in—"

Jennifer watched him in keen anticipation, hanging on his every word.

"—a fortnight. Two weeks."

45

Jennifer's teacup was raised to her lips. Drops of liquid splashed slightly as her arm jerked.

"You'll have to take it easy even then, mind you," cautioned Dr. Kirby. "No running, no lifting, no strenuous activity. Just because you're healed outside doesn't mean you're healed inside."

"Well," said Savage, "a fortnight it is then." He glanced cautiously at Jennifer, but turned his eyes away quickly when he saw she was looking at him.

"I weel come for you zen," said D'Arcy, "and take you weeth me to ze trading post. From zair we bring ze men together, and plan ze attack to take back *la belle Liberty.*"

Savage said nothing. He took a sip of his tea.

"Eet weel be ze life of adventure once more!" continued D'Arcy enthusiastically. "On ze high seas, fighting ze Engleesh. Ze men have been waiting for zis day all ze time. Now ze day is here! We have our Captain back!"

"Yes," said Savage somberly. "The day is here." He did not glance at Jennifer this time.

The men continued talking amongst themselves, drinking tea and later smoking cigars. Jennifer had no part to play in their conversation. She could not bring herself to speak. She would not trust her voice. She tried to keep her eyes looking from man to man, at whomever was talking, but she knew she was failing. She was looking far too hard and too long at Savage. As she looked at him, her thoughts kept drifting to the way it had been before he had come out of his coma. . . .

He had been lying in bed then, his eyes closed, with no hint as to whether he would live or die. She had sat in the chair by the side of the bed looking at him for hours on end, day after day. She had bathed him, covered him with blankets, fed him broth when he was able to swallow. And there was something else that she had done, too, which she had pushed from her mind and not thought of since then, until just now.

46

There had been times when she raised his hand to her cheek and rubbed her face softly against it. And she had looked at his beautiful face, which looked boyish in repose, and said to him, though he could not hear, "Please live. I want us to be together. Please don't die. Don't leave me."

She thought of this now as she watched him smoking his cigar and joining in the conversation.

"Well," said Dr. Kirby, jarring Jennifer back to the reality of the smoke-filled room, "it's time to be on my way."

"You can't stay longer?" asked Savage.

"If I start back now, I can tell the Redcoats I was in the forest, searching out roots for my medicines. If I wait any longer and show up too much after dark, they'll know it's a lie. You can't search in a forest past sundown."

"I go too," said D'Arcy rising.

"You can stay if you like," Jennifer said, extending the common courtesy. "There's plenty of room and you could leave in the morning."

"*Non, non,* though many thanks for ze invitation. Eet eez better to travel under ze darkness." He bowed formally. "*Adieu, ma cherie.*"

"Take care, Jenny," said Dr. Kirby. D'Arcy and Savage bid each other farewell. Then the two visitors were out the door and mounting their steeds. Jennifer and Savage stood on the porchstep in the cool night air, watching as the two men rode away.

Then they went back inside and Savage closed the door. Jennifer immediately went to the table and began cleaning up. Neither of them said anything. Then, because she could not stand the silence, Jennifer began speaking. "So you're leaving," she said in a harsh, nervous voice, not looking at Savage, but at the cups and utensils she was attending to. "Good. I . . . I'll be happy to have you gone."

Savage just stared at her, a strange look of gentleness on his face.

She put the cups and utensils on the tray with fumbling hands that she could not stop from shaking. She brushed a lock of hair away from her face with the back of her wrist in a sharp, abrupt gesture. Then she picked up the tray and started toward the kitchen.

When she passed near Savage, he reached out his hand and clasped her arm, stopping her. She stood for a moment, not moving, still holding the tray in both hands. Savage remained facing her holding her arm, the look of surprising gentleness still in his eyes. His hand went to her face and he touched her cheek softly.

Jennifer dropped the tray and slapped him stingingly. The mugs crashed to the floor, splintering into shards. She backed away from him. "I'm not to be *toyed* with!" she screamed at him, half crouched forward, her eyes filled with pain. "You don't think I'm good enough for you to *care* for—oh no, I'm not good enough for that!—but I'm fine enough for you to *use*, aren't I, for you to take for your pleasure? For you to treat like a cheap *whore!*"

He started coming toward her. When he was close enough, she slashed out at his face with her half-clenched fingers, scratching him deeply with her nails. "You'll have to kill me before you'll have me that way again!" she shouted.

He grasped her arms and looked into her fiery, raging eyes. "Jennifer," he said, his voice thick with emotion. "I love you."

She was shocked. Startled. Uncertain. Had he really said that?

His eyes were intense, his expression strong but gentle, with a trace of anguish. "I tried not to say it to you, not to let you see it. It wouldn't be fair to you, I told myself. You'd want to wait for me during the coming war. You'd waste your best years. And for *what?* My life is so full of danger, I'll surely leave you in mourning."

He narrowed an eye at her. "I told you before, my future involves my men and my ship and a good chance of being killed. It's not fair to claim your love, not when the odds are so against me ever returning to you in one piece. It's not fair to say this to you, but ... *damn* it all, I can't stop myself." He clutched her to him. "I love you, Jennifer. You're all I love."

He kissed her hard, his lips searing her mouth, his body pressing full against her from her knees to her breasts. Jennifer was dizzy, reeling, her mind spinning crazily. She barely managed to push slightly back from him and say in a tremulous voice, "But you ... you..."

"Raped you?" His voice became bitter. "I had to make you hate me. So there'd be no chance of my weakening and telling you my true feelings. If you hated me, I figured, I'd never be in danger of telling you my feelings, since you wouldn't *care* what I felt about you—you'd still hate me." He grinned in sardonic amusement at his folly. "I underestimated how weak I really am ... or how strong my feelings are for you."

She stared at him like an awe-struck child, her blue eyes wide with uncertainty and wonderment.

"I love you," he said softly. "If I'm alive at the end of this war, I'll be back for you. And we'll be married." He swept her up in his arms and carried her into the bedroom. He laid her gently down on the bed—the same bed where last night she had been so brutally raped; the bed where she had lain while vowing never again to let him touch her.

He began unlacing her dress, pushing her chemise down off her shoulders ... his hands were everywhere. She made a gesture to fend off his hands, to stop him from laying her bare. But it was only a gesture, with no conviction to it. Her mind was so clouded by the powerful emotions surging through her, she could not think clearly about whether she should stop him or leave him do as he wished. The single thought kept running through her mind: he loves me. He *does* love me.

49

Soon she was completely naked, sitting up in the bed with her legs curled under her, her arms crossed over her breasts protectively. She felt shy and horribly exposed, even though she knew her body was no longer a stranger to his hungry eyes. She watched Savage remove his blouse, baring his muscular arms and chest. He put his hands on her arms and drew her forward so that she was standing on the wooden floor in front of him. She looked in his face searchingly, at his slate gray eyes, his pronounced cheekbones and flaring nostrils.

He kissed her passionately on the lips, then on her throat and shoulders. His hand traveled down her stomach to her loins. She pushed his hand away. His body came close, and the flat planes of his chest brushed against her straining nipples, exciting them. She pushed him back.

"What's this?" he said, astounded. "You don't want it? I told you I love you."

"Please," she breathed. "It's not that I . . . it's . . ." She was stumbling over her words, unsure of herself. Conflicting crosscurrents battled each other in her mind. He did love her, yes, but still. . . . "It isn't right," she finally blurted out.

"Not right? Whatever do you mean 'not right'?"

"Everyone says it's not. Good girls don't . . . decent girls never . . ."

"Jennifer, what tripe," he said, losing patience with her. "If you're to be my woman, then you're to be my *woman*. Not some silly schoolgirl filled with cockeyed notions. You must learn to know what you want and to take it." His jaw set hard and he looked at her with serious, purposeful eyes. "I'll have to teach you, I suppose."

She reached for her dress to cover herself, now that she had made her decision. But Savage grabbed it out of her hand and threw it across the room. He put his hands to her slim shoulders and moved them slowly down along the swell of her breasts. She grasped his

50

wrists and tried to push his hands away. He was too strong for her, though. She watched his fingers begin to close over her breasts. She could not stop him! His hands cupped her breasts and began kneading them softly, his thumbs swirling in small circles around her nipples.

"Do you want it?" he said in a low taunting voice, a tight grin crossing his lips.

She looked at him with helpless eyes. His palms rubbed her breasts, his thumbs flicked her pert nipples that were now ablaze with sensation. Her hands were still gripping his wrists, trying ineffectually to pull them away. "Please . . . I . . . *stop it!*"

His hands moved down her stomach and touched her thighs, passing near her womanhood though not touching it. They moved up across her lower stomach, back down to her thighs, roaming over her body at will, touching her everywhere but at her loins, which soon began throbbing with expectation each time his hands passed near. "Do you want it?" he said tauntingly. His hands roamed across her breasts, over her arms, hips, belly, igniting small fires of passion everywhere they touched. His fingers began moving in circles around her loins, still not touching her there. She felt her lower body begin burning up with desire.

Then he touched her at her sex, rubbing frenziedly against her before quickly withdrawing his hand. A flame of pleasure burst from her loins, but then died away. He was only teasing her. His finger flicked in and out of her suddenly, making her gasp with the rapturous sensation that blazed up and then died down. In and out quickly, once more. She moaned. Both her hands gripped his wrists tightly, which was down between her legs. Her face pressed against the bulging muscle of his upper arm, her eyes closed tightly, her features contorted in tortured agony. She was breathing rapidly and loudly and felt beads of perspiration break out all over her burning skin. His finger flicked in, slid up and down, withdrew quickly.

51

"Stop it," she moaned, *"I can't stand it!"*

Once more, in and out, teasing her, driving her mad with the rapturous feeling that carried her to new heights of sensation each time he touched her there. He wanted her to ask for it, she knew, but no, she wouldn't—she couldn't; if the feelings she had experienced before were unleashed once more, she might never be able to hold them back again, to deny herself.

Suddenly his fingertip slipped inside her and touched her at the very knot of her being, pressing hard against it, flicking it about, driving her mad with the swirling passion and burning pleasure that became more and more intense, not giving her a second's respite, driving her higher and higher into tumultuous rapture.

She gasped and panted for breath, her entire body awash in the powerful sensations shooting through her fiery loins. She moaned loudly, holding tightly to his wrist as if for dear life, her nose and chin pressing against the muscle of his arm. Then, just as the sensations were carrying her toward a peak of pleasure she had never in her wildest dreams imagined possible—he stopped. He removed his hand, stepped away from her.

She almost collapsed forward. She stood there with her knees half bent, weak, sobbing, her loins aching with sensuality, almost there . . . almost there. . . .

She looked up and saw him pushing down his britches and stepping out of them. His sex was hard and rigid and pointing like an arrow toward her face. He put his hands on his narrow hips and stood with his legs braced apart, his waist thrust slightly forward. He grinned at her with a smug, stern look. "You must learn to ask for what you want, my love. It's a rule of life you'll thank me for teaching you."

Her gaze fixed upon the long, hard shaft of his manhood. Her loins, which he had deliberately teased into fiery desire, ached with the need of it.

"Do you want it?" he said, as if reading her mind. His voice was low and manly.

"Only a tramp would say—" She could not take her

eyes away from it. Her body was sweating and aching and burning up with passion. "I'm not the sort of girl," she said weakly, "who—"

"Do you want it!"

"*Yes!*" she shouted.

She did as he ordered. "Onto the bed. On your back."

Savage's voice was thick with excitement. "If you want it, then show me, my love."

She closed her eyes tightly. No, she wouldn't do this. She wouldn't. . . . But could she stop herself? Her loins throbbed with sensuality. Slowly she spread her legs far apart, and then farther still. She began undulating her hips up and down.

God, what was wrong with her? What manner of shameless hussy had she become? What were these strange, powerful cravings he had aroused in her which she could not fight down? She was thrusting her hips wildly up and down now, in the most brazenly shameful act she had ever committed. A wild thrill shot through her as she lay with her arms flung back, her head rolling from side to side, thrusting violently with her hips. She knew that this was what he wanted her to do. She was giving him pleasure by doing it. She looked at him and saw that his face was sheathed in sweat, iron hard in torment.

He bent over and kissed her on the lips. Then he came onto the bed on top of her. She moaned loudly with pleasure as he entered her, arching her back. Savage began thrusting slowly and steadily, but soon he became lost to the same unbearable passion that engulfed Jennifer. He began thrusting violently, relentlessly, tearing her apart, making her move frenziedly to the rapture of the lightning bolt between her legs. The flames inside her were blazing in an inferno of ecstasy as she came closer to it, and closer . . .

Finally her loins exploded with unbearable pleasure in the most devastating, liberating feeling she ever experienced. She cried out and grasped Savage's hot, sweating body tightly to her as the feeling overwhelmed her in endless bursts of sensation. She hugged him with all her might, her arms and legs locked tightly around him. Then Savage too shuddered with the ecstasy that made his hard body tense in excruciating torment. As Jennifer watched him surrender helplessly to the rapture she, Jennifer, had given him, she felt a sense of strong satisfaction. *I* made him feel this way, she thought. I brought him to this.

After a moment, his body relaxed. He raised his head and looked down at her with his strong, handsome face. Love was in his eyes. She moved her fingers through his wet curly black hair, tousling it. "I love you," she said. Relief, happiness, warmth flooded through her. She felt fulfilled. This was what it meant to be a woman, she thought. This was what Savage had made her feel. She looked at him and thought of the happy life the two of them would have together when Savage returned from the coming war.

The following days were filled with love and tenderness and violent, searing passion. Jennifer had never felt more like a whole woman, or been so emotionally and physically fulfilled. The only thing that disturbed her was the speed with which the days flew by. Then, the very day before he was to leave, a loud rapping at the door startled them as they sat at the table, Savage eating a serving of apple pie she had just baked for him.

"Who is it?" Jennifer asked, trying to keep the apprehension out of her voice.

"Matthew Armitage, Miss VanDerLind! I have come to call on you."

Oh no, she thought. Not *him*. Not *now*. "One moment, Mr. Armitage," she said, as she scurried about putting the dishes into the kitchen, and as Savage took the musket from the mantle and disappeared into Silas's room.

Matthew Armitage was one of the most cretinous young men in the village. Jennifer could not stand him. Unfortunately, he had taken a liking to her and had been courting her for almost a year.

Though she had made it very clear that she was not interested in his attentions, she had never gone so far as to be openly rude in emphasizing the point, as she would have liked. Silas had warned against this. One did not offend Matthew Armitage if it could be avoided, he cautioned. The man had a mean streak in him and a petty nature that was almost feminine in its vindictiveness. And though he was only in his young twenties, he already wielded unusual influence within the Colony, mostly owing to secret "connections," the true nature of which few people clearly understood.

Jennifer hurriedly scanned the room to make sure no sign of Savage's presence remained, then opened the door.

Matthew Armitage bowed formally, removing his tricornered hat, bending deeply at the waist. "Good afternoon, milady. How *won*derful of you to receive me." He was a short man and was dressed in the most pretentious finery imaginable: fancily embroidered coat, lace-front shirt, shoes sporting ostentatiously large buckles. His goal was to show the world he was an up-and-coming man of the highest ambitions. It was unnecessary—no one doubted it; everyone in the Colony was wary of him, certain he would stop at nothing to achieve his goals.

"I'm honored at your visit, Mr. Armitage. But . . . actually, you see, you caught me about to nap and—"

"So early?"

"When you live alone, sir, the diversions are few. Sleep is more welcome than boredom. And once you develop the habit—"

"Well, perhaps I can spare you the boredom, milady," said Matthew, smirking conceitedly. "I *am* an entertaining sort, if I say so myself, and I'm *quite* sure

I could endure spending a few moments in your presence. So if you'd care to invite me in? . . ."

"Ummm, well . . ." Jennifer was at a loss. When Silas was alive, Matthew was no problem. Whenever he came courting, Silas would engage him in constant conversation, sparing Jennifer from having to respond. Jennifer could sit at the table with the two of them, confident that Silas would jump in and turn the conversation to other matters whenever the dandy attempted to personally address her. Now, though, she had no such defense.

"It's probably quite comfortable inside your domicile, Miss VanDerLind, and I'm most certain you brew an *ex*cellent spot of tea. So, 'Jennifer'—" He had never been this bold when Silas was alive. "—if you will permit me? . . ." He took a step toward the doorway.

She raised her hand. "That would hardly be proper, Mr. Armitage. Unchaperoned as I am and—"

"Oh Jennifer, what rot! Surely we needn't be bound by convention. I've been coming round for . . . what, a year now? You know where my interests lie. Surely you're not afraid I'll make untoward advances toward you, as they say."

"It isn't that, Mr. Armitage. I know you're a man of impeccable manners. It's just that—"

"And stop this blasted Mr. Armitage nonsense! You've known me long enough to cease such formality." Suddenly he raised an eyebrow suspiciously. He began peering into the room blatantly, standing on his tiptoes to look over Jennifer's shoulder.

"Mr. Armitage, what are you doing?"

"Not a thing, not a thing. Don't mind me, I'm just . . ." He looked at her piercingly through narrowed eyes. "Certainly there's no *other* reason you might prefer to keep me outside?"

"What other reason could there possibly be?"

He did not answer. He resumed attempting to peer into the room from over her shoulders or around her sides.

"Mr. Armitage, if you please! It's simply that, convention aside, I'm very tired and need a nap. Since Grandfather's death I've been spinning and weaving and doing unending chores for the women of the Colony and it's really quite exhausting. And—"

"*Well*, Jennifer," Matthew interrupted caustically, pursing his lips, "if you're all *that* tired, then perhaps you *should* get your rest, now *shouldn't* you? And I *beg* your leave, Madam." He bowed, turned angrily, and stalked away.

Jennifer frowned sharply and bit her lip. She couldn't let him leave like this. He was too suspicious at not being invited inside. "Wait!" she called.

He turned back to face her, eyebrows raised quizically.

"You can't stay long, as I say. But before you go, you . . . um . . . you must have a taste of my greenapple pie! I just baked it."

He looked startled, as if he had imagined a very suspicious situation and now that he was being invited in after all, the situation crumbled. "Pie, you say. Yes, well . . . thank you, I'd be delighted." He seemed more disappointed than delighted.

After she sat him down to the table, Jennifer fetched the serving cart from the kitchen, where she had just put it, and gave Matthew a large slice of the still-warm pie. Then she sat down with him at the table to watch him as he ate.

"You're not joining me?" he asked, taking a silk handkerchief from his sleeve, whipping it in the air with a flourish, then tucking it primly into his shirt collar.

"I had quite a bit already."

Matthew looked at the remaining pie, which was shy by a half thanks to the large serving Savage had eaten. "I should say so." As he began eating, his eyes darted about the room. "Listen, Jennifer," he said between swallows, "it's indecent of you to be treating me so formally. You know how I feel about you. Why do you continue living in such poor circumstances, doing lowly

chores for the local biddies and gossips, barely sub-
sisting when you could become my wife instead?
I'd provide you a far better life than this."

Forgetting himself in his enthusiasm for his subject,
he began betraying his show of manners by talking
with his mouth full. Jennifer felt disgusted watching
him.

"Why, you don't even have the security of your own
cabin!" Matthew exclaimed. "Everyone knows that
when old VanDerLind was arrested the property was
confiscated by the Crown to be sold over to Lord
knows who. You could be turned out at a moment's
notice! What kind of life is that to lead?"

Jennifer gave him a sharp look of disapproval at his
mention of Silas, but Matthew was oblivious to it.

"A woman of your grace and beauty is *wasted* in
such circumstances as you live in, utterly, *utterly*
wasted! Dealing with these Philistines. Why, with me
you'd soon have fame, wealth, position. All the luxuries you could dream of!"

"Im grateful for your offer, Mr. Armitage, to be
sure, however—"

"Of course, of course, you look at me now and I
seem far from the wealth and position I'm promising
you. But if you only knew what exists beneath your
preceptions, dear Jennifer! I have more irons in the fire
than you can imagine. Any day now one or several of
my sundry undertakings will bear fruit. And when that
happens, when all of it begins to coalesce, why no
power on earth will be sufficient to stop me!"

He was so impassioned with his own ambitions that
he was waving his fork around in emphasis. Jennifer
did not know what do say. When he paused for her to
respond, she tried a new approach: "I'm flattered at
your proposal, Mr. Armitage, truly. But . . . there are
so many other women in the Colony who would be
overjoyed to receive your attentions, perhaps you
should—"

He bent forward over the table, surprising her with

the nearness of his unpleasant face. His eyes became sly. "You could do me much good as my wife. None of the others could come even close. It counts a great deal, Jennifer, among pedestrian minds, to have a lovely and gracious woman as one's wife. And when I commence my ascent through the ranks, you'll become even *more* valuable. Those of a higher social strata are unbe*liev*ably susceptible to the impact one makes with a true lady on his arm. Why, we could do so *much* for each other."

He threw down his fork, forgetting about the pie entirely. This was the first time he had been able to talk to Jennifer without the interference of old Silas and he was getting carried away with the opportunity. "Oh, you're so lovely, Jennifer, so lovely, and so *wasted* here. These other morons who come a-courting, they have nothing to offer you. They have nothing in their empty heads but the thought of your beauty, and even that only for—" he frowned disgustedly as he uttered the word "—*sex*ual purposes. They give no thought to what you can do for a man's *career!* But *I*, Jennifer, I'm not like that!" He leaned even further over the table toward her, and grasped her hand. "I'm a man who can truly app*rec*iate you, who can—"

She pulled her hand out from under his and placed it on her lap. She lowered her eyes demurely.

Matthew Armitage ceased speaking and glared at her. Then he kicked back his chair as he stood. "Perhaps you think I'm like those other dolts *after* all, who come drooling after you with no more in mind than *the shape of your bosom!*"

"Mr. Armitage!"

"You narrow, shallow woman. You're like all the others. I gave you undue credit. Beauteous outside, verily, but with only the usual great yawning chasms within." He fetched his hat. "Thank you for the ex*ceed*ingly mediocre apple pie."

Jennifer followed him as he started for the door. Instead of leaving, though, he turned suddenly, a curious, keenly attentive look on his face. He glanced about the room swiveling his head sharply as he surveyed each part of it. "Where's Silas's musket?" he said. "It's gone from the mantel."

"It's . . ." She started her answer quickly to show no hesitation—but now she faltered, uncertain what to say. "It's in the bedroom!" she concluded. "I keep it there to protect myself at night."

He glanced toward her bedroom and then toward the closed door of Silas's room. Then he pivoted on his heel and left the house.

Jennifer went to the door and looked after him as he strode through the yard without a backward glance. She felt very uneasy at the way the situation had turned out. But what could she have done differently? Biting her lower lip, she shut the door.

Immediately upon hearing the door close, Matthew Armitage stopped in his tracks and turned around. He stood for a long moment staring at the cabin, squinting his eyes in concentration. Something was amiss here, he was certain of it. A cruel, thin-lipped smile crept across his features. Yes, he thought, something was definitely amiss and he was *just* the sort of man to find out what it was—and turn it to his advantage.

That night—their last night together—Jennifer and Savage were standing up, embracing, just on the verge of undressing and going to bed . . . when suddenly there was the sound of night riders coming up the road, working their mounts hard. Savage rushed to the window. He pulled the curtain aside and looked out, just as the sound of the horses being reined to a halt came from outside the cabin.

"What is it?" Jennifer asked, a chill of terror flooding over her. Savage did not answer. For a moment he stood looking out the window, transfixed. Then he let the curtain fall back into place. Without any hesitation he rushed to the front door and unlatched the bolt.

"What are you doing?" Jennifer asked, shocked.

Still he said nothing. He came right up to her.

Instinctively she started to go for the musket, to hand it to him. Savage grasped her arm, though, and stopped her. He held her arm and then came up very close to her, so that his face was only inches away. In his eyes Jennifer saw such an overpowering look of love—and sadness—that it made her catch her breath. *"What is it?"* she said. *"Who's out there?"*

There was the sound of heavy boots marching up to the doorstep and then the door he had just unlatched burst open with a kick. At the very instant of the door's swinging full open so that he and Jennifer were visible, Savage slapped Jennifer hard, sending her reeling across the room.

"You scummy bitch!" he screamed at her, "denying me shelter! I come not minutes ago and ask you to hide me and you *refuse!*" He advanced on her as she lay on the floor, as if to slap her again. "And now I'm captured!" As he raised his arm to strike her again, the sergeant of the Redcoats rushed up to him from behind and smacked him in the head with the barrel of his musket. Jennifer screamed.

Savage crumpled to the floor. He was unable to speak or gain his footing, but he was not unconscious. His legs kicked about ineffectually, as if beyond his muscular control, and blood poured out of the cut in his scalp where the rifle barrel had struck.

"Get him out," the sergeant sneered to the soldiers in his detail. There were five Redcoats in all, Jennifer saw; Savage could not have fought them off without endangering her. She watched as the soldiers dragged him by his wrists out of the cabin.

The sergeant strode up to her as she lay on the floor. "So he come just minutes ago, did he?" he asked, his voice contemptuous.

Jennifer was too shocked to speak. She did not even look at the sergeant, who was towering over her, glaring down at her. Her eyes were on Savage. She

61

watched through the open doorway, feeling the coolness of the incoming breeze on her face, as the soldiers slung him up on a horse and tied his wrists together around the horse's neck. Blood gushed from his scalp into his face now that he was almost horizontal. It began to hide his features.

"Lucky for you, missy," the sergeant said to Jennifer, "him bein' here only a short minute. For if'n he'd been here longer'n just that, ye'd be coming in with him now, I'll promise ye that, as a harborer of a dangerous fugitive."

Jennifer still said nothing. She watched through the doorway as the soldiers mounted up. Savage seemed to come out of a trance for a moment for she saw him try to jerk upright, but the way his wrists were tied prevented this. Then the sergeant left the cabin and mounted up also. The detail rode off, the sergeant holding the reins of Savage's horse, Savage's head still down, sheathed in blood.

The riders disappeared into the darkness, leaving Jennifer alone in the cabin—absolutely alone—listening to the sound of the receding hoofbeats and staring at the empty blackness framed by the doorway.

Chapter 4

Savage's trial was a travesty.

In most cases involving capital crimes such as treason and piracy the accused person was removed to England to stand trial there. In Savage's case, however, the evidence was so overwhelming and the governor of the province so anxious to have him tried, hanged, and forgotten about, that a special court was convened right in the village meeting hall.

A Tory magistrate was hastily brought in from the neighboring township of Ellingsley, where the elderly jurist spent the majority of his time overseeing the management of a prosperous tavern in which he held half interest.

Jennifer sat in one of the rear rows of the audience gallery, watching as the various witnesses were called forth to identify Savage and to testify against him. Dr. Kirby sat next to her to give her emotional support. Savage himself was seated at a stool on a raised platform off to the side of the newly installed judge's bench. He was facing the gallery, but he did not once look at Jennifer. His wrists were manacled and chained together, as were his ankles. He wore rough, baggy prisoner's clothing. Though he had a bandage wrapped around his head near his temple, he seemed to have recovered from the blow he had received.

Rather than paying attention to the procession of witnesses called against him, he let his eyes wander out the window of the meeting hall. Occasionally he would smirk at a remark uttered by the magistrate or a witness. There was no defense he could make in his own behalf. Several witnesses were brought up in rapid succession to identify him and to say that he was the one who had boarded their merchant vessel after firing upon them, and he was the one who had seized all the goods bound for England. Or that he was the one who had engaged the British naval vessels and sunk two of them. One sailor recognized him as the man who had thrown a buoy keg over the side to save him as he lay in the water wounded after his British man-o'-war had been sunk in battle.

The trial proceedings had settled into a bland sameness of mood with nothing unusual to spark interest, when, suddenly, Jennifer received a shock of recognition as a new witness was called. The man entered from the entrance door at the rear of the gallery and stomped down the aisle, passing right by her. She recognized his features: the narrow eyes, the wind-calloused face. Her eyes went wide and every muscle in her body tensed at the memory of where she had seen that face before.

"Captain H. C. Trevor," announced the clerk, as the man strode briskly forward to the front of the meeting hall and approached the bench. His bearing was still militarily stiff, but Jennifer noticed that it was different than she remembered it. This was due to the fact that he was missing his left arm, she could see, and was altering his stride to compensate for it.

Captain Trevor went directly up to Savage, very close to him, and looked him in the face. "Aye, this is the one," he said, his voice cold steel.

"Over there, over there first," ordered the magistrate, flustered at the breach of protocol. "Go over there, will you, over there by the clerk and take the oath of honesty."

"I'll take any damn oath you like, if it pleases you. But here's what I come to say and no oath will change it: this be the one. This here be the vermin what shot my shoulder at two-foot range, and me unarmed at the time."

"Captain Trevor," said the magistrate, becoming more flustered and irritated at this breach in the smooth running of his court, "if you'll please go to the clerk for the—"

Trevor raised his fist and smashed Savage hard on his right temple, knocking him to the side. A stunned gasp rose from the gallery and there were sudden shouts of rebellion as the anti-Tory villagers in the audience rose to their feet.

"Quiet!" the magistrate yelled, banging his gravel. "Shut up! Everyone shut up and sit down or the troops will clear ye all out!" The audience took their seats. Savage had fallen almost off the stool with the force of the blow. Now he righted himself and looked the angry-faced Captain in the eyes. Without warning he spat at him, full in the face.

Captain Trevor shrieked a curse and hit him again, this time in the jaw, knocking him completely off the stool and on to the floor. He began kicking him, but before he could do any further damage the magistrate ordered the two British soldiers at the front of the room to pull him back.

"We have *justice* here!" shouted the magistrate, furious. "We are English *gentlemen,* not barbarians! We do not strike chained prisoners!"

The courtroom had erupted in shouting and foot-stomping and immediately a squad of British troops filed into the hall at double-time to secure order. They had been stationed outside the building to prevent any attempt that might be made by the Sons of Liberty to free Savage.

Finally the Captain stood straight, shook off the guards holding him, and made a show of regaining his dignity and self-control. "All right," he said, "ask me what ye will. I've business to attend to. No time for this frivolity. Hang the vermin and be done with it, that's my advice!"

Cheers went up from the Tory Loyalists in the audience.

The clerk tried to give the witness the oath now, but Captain Trevor waved him away angrily, sending him retreating in fear. "Get on with it, by God! Ask me your questions or give me my leave!"

"Captain Trevor," began the white-wigged barrister who was prosecuting the case, "you were captain of His Majesty's vessel the *Rubiyat*, were you not, when it was taken over by the accused Lancelot Savage, who—"

"Yes, yes, yes! Who ordered my crew overboard at gunpoint and shot me coldbloodedly in the shoulder. Yes! And who blew her up then, when the *Serapis* came to the rescue. Late, I might add. If'n I'd had some decent reinforcement when I needed it, why I'd have—"

"I believe you no longer hold your commission in His Majesty's Navy, is that right?" interrupted the barrister. "Thanks to—"

"Thanks to that bloody vermin *pirate!*" exploded the Captain. "Who cost me my arm and made me unfit for sea command. *Me,* with an admiralty within me very grasp. And now I'm—"

"Thank you, Captain," interrupted the barrister, "that'll be all."

"And now I'm landlocked here in your stinking Colonies, with the stinking job of serving King George as commandant of his stinking—"

"That's fine, Captain, thank you!" interrupted the barrister, trying to shut him up now that he had given the evidence and pointed the accusing finger. "Your Honor, that's all we need from this witness, if you please."

"Captain—"

"Yes, yes, I'll shut up! But first let me tell you what to do with this prize criminal here. Don't hang him! Give him to me, let me have him, just for an hour, just for a few minutes. Give him to—"

"Next witness!" exclaimed the magistrate. "Moving

along, moving along here, we've a busy schedule! Next wit . . . I say *next witness!*"

The Captain stormed out of the courtroom, slamming the double entry doors behind him. Jennifer hid her face behind a kerchief as he passed her by. Had he recognized her, it could have been bad. He could have pointed her out as the woman Savage had rescued, during that earlier episode on his ship. Suspicions would have been incurred about a possible relationship between Savage and herself and that would have affected the question of whether or not she had indeed harbored Savage. As it now stood, the story of her rescue remained clouded. Captain Trevor had been too humiliated to relate the true facts of how he had been about to whip her when Savage sprang to the rescue.

"Come on, come on," ordered the magistrate to the clerk, who was putting his papers in order, trying to determine who the next witness was. The clerk was turning red with embarrassment, and in response to the pressure.

Dr. Kirby leaned over toward Jennifer and whispered, "If you be the next witness, remember what I told you: you must follow up on the story Lancelot prepared for you. He came just minutes before the British arrived. He ordered you to shelter him and you refused. And he held you there by force to prevent you running to the authorities to report his presence."

"I won't say that."

"Don't be foolish, girl! Listen to me. You want to end your life in a dungeon?"

She was spared having to make the choice, however, for the witness called to testify about Jennifer's role was not Jennifer herself, but the sergeant of the Redcoat detail that had taken Savage in.

"Aye," answered the sergeant in response to the magistrate's question. "When we just come in, he, that one there, he hit the young woman straight across the face. Hit her so hard she fell to the floor, she did. And

he cursed her for refusing to shelter him like h
asked."

"The woman you're speaking of, that's th
granddaughter of old Silas VanDerLind, the printer?"

"She be the one, aye. That's her, right there." H
pointed to Jennifer, leaning forward in the stand. "Re
fused to shelter the pirate, she did. Refused to hid
him. That's why he hit her—at least that's why he said
And he'd of hit her again, too, if'n I hadn't stepped i
smartly."

The faces of the audience turned to look at Jennifer
There was deep scorn in many of their eyes. Jennifer
kept her eyes looking straight ahead. She felt th
townspeople's hatred burning into her, as if it were a
physical thing.

Dr. Kirby reached over and patted her hand. "It's a
necessary lie, Jenny. We can't let out the truth while
you're in danger of being accused as a harborer. You'll
just have to bear up under it, girl. Those that know
you well have an idea of the real facts of the matter."

The magistrate said something further and suddenly
all the eyes that had been boring into Jennifer were no
longer on her, but were directed attentively toward the
front of the hall. There had been an undercurrent of
murmuring while the sergeant pointed out Jennifer as
the one who denied Savage shelter. Now, though, a
deathlike hush fell over the room as the magistrate repeated his question to Lancelot Savage. "Does the accused wish to remark in his own behalf before hearing
the verdict?"

"No," said Savage. "Say it and get it done with."

The magistrate was not yet ready to pronounce his
decision, though. First he wanted to try to get some
concession from the prisoner, something that might
make the magistrate stand taller in the eyes of his English overseers. "Young man, I want to help you," he
said.

Savage smiled in amusement. There were snickers
from the audience.

"Quiet!" the magistrate yelled at the gallery. "Young man," he began again, "I want to give you a chance to lessen your sentence. It's widely known that you're a member of the clandestine group of traitors calling themselves the Sons of Liberty."

Savage raised his manacled hand to his ear, suggesting he had not quite heard right. "Sons of Puberty, you say?"

A roar of laughter erupted through the hall, despite the tension and pinpricking suspense that hung in the air.

"Silence!" yelled the magistrate, turning red-faced, banging his gavel repeatedly. "Don't trifle with me, you blighter!" he said to Savage. "You scalawag! Now hear me: I know you belong to this treacherous group. If you divulge the names of your fellows, I'll see that it goes easier for you. If you don't . . . you'll feel the full weight of English justice!"

Savage hung his head, as if in despair. Then he raised it and said, "There is one man I could make known to you."

"Tell me," said the magistrate, leaning forward excitedly. "Who is it? It'll go easier on you, I swear it will."

"I don't know if I should," Savage said, hesitation seeming to creep into his voice. "He's quite highly placed among the British."

"So many of them are!" exclaimed the magistrate. "Passing themselves off as loyal supporters of the Crown, but really just waiting for the moment to rebel!" He pointed to his clerk. "You there! Get this down, take careful note! Now, lad, who is it, who is the traitorous member of this revolutionary faction?"

Savage motioned to the magistrate with a bent index finger, indicating that he wanted to whisper the name. The magistrate leaned far over toward the prisoner's dock. Savage whispered in his ear.

"That's *calumny!*" shouted the magistrate, jerking his head back violently.

69

"It's true," said Savage, a look of wounded sincerity on his face. "The highly placed member of the Sons of Liberty is King George III. Why . . . just ask anyone."

The courtroom erupted in laughter. The magistrate, infuriated, ordered the hall cleared. "Get them out!" he yelled to the English troops. "Out, out, clear the hall of the bastards!"

As the British troops started rousting people from their seats, ordering and shoving them toward the rear exit, Jennifer stood up and looked desperately toward the front, trying to peer over the top of the crowd. The magistrate was stomping off to a small office at the front of the hall, shouting his verdict over his shoulder, angrily. "Hang him, that's his sentence! Hang him by the neck on the morning after Sabbath! And may the devil take his foul soul!"

Jennifer stood up on the pew to try to see Savage, ducking and weaving her head to look through the onrush of people who were jamming the aisles trying to escape from the British troops, who were pushing forward now with wooden clubs.

Peering through the crowd, desperately, Jennifer finally caught sight of him as he was being taken from the prisoner's dock and led away, guarded by a full phalanx of British troops. He turned his head, and for the first time since entering the hall, he looked at her. His eyes stared deeply into hers as the guards shoved him toward the side exit. As they stared at each other, Jennifer felt the bond between their eyes as if it were a streak of lightning that electrified the space between them. Then, with an abruptness that jolted her, Savage was pushed through the side exit and was gone. Jennifer kept staring at the exit, but there was nothing to see now.

"Back, I say. Back!" The sound of Dr. Kirby's voice forced Jennifer to return to reality. She looked down to see whom he was talking to and saw that he was pushing away two English soldiers who had been trying to advance on him and Jennifer to evict them from the

70

hall. "Back now, you heard me!" he said to the soldiers.

He had managed to keep the soldiers at arm's length so that Jennifer could continue looking at Savage. He had managed this by taking advantage of the fact that the troopers were reluctant to become brutal with him, since he was an old man. Now, though, they were getting fed up with his resistance, and one of them raised his club threateningly.

"You stop that!" Jennifer shouted to the soldier, jumping down from the pew. "You go beat up old men elsewhere, if you have to prove yourself." She led the way toward the exit with Dr. Kirby following behind her, glancing nervously over his shoulder at the stunned soldier who still stood holding the club raised for action.

The sun was shining outside and the brightness hurt Jennifer's eyes. "Is there nothing we can do to help him?" she asked Dr. Kirby as they walked down the road.

He shook his head sadly. "They're keeping him too highly guarded. We can't rescue him. And with this informer in our midst, we can't even hold meetings to discuss a plan of action."

"There must be *something* we can do!" she exclaimed in rage and frustration.

There was a slight sound of a stone being kicked up behind them, barely audible. Jennifer turned around to look. There, walking a few paces behind them, was Matthew Armitage.

When Jennifer looked at him, Matthew cast his eyes down as if he were simply minding his own business, unaware of their presence. Then he looked up as if in surprise. "Ah, Jen—uh . . . Miss VanDerLind. And Dr. Kirby. Hello." When they stopped walking, and turned full round to face him, Matthew came right up to them. "Miss VanDerLind," he said, "my condolences at your being mistreated by that brute. Yes, I was at the trial, I heard all about it. What cowardice, striking a woman! If only he'd come earlier in the day, while I was visiting. I'd have spared you such brutality, you can be sure of that."

"Matthew," said Dr. Kirby quietly, "you're headed in the wrong direction. Why are you going this way, when your home is to the south?"

"A constitutional," said Matthew Armitage.

"Well," said Dr. Kirby, "don't let us stop you."

Matthew looked at him for a moment, a specter of rancor in his eyes. Then he tipped his hat politely and said, "Good day to you, Sir. And to you, Madam." He continued on down the road. After several minutes he glanced over his shoulder, saw that he was not being followed, and cut sharply to the left in the direction of the Governor's mansion.

He thought of the way Jennifer had looked just now—distraught, deeply saddened—and he savored the image. She'll pay for refusing me, he thought to himself. That bitch will pay.

True, he had wanted her for his wife. But all was not lost just because she had refused him. There was another way he could take advantage of her beauty, another way he could *use* her to further his ends. The stupid girl. She'd have been so much better off as his wife. Even *she* would admit this, he thought, if she only knew what it was he had in store for her *now*.

He grinned to himself tightly as he turned into the grounds of the Governor's estate. He enjoyed thinking of the horrors Jennifer was about to suffer. He felt no guilt at the fact that he enjoyed it. After all, he thought philosophically, that was what made the rich and famous rich and famous: the ability to find benefit in the misfortune of others.

He turned onto the cobbled road that cut across the spacious green lawn which fronted the magnificent white mansion. He went up the steps of the building and past the guards who knew him by now and did not stop him. He walked down the marble-tiled entrance-way and up the stairs to the Governor's chambers on the second floor. When he arrived the Governor's secretary, a nervous looking man who sat behind a tiny desk in the outer office, disappeared into the inner office to announce Matthew's presence.

When the doors of the office opened again it was the Governor himself who stood on the threshold, beaming. The secretary stood behind him, waiting for a chance to go past.

"Dear boy, dear boy!" the Governor clucked, coming forward to pump Matthew's hand vigorously. "How good of you to favor me with a visit! Do come in." He stepped aside and extended his arm with a flourish to invite Matthew inside. The secretary took the opportunity to walk quickly out and retake his seat behind the small desk.

The Governor closed the double doors behind them once they were in the inner sanctum of his enormous, luxuriously appointed office. Matthew sat down in a thickly upholstered chair under which was a fancy decorative rug imported from the Orient.

"A sip of brandy?" asked the Governor solicitously.

"Yes, I'd like that. Thank you, Excellency."

The Governor poured the brandy from the snifter into two crystal goblets and offered one to Matthew. He looked on with apprehension as Matthew passed the glass under his nose, then took a tiny sip and rolled it around on his tongue before swallowing it. "Very nice," Matthew said courteously.

"Wonderful, wonderful," exclaimed the Governor delightedly. "You know you're the only one in this entire godforsaken Colony who appreciates the finer things in life. Who else do I have to share such pleasures with? As a matter of fact—" he went to a snuff box on a decorative table and held it out to Matthew "—may I offer you a touch of the divine dust? Imported all the way from India, I might add."

Matthew waved away the offering. "Thank you, Excellency, but not right now. I've had your snuff before, though, and I *do* recognize it as being of the most sublime quality."

"Why, of course you do, dear boy! You're so refined! So cultured! Speaking of which, Matthew, allow me to show you some absolutely exquisite . . . oh, wait, wait, let me find them." He went to his mammoth desk and searched feverishly through a top drawer. "Ah!" He took the heavy parchment cards he had been looking for and handed them to Matthew. "A true artist rendered these, my boy, a gentleman from Paris, France, who—"

"Excellency, *please!*" exclaimed Matthew in a whining, shocked voice, as soon as he saw that the cards he had been handed were erotic drawings. He leapt up from his chair and threw the drawings down on the floor disgustedly. He was shaking with revulsion. "You *know* that I find such . . . *filth* . . . extremely distasteful."

The Governor regarded him with disappointment. "I beg your pardon, Matthew. I forgot."

"I *never* indulge in such . . . *trash.*"

"A pity. Your one failing. Ah well," said the Governor, brightening again, "we can't all be perfect now, can we?" He picked up the drawings from the carpet and put them in his desk drawer. Then he sat down in the chair facing the one Matthew had just leapt up from and pressed the spread fingertips of his left hand against the spread fingertips of his right hand.

"Well, now," he said, "let me guess what it is that you've come for. It can't be your reward for turning in the pirate, since we already deposited that in the Bank of London, as per your wishes." He looked perturbed. "By the way, dear boy, why is it you keep insisting we deposit your money there, instead of giving it to you here in gold? You don't *really* expect to get to England, now do you?"

"I told you, Excellency. I will get there."

"Yes, yes, you've told me this balderdash before, about how you expect to be granted a title and position in London itself. But surely you're jesting, Matthew? Even though you have done quite a few favors for the Crown, you can't really believe that you, a commoner, could do enough to actually come to the attention of the peerage?"

"You don't have faith in me," said Matthew, half-grinning. He had recovered his composure and now sat down again.

"Dear boy, dear boy," clucked the Governor, "quite to the contrary! I have *every* faith in you. Why, you're one of the most deceitful, conniving, ambitious young men it's been my pleasure to know. It's just that . . . well really, sir, a titled position? That's *quite difficult* to get, even for a man of your diverse talents, don't you think?"

"I'll get it," said Matthew calmly.

"Quite so, quite so, if you say so. Do put in a good word for me with His Majesty, won't you, when you make it to London?" His expression was amused and jesting.

"I may," said Matthew, smiling.

The Governor broke up in laughter. "Such arrogance! My, but I wouldn't trust you a farthing's throw out of my sight." His shook his head, grinning. Then he sighed deeply and glanced over at his gigantic desk, which was piled high with waiting work. He put on a businesslike expression. "Well, now, Matthew, what *did* you come for?"

"I just left the trial."

"Of that pirate, yes, I know. Bloody glad to have that over with. Now he'll be hung and we'll have it behind us. Quite a poor reflection on me, don't you know, to have him running around the province for so long with no one able to track him down. But now we'll stretch his neck a bit, and—"

"I don't think so," said Matthew.

"Eh?"

"You're far too magnanimous a soul to carry out the

75

sentence," said Matthew, grinning his supercilious, thin-lipped grin.

"I certainly am not. However, do I detect in your manner the hint of a benefit about to accrue to me?"

"Excellency, you are familiar, are you not, with the VanDerLind girl?"

"The granddaughter of that printer you secretly turned in to me. Yes indeed, a lovely girl. In fact, I'm curious why you haven't used the threat of eviction to gain certain 'favors' from her, now that you own title to the printer's property."

"She doesn't know I own the title. Besides, she'd never compromise herself simply to avoid eviction."

"A pity. She is *such* a lovely girl. Even more's the pity that Royal Governors are subject to the law of the land and prohibited from performing certain forcible acts of passion upon the populace."

The Governor licked his lips at the thought of the girl, whom he knew he could never have. But then he looked at Matthew, who was gazing at him with malevolent amusement, and it occurred to him that if Matthew Armitage was bringing up the subject, perhaps his longing for the girl might not be so hopeless as he thought. "Tell me, Matthew, do you have something of interest you might wish to impart to me regarding this ravishing young creature?"

Matthew grinned tightly. "Excellency," he said, "you're going to be very grateful to me for this information. Now about Miss Jennifer VanDerLind. . . ."

Jennifer stared at the vial of arsenic on the workbench in Silas's room. Silas had always used it to keep insects away from his garden.

Arsenic was painful, she had always heard. She wondered how long the pain lasted until . . . it was over. Well, she thought, the answer to that question might not be long in coming. Savage was to be hanged at the first break of day, tomorrow morning. She had no desire to live past that time. She was gazing at the

76

vial—seeing in her mind's eye the image of Savage's face during the times he had looked at her so tenderly, so lovingly—when there was a knock at the cabin door.

She did not want to answer it. There was no one she wished to see or talk to. But the chance that it might be someone with word about Savage made her go to the door and open it.

Matthew Armitage stood on the porch, his hands holding the lapels of his waistcoat. "*Good* afternoon, Jennifer. I'm sure you're simply de*light*ed to see me, after—"

"Go away, Mr. Armitage," she said wearily, not caring now whether she was rude to him or not.

She started to close the door, but he slithered in very quickly and was then in the room with her. "Oh, but Jennifer," he said, "I came to help you. You wouldn't turn away an ally, would you, who comes offering aid?"

"Help me do what?" she said still standing at the door, holding it open for him to leave.

Matthew turned to the room and inspected it, began walking about carelessly, as if he owned the place. He picked up a wooden humidor still filled with Silas's tobacco, sniffed inside, raised an approving eyebrow. He glanced at the pleated ruffled skirt of Jennifer's pink dress, and at the square-cut bodice which highlighted the lacy white chemise that covered her breasts.

"I have come to help you in your humanitarian pursuits," he said. He raised a finger to make a point. "Now don't misunderstand me. I'm not suggesting you have any, shall we say *personal* interest in a certain buccaneer pirate. Why, everyone knows you refused him shelter and he slapped you, so *nat*urally you have no af*fect*ion for the man." His lips compressed in a mocking sneer. "But perhaps you might like to help the poor devil for purely philo*soph*ical, humanit*arian* reasons . . . before they snap his silly neck at daybreak on the morrow."

77

"Oh, stop it, you cretin! What do you want! What have you come here for?"

"Merely to suggest, *dear*est, that were you to ask me in a polite manner, I might see fit to use my influence with the Governor to get you an audience with him."

Jennifer stood very still, not moving a muscle in her body. She stared at Matthew intently.

"Once I gain you an audience, you might speak to him of such things as . . . oh, the weather, or the tea tax, or . . ." he yawned affectedly, covering his mouth with the back of his wrist, ". . . *clemency*."

"He wouldn't listen to me."

"He would."

"How do you know that?"

"His Excellency is a very generous and lenient soul."

She slammed the door violently, to show her feelings.

"*No* one seems to believe that," said Matthew, frowning, looking reflectively off to the side. "Ah well, in any case, the fact is that I've already dis*cuss*ed the matter with him, and he's *more* than willing to entertain a plea of clemency. If it comes from you. He will listen with an open ear and an open heart, he assures me."

Jennifer stared at Matthew coldly and appraisingly. "Why is he willing to grant this audience? Is there more to it than just his being lenient, as you say?" She raised her hand and rushed toward him, fire in her eyes, her cheeks flushing. "Because if there *is*, and if it's—"

"Jennifer, I swear!" said Matthew, raising his hands in protection and backing away quickly. "Would I even sug*gest* anything that would displease you?"

She lowered her hand, but there was still fire in her eyes. And there was a chill which had crept up her spine, which she felt very strongly. She had a premonition. She knew what this was all about. But Matthew was too sly to say so openly, knowing that she would indignantly refuse and would turn him out bodily. And so long as the thing was left unsaid . . .

"Shall I tell the Governor then that you're coming?"

She did not answer.

"*Well*. I can see you're not interested in the slightest. So we'll simply for*get* the entire matter. *Sorry* to have troubled you. Good day, Jennifer." He started for the door, opened it, but then halted. He was too smart to expect her to bid him wait. He seemed to know that she would not go that far . . . but that there was a way to make the proposition amenable to her, so long as it was not stated directly, so long as it was camouflaged and disguised. "Perhaps you *should* go after all," he said. "For humani*tari*an reasons, as I say." He paused. "Shall I arrange it?"

When she lowered her head because she could not look him in the eyes now, once the decision was made, Matthew Armitage knew he had won.

"Six this evening would be perfect, I think. That's . . . why, oh my! . . . that's only two short hours away. What a con*ven*ient co*in*cidence." He smiled at her, then left.

Jennifer paced the room, feeling tense and nervous. She knew Savage's life depended on the outcome of her audience with the Governor. She felt a piercing sense of foreboding. Far down in her mind, hidden away in the darkest depths, she had an inkling of what was to take place during this audience . . . of what was to be expected of her. The notion tried to rise up to the surface of her mind, but she fought it down viciously. She could not think about it. She could not admit it to herself. Or there would be no way of letting herself go to this audience.

When it was time to leave, she put on a shawl, took a deep breath, and stepped outside to walk to the Governor's mansion.

Chapter 5

Jennifer was ushered into the Governor's private office as soon as she arrived at the mansion. The Governor was sitting at his desk when she entered the room and he remained seated, writing with a quill pen, not bothering even to look up at her. After several minutes, he did look up. He stared at her appraisingly with a lecher's eye, sizing her up slowly from head to toe. Then he returned to his writing, ignoring her.

"Excellency," she said, "I—"

"Keep still."

She stood by the doorway, silent, unmoving. She glanced nervously at the plush red carpet and the colorful, wood-framed paintings on the walls.

The Governor looked up from his work and glanced at the clock. He seemed to be awaiting some event that was to take place at a prearranged time. He leaned back in his chair, folded his hands together over his large belly, and regarded Jennifer in silence. Soon, a thumping sound came from the courtyard below the room's second-floor window. When he heard the sound, the Governor stood up and walked over to Jennifer. He did not stop until he was extremely close to her, so close that Jennifer found herself backing away.

"Stay still," ordered the Governor, moving forward again. He was just inches from her now and the smell of the too-sweet cologne on his skin made Jennifer want to raise her hand to her nose. The Governor's fat face was very close to hers. He had thick blubbery lips and very heavy eyelids over his protuberant eyes. The thumping sound continued to come from the courtyard below. Jennifer wondered what it was.

Without warning the Governor went behind her, bent down, and stuck his hands under the hem of her pink dress and petticoats . . . he rose quickly and grasped her buttocks tightly through the thin cloth of her underdrawers. Jennifer yelped in shock and tried to turn, but he was clutching her too tightly. Finally she managed to jerk around and step away from him, her eyes wide in horrified outrage, her mouth open. She raised her hand to slap him—but then hesitated in midmotion, her hand just inches from his face.

The Governor smiled maliciously at her hesitation. "You do have an idea what this is all about then, don't you?"

She slapped him. Then she rushed for the giant double doors, only to find them locked. She turned back to face him, breathless, and fearful, her palms and back pressed against the doors. "You can't do this," she said under her breath. "Even a Governor can't rape a citizen—"

He laughed an evil, sneering laugh. "Rape?" he scoffed. "That will hardly be necessary." He went over to the windows overlooking the courtyard and drew aside the brown velvet curtains. Jennifer looked out and now saw the source of the thumping sounds emanating from the courtyard. Lancelot Savage was down on the ground, his hands manacled, being beaten by two large burly guards. His expression as each new blow landed on his body was one of pure agony.

Jennifer screamed in shock and revulsion, then covered her mouth with her fist. "Make them stop!" she cried. The Governor did not budge. She said it again this time with pleading in her voice. "Make them stop?"

The Governor smiled. He came forward and put his hands on her breasts, over the thin bodice of her dress. Jennifer started to pull away from him, but the sight of Savage being beaten to death in the courtyard below

81

made her stop. She forced herself to remain motionless, her face wincing in torment.

The Governor smiled even more maliciously. As Jennifer stood there, he pushed her shawl off onto the floor, then unlaced the front of her dress slowly, as if time meant nothing to him. Then he jerked down the bodice and the white chemise beneath it. He pulled the bodice and chemise down to just below her breasts. Her full young bosom stood nakedly exposed, rising and falling with her quickened, fearful breathing. The Governor looked her right in the eye, smiling as he put his hands to her breasts and began squeezing and kneading them. He pinched her nipples, hard. She tried, but could not stifle the groan that came to her lips. Still she did not pull away from him.

In keeping with his end of the unstated agreement, the Governor now went over to the window, opened it, and yelled down to the guards below. "Cease that barbarism, you heathen scum! This is a civilized age. Prisoners are not beaten . . ." he closed the window and pulled the drapes shut again, and turned back to Jennifer, ". . . only hanged," he concluded.

Jennifer now stood with her arms crossed in front of her, a hand on each shoulder. The Governor slowly walked around her, looking at her appreciatively. "You will be my mistress," he said, "for a period of one year. In return, I will pardon your pirate from the gallows. And when the year you spend with me is over, I will let him go free."

Jennifer said nothing. Tears welled up in her eyes and streamed down her cheeks. She pressed her arms tighter against her breasts, as if that somehow protected them.

"Come, come," demanded the Governor harshly. "I haven't all day. Do you accept my conditions or do you not? I'd really as soon hang the bugger anyway."

Jennifer's eyes showed her agony. She could not make herself speak. Slowly, with deep anguish, she nodded her head.

"Excellent," said the Governor. He grasped her dress and chemise and jerked them down past her hips to her knees. His hands went to her petticoats and pulled them down also to around her knees.

She could not just stand still and take it! It was impossible! When his hands went for her underdrawers, she lost control and shoved them away. She tried to scratch his face. He grasped her wrist. She swung at him with her other hand, nails bared, and he grasped that too, then pushed her backward until her buttocks and shoulder blades slammed up against the wall.

"A spirited one, eh?" he said, grinning cruelly, his face almost touching hers. "Fine, fight me if you can. It'll only make your degradation all the sweeter when I finally break you. And break you I will! I'll have you cringing and broken long before your year is through!"

He forced her hands back against the wall, above her head, then mashed his bulky body tightly against her, pinning her to the wall. The silken fabric of his lavender waistcoat pressed against her breasts and she felt the rigidity of his manhood poking hard behind his britches against her loins. He tried to kiss her, but she turned her head away, grimacing in disgust.

This only infuriated him and he began thrusting his hips against her with violent force. She tried to bring her knee up into him, but her legs were locked together by the bunched-up dress and petticoats around her knees. She groaned sharply as his ramming thrusts became more frenzied, his shaft prodding her repeatedly behind the layers of clothing. His bulk was so great that each of his thrusts against her felt like a hard blow upon her body. His chest continued to mash against her naked breasts.

He moved her wrists together so he could grasp them both in a single hand. Then he moved his free hand to her face and put his palm over it, lightly pressing against her features—not to hurt her but to further degrade her. She tried to bite him. He moved his hand away before she could do so, then slowly moved it down her throat, down past her collarbone, lower still. He grasped her breast and squeezed it tightly. She moaned loudly.

He pinched her pert nipple between his thumb and forefinger and began jerking it up and down, hurting her. He moved to her other nipple and did the same thing, grinning in vicious malice, his face beaded in perspiration. Jennifer rolled her head from side to side against the wall, moaning in torment. Through her despair, she realized a terrible truth: this man wanted more than just to use her body for his pleasure, he wanted to defile and debase her as well. He took perverse enjoyment from doing so. And *this was the man she would be at the mercy of for an entire year!*

The Governor laughed with evil pleasure at the look of horror that came to her face. He began slapping her breasts with the front and back of his open hand. The pain she felt was only slight, but the humiliation was as intense as pain. His hand slid down her stomach to the top of her underdrawers.

"No," she pleaded, "don't? . . ." She tried to pull her hands free, but they remained locked tightly in his grip. She tensed, waiting to hear the ripping sound of the flimsy garment being torn away. Instead, she felt his beefy hand move inside the waistband and rub against the soft silken hairs of her womanhood. Then his hand moved down and covered her womanhood completely, his fingers pressing up against the bottom of her.

"Stop it!" she cried, beginning to sob.

He pressed his fat fingers inside her and began wiggling them about. She cried out tormentedly and twisted and squirmed against the wall. The Governor became so excited at the sight of her writhing about so furiously, he neglected to keep up the tightness of his grip on her wrists. She managed to pull her hands down. She beat wildly at his chest and shoulders.

When he stepped back, cursing, she broke free. His hand grasped her underdrawers, though, and as she ran

84

away from him the garment ripped apart and came off in his hand, baring her loins and buttocks.

She ran only a short distance from him before tripping and falling to the ground, due to the dress and petticoats that were bunched up around her knees. She tried to get to her feet, but her locked-together knees made it difficult. She did not have time to move the garments up or down, for the Governor was advancing on her now. He was twirling the remnant of her underdrawers on his finger in malicious humor.

She pulled and pushed herself along the carpet away from him, until finally she was against a backless banquet couch and he was towering directly over her. She cowered back, one hand covering her naked sex, the other pressed over her breasts. She gazed up at him with pleading, fearful eyes.

He raised an arm sharply, as if to strike her. She put up her hand, fingers spread, to protect herself. No blow came, though. He was just toying with her. He had done this to make her raise her hand and now he stared leeringly down between her legs where she had just exposed herself. Before she could move he grabbed her wrist and jerked her forward. She toppled over in front of him, her face coming into contact with the top of his black leather boot.

He bent forward and put one hand on the back of her neck. His other hand, the one holding the torn remnant of her underdrawers, went to her derriere and began pinching her. She moved her hands behind her to shove his hand away, then realized too late that she had done exactly what he wanted. He grasped her wrists together and bound them tightly with the torn undergarment.

He stepped back. She looked up at him, her hair falling into her face. He unbuttoned his britches, slowly, making a show of it, delighting in the terror that came to Jennifer's eyes as she watched him. He pushed his britches down, and pushed down his linen underdrawers too. The sight of his stiff pink mast made her cringe in horror and apprehension.

He shoved her down on the backless banquet and laid her lengthwise atop it. He tugged her bunched-up clothing away from her knees, down to her ankles. Then he grasped her bound wrists and pulled them sharply upward, forcing her to rise on her knees on the thickly cushioned banquet. She had to spread her knees apart to keep from toppling over onto the floor. The Governor jerked her wrists up higher still, making her scream with pain and forcing her to double over at the waist. She was on her knees now with her backside raised up toward him, her face pressing humiliatingly down into the cushions of the banquet. He came up onto the banquet behind her.

Though Jennifer despised herself for giving him the satisfaction of seeing her beg, she could not stop herself. "Please don't, please don't!" she cried in desperate panic, as the shame and degredation overwhelmed her.

The Governor snorted in reply. His beefy hand moved about her loins, roughly rubbing and pressing and then . . . guiding him in between the sensitive lips of her womanhood. She screamed, her voice muffled by the thick upholstery her face was pressed down into. He thrust violently in and out, pinching her backside repeatedly with his free hand, all the while keeping her wrists raised painfully high behind her. Her screaming continued and did not cease until finally, after a vicious thrust, he issued a gutteral grunt from deep in his throat, and then it was over. He began pulling his clothing back into place, leaving Jennifer in the most debasing position she had ever in her life imagined. When he finished buttoning his trousers, he untied her wrists, then went over to the giant, black, overstuffed chair behind his desk and sat down.

Jennifer got up slowly, achingly, hot tears streaming down her cheeks. She did not try to cover herself to hide her nakedness. It did not matter any longer. She was dirt. She was filth. She was the scum of the universe, and nothing could ever change that. The rest of the year would not be worse than this, she thought. Nothing could be worse than this. Nothing could make her feel lower than she felt now. She would survive this next year, she would endure the tortures so that Savage could go free. But once he was free and away from their clutches, there would be no reason for her to go on living. She was not worthy of Savage any longer. Not now, not after this. . . .

The Governor leaned back in his chair. "Now," he said, "here's how we'll arrange this little *liaison* of ours. You're to move into the mansion here with me. No, don't look so surprised. How else could we manage it? I certainly can't be sending a messenger after you every time I get the urge, now can I? After all, my needs are rather immediate, you know, and I do hate having to suffer undue delays."

He paused to stick a pinch of snuff into his nostrils and sneeze into a handkerchief. "We'll put you in the east wing. You'll find it quite pleasant, I daresay. Small, but very stylish. Louis XIV is the dominant mode. And, pay attention now, this is important: you're not to tell any of the townspeople about our little agreement. They'll know you're living here, surely, but the *reason* must remain our secret. You can imagine why, of course. King George is a most understanding monarch, but I daresay even *he* would not approve of his Royal Governor staying the execution of a pirate—one who has been preying upon his shipping for years mind you—simply for the Governor's personal gain. No, my dear, my position would be quite untenable if word got out about our agreement. In fact, if word did get out, I would be obliged to have your pirate hanged immediately, just to show there was no truth to the vicious rumor. You understand, I'm sure?"

Jennifer said nothing.

"Do you understand!?"

She nodded.

"Good."

She had been dressing as he talked, and she now wore the tattered remnants of the clothes she had arrived in. She recovered her shawl from the floor and wrapped it around her shoulders, hugging herself tightly once it was in place.

The Governor smiled at her pleasantly. Then he got up from the chair, grasped her by the arm and pulled her toward the closed doors. "Open up out there!" he shouted through the doors. A key jiggled in the lock, then the doors were opened by one of the guards standing outside. The Governor pulled Jennifer forward and flung her out through the doorway. "Now, *slut*," he said harshly, "get out of my sight."

When she returned to her cabin, taking care to pass no one she knew along the road, Jennifer found a big white-painted board nailed to her front door, with bold black lettering on it:

NOTICE OF EVICTION
(And Solicitation of Bids)

The absentee owner hereby orders this property sold forthwith to the renderer of the highest bid. Direct inquiries to R. Cromwell, Esq., agent for the owner. Tenant must evacuate premises immediately.

Jennifer stared at the sign, too dulled and emotionally drained to feel anything more than a sense of resignation and horrible fatefulness. The universe was caving in on her now. She went inside, filled the tub with water from the well—without taking the time to heat it first—then took a very long time bathing herself. She scrubbed her tender skin harshly with the cloth, trying to wash away with lye-soap and water the defilement and mortification that had been visited upon her body.

Afterward, she dressed in fresh clothing. Just as she was finishing putting on her shoes, she heard a knock at the door and Mrs. Fiske's voice call out, "Jennifer, are you home?"

Jennifer went to the door and opened it.

"Oh, you poor dear," said Mrs. Fiske, eyeing the white-painted board. "So it's true after all. Signs are posted in the town square, too, but . . . I never imagined!" She shook her head in sympathy. "What'll ye do now, child?"

"I . . . I'll move someplace else."

"Oh, as easy as that, is it? With no money and you being all alone as you are."

Jennifer did not want to talk now. As kindly as Mrs. Fiske was, Jennifer wished she were gone. She went to the shelf where she kept the sewing she had done for her and handed it to her in a bundle. Mrs. Fiske was almost oblivious to the bundle as she accepted it. Her eyes were on Jennifer and she looked concerned. "I'll tell you what," she said. "You come live with Mr. Fiske and myself. We'll welcome you. And you can work for your keep doing chores and the sewing."

Jennifer did not know what to say. What could she tell her? No thank you, she was moving in with the Governor instead? But then, she would find out soon enough. The entire town would find out. There was no way of keeping a thing like this secret. If only the eviction sign had not been posted! Now it would look like she was moving in with the Governor as a result of being evicted, to avoid moving in with a family and having to work for her keep.

"Thank you, Mrs. Fiske, but I . . . I already have a place to go. Now, I have a headache, so—"

"So soon you have a place to move to?" Mrs. Fiske looked surprised, then suspicious, and finally disapproving. Her eyes seemed to say that any place Jennifer had found on such short notice *had* to be illegitimate. "Well," she said, "in any case, you'll need help moving, wherever it is you're moving to. I'll have Mr. Fiske hitch up the wagon and—"

"No. But thank you kindly." She had to get rid of this woman. She could not talk now. "Thank you, Mrs. Fiske, really, but I have to go now. I have a headache, you see, and . . . I'm sorry." She closed the door firmly. After a minute, she heard Mrs. Fiske's retreating footsteps. They were loud, angry footsteps.

Jennifer put her hands to her eyes. Her head pounded horribly. True, she thought, she did need help moving, even though her belongings were few. But Mrs. Fiske's offer would not have remained once the matron knew the destination where Jennifer's things were to be moved.

She could not tell Mrs. Fiske, or anyone, that she was making this move to the Governor's mansion in order to save Savage's life. And the townspeople would never guess it by themselves. As far as they knew, the only relationship she had with Savage was the one that had come out at the trial: she had refused him shelter and by doing so had contributed to his capture. That in itself had not set well with the townspeople. But now this—seeing her move in with the Governor—this would be the last straw. She would not have a friend left in the Colony.

Abruptly she made a decision. She would not ask anyone for help in moving. She would leave her belongings, everything but her clothing. She needed nothing, and there was nothing she wished to take for pleasure or to comfort her. She did not want to take pleasure in anything or to be comforted. This was to be a year of solid torture and she would make no attempt to lessen the pain of it. Just as she was thinking this, the creaking sound of a team-drawn buckboard wagon came from outside. She opened the door and went outside in time to see the wagon pull to a stop in front of the cabin. Two Redcoat privates were seated in the buckboard.

The older of the two soldiers climbed down from the

wagon slowly and came up the walk to Jennifer. "Orders of the Governor," he said. "We're to help you move."

The younger soldier jumped down from the wagon gaily and came up to Jennifer. His expression was leering and snide. "The Guv's extended the royal courtesy fer you, missy. 'Course, word's got out why. We all know how 'courteous' ye've been to him, now don't we?" He grinned lewdly.

Jennifer's eyes went wide and she slapped him stingingly.

Surprised and enraged, the soldier pulled back his arm to slug Jennifer hard, but his movement was arrested by the older soldier, who grasped the man's elbow, exclaiming, "Anson, think! This be the Governor's woman you're about to strike! The *Governor's woman*, Anson!"

That stopped the soldier cold.

And it made Jennifer scream at the older man, "I'm *not!*" But it was no use. She ran into the cabin and slammed the door. She stood there with her eyes shut tightly.

At least she had saved Savage, she thought. That was the only consolation that lessened her present agony and the agony she would have to endure over the next twelve months. At least, come the morning, Savage would be spared from visiting the hangman. . . .

Chapter 6

On the morning he was to be hanged, Lancelot Savage
lay on a pile of stale, matted straw that served as his
mattress, his legs in irons, his hands behind his neck.
He stared up at the single barred window of his cell.
Cool morning air was wafting in through the window,
along with the first rays of sunlight which signalled that
it was time for his journey to the gallows. Off in the
distance, beyond the fortress walls of the prison compound, he could hear crickets still chirping.

He breathed in the cool air, listened to the crickets,
and thought of Jennifer. She was a unique experience
in his life. She was the only woman he had ever felt so
deeply about that he wished to spend his life with her.
No other experience in his life had been so sharp, so
vivid. No other woman in his life was as desirable to
him as Jennifer. This was his one regret now that he
was only minutes away from dying: that he had found
her at last and would not be able to have her. . . .

It hurt. God, it hurt. He would almost have been
better off not meeting her at all, so that he would not
have to suffer this agony of losing her now that he had
found her. But no, he thought, it was better having
been with her, having shared the few weeks they had
together. It was better having these intense, strong
feelings for her, though they pained him now deeply.

Footsteps sounded heavily beyond the thick cell
door and there was the sound of a key rattling in the
lock. The door came open with a creak and a British
lieutenant entered the cell, flanked by two guards.

"Been 'aving pleasant enough dreams, 'ave ye?" asked the lieutenant sarcastically. "Well, we'll put an end to that soon enough. No more dreams for you. Plenty o' sleep, though. A long, long time to sleep, yes indeed." He chuckled at his own joke. He instructed the two guards to chain Savage's arms behind his back and to free his legs from the restraining irons. As the leg irons were being removed, an orderly came to the door of the cell carrying a pot of gruel.

"What's that?" the lieutenant asked, astonished. "Breakfast?"

"Aye, sir," the orderly said, nodding, "it's—"

"He'll have no need of breakfast! What hunger he has now he won't be suffering much longer, eh? Go on," he ordered sharply, "give it to someone it won't be wasted on!"

The orderly left quickly. When Savage was on his feet, the lieutenant instructed the guards to take him by the arms and march him out to the hanging tree.

Savage shook off the guards with a violent twist of his body. "I can walk unaided!" he said.

"Can ye now," said the lieutenant. "All right, lads, let the man march by his own power. Seeing as it's his last stroll, 'e may as well 'ave it to his own liking." He indicated the open door, with a gesture of his hand. Savage walked through it into the corridor, preceded by one of the guards. He walked down the dungeon corridor, not looking at the faces of the other prisoners as they peered out from behind the iron gratings in the upper centers of their closed cell doors. He walked with his back straight, moving forward down the corridor, then up the steps. He came out of the dark, dingy dungeon into the just breaking sunlight of the new day.

As he walked across the dirt field toward the north wall of the prison compound, he looked around him. The compound was enclosed by high walls of sharpened wooden palisades with guard towers at each of the four corners. The field itself was strewn with rocks and stones, far too many to ever be cleared away to make the land tillable; that was one reason the prison was built here—the rocky land was unsuitable for any other purpose.

The wall he was being directed toward had a sturdy oak tree in front of it and from the lowest branch of the tree hung a hemp rope, its base knotted into a hangman's noose. A lightweight shoulder-high platform was positioned directly under the noose with steps leading up to it.

When Savage reached the oak tree, he stopped.

"Well, let's get to it," said the lieutenant, slapping his palms to his belly. "I've got a powerful hunger this mornin', and I want to make messhall afore the food's all gone cold."

Savage looked up at the noose as it swayed slightly in the breeze. He thought of kicking and biting and giving these Redcoats hell before they finally overpowered him. But what would be the use? He would end up there on the platform anyway, the noose around his neck. The only difference would be that he might not be conscious then. He did not want that. He wanted to go out with his eyes open, if go out he must.

He stepped onto the first step leading up to the top, then took each succeeding step until he was standing on the small platform itself. It was very wobbly and poorly built. When one of the guards went up after him, the platform began to shake so much that it seemed it might collapse right then and there. The guard grasped the swaying noose, slid it down over Savage's head, then pulled its knot down tight. The rough fibers of the rope bit into the skin of his throat. The guard pulled the knot around to the side of his head, just under his left ear, scraping the circle of the noose roughly against his throat as he did so. Then he stepped down from the platform onto the ground.

"Any last words before I kick it out from under ye?" the lieutenant asked Savage good naturedly.

"Yes," said Savage. "The plague on you and your mongrel mother."

"Swine," sneered the lieutenant. He motioned for the first guard, who had now strapped himself into a drum harness, to begin the drum roll. As it started, Savage looked across the yard and saw the scores of faces that were staring out at him through the iron-barred windows of the main barracks compound. He could not see the expression on the faces at this distance . . . only the staring eyes.

His body tensed. The drum roll reached its crescendo, then ceased abruptly on a powerful beat. "Now!" yelled the lieutenant and suddenly Savage felt the wobbly platform being kicked out from under him and go clattering to its side on the ground. He began falling. He felt the snap of the rope against the side of his head.

But then, instead of coming to an abrupt, dangling, bouncing-around halt in midair, he continued to fall through the air and came crashing down to the dirt ground.

He was stunned and shocked, and it took a moment for him to come to his senses. The lieutenant was laughing uproariously, holding his sides, bending over with hilarity, his eyes tearing.

"Heee, heee, heee," he laughed, "did y' see 'is look, did y' see the look on him when the platform got kicked away from under 'im? Heee, heee, *heee*," he laughed, doubling over in merriment.

Savage slowly got to his feet, with great difficulty since his wrists were still shackled behind him. He went up to the lieutenant.

"Oh, didn't I tell ye?" laughed the lieutenant uproariously. "New orders 'ave come in. Yer sentence 'as been changed a bit. Pity I neglected to tell ye, eh wot? We didn't tie the rope to the branch, as y' can see, just draped it over."

Savage kicked him *hard* in the stomach, doubling the man over and knocking him backwards, his cheeks billowing out with the expulsion of breath. The lieutenant lay on the ground, his face turning red as he

95

tried gaspingly to catch his breath. A cheer rose from the men in the barracks across the field. The multitude of eyes lit up joyously.

Savage advanced on the lieutenant, but was felled suddenly by one of the guards wielding a truncheon, which crashed down along the side of Savage's neck. Then the lieutenant got to his feet, red-faced and cursing wildly, and began kicking Savage in the side and back as Savage lay on the ground writhing, his arms manacled behind him.

Finally the lieutenant stopped. His expression was that of a schoolyard bully who had forgotten he was not supposed to beat up on the weaker, helpless children because it made him look bad. He pulled a scarf from his pocket and mopped his sweating, red face. "We'll leave you a bit alive now, lad," he said wheezingly. "Fer ye've got yourself another appointment, this one with the prison commandant. And it's bad form, don't ye know, to arrive for it half-dead."

He turned to his guards. "Get him on his feet." When they did so, the lieutenant led them across the field toward the garrison building and the commandant's quarters. Savage walked slightly bent forward, unable to stand straight because of the pain in his stomach. The lieutenant had kicked him in the area of his previous wound and a sharp pain shot all through Savage and refused to abate.

To enter the garrison area, they passed through a palisaded gate in an interior wall within the compound, which separated the main prison yard from the guard's quarters, armsroom, and garrison area. The guards on duty saluted the lieutenant as the small detail passed through. The lieutenant did not answer the salute. Savage was led up wooden steps to the upper level of a fortresslike building, arriving at a door. The lieutenant knocked, then entered. After a moment, he came out again. "The captain will see you now," he said to Savage, shoving him forward through the doorway, so that Savage lost his footing and ended up on the wooden floor of the room. The guards entered after him and quickly pulled him up so that he was standing on his feet, though very shakily. They continued holding him up, to support him.

The captain's back was to Savage, as he stood gazing out a window. But Savage recognized him instantly and felt a fearful hollowness inside him as he realized that he was now at the mercy of this man.

"We meet again, do we, pirate?" said Captain Trevor, turning around to face him, his one arm holding a swagger stick. He still wore the blue coat of a Naval officer, though he was no longer in the Navy, but instead held the position of prison commandant. The empty sleeve of his jacket was pinned to the side of the garment.

"You don't know how I've longed to have you here like this," Captain Trevor said in almost a whisper, his mouth contorting into a wicked sneer. He stood staring at Savage for a long moment. "Did ye enjoy your little charade at the hanging tree? I enjoyed it. I stood here watching, thinking good, good, knowing that afterward, in just minutes after, ye'd be here, standing here right before me. As ye're doing right now.

"Stand aside," he ordered the guards who were holding Savage up. When they did so, Savage teetered, but did not fall.

"Why wasn't I hanged?" Savage asked. "The sentence—"

"—has been changed. Ye may believe it was out of the goodness of the Governor's heart that he temporar . . ." He let the word fade out and instead said, "that he reprieved you. Or you may believe it was because I wanted you here so badly. Or ye may believe anything ye damn well please. But here's as it stands now: you're to be imprisoned here at Haverhill for the space of one year."

"And at the end of the year?"

"Why, ye'll be set free, of course." He grinned wickedly. "If'n you're still among the living, that is. Do you think ye will be, pirate? Eh?" His hand suddenly slashed forward viciously and the riding crop struck Savage in the chest, dropping him to his knees, leaving him choking and gritting his teeth to stop himself from screaming.

"You have one year here with me, before ye get your 'freedom'," said the Captain. "All you have to do is live it out." Then he began thrashing Savage with the crop, until the blackness descended on Savage, whisking him off into merciful unconsciousness.

Living in the Governor's mansion was sheer hell for Jennifer. She had been here over half a year now. The only good thing was that the Governor's raping attacks had become less frequent than they were at first, due to the fact that she always fought him wildly—kicking and scratching and biting—making him pay dearly for his pleasure. He had been wrong when he assumed she would be "broken" early and cease resisting him. Now he was too prideful to order her to stop her resistance, since to do so would be an admission that he was not man enough to break her as he had promised.

Although Jennifer was permitted to come and go as she pleased, beyond the mansion's walls, in the village, there was only hatred for her. Everyone knew she was living with the Governor, but no one knew the true reason. So Jennifer did not venture out. Because of this, she had no one to talk to, no one to give her sympathy, or help lessen her burden in any way.

To counter the unbearable misery and bleakness of her days, she had found a way to keep herself busy. It was a way that let her secretly aid the Colonial cause. She had come upon it accidentally some time before by overhearing a conversation. She had been in the hall when she happened to hear the Governor yelling at the young man who scripted his correspondence, most of which went to the Minister of Colonial Affairs in London—the Governor's superior.

"You blithering moron!" the Governor shouted at

the cringing man. "Can't you write gracefully? Have you no sense of style, of elegance? These are official communiques, you fool! Their appearance is utterly crucial!"

He slapped his hand to his head, as the young man cowered back fearfully. "Can't you understand? The Minister forms his impression of me by the look and style of my missives. He sees me personally only once a year, when he comes for his tour of the Colonies. The rest of the time it's only my communiques he has to form impressions of me by. They must look sublime! Not cramped and angled like *this*." He waved a sheaf of pages in the air, then slammed them down on his secretary's desk. "These look as if they've been written by some rummy in the midst of an epileptic seizure!"

"I'm *terribly* sorry, Excellency, I—"

"Oh, shut up, shut up. I'd replace you in a minute if there were anyone better. But I've already gone through a dozen of your ilk. Is there no one in the entire province who can write His Majesty's English with style?"

That evening at dinner, which she was always required to attend, Jennifer mentioned the subject to the Governor. "So your correspondence with the Minister looks bad, does it?"

"What's this?" said the Governor, feigning shock. "She can actually speak?" Jennifer had not said a word to him in all the months she had been here, except when forced to.

"I hear Governor Rasmusson of Carolina has a wonderful Secretary, and receives the Minister's compliments often."

"Oh, quiet," said the Governor, upset. "It's enough of a cross to bear without the need of constant reminder."

"If your missives look stodgy and crippled, perhaps the Minister will assume from them that you yourself are stodgy and—"

"Hold your tongue, girl! Or you'll find yourself without it!"

"I'm merely trying to help, Excellency."

"Pah!" he spat. "Help?! Help?! How, by ruining my digestion?"

"No," she answered quietly, "by offering to script your letters."

The Governor's eyebrows raised suddenly in interest. He held his soup spoon suspended halfway to his mouth. "I say," he commented, surprised, "you do that sort of thing well, do you?"

"I used to script Grandfather's letters. His own handwriting was awful."

The Governor slurped his soup from the spoon. "Writing someone's letters, that's hardly such a high recommendation. Here, let me see your writing." He motioned to a servant and asked for a quill and inkstand and paper. When it arrived, he ordered it given to Jennifer.

"What would you have me write?" she asked, dipping the quill in the ink.

"Anything, anything. Just something for me to look at."

She bent over the paper and began writing. The Governor watched with interest from the far end of the long table, craning his neck to see. When Jennifer finished, she gave the paper to the servant, who brought it to the Governor, bowing fawningly.

The Governor first looked at the visual appearance of the beauiful, elegant writing, at the wide swirls and intricate loops. His face lit up with delight. Only afterward did he notice what the writing actually said: *"You are a cruel, wicked, selfish man, with the blackest of souls."*

He grinned bitterly at Jennifer across the table as he crumpled the paper in his fist. He rose from the table, went over to her, and shoved the wadded paper into her face, trying to force it down her mouth. She pushed

100

backwards in her chair and finally managed to scoot away from him.

"You go too far, girl," he said broodingly. "But you're quite right. Your script is excellent. From this day on, you'll do my correspondence." He glared at her. "If you think you'll receive any concession in return, however, you're deluding yourself." He began advancing toward her, the familiar evil, leering glimmer in his eye. She backed away, crouched half-forward with her nails bared, and prepared to fight. . . .

That had been several weeks before. Now, as Jennifer sat at the small, round table in her room, scripting a communique, she felt greatly distressed. She had just come upon a valuable piece of information the Sons of Liberty could make much use of. It had slipped through, despite the Governor's efforts to keep secret information away from her, because it had been written on a small sheet of paper that had stuck unnoticed to the back of a larger sheet—thanks to sugared-tea stains.

She was feeling distressed because the information had to be relayed to Dr. Kirby, but Jennifer did not want to go into the village. The feeling of distress persisted as she continued scripting the letter she was presently working on, trying to ignore the feeling. Suddenly she scratched a giant X across the page, turning the quill at a contrary angle, causing speckles of black india ink to splatter all over the paper. She threw the quill down angrily and went to the large French windows.

Damn! she thought. She didn't want to go into town! There was only hatred and pain for her there. She had too much hatred and pain to live with already, she did not need more!

She stared out at the well-tended flower garden warming in the bright afternoon sunshine. She was seething. She *detested* the idea of going into town. But

. . . she knew she had to do it. The information had to be delivered. She put on her bonnet and left the room.

Down on the first floor, when she began to walk out through the front column of pillars, leaving the marble foyer, she was stopped by Barczic. The tall, blue-coated Hessian guard stepped quickly in front of her and looked down his sharp nose at her as she almost collided into his chest.

Jennifer loathed Barczic. He was the worst of all the mansion guards she had to deal with. He was continually leering at her in obscene glee at her situation.

Jennifer looked up at his pock-marked, tight-skinned face.

"Going for a stroll, *Jennifer?*" he asked in his nasty, Hessian voice. He was the only one who showed utter disrespect for her by being so out-of-line as to address her by her first name. He did so to taunt her and only when no one in authority was nearby. Jennifer hated him with all her might.

"Out of my way. You have no right stopping me."

"You have the Governor's permission to leave then? Is that right, *Jennifer?*"

"I don't need his permission. He's never confined me to—"

"Here now, here now," exclaimed the sergeant of the guard, a stout, pleasant-faced, gray-haired man, as he hurried up to them. "What's the to-do here, eh?"

Jennifer explained that she simply wanted to go outside. The sergeant was apologetic, but said he would have to check with the Governor before he could permit such a thing.

After a minute, the Governor himself came down, upon receiving the sergeant's request for instructions. He had been in the midst of being fitted for a new set of finery. His white shirt was out of his britches and a partially finished jacket was half on and half off him. As he came up to them, his tailor ran along after him, a tape measure around his neck, a distraught and harried expression on his face.

"Well, where do you think you're off to?" the Governor asked Jennifer, stomping toward her as she stood with the two guards. Barczic and the Redcoat sergeant came to attention immediately.

"Am I a *prisoner* here?" Jennifer asked defiantly. "You said I was not."

"Well . . . well . . ." stammered the Governor, unsure of himself. "You're not!"he blurted angrily. "But . . . that is . . . well. Where the devil do you think you're going?"

"To town. I have a pain. I wish to see the doctor."

"We have a perfectly good surgeon in attendance here. There's no need for you to—"

"Are you afraid?" Jennifer asked, feeling a fearful sensation at her own boldness. She saw the horrified expression that came to the sergeant's face as she said this, but she continued on quickly, "Afraid I won't be back once I leave?"

The Governor's face became stern. For a moment Jennifer thought he would strike her. But he sneered instead. "You'll be back." To the sergeant of the guards he ordered, "Let her go. I've got a stronger bond to insure her return than mere sentries."

Barczic, the Hessian, stepped aside, then immediately returned to attention. Jennifer walked past him, down the steps, out to the front lawn. She did not turn around when she heard the Governor yell after her, "And when you do return, we'll have some fine recreation for you! A *new* kind, you hear me, girl? A new kind, you go ahead and look forward to *that!*"

He would make her pay, Jennifer knew, for challenging him like this. What sort of new humiliation could he have in store for her? she wondered. But that was something to be worried about later. For now . . . at least she was out. At least she was on her way to see Dr. Kirby.

It was a strange feeling, walking down the dirt road that led into town, passing the tall trees and the clumps of greenery along the sides. It had been a long time

103

since she had been beyond the grounds of the mansion. She was feeling very nervous when she reached the boardwalk. People were turning to look at her as she passed, and though many of them knew her, not a soul said a single word of greeting. One girl whom Jennifer had grown up and been friends with came toward her. Jennifer smiled as the girl came close. The girl raised her nose into the air sharply and went past without a word. Across the street, Jennifer saw a small group of people talking in whispers, one man in the group pointing a finger at her as he spoke to the others.

When she reached Dr. Kirby's residence where he also kept office, Mrs. Bredlinger was there, complaining to Dr. Kirby about her gallbladder, holding a bottle of medicinal powder which the doctor had just made up for her. When she saw Jennifer, her eyes went wide.

Dr. Kirby, in the midst of spooning a pasty lotion into a jar, saw Jennifer too and exclaimed in happy surprise, "Jenny!"

Jennifer nodded and tried to smile at him.

Mrs. Bredlinger, overcoming her shock, began scolding, "Jennifer VanDerLind, have you no decency! Showing your face here among the good people of—"

"Oh hush, Emma!" ordered Dr. Kirby.

"Well! Am I to understand you're siding with this ... this slatternly woman who—"

Jennifer could not bear to hear the rest of it. She rushed out of the room, through the curtained doorway into the main living quarters. She stood with her hands pressed over her ears, her eyes shut tightly. These were people who had known her all her life! she thought. How could they believe such things about her? They should know better. They *should,* they *should!*

Even through her closed-off ears she could hear Mrs. Bredlinger arguing in accusing tones with Dr. Kirby as he tried to get rid of her. Finally, the sound of the woman's whining voice ceased and then Jennifer felt Dr. Kirby's hand gently touch her shoulder. She opened her eyes. She took her hands away from her ears.

"I'm sorry, Jenny," said Dr. Kirby. His expression was very sympathetic.

Jennifer felt so weak suddenly at hearing a few words of kindness and sympathy that she wanted to collapse against him and let old Dr. Kirby hold her up, and . . . maybe . . . hug her. But no, she would not do that. She might have done it once, but she was older now. God, she felt older, so much older than the young girl she had been just a few short months ago!

"Hello, Dr. Kirby," she said. "Please, I'd like to sit down now."

He led her to a chair and gestured for her to be seated. "I won't ask how you've been, Jenny. I can see it just looking at you. Don't you eat anymore? You've lost maybe ten pounds. And you're so pale. It must be horrible for you. It is, isn't it?"

She nodded solemnly.

"Ah, you poor girl. And the awful part of it is, no one knows about your sacrifice, except'n me and anyone else with even a pea-sized brain in their head. Which no one seems to have these days! That's what galls me, that's what really strikes me full o'fire: they're so quick to condemn and so slow to *think!* Our noble, high-minded citizenry, so quick to believe the absolute worse. And the only way——"

"Dr. Kirby," she interrupted, "tell me about Lancelot."

"——they'd believe the truth about your sacrifice," he continued, "would be if they first learned of your sheltering Lancelot and nursing him back to health. But if word of that got out, you'd be up before a magistrate yourself and——"

"Dr. Kirby!"

"Eh?"

"Tell me about Lancelot. Is he all right? Have you heard any word?"

He took her hand and patted it. "Nary a rumor. We

105

can get word into the prison by having our own people arrested. But no word comes out. Security at Haverhill is tighter than a hide-dried keghead. But I'll say this to you, Jenny. He is alive. We know they didn't hang him, if from nothing else than from the lack of public gloating, which they'd surely indulge in once they *did* put the noose to such a celebrated fugitive. But as for how he is, we know nothing."

She hung her head. She had hoped for more. At least for news that he was well and not being mistreated.

Dr. Kirby clapped his hands together. "And while I'm remembering! Jenny, I have something important to tell you."

"Yes?" She looked up at him.

"It's that Frenchman, D'Arcy Calhoun. He wants to meet with you. The matter is important, he tells me. He come by, oh, not a month ago. Here, can you stay for a while? Long enough for me to send a messenger to see if he can come now?"

"He's near?"

"No, not near. But near enough. He can be reached within a quarter of a day's ride and then arrive here in another quarter. Must you return this evening? Or can you stay?"

She was trying to think, but it was difficult. She felt disoriented. D'Arcy Calhoun wanted to see her? Why? For what reason? Thinking about him, the thing she remembered most vividly was his strong handsome face and his long, golden locks of hair. And the way he had squeezed her hand supportively the morning she had been taken off the *Liberty*, when Silas was dead and Lancelot was feeling too guilty to speak to her.

"Jenny, I'll send a messenger right now. 'Scuse me while I—"

"No! That is, I . . . I can't stay now. I have to get back soon or the Governor will be suspicious. If that happens, I won't be allowed to come here again to see you." She paused. "How did he take it, when he found that Lancelot was captured? He didn't show up the next morning, as he said he would."

"He figured the place would be under surveillance after Lancelot's capture. And as for how he took it, well, he near as raided the prison by himself, that's how he took it. It was hard for him, very hard. But no worse than it was for you. And listen, he's also one who knows your true reasons for living where you are. You can be sure of that."

"I won't be able to leave the mansion for a few days more," Jennifer said, thinking as she spoke. "Tell him a week. A week, and I'll meet him by the tallest oak, out by the north hedge in Waterbury field."

"A week it is. I'll send a messenger on the morrow."

"He didn't say what this is about?"

"Not a word. Only that it's very urgent."

The clock in the front office chimed five times. Jennifer stood up. "Dr. Kirby, I have to go soon. Let me tell you what I came to say. I discovered something from the Governor's personal communique to the Colonial Affairs Minister in London. This may seem strange, but . . . the Governor does *not* have an informer in the Sons of Liberty."

"How's that? But he must! The information that's leaking out, only someone within the group could—"

"Wait, Dr. Kirby. Let me tell you what the communique said. It said the Governor was *planning* to plant an infiltrator among you. That he knew how important it was to find out about the group and that this idea had just come to him. And he would try to follow through on it."

Dr. Kirby narrowed his eyes in concentration and rubbed his chin with his thumb and forefinger. "There is an informer," he said, "I'm certain of it. But he's not responsible to the Governor, eh? And the Governor is not even aware of him. So who planted him then? And who *is* he responsible to?"

Jennifer shook her head.

Dr. Kirby put his hands on her back and shoulder and guided her out through the curtain to the front office. "This is very useful information," he said, as he began pouring some golden liquid from a flask into a small bottle. "I'm beginning to think up a plan on how best to take advantage of it." He held the bottle up to the window to survey the colored liquid against the light. Then he stoppered the bottle with a medicinal cork. "In the meantime," he said, handing it to Jennifer, "you'd best take this back with you. If you return without some kind of medicine, your visit here will look suspicious."

"Thank you. What is this?"

"One of the most effective potions known to medical science. Take an ounce of it whenever things seem very bad. At least once a day." He was putting on his coat. "Come Jenny, I'll take you back in my carriage."

Jennifer uncorked the bottle and sniffed at it. "Why, this smells like whiskey!"

"Purely a coincidence, I'm sure," said Dr. Kirby with a faint smile. He put on his hat, and then held the door open for her.

During the ride back in the carriage, Jennifer's mind was on her coming visit with D'Arcy next week. Why did he want to see her? Did he possibly have word about Lancelot? It was not until Dr. Kirby let her out just beyond the grounds of the estate and she began walking up the cobbled path toward the steps of the mansion that she remembered the scene that had taken place this afternoon. The Governor had been angry. She remembered his ominous words about some "new form of recreation."

She looked warily at the guards as she mounted the steps, thinking of this. She was relieved to see that Barczic was not there. The last thing she wanted to see now was his smug, leering, pock-marked face.

The guards let her pass without comment and she went inside quickly, down the long hall, then up the stairs to the second floor. If she could only make it to her room without being seen, she could possibly avoid whatever it was the Governor might have in store for her. She was only scant yards from her door when she heard a sharp call from behind her. "You there! Halt!"

She halted. Her eyes darted from side to side, nervously, but she did not turn around. She heard footsteps coming up to her and then she recognized the voice, now that it took on its normal tone: "Hello, *Jennifer*," said Barczic, behind her. "Back so soon?"

"*You* have no right to stop me," she said and started rushing off again toward her room.

He grabbed her arm and stopped her. "I'm under orders from the Governor, to take you to him the moment you return."

She turned and looked at him, her head held high. "I'll go to him if he wishes it. I don't need *you* to escort me." As she started forward, though, Barczic fell into step with her. Jennifer's eyes were pointed straight ahead, her chin raised. Even so, she could sense Barczic's lecherous, wicked grin as he walked apace with her, staring at her profile

"I've been waiting for you, *Jennifer*," he whispered tauntingly, looking around to see that no one could hear him. "The Governor had me posted here, to bring you right to him. I wonder why? I wonder what he has in mind that he orders me to make sure we arrive *together?*"

Despite her fear and nervousness, she remarked, "He probably wants to see us both at once so by contrast he can truly appreciate the depths of your ugliness."

She sensed the expression on the Hessian's face; it was violent. She was almost relieved that they were now at the Governor's office and that two guards were in attendance outside the door. This prevented Barczic from taking any action against her.

"I'm bringing the girl." Barczic told the guards in a clipped, staccato voice. "As ordered."

The ranking guard nodded his permission, allowing

Barczic to knock on the door. After a moment the door opened. The Governor's secretary poked his head out. "Yes?" he said uncertainly. Then he saw Jennifer and said, "Oh." His head withdrew back into the room and the door closed. A moment later the door opened again and the secretary hurried out, brushing past Jennifer and the guards. He went only a few steps past them when the sound of the Governor's voice from within the room made him pivot on his heel and return to the doorway.

"Get that corporal I'm supposed to reward," the Governor shouted at him. "He's downstairs waiting, you know the one. Get him and send him in."

"Yes, Excellency," said the secretary, bobbing his head up and down obsequiously.

"Stop bobbing, damn you! You make me dizzy, I've told you a thouand times."

"Yes, Excellency, yes, yes, I'm sorry, Excellency." His head began to move, but he stopped himself in mid-bob. He rushed away to do as he was bid.

The doors remained open. The Governor's voice from within the room said, "All right, guard, bring her in. Come, come, come, I haven't all day."

Barczic pushed Jennifer in the small of her back, though it was not necessary since she had already started walking in. She almost stumbled with his push. She turned and shot him an angry look. But Barczic was absolutely formal now that he was in the Governor's presence. He simply stared straight ahead, stone-faced, while assuming an at-attention stance. The outer-office guards closed the doors quietly behind them.

"Well," said the Governor to Jennifer, somewhat pleasantly, coming out from behind his mammoth desk, "I see you're still among the living."

"I beg your par— Oh! It was just a . . . a cramp of sorts." She held up the bottle which was still in her hand. "It's not serious," she said, "but the doctor gave me this and said for me to . . . to rest a lot and not engage in physical activity."

110

The Governor laughed merrily, "How obvious you are. So you remember my promise of recreation, do you, and you fancy that concern for your 'health' might stop me?" He came up close to her and put his beefy hand on her shoulder, then moved it slowly down toward her bosom.

Jennifer backed away from him so quickly that she stepped into Barczic, hastily regained her footing, and moved off to the side. She threw down the bottle so both her hands would be free. She half-crouched forward and spread her clenched fingers so that they were like claws.

The Governor smiled gaily. He was in an unusually good mood for some reason. "So you intend to fight me again if I want to have you, eh? That's how you've prevented me taking you as often as I would have liked. At least, so far. You never gave in to me, always fought viciously, always made me exert myself for whatever pleasure I might take. And yes, yes," he said, waggling his index finger, still smiling, "you have been successful, haven't you? Since I'm not usually in the mood for battling a fierce she-demon, you've had your way far too often. You knew I would consider it an insult to have to call in reinforcements to aid me. You knew—you clever girl, you!—that my pride would make me insist that if I could not take you by my own power, that I simply would not have you."

He glanced at Barczic now, who was standing dutifully at attention. He returned his gaze to Jennifer, who had followed his eyes as he looked at Barczic, and who now seemed very frightened and apprehensive.

"Now you're wondering if I've become less fastidious about insisting upon not needing reinforcements, aren't you? Well, dear girl, leave me put your fears to rest. I haven't changed. I still will not request the aid of outside force when I wish to bed you. I'm still man enough to take you by myself." He paused. "That is, when I wish to have you badly enough to put up with your wild scratching and clawing resistance."

There was a knock at the door. The Governor ignored it. "But the question you must now ask yourself is this: do I still have the same dislike of using outside force when it is not I, myself, who is to partake of your favors?"

Jennifer felt a cool, clammy fearfulness sweep over her. She wanted to run from the room.

There was another knock at the door, this one louder than the first.

"Yes," the Governor bellowed to the guards beyond the door, "send him in!"

The door opened and Jennifer was so stunned at the sight she beheld that it made her gasp. Even when she realized after a second that the sight was not what it at first seemed, she still was stunned and breathless. There standing in the doorway was a tall, exquisitely handsome, curly-black-haired man, who looked as if he could be Lancelot Savage's mirror image. At first, she had thought it was Savage himself.

"Ah, Corporal . . . um . . . um . . . whatever the deuce your name is. Yes, well don't just stand there, come in, come in! And you, you two door-guards, you come in too."

When the black-haired man came closer, walking up to the Governor and saluting, Jennifer saw that there were clear differences between him and Savage. This man's eyes were dull and vacuous, whereas Savage's eyes were bright and alert. And Savage's face had intelligence written all over it. This man was clearly a plodder. But he was very handsome and tall, as was Savage, and he had the same trim, well-muscled physique. What was he here for, Jennifer wondered apprehensively.

"Corporal," said the Governor, his voice becoming excited, "your platoon leader tells me you distginuished yourself during tax collection duty recently. You became a bit rough with some of the local citizenry, who were hesitant about keeping the King's coffers properly filled."

112

"Uh . . . aye, Excellency," croaked the corporal, "that's God's own truth." He was clearly nervous before such an eminence as the Governor.

"Well, we have a reward for you." He smiled. He made a flamboyant sweeping gesture with his hand, ending with his palm up, fingers pointed toward Jennifer.

"No," Jennifer gasped, backing away.

The Governor looked at her, his face stern and unforgiving now. "You embarrassed me this afternoon. You will learn not to do it again."

Jennifer's eyes darted about the room frenziedly and she bolted for the door. Barczic intercepted her, grabbing her by the shoulders, jerking her arms behind her. He pulled her so that her back was against his chest and her wrists were firmly pinned behind her in his grip.

Jennifer kicked at his ankles, but the two other guards, sensing their instructions from the Governor's approving nod at Barczic, quickly came forward. Each grabbed hold of one of Jennifer's ankles. They did not know what to do with her then, and in confusion, seemed about to lift her onto the divan.

"No," the Governor said. "Just hold her there, standing as she is now."

The guards seated themselves on the floor, each grasping one of Jennifer's ankles, holding them far apart. The Governor went to a straight-back chair, picked it up and placed it directly in front of Jennifer, a few feet away. He sat down, took a silk handkerchief from his sleeve, and wiped his sweating forehead and face.

Jennifer looked at him with terrified eyes. Squirming, twisting her shoulders, she begged, "Please. Don't. I won't embar—"

"Corporal whatever-your-name-is," the Governor interrupted, smiling. "Never let it be said the Governor fails to reward a job well done. You may claim your prize."

The corporal's eyes lit up in excitement and lust, and he licked his lips. He looked at the Governor, his head cocked to one side, not really believing his good fortune. But then, seeing the Governor urge him on with an impatient flutter of his hand, he turned to Jennifer and walked up to her. He was smiling gleefully with the simple-mindedness of a moron. Jennifer looked at him with pleading, helpless eyes. The corporal tried to kiss her. She jerked her head to the side. Unperturbed, the corporal put his hands to the collar of her dress and then suddenly there was a ripping sound as the front of the dress was torn open down to Jennifer's waist, sending buttons flying. Only Jennifer's chemise prevented her bosom from being exposed. She breathed in short gasps as she waited. Then she felt his hands on the top of her chemise and she screamed as the garment was ripped down and pulled away from her, so that it remained dangling down from her waist, exposing her creamy breasts to the eyes of the corporal and the Governor and the guards who were looking up at her feverishly.

Suddenly she heard the ripping sound of the cloth as it was torn apart, all the way down to the hem. He pushed the dress flaps away to the sides. All Jennifer had on now were her petticoats and pantaloon underdrawers and the remnant of her chemise. The corporal pulled the chemise down to her knees and yanked down her petticoats. His fingers went to her hips at the top of her underdrawers. He grasped hold of the top and slowly, excruciatingly slowly, pulled it all the way down.

Jennifer squirmed and wriggled and tried to free her arms and legs from the iron grip of the guards. She was completely naked before the corporal and the sweaty faced Governor and the wide-eyed guards. Barczic, behind her, was looking down at her bosom from over her shoulder. His foul breath offended her nostrils, and the stubble of his beard scraped against her cheek and neck and shoulder.

Then came the worst of it. The corporal got down on his knees and moved close to her stomach. "No!" Jennifer screamed when she saw what he was about to do.

She threw her head back and stared in wide-eyed panic at the ceiling, her mouth wide open.

"Force her head forward!" the Governor barked. "Make her look! It took a lot of effort to find such a close lookalike for her beau, I'll not have him wasted!"

Barczic's hand grasped her hair and forced her head down. She tried, but could not make herself close her eyes. She could only watch in trembling horror as Savage—*No!* she screamed to herself, *it's not him! It's not him!*—as the exquisitely handsome man who looked so much like Lancelot Savage put his mouth to her belly below her navel and began moving it down, wetting her skin with his lips and tongue.

Jennifer jolted rigid and her eyes bulged when the man's fingers touched her between the legs. The fingers pressed in and played up and down her. Horror of horrors, her body was *responding*! *Please God, please God, don't let me be*—

Suddenly his mouth was at her sex, his tongue probing her womanhood. She screamed. A torrent of tears flooded from her eyes. "Stop it, stop it, ahhhnnnn!" And looking, seeing Lancelot Savage's face down there—*It's not him, it's not him!*—an unstoppable throbbing, yearning, tingling sensation became more and more intense and then exploded through her lower body in an excruciating wave of pleasure.

She moaned and gasped and wildly tried to wriggle free, to stop the shuddering explosions of pleasure that flooded over her. Nothing stopped the sensations, the tongue, the lips, the rough hands that crept up to her breasts and began squeezing and rubbing. A warm wave of sensation lingered over her body, making her hate herself, detest herself . . . making her feel so vile and guilt-ridden that she wished she were dead. Dear God, she had *responded* to him!

"All right," said the Governor, sighing deeply, "release her."

The hands holding her ankles and arms vanished from her body. Jennifer sank down to the floor and lay there, her tattered clothing clinging in remnants to her wet body. She was sobbing, her head buried in the crook of her arm.

"Get out," she heard the Governor say to the guards, then heard their footsteps as they departed. The doors closed after them.

"You're a slut, Jennifer VanDerLind," said the Governor. "You are a filthy, common trollop. You are *dirt*. And you will never forget it. You will never be the same again. *I* have broken you."

As if to emphasize the point, the tip of his hard leather boot pressed rudely up against the inside of her thighs from behind, as she lay half-curled, face down on the floor. She jerked her hand back and tried to push the boot away, but she could not manage even that, she was so weak and faint. The Governor laughed wickedly, the sound echoing resoundingly in Jennifer's head. She felt his boot press even harder against her womanhood, from behind.

She deserved to die. The thought would not leave her: she deserved to die, to die, to die. . . .

Chapter 7

Savage leaned against the wooden wall of the prison barracks, watching the men strain their muscles at the barnlike front door as they pried out the last remaining bolt holding the lock in place. As the leverage of the makeshift crowbar took effect, the final bolt shot out of the iron lock-latch. A wave of nervousness spread through the group of prisoners. There was nothing to stop them now. The escape would begin in just seconds.

It was dark inside the barracks. The moonlight coming in through the windows provided the only illumination. Savage's eyes were adjusted to the darkness, though, and when he saw the huge, hulking figure striding down the length of the barracks toward him, he recognized the man as Mighty Mike Mulligan.

Mulligan stopped when he reached Savage. "This be yer last chance to join up with us," he said.

Savage shook his head.

Mulligan glared at Savage and at the group of prisoners—roughly half of the barracks population—who had sided with him in opposing the escape attempt. "Yer yellow-belly cowards all of ye," he said, spitting out of the side of his mouth to the dirt ground. "Them of us with backbone'll be breathing free air, miles from here, while you jellyfish'll still be here rotting."

"Those of you with 'backbone'," said Savage, "will be dead, for the most part. You're a fool, Mulligan. I told you, you can't storm that gate without knocking out the guard tower first. All you'll be doing if you try is killing off the men that follow you."

Mulligan snorted disdainfully. His Irish face was

sweating and it shimmered in the moonlight coming through the windows. He turned and went to the men standing by the barnlike doors. "Stand ye ready, me laddies," he told the prisoners converged near the doors. Then, with a violent kick, he knocked open the doors.

The prisoners rushed out in a wave, shouting, screaming, surging forward toward the gate that separated the main prison yard from the gunroom and guards' quarters. Mulligan let out a shrill banshee wail and rushed into the wave of prisoners, running with all his might, surging forward through their ranks to the very front, to take the lead.

The charging prisoners would have had several seconds extra before being spotted by the guards in the tower had they not been yelling and screaming. As it was, the guard's were immediately alerted and began firing at the mob with their already loaded muskets.

Savage had warned Mulligan that having the prisoners yell as soon as they left the barracks would be costly in lives. But Mulligan, a mountain man and trapper by trade, said he had learned from experience that the best way to startle and frighten dangerous beasts was to yell at the top of your lungs while attacking them. He scorned Savage's attempts to reason with him.

Looking out through the barred barracks window, Savage watched the massacre that was taking place. The prisoners reached the gate as planned and half were attempting to climb over it, standing on the shoulders of their fellows. Once on the other side, they planned to push open the wooden bolt, so the gates could be opened. The other half of the prisoners were pelting the tower at the left side of the gate with rocks from the yard, hoping to prevent the guards from having clear shots at the men storming the gate.

The effort was doomed as Savage had told them it would be. One of the guards in the tower fired down at the prisoners trying to climb over the gate, easily picking them off. The other guard concentrated his fire on the rock throwers. The men on the ground dropped like

118

flies as the buckshot and balls rained down upon them. A few men managed to reach the top of the gate, but ended up draped over the palisades, dead or dying.

Above the blaring cacophony of sounds—the shouts of the gate stormers, the screams of the wounded, the crackling of the muskets—Savage picked out Mike Mulligan's banshee wail and his rumbling voice as he yelled, "Over the gate, laddies! Over the gate! It takes but one of us to open the bolt! Go for the bolt!"

Savage turned his eyes away. The sheer wastefulness of it was too much for him. Any minute now the guards from their quarters on the other side of the gate would secure arms from the gunroom and would be up in the tower with the original two guards, firing down on the unarmed mob.

"Over the gate, laddies!" Mulligan yelled. "We can still make it!"

Savage heard a fusillade of musket fire, at least half a dozen weapons at once, and knew that the contingent of guards were now up in the tower reinforcing the original two.

"It's a bloody massacre," whispered one of the prisoners who had sided with Savage and remained in the barracks. He was looking out the window still, at the moonlit field and the carnage taking place. "They're—"

"I don't want to hear it," said Savage. He lowered himself to the straw matting on the ground, his back against the wall, and waited for it to be over with. After a moment, the firing stopped and he knew that the prisoners had surrendered.

It was only a few minutes more before the surviving prisoners—those who could still walk—began arriving back in the barracks. They were being shoved and herded by the British guards, who were swinging musket butts wildly and kicking those of the prisoners who stumbled to the ground. A shot rang out and one of the prisoners fell, though he had not been resisting. He had simply been moving too slowly to suit one of the guards. The other prisoners quickened their pace as they rushed into the barracks. Once inside, they fell down on the straw matting or sank to the ground. The foul, tangy smell of their sweat and blood was overpowering in the enclosed area. Many men were coughing or moaning. Moonlight streamed in through the windows, shimmering on their sticky wet faces and necks.

Savage had been helping the wounded as soon as the men started coming into the barracks. Now he saw a very skinny, mustachioed man who had entered the doorway, but just stopped in the middle of it. He stood there in a daze, his eyes wide and blank, his mouth sagging open. Savage saw a guard rushing toward him with a raised truncheon. Savage ran over to the man to pull him out of the doorway, where he was a target, before the guard reached him. But the guard got there first and swung with his truncheon at the man's face. Savage raised his forearms and stepped inside the guard's swing, taking the blow just beneath his wrists, blocking it from reaching the man's face.

Incredible pain shot through his arms. He knew that nothing was broken, though, because his hands and arms were still functioning, as he grasped the dazed man by the arm and pulled him off to the side of the barracks and down to the ground.

When all the prisoners who could walk were back inside, the guards formed a line at the doorway. They were waiting for something. After a minute, it became clear what they were waiting for: the commandant, Captain Trevor, arrived.

Captain Trevor strode forward a few paces in front of the line of guards and regarded the prisoners scornfully, a crop in his hand, his legs spread apart. Though he had undoubtedly been wakened out of sleep at this late hour, he had taken time to put on his blue Naval officer's coat before coming to confront the prisoners.

He stood smirking at them now, looking them over. "I won't ask who the leaders of this insurrection are." he said. "If they're still alive, I have no desire to punish them. Rather, I'd like to reward them. In a single night, they have reduced the population of this barracks by a full quarter. Roughly half the men in here participated in the riot, I estimate. And half of that half are lying outside by the gate in puddles of their own blood. Some of them will live, of course. But that fact is balanced, happily, by the fact that some of you listening to me now won't last out the night."

A guard came into the barracks carrying two blazing torches, so the Captain could see the men he was addressing. He handed one to a guard at the Captain's left and the other to a guard at his right. The Captain's face was lit up in bold relief now, yellowish in the flickering flames.

"So, gentlemen," the Captain said, "we won't bother with reprisals. On the contrary, I heartily invite you to try your escape attempt again. And again and again! The less of you there are alive, the less I need spend on rations to feed you. In fact . . ." He yelled over his shoulder, "Lieutenant!"

"Aye, Sir!" said the duty officer, stepping forward.

"I order double rations for this barracks at the morning meal. As an added treat."

"Very good, Sir!"

The Captain turned to leave, then stopped before moving away. He turned back to the prisoners, his eyes scanning their faces in search of someone. When he saw Savage, he pointed with his crop. "Kick that man," he said. Before Savage could move away, the guard standing nearest him came forward and kicked him hard in his side. Savage grimaced in pain.

"A pleasant ending to a pleasant night," remarked the Captain. He turned and marched out of the barracks.

The duty officer addressed the prisoners. He told them that there would be a burying detail first thing in the morning. Those with wounds could visit the prison doctor in a few days, but not before; it would take that long before the doctor could dispose of the critically wounded who lay near the gate. After saying this, the lieutenant turned sharply on his heel and left the barracks, ordering the guards to follow him out. The heavy

121

wooden doors were swung shut, but—significantly—no effort was made to install a new lock to replace the pried-off one.

As soon as the barndoors were shut, Mike Mulligan came stomping over to Savage. Savage could see that he was not wounded but he was madder than hell. "Well, I hope you're satisfied!" Mulligan roared.

Savage just looked at him. "*You* hope *I'm* satisfied?"

"It's all your fault that this thing failed! If ye hadn't been so lilylivered, we mayhap could have done it. If'n we'd a had *all* of us pitching into the effort, instead of ye and yer yeller band here holding back, we'd surely have—"

"You'd surely have lost twice as many men," Savage said angrily, rising to his feet, despite the pain in his side where he had been kicked. "It was a stupid plan. The Redcoats didn't kill all those men out there, Mulligan. You did!" He wanted to say much more, but he stopped himself. He had to control himself, to hold his temper . . . because Mighty Mike Mulligan was mighty indeed. He was a giant grizzly bear of a man. He had come into the prison several weeks ago after being sentenced for crushing the ribs of a trading post owner he said was trying to cheat him.

Savage had had run-ins with him ever since the man arrived, mostly over Mulligan's constant attempts to put escape plans into operation, even when the plans had practically no chance at all of succeeding. Savage was desperate to escape himself. But he had scrutinized all the possibilities and come to the conclusion that, at the present time, there wasn't any attempt they could make which would not be suicidal.

Tonight was the first time Mulligan had succeeded in actually convincing anyone to go along with his insane plans. He had done so mostly by bullying and by taking advantage of the desperation of many of the prisoners. Now that the attempt had proven so disastrous, he needed a scapegoat.

"I say it was *you* what killed those men," Mulligan declared. "By not joining us and making us stronger. As

122

fer the plan, why there weren't nothing wrong with the plan!"

In frustration, Savage slapped his hand on the back of the man's neck and pointed him toward the window. "*Here's* what's wrong with your damn plan," he said, pointing out the window as he spoke. "So long as those guards are in the tower over the gate, anyone storming the gate will be cut down. Like they *were* cut down, just now. The only way to make the plan work is to get rid of the guards first. And the only way to do *that* is for someone to climb up on that horizontal beam that runs along the top of the gate and to run along it straight to the guard tower. I know. I've thought this thing through a thousand times."

Mulligan's face brightened at this idea of having someone run along the beam to attack the guard tower, and to stop him from considering it further, Savage said, "And it can't be done, because it's *suicide* for the man who tries it! Can't you see that? Here, look." He pointed at the structural beam that was high above the palisaded points of the gate. "The far end of it connects to the base of the booth where the guards are. The guards would have an open bead on anyone attacking them that way, since the man would be running directly head-on toward them. Do you understand? Do you see now why it's suicide to try it?"

"Aye, I see, laddie. Mighty Mike Mulligan never misses seein' nothin'. And here's how I see her: yer afeared a' dyin'. Ye'd let yer mates risk their necks fer ye, and then ye'd walk out clean and unmussed once the deed's been done and the gate been breached." He glared at Savage. "Yer yeller like a chicken." At this, he stuck his thumbs under his armpits, flapped his elbows, and began squawking like a chicken: "Pok, pok pok pok!"

Savage wanted to hit him so badly he could feel the bilious taste of it in his mouth. But he knew Mulligan was deliberately trying to provoke him. And he knew that if he did fight Mulligan, he would probably lose. Aside from the fact that Mulligan was much bigger and

123

stronger than he was, there was also the fact that Savage was weakened and bruised from the frequent beatings he received at the hands of Captain Trevor. And right now, his side burned from where the guard had kicked him, and his forearms ached from the blow of the truncheon.

He turned and walked away from Mulligan.

"Pok pok pok!" Mulligan squawked, dancing in a small circle, flapping his elbows.

All eyes in the barracks were on Savage. He felt them burning into him. He continued walking away, found an open space near the wall and lowered himself onto the straw matting.

"Yer yeller!" Mulligan yelled at him, the words ringing through the tense, still air of the barracks.

Savage ignored him. So long as he was in charge of his emotions, he would not let himself be provoked. He'd have to be crazy to fight Mulligan under these conditions.

"Aye," Mulligan announced to the room at large, "but what der ye expect from a man what slaps around the ladies?"

Savage ignored this too. So Mulligan knew about the story of his capture. So what?

Mulligan was beginning to weary of his efforts at provoking Savage. He spat out of the side of his mouth and prepared to give up. The man simply would not be provoked. Turning toward the wall and looking for a place at the other end of the barracks, where he could sit down too, he muttered one last remark under his breath, intending it as a meaningless throwaway line before shutting up entirely. "She wer'n't no lady anyhows. Bedding down in the Governor's mansion, when she's evicted from her own."

"What did you say!"

Mulligan turned back. He was surprised to see Savage rising to his feet and striding toward him angrily. In genuine bafflement, he said, "Eh? Yer mean about the VanDerLind wench? About her sporting with the Governor?"

124

Savage was right next to him now, staring up into his face, his eyes blazing with fury. "You lying scum."

"Eh?" Mulligan could not believe it. How could this possibly be the remark that would set him off? "Why . . . it's common knowledge," he said, puzzled but preparing to take advantage of the situation. "Ask anyone what's come in recently. Here, you with the red beard—"

But before he could put the question to the man, Savage smashed his nose in with a vicious blow. Mulligan shook his head to clear it, hearing the shocked gasps of those around him. He stared at Savage in absolute surprise. Then he started to smile. Hell, what did it matter what was the cause of the pirate's rage? Mulligan was thankful for it, regardless of its cause. He broke into a big, toothy grin and prepared to rip Savage into tiny pieces.

Before he could raise a fist, though, he found himself suddenly on the ground gasping for breath, after a lightning series of mulekicks to his belly and knees. He flailed out and grasped Savage's upper arm, and prepared to snap it like a twig. But suddenly he was rocked by stinging, smashing blows to his forehead that made his grip slacken and the arm pulled free.

All at once, Mulligan felt he was at the center of a whirlwind. He was vastly bigger and stronger than the pirate, but who could have known that when the man flew into a fury, he went stark raving *insane*? He was like a whirling, spinning Chinese firewheel, his legs snapping in lethal kicks, his knuckles slamming maniacally into Mulligan's gut and groin and face, his elbows and knees striking in lightning motion.

Mulligan was doing more than his fair share of damage to Savage, but he could not see this for the blood that poured down into his eyes from his cut forehead.

Savage was feeling the pain and force of the big man's pulverizing blows, which landed on his arms, his chest, his side that was already exploding from pain. But he kept his mind focused on avoiding grips and

125

bearhugs; so long as he could move fast enough to avoid the grips, he would be all right. A glancing blow smashed into his forehead now and sent him reeling halfway into blackness. He caught himself and forced himself back.

The two of them struggled ferociously on the ground, tumbling and rolling onto the prisoners who could not move out of the way quickly enough, kicking and lashing out wildly. After a while, both of them began to lose steam and the fight seemed to progress in slow motion, the two combatants huffing and puffing and staggering about.

Savage seemed at the disadvantage now. If he lost his speed and agility, he would not be able to avoid Mulligan's bone-crushing grips. But then, finally, Savage stumbled to his feet and, when Mulligan began to rise also, Savage grasped the man's thick mane of hair in his two hands, jerked his head back, and jammed his knee into the man's throat.

Mulligan choked loudly, his arms shooting out to his sides, fingers clawing the air. Savage jerked his knee up into the man's throat a second time and then released him to fall back onto the ground, writhing and choking and clutching his throat.

Savage wanted to stand over him a minute, but he stumbled backward involuntarily. He tried to move forward again, but staggered to the side instead and fell down. He got up again, shakily, and stumbled forward in the direction of Mulligan. He fell down. He got up again. Finally he managed to stagger over to Mulligan, who lay still choking, breathing in loud, rasping drafts as he tried to force air in through his throat.

"You want to say it again, liar?" Savage demanded, speaking through lips that were puffy and bruised. "You want to say it—" He began coughing and sank down to his knees.

There would be no response from Mulligan, he could see. The man was too busy just trying to stay alive. Savage stood up and went to the recently imprisoned red-bearded man whom Mulligan had called on to support his statement. "You have something to say about the VanDerLind girl?" he asked.

"I don't know nothin', I don't know nothin'!" the man exclaimed fearfully, cringing and holding up his palms to protect himself.

Savage was drunk with pain and exhaustion. "She is the finest, most faithful woman," he mumbled. Then, quietly, as if to himself, "And it's only the thought of her that keeps me alive and gets me through these days." He spied an empty spot in a corner and staggered off toward it. He collapsed to the floor before he could reach it.

Chapter 8

D'Arcy Calhoun stood under the low-branched tree, smiling warmly and waving both hands at Jennifer as she came riding toward him. Jennifer's expression was grim and severe. She did not want to see D'Arcy now. She did not want to see anyone, but especially not someone who knew her. How could she pretend to be the way she was before? How could she pretend to still be . . . decent?

All week long, ever since that horrible experience with the Redcoat who looked like Savage, she had remained barricaded in her room, unable to face anyone. But as this morning drew near, Jennifer realized she could not avoid the meeting. It was too important. It probably involved information about Savage. So at the last minute, she had left her room, taken a horse from the stable, and rode here, making certain she was not followed. No one had tried to stop her this time.

Now that she was here, she wondered how she could possibly deal with him. Certainly not as one decent person to another. She felt too vile and degraded inside. As she reined her horse to a halt and he came up to her smiling warmly, she realized that she also felt very cold and remote.

"Jennyfair," D'Arcy exclaimed, "you make me so happy that you came."

Jennifer raised her leg out of the stirrup and passed it over the top of the horse to dismount. Just as she was beginning to slide down the flank, D'Arcy put his strong hands to her waist, and in a gesture of chivalry, pulled her forward and began lowering her to the ground. Jennifer was forced to put her hands on his shoulders to maintain her balance.

"I can dismount quite well by myself, thank you," she said icily as her feet touched the ground.

D'Arcy's smile, which had been so bright upon seeing her again, now turned into a frown of puzzlement. "What eez eet?" he asked. "What eez ze matter?"

"Nothing is the matter." She was not looking in his eyes or even at his face. She stood with her head averted, waiting for him to take his hands away from her waist. In his puzzlement, though, he completely forgot that he was holding her. "Kindly take your hands away," Jennifer said.

He did so and Jennifer then walked away from him toward the base of the tree. "Well," she said, still not looking at him, "Dr. Kirby said you had something important to tell me. So if you'll tell it to me now, we can discuss it, and then I can go back."

D'Arcy said nothing. When several seconds passed, without him saying anything at all, Jennifer finally looked at him to see why he was not answering. She saw a look of deep hurt on his face and this stung her. She did not mean to hurt him. It had not occurred to her that he would take her behavior personally.

She closed her eyes.

D'Arcy came up to her and she felt his hand gently touch her elbow. "Eet eez all right, Jennyfair. I undairstand. I know how hard eet has been for you."

"No you don't," she said, her voice softer and full of pain.

"Come weeth me," D'Arcy said, guiding her by the elbow. "We go for a stroll, and I tell you ze good news to take your mind away from your unhappiness." He guided her through the field of tall grass to a rushing stream. They walked along the bank of the stream. The sound of the rushing water was pleasant. After a few minutes, Jennifer felt the emotional tension within her begin to ebb.

"Ze good news," D'Arcy said, "is zat we will soon try to rescue Lancelot from ze prison."

Jennifer looked at him, wide-eyed.

"Zair are almost twenty of us now, from ze old crew. We have ze plan to—"

"D'Arcy," she interrupted, "just twenty of you? You won't stand a chance! The prison is like a fortress and it's garrisoned by half again as many men."

"*Pardonnez-moi, cherie*, but we do stand ze chance. Eet eez not so good a chance maybe, but weeth your help—"

"But why take such a risk! You could lose all of your men. And, here, D'Arcy, there's something you don't know that's important. You see . . ." she hesitated. How could she say this? "D'Arcy, do you know why I'm living in the Governor's mansion?"

He looked insulted. "Do you take me for ze fool? I see zat Lancelot he is spared from ze hangman and at ze same time you move in weeth ze Governor. *Bien sur* I see ze relationship, of course I see eet!"

"It's more than that," she said. "The Governor didn't agree to just not hang him. He agreed to let him go free, after one year. And so many months have gone by already that . . . well you see, for you and your men to risk your lives, and to risk Lancelot's, in a plan that faces such great odds, it's . . . well it's not necessary, D'Arcy. He'll be free soon and without you risking your life."

D'Arcy stopped walking. He took her hand, making her turn to face him. "Jennyfair . . ." he said. Then he just shook his head slowly.

"What do you mean?"

"No more telling ze fib to yourself now. *Le Gouverneur* he is not ze crazy man. He knows zat if Lancelot is freed, he weel go back to pirating on ze Breeteesh sheeps. He knows zat ze King George weel esteem him highly if he can send him ze head of ze infamous American 'pirate.' When ze Governor says he weel free Lancelot at ze end of a year, what he really means is he weel free him from ze land of ze living."

She thought of all she had suffered during the past half year. "Then, all of this has been for . . . nothing?"

she asked, her voice cracking. "They're going to kill h—"

"Not for nothing!" declared D'Arcy, grasping her shoulders firmly. "For Lancelot! You have saved heez life! You have kept heem alive thees long. Eet eez because of you that he eez alive today, Jennyfair, and only because of you."

She was feeling shaken and disoriented. So Lancelot would *not* be freed at the end of the year? But then she wondered: had she really known this all along and just not admitted it to herself? By not admitting it to herself she had let herself continue acting out her role as the Governor's whore. And each day she continued acting out this role was another day that Lancelot stayed alive. . . .

"Jennyfair," D'Arcy said softly, "you have made eet so he eez steel alive today. And now you can help him *stay* alive. For our plan, eet weel not work weethout you."

She put both her hands to her temples and brushed back her mane of hair. "How can I help?" she asked.

"You must go to ze prison to see Lancelot."

The idea startled her. Before she could respond to it, D'Arcy continued.

"Our plan eez thees: we have deescovered an old sheep's cannon, and weethin a month we will have transported her here, secretly. Zen we weel put her outside ze main gates of ze prison and blow zem open! Zen we attack. Though zair are less zan twenty of us, we have ze surprise on our side. Eef we can storm ze prison before ze guards can arm zemselves from ze gunroom, we can win ze battle."

He narrowed his eyes at her. "But you see, someone must tell Lancelot ze date of ze attack, so ze prisoners can stage a commotion and riot. Zat way we can move ze cannon into position without being seen, without losing ze element of surprise. And also, we must have information *from* heem. Are zair any cannon inside ze compound? How many? Is ze gate that separates ze guard quarters from ze main prison yard to ze left or to ze right? We must know so we can move in ze cannon and blast open ze interior gate immediately. That is why we need you. We can get information into ze prison, but nevair out. You can get in to tell Lancelot our plan and zen back out again weeth ze information for us."

"D'Arcy," she said, "I don't think I can."

"You must."

"But I can't!" The fierceness and anguish of her reply surprised both of them.

D'Arcy looked at her with probing, analytical eyes.

Jennifer turned away from him and walked toward the stream. She watched the water babbling over the smooth rocks in the streambed. The truth was, she knew, that *she did not want to see Savage now*. The idea frightened her. She had such a strong, clean, pure image of him in her mind's eye, based on the memory of the way he had been when they were together. To see him now in some filthy cell, manacled, helpless, possibly being beaten right before her eyes—she could not bear it. And she knew he would not be able to bear it either, having her see him that way.

But then she thought: no, that wasn't the entire reason she did not want to see him now. That didn't apply because Savage would never really be weak, no matter what they did to him physically. They could never touch his spirit, or the sense of dignity and strength that he would have in her presence no matter what external circumstances she found him in.

So why was she so frightened then at this idea of seeing him again? Was it her own hatred of having to face him now that she had been so defiled and degraded? Yes, that was a large part of it. She could not bear for him to know that about her, to think of her in that way. Yet it would be horrible for her to have to lie to him, to pretend the defilement and humiliations had never taken place . . . to pretend that she was still the same virtuous girl she had been when he had seen her last.

There, she thought, there was the real problem: She was repulsed by the idea of having to lie to him, of having to put on this false act of still being untouched by others. *But she would have to do it.* She would have to lie to him, right to his face. For his life would depend on it. If she told him the truth about the agreement she had entered into with the Governor, she was absolutely certain that he would not permit it. He would become enraged and insist that she stop sacrificing herself for him . . . even though it would mean the end of his life. In fact, he would probably take some action himself to end the need of her continuing the sacrifice.

It would be hard lying to him, playing out a role in front of him. She would feel so wickedly false! She did not know if she was even capable of doing it. She had never lied to him before. Could she maintain her composure without giving herself away?

Jennifer looked into the rapidly rushing clear water now and realized that the answer was a simple one, because there was no other choice. Yes, she would do it. Because she had to do it. Because Savage's life depended on her doing it and nothing was as important in the entire world as saving Lancelot's life and helping to rescue him.

As much as she loved him and wanted desperately to be with him, she dreaded the thought of going to the prison in the next few days to see him. It would be unbearable agony for her to see him again under these conditions, and to be forced to act out a false role in front of him. Still, she turned back to D'Arcy now and said, "Yes. I'll do it."

D'Arcy simply nodded his head, as if he had realized all along that this would be her answer.

Jennifer began walking along the stream again. D'Arcy came up to her and walked beside her. For several minutes neither of them spoke. Then D'Arcy, seeing how distraught she was, said in a mischievous voice, "I will tell you how I first met Lancelot. You weesh to hear?"

She did not answer.

"Eet eez ze very funny story," he said, grinning slightly with a boyish half-smile.

"You're trying to change my mood," she said.

"But of course!"

She did not say anything.

"Eet was like thees," D'Arcy began, as they continued walking alongside the stream. He gestured animatedly with his hands as he spoke. "Zair I was, running out of ze tavern in Paris. I rush out through ze door, and I am running so fast I knock over zis man who eez passing by outside. We stumble and roll and he ends up on top of me. He ees in ze foul mood already, from a bad day trying to raise financing to arm heez sheep to attack ze Briteesh.

" 'You clumsy oaf!' he yells at me, and I curse at heem in my native tongue, trying to get him off me so I can keep running. But *alors*, eet eez too late! Ze men I am fleeing from, zay come out from ze tavern and find me there, trapped under thees English American. One of zem has ze cocked pistol in heez hand and ze other three zay have drawn swords.

" '*Out of ze way!*' ze one weeth ze pistol yells at Lancelot. '*Move aside, so we can slay zis dog!*' Meaning *me*," D'Arcy said to Jennifer, gesturing dramatically at himself. "Meaning yours truly, your humble servant D'Arcy.

"Now Lancelot, he does not know me from Andre. To heem I am only zis stranger who comes running him down and zen curses him in French. But he sees zat zair are four of zem and only one of D'Arcy, and so as he is getting up he turns to the side, showing me ze pistol in his scabbard. I take it while he eez still between me and ze others, who cannot see. '*Hurry, you English dog,*' zay yell at Lancelot, '*or we'll lay into you too! With pleasure!*'

"So Lancelot stands, still between me and ze others, and zen for ze first and only time in heez life he eez 'gallant.' He puts heez hand to his shirtwaist and bows over it, a deep, very gracious bow. Which allows me, of course, to raise ze gun, steady my arm on Lancelot's backside, and fire at ze man before he knows what eez transpiring."

134

Jennifer found herself smiling at the humorous image of Lancelot Savage bowing in a graceful, formal bow, while D'Arcy on his knees behind him steadies a pistol on his backside and fires.

"Zen zair are only three of zem left," D'Arcy continued, "and between Lancelot and I, we make ze short work of zem weeth ze blades." He mimicked a humorous, fancy-stepping sword fight, pantomiming thrusts and parries and quick flamboyant dances forward and back. He pantomimed one series wherein he was parrying off attacks while inspecting his fingernails, blowing on them, rubbing them against his shirtfront, inspecting them again. Jennifer laughed out loud. D'Arcy looked at her and smiled broadly, pleased at his success in changing her mood.

"But why were those men after you?" Jennifer asked, curious.

"Oh . . . this reason and that."

"But there must have been a main reason, though, wasn't there?"

"Well . . ." he hesitated. His mood seemed to go quickly from festive to somber. He bent down and picked up some stones, began pitching them into the brook. "I killed zair master in ze tavern, ze Earl of Lourdes. Ran heem through weeth my blade while he sat at ze table eating veal."

Jennifer was shocked. "He hadn't even drawn his sword? You killed him when he wasn't armed?"

"Jennyfair, in my country we have ze expression, *'premier venger, deuxième honneur'.* 'Revenge first, honor second.' If I challenged heem to ze honorable, fair duel, he, being ze better swordsman, would be steel alive. And I would be dead."

"What were you taking revenge for?"

His mood became very somber now, and the idle tossing of stones into the stream became violent overhand pitches. "Zair was a girl. Adreana. We were to be wed. Ze Earl he calls her to heez castle one day, to take shoes to her father ze cobbler. Zese aristocrats, Jennyfair . . . in my country zay can do *anyzing.* He tries

135

to rape her. She backs away from heem, out of ze room, onto ze high balcony. He pursues her, tearing her clothes, and as zay struggle, she falls over ze side, down to ze steenking mud at ze base of ze castle." He stopped talking. He continued pitching the stones violently into the stream.

"What was she like?" Jennifer asked softly.

He turned to her and the very personal, intimate, yearning look in his eyes made her wish she had not asked the question. "She was very much like you, Jennyfair."

She lowered her eyes. After a minute, she turned and began walking back toward the horses. D'Arcy followed. When they arrived, D'Arcy did not mount up immediately, but simply stood stroking his horse's neck. "You have to go now, yes?" he said, a note of sadness in his voice.

"I have to," she said, mounting her steed. "If I'm not back soon, it will look suspicious."

"*Oui*," he said, "*naturelment*." His voice became businesslike again. "Well, you will see Lancelot soon zen. Tell him zat thirty days from today, just after ze night falls, he must make ze commotion. When we hear eet, and ze guards turn away their attention, then we roll ze cannon onto ze road and begin our attack. And you will get ze information for us, too, zat I ask you for, *non*?"

"I will, D'Arcy. I'll do it. Goodbye. You're very nice."

"*Au revoir, cherie.* Give my love to Lancelot."

She rode hard back to the mansion, and then marched straight up to the Governor's office, without even taking time to change out of her riding clothes. She did not know for sure if the Governor would permit her to visit Savage. She had to find out now, right away, for the uncertainty of not knowing whether she would soon see him again, face to face, would be unbearable, now that the possibility existed. And if the answer was that she was to see him, she would have to prepare herself for it emotionally.

136

The two guards stationed at the Governor's door stopped her from entering when she tried. " 'Ere now," declared the shorter of the two, "you can't just go barging in as if'n you own the place. You just 'old your 'orses now whilst I announce you." But when he knocked on the door and then opened it to announce her presence, Jennifer scooted between the two guards and slipped in past them.

The Governor was in the midst of pacing the room angrily, shouting to his secretary, who stood cringing obsequiously. "That treacherous young man!" the Governor ranted. "Who would have thought he could *manage* something like this? All the while that he was informing for me, he was at the very same time—"

The Governor's thoughts were interrupted by a shout from the guard at the door. "Here now, you come back here!" The Governor looked up, annoyed, to see what was the cause of this interruption. He saw Jennifer striding up to him angrily and announcing "You lied to me!" and at the same time he saw the guard come forward angrily, grip her by the forearm and start to tug her out of the room, saying "Terribly sorry, Guv'n'r, she slipped right past us she did."

Jennifer continued trying to speak to the Governor, resisting the guard, while the guard kept struggling to yank her out of the room, all the while apologizing profusely to the Governor.

The Governor watched the scene in disbelief for several seconds, finally shouting, "Shut up! Both of you! What the hell is going on here?"

"Well, Guv'n'r, the missy here, she just—"

"You! Out! Out out out *out* OUT!"

The guard left the room quickly, bowing repeatedly as he backed out the door and shut it after himself.

"Now what the devil is this all about?" he asked Jennifer. He was upset, but Jennifer could also see that he was very curious; this was the first time she had talked to him since the incident a week ago.

"You lied to me!" she accused, her eyes fiery. "You told me Savage would be saved. But he wasn't, he was

137

hanged! He's dead and you reneged on our agreement!"

"Dead? Dead? Of course he's not dead! Wherever did you get such an idea?"

"In town. Everyone's saying it, that—"

"Well it's balderdash! Don't you think I'd know if he were dead? I am the Governor of the province, after all. I told the prison commandant that your precious pirate was to be spared, and he *was* spared. My edicts aren't taken lightly, you know, by anyone other than . . . you. And what do you mean barging in here like this when I'm in the midst of—"

"I don't believe it!" she exclaimed. "You'll have to let me see him. If you don't let me see him and talk to him and see that he's well, then I'll know that he's dead. And our agreement will be off!"

"My dear girl, do you really think I need your 'cooperation' for our little agreement to continue. I don't have your cooperation as it is. Every time I want you I have to fight a pitched battle to gain my way. I can continue doing so, whether you want to end the agreement or not."

"Not," she said slowly, "if I take my life."

That stopped him. "No," he said, "not if you do that." He paused, looking at her. "So you're willing to remain alive and 'endure' my tender affections, so long as your pirate's life is at stake. But not if it is only your own life at stake."

"Excellency, if it was a choice I had to make between taking my life . . . or submitting to someone as odious as you . . . I'd welcome the Grim Reaper with open arms."

"Hmmm." He began pacing in front of his desk slowly, his head down, hands clasped behind his back. "Well go see the blasted villain then!" he exclaimed suddenly, looking up. "You think I care enough about your insignificant comings and goings to wish to prevent you? Go, go, I've wasted enough time on this as it is!" He turned to his secretary. "Inform the commandant, make the arrangements."

"Yes, Excellency."

"Now," the Governor yelled at Jennifer, "will you get the devil out of my sight and leave me attend to my business!"

As Jennifer turned and began to leave, the Governor started ranting again to his secretary on the subject he had begun initially, before the interruption. "We must find some way of making the deceitful bastard pay, of—" Suddenly he stopped, at an inspiration. "You girl!" he shouted at Jennifer, just as she was walking through the door. She turned and looked back at him.

"You may visit your pirate on the day after the morrow, but on one condition only: you must be back here by midafternoon. I've just had the most wonderful idea about how to give comeuppance to a certain duplicitous cretin dandy. And you, dear girl, are to lend a helping hand." He smiled a big, malevolent fox's smile, baring all his teeth.

Jennifer did not know what event the smile portended, but she did know this: it frightened her.

Chapter 9

Savage knew something unusual was about to happen. He had not been beaten in two days. And now, after having his wrists manacled in front of him and his ankles manacled with enough chain to allow walking, he was being led through the interior gate, to the guards' quarters and administration area beyond.

At first he assumed they were taking him to a new area for the purpose of the same old beating. But when they put him into a cubicle that resembled a waiting room, he began to think differently. There was no post for him to be tied to and whipped, and the room seemed too clean and airy.

There was a bench against one wall and a barred window high up in the opposite wall. The door was not heavily bolted with a barred aperture in its center—like the sort he had seen when they kept him in the dungeon. It was simply a regular wooden door. He tried it and found that it was locked. He scrutinized every inch of the sunlit room. Why had they brought him here? His mind raced to consider the possibilities, so that he could find the reason and best prepare himself for it. Of the various possible reasons he came up with, none prepared him for the shock he experienced when he heard the key clicking in the lock, then saw the door open to reveal Jennifer standing there next to the guard.

She wore a sky-blue dress with dark blue ruffles bordering the square-cut neckline and cuffs, and encircling her waist. Her hair was brushed back, with ringlets falling about her temples. Her eyes were wide and apprehensive and slightly fearful as she stood staring at him. She looked as lovely and innocent as she had that last day he had seen her close up, the day the British came to drag him away from the cabin. A white crocheted shawl was draped over her shoulders.

"All right," the guard said to Jennifer harshly, indicating with a sharp gesture of his hand that she could enter. "But remember now, ye can't be long."

She walked a few steps forward into the room. The door was shut behind her and the key turned in the lock.

"Jennifer," Savage whispered, the sound almost like a gasp.

For a moment she just stood looking at him, unable to move. At the handsome familiar face that had dominated her dreams and waking hours every day of the last months. Then she cried out, "Oh, Lancelot!" and dropped to her knees before him, wrapping her arms around him and hugging him, burying her face against his leg. She felt the heavy weight of the manacle chain press down on her back as his hands lowered and he put his fingers to her tawny brown hair. She was crying, shudderingly, against his leg, dampening his trousers with her tears. His fingers were in her hair, tousling it, touching it.

It took a long time before she could make herself stop crying. When she finally managed it, she said, "I came here to—"

"I love you, Jennifer." His voice was deep and low.

She closed her eyes tightly and began crying again. "Th . . . there's an important reason I came," she continued. "It's to—"

"I love you."

She found that she was smiling crookedly through her tears. How crazy, she thought, to be smiling and crying both, her face buried against the rough cloth of his pants.

Savage lowered himself so that he was on his knees too and he took her face in his hands and looked at her. Then he kissed her. His hands on her face were gentle,

141

but his kiss was raw and forceful, as if he were too overcome with emotion to know his own strength. His lips pressed hard against hers, bruising them. But she did not care. She wanted the feel of it, the hurt of it. His lips were on hers for a seemingly endless time and then he pulled his head away and looked at her with his deep intense eyes. She started to speak, but he did not listen. He put his lips to her face and he began kissing her on the forehead and eyes and cheeks and chin. He kissed her on the throat. Her arms went over his shoulders, around his neck, and she felt his arms hug her tightly about the upper torso, so tightly she almost could not breathe. The chain connecting the manacles was draped heavily against her back.

"Jennifer," he said. "I thought of you night and day. The image of you, it's all that kept me going. Knowing you were out there, untouched by this. Knowing that no matter how bad it got for me, no matter how hard it was to keep going . . . somewhere out there things were normal and there was you, in your cabin, living each day peacefully, wait—"

He broke off the sentence. She had a powerful intuition that he was about to say "waiting for me," that he wanted to say it, but would not permit himself to do so. Why? Because he . . . doubted it?

"I'll wait for you," she said. "I'll wait for you always. I love you, Lancelot. I'll never be anyone's woman but yours."

"Jennifer . . ."

"I love you."

"*Oh God, Jennifer!*" It had the intensity of a scream, though his voice remained low. He hugged her so forcefully and suddenly that she really could not breathe. Then, slowly, he relaxed his arms. He pulled them up over her head, so that he could remove the chain from her back. Then he moved away a slight distance so he could look at her. His back was against the wall. He held her hands in his and could not seem to stop touching her. He moved his fingers all over her smooth hands, all over her wrists . . . brushing his palms over her fingers and against the heel of her hands.

"How . . . how have they been treating you?" she asked.

"Forget that," he said, more harshly than he seemed to intend. To compensate, his voice became more normal when he asked, "How did you get them to let you come here?"

She had a story already made up to answer this question. But she could not look him in the eyes as she said it. She looked away, at the far wall, as she said, "They think I can get you to tell me secrets, like who are the members of the Sons of Liberty. They can't prove it, but they suspect you and I are close, that your slapping me was only to mislead them."

"So they think they can use you to get information from me," he said, half-grinning.

"Lancelot, I have a message from D'Arcy. Yes, he's still free. He wants me to tell you that he and your men have a rescue planned for you, on the seventh day of next month. Just after nightfall you're to start a commotion inside the prison yard . . ." She continued, explaining the details of the plan as D'Arcy had explained them to her. Then she asked him for the information D'Arcy needed and he told it to her.

Afterward, when the details were settled, it was clear that he did not want to talk about the escape plan anymore. Instead, he wanted to talk of something else. He settled back, still touching her, seemingly not able to stop from touching her, and said, "Tell me about your days."

She did not know what to say.

"You wake in the morning," he began, prodding her gently. "And you get the banking iron from Silas's room to air the smoldering ashes in the hearth. . ."

"Yes," she said, hesitantly, picking up the thread. "I—I air the banked ashes in the hearth and put in a fresh split of firewood. And then I—I . . ."

"You wash at the basin . . ."

"Yes, I wash and then I start making the biscuits for

143

breakfast. And when they're ready I put them in the hearth. And then I—I—" She was stammering. "And then I *dress*," she blurted out, "and go outside the cabin to see what the night's frost did to the vegetables . . ."

It hurt at first to be talking like this and thinking of these things, these familiar things that were now so foreign to her and hurt her with the memory of how pleasant they had been. But she could see Savage wanted these words, that he needed them. He seemed content during the few minutes left them now to sit back, touching her, and gaze at her somewhat glassy-eyed as his thoughts wandered to the appealing scene she was describing. She realized, looking at him, how hard it must have been for him these past months.

Now that she had gotten over the initial shock and joy of seeing him again, she could notice the changes that had taken place. His face was leaner—too lean. His lips were dry and cracked. His right eye, now that she looked at it closely, seemed too heavily lidded, as if from a wound that had not fully healed.

". . . and then I begin spindling the thread for the day's sewing . . ." she continued. Her words seemed to give him pleasure and it became easier for her to say them now, knowing that they were sparing him—even though only for a short while—from the pain of his existence. A slight smile played along his lips as he listened to her recite this charming lie about her daily activities.

God, she loved him, she thought, looking at him. She loved him so deeply, so fiercely. And she hated these men who were doing this to him. But at least now there was a good side: he would be free in twenty-eight days.

He might be dead in twenty-eight days, a voice inside her head said. Killed during the attempt to escape.

No! she protested. He would live! He would escape! He would be free in twenty-eight days, she knew it was true, she knew he would be free and he would come back to her. She knew this with more certainty than she had ever known anything.

"Lancelot," she said softly. "When D'Arcy and the

144

men rescue you . . . when you're free . . . I want to go with you. Don't leave me alone to wait for you. I can't wait any longer. You have to take me with you."

"Yes," he said.

"On your ship?"

"No, not on the ship. But I'll be on the ship for only part of the time. The rest of the time we spend in port, in a secret cove, preparing for our sallies. You'll be with me there. I'll take you with me, and during the weeks and months the ship is docked in hiding, we'll be together."

"And we'll be married?"

"Yes, my love. The instant I'm free."

She put her head against his shoulder. He put his hand on her hair and began stroking it. Nothing else mattered now. Her earlier thoughts about how she could never be with him again because she was unworthy . . . her fear for his safety during the escape . . . none of it mattered. He would escape and he would return to her.

"You're to be ready on the day of the escape. Have D'Arcy come for you that morning and move you to the hideout that will be our temporary rendezvous. Tell him I said to do this. Then, when I'm out, we'll all go to whatever new staging area D'Arcy's found. And we'll be together. . . ."

The key jangled rudely in the doorlock, making Jennifer cringe. No, she thought. Not yet. Please, just a few minutes more. She felt Savage squeeze her shoulder in an attempt to reassure her.

"All right, pirate," said the guard, entering the room. "On yer feet. 'Tis time to rejoin the other swine in the main compound."

"Take her out first," Savage said. It was clear he did not want Jennifer left with the sight of him being shoved or kicked into the corridor.

"Don't be givin' *me* orders. When Private Chivers commands ye to be on your feet, ye'd darn well best get on yer—"

"I said," said Savage slowly, his voice low and men-

145

acing, his eyes riveted like steel on the man, ". . . take . . . the girl . . . out first."

The private stared back for a moment, blank-faced, disoriented by the commanding resolve in Savage's eyes. He was not used to seeing such strength in prisoners. At least not after they'd been here for a few weeks. He stared in Savage's eyes and it became a contest of wills. And then—though the guard was armed and unchained, while Savage was manacled and unarmed—the guard abruptly jerked his eyes away.

"All right," he said to Jennifer, his voice unusually high, "ye be first. On yer feet, git on back home."

Jennifer stood and went to the doorway. She turned before walking through it, to look at Savage one last time. She saw him putting a confident expression on his face as he looked at her, and she knew what force of will it took, and what his words to the guard would cost him once she was out of sight. She tried to look confident in return, but failed. Afraid her composure would crack completely if she continued looking at him, she turned away and walked out through the open door, then down the corridor and out of the building.

Twenty-eight days, she repeated to herself, over and over in her head. Twenty-eight days and he'll be free. Twenty-eight days and we'll be together. Repeating it over and over to herself was the only way she could block her mind from other thoughts—it was the only way she could survive.

She stopped to see Dr. Kirby in town, before returning to the mansion, to tell him the information Savage had given her. He promised to relay it to D'Arcy. He was full of questions about how well Savage was holding up, but Jennifer did not have time to stay and answer them all. "The Governor ordered me to be back by midafternoon. He made a point of insisting on it."

"What's so all-fired important that he wants you back specifically by then?"

She did not know. All she knew was that she did not want to risk causing any upset, now that Savage was so close to gaining his freedom.

When she arrived back at the mansion, Barczic was there at the top of the stairway, telling her in his obscene, slimy voice that the Governor was expecting her. She went past without looking at him and continued on to the Governor's office.

"He's waiting for you," said the secretary when she arrived. "Go in, go in." One of the guards opened the doors for her, and she entered.

"Good, you're here," said the Governor, glancing up from the paperwork he was attending to at his desk. He was wearing half-spectacles and his white-powdered wig. Jennifer could tell from his sharp tone that he was in a foul mood. "So how was the bugger?" he asked. "Our handsome young buccaneer?" He returned his eyes to his paperwork.

"He's being treated horribly. He's bruised and chained and half-starved. You're not keeping to our agreement, you said you would—"

"Spare him from the gallows. That's what I said I would do. And it's exactly what I did. I also said I'd set him free, if you stayed with me a year, and I'll do that too. So cease this unconvincing outrage, if you don't mind. We're both well aware what was agreed to and what wasn't."

He picked up a quill, dipped it in ink, and scribbled his name on a piece of parchment. He replaced the quill and looked at her. "I would like to announce a change," he said, "in the manner of our relating. We're going to do things my way from this instant forward. So far you've had your head much too often. I thought I'd be able to break your spirit, but evidently I was wrong. You've fought me every time I tried to take you. That's going to stop. That is a thing of the past. Do you understand me?"

She said nothing.

"From now on, you will do as I say, when I say it, and you will offer no resistance whatever. I've quite made up my mind that that's how it will be and that *is* how it will be." He glanced at the wallclock in the corner. "Now, my dear," he said, smiling his evil foxlike

147

smile at her, "if you would be so good as to remove your clothing."

She raised her chin. "You'll have to fight me if you want that. I'll take off not even a hair ribbon of my own free will."

"You've just seen your young gallant," the Governor said menacingly. "You know he's alive. Whether he stays that way depends on you." His voice turned sharp: "Now take off your clothes!"

She returned his stare and made no move to undress.

The Governor rang the summoning bell on his desktop. The secretary instantly came into the room. "Send a messenger right away," said the Governor. "Send him to Captain Trevor with the instructions that Trevor is to shoot the pirate Lancelot Savage within the hour. And have his head brought to me in a box."

The secretary blanched. "Yes, Ex—Excellency," he stammered, bowed, and backed out of the room.

Jennifer's expression was one of gaping horror. "No!" she screamed.

The Governor leaned back in his chair, folded his fingers together across his large belly, and said nothing.

"Get him back!" Jennifer screamed. When the Governor still did not respond, she said, "I'll do what you ask."

The Governor reached a hand forward and jingled his bell again. The door did not open immediately. It took several seconds before the secretary again entered the room and bowed.

"Hold back the messenger. I've changed my mind."

The secretary leapt for the doorway and disappeared into the corridor. Jennifer heard him shouting, "You there, guard! Hold! I say there, guard—wait!" A moment later he came back into the room. "It's taken care of, Excellency. Will there be anything else?"

"No, no, no," he said, shooing him out of the room with a fluttering wave of his hand. He turned his attention to Jennifer. "Now. Take off your clothes."

She closed her eyes and took a deep breath. Then she removed her shawl and let it drop to the floor. She unlaced her dress from behind and pulled it down her shoulders, removing her arms from the sleeves. She pushed it down her waist and let it fall to the floor. She was wearing a long cotton slip and petticoats. She pulled the slip off over her head, feeling the Governor's hungry eyes on her naked breasts as if they exerted an actual physical pressure. She stood still, her hands at her sides.

"The rest of it, too," said the Governor, his voice thick with excitement.

She turned away from him as she pushed her petticoats down her legs and stepped out of them. She turned away out of a desperate sense of modesty that seemed ridiculous to her under the circumstances. What did it matter if he could see her naked backside rather than her front? She was bare and exposed either way. And he would see all of her soon enough, there would be no escaping his eyes . . . and worse.

"Face me," he said. "And open your eyes, damn you!"

She did as she was ordered. She felt the slight breeze coming in through the open veranda windows, over her entire body. Goosebumps rose on her skin.

The Governor smiled and looked her over appraisingly. He had rarely had such a chance to see her like this, without having to do furious battle. And he had almost always been too occupied trying to protect himself from her scratches and blows to be able to savor the beauty of her voluptuous young body, as he was doing now.

His eyes traveled down the length of her pale white torso. Jennifer felt herself blushing wildly and knew her whole body must be turning a fearsome red. She began to perspire.

This was much worse, she thought. Much worse than when he was forcing her and she could fight him. Having to stand here like this, exposed to his stare, not being able to offer the slightest resistance . . .

The door opened suddenly behind her.

She swiveled sharply to see Matthew Armitage being

149

pushed into the room by the Redcoat guards, as he protested to them, "You must *check* first, to see if it's all right! I can't just *enter*, you must first check, and then an*nounce* me!"

Jennifer grabbed up her dress from the floor and held it in front of her.

Matthew was facing the doors he had been pushed through. Now he turned, saw Jennifer, and his mouth dropped open. Instantly he rushed back to the doors, exclaiming "Beg your *par*don, Excellency!", as he tried to pull open the doors. He found that they were locked. He jiggled the handles feverishly, but could not open them. He began pounding on the doors.

"Ah, Matthew," remarked the Governor pleasantly, "so good of you to come. And right on time, I see."

"I . . . I . . . I *beg* your *par*don, Excellency!", he stammered, flushing a crimson red. "I'll leave at once, of course, if I can just—open the doors!" he yelled, panic-stricken. "*Open the doors!*" He pounded on them violently.

"No, no, Matthew, please. It's quite all right. We do have business to discuss and it's certainly not your fault if I was neglectful in keeping my appointments straight. How unforgivable of me. Do sit down."

Matthew glanced at Jennifer's nakedness again and his expression was one of unbridled horror. "Thank you, Excellency, but no, I'll return at a more—open the doors!—at a more convenient—"

"I said *sit*, Matthew," commanded the Governor.

Matthew came forward very hesitantly, eyeing Jennifer in quick nervous glances as he took a seat in front of the Governor's desk. He pulled his collar away from his neck with an index finger and swallowed hard.

Jennifer began dressing quickly, still holding the dress in front of her, trying to cover her nakedness.

"My word," said the Governor in an apologetic tone, "damned if I didn't forget you're quite squeamish about naked women and sexual matters. Aren't you? As a matter of fact, you're quite repulsed and disgusted by such things, if I'm not mistaken."

"Yes, Excellency, so if I could kindly beg your leave while you—"

"But I'm afraid you can't, dear boy. We do have an appointment to discuss urgent matters, don't we, and that's exactly what we shall do. You will forgive me, won't you, if I 'indulge' a bit during our discussion?" He now said sharply to Jennifer, who had managed to get her slip back on, "I told you to take your clothes *off*, not to put them *on*."

She froze.

He raised an index finger. "Remember our new arrangement. You do as I say or I send out that messenger. And I'll tell you frankly, if I have to send him out again, I shan't recall him this time. It just doesn't do to have the Royal Governor appear wishy-washy."

When she saw his hand begin reaching for the bell, she said very quietly, "Wait." She pulled her slip up over her head. She heard Matthew gasp.

"Here," directed the Governor, pointing to a spot between his desk and the chair Matthew sat in, only a few paces from each. Jennifer walked to the spot. She tried to cover herself with her dress, but the Governor slapped her hands away and made her drop the garment. She stood before him naked once more. Behind her, she heard Matthew's loud asthmatic breathing.

Despite the seemingly pleasant tone of voice with which he addressed Matthew, the Governor now showed what a truly foul mood he was in. He stood up and with his arm fully extended, he swept every item off his huge, polished, mahogany desktop. Ink bottles, trays, penstands, knick-knacks—all crashed to the floor. Papers fluttered about. "Up here," he said to Jennifer, indicating the now empty desktop. "On your back."

She began to cower back, but stopped herself. A tingling, burning sensation went over her skin.

"Now!" commanded the Governor.

She moved forward to comply with his order. All that was in her mind was the thought that the bell must not be rung again, the messenger must not be dispatched.

She felt the hard, cool smoothness of the polished mahogany against her shoulder blades and elbows and backside. She watched the Governor's beefy hand descend on her belly and begin to rub it in small circles.

"Now, Matthew, where were we? Ah yes, the urgent matter I spoke of. By George, you know what it is? Why, you've succeeded, Matthew! You're to be awarded a title—oh, a minor one to be sure—but a title nonetheless! And you're to be transported back to England."

Matthew's face was too contorted in revulsion to register any joy. He seemed physically sickened by the sight he was being forced to witness. He tried to turn his head away, but the Governor exclaimed, "Pay attention when I speak to you! I command it!"

Matthew turned his eyes back.

"Pay particular attention to my hands," said the Governor.

Matthew seemed to be fighting his own eyes, which did not want to look at the Governor's hands. Finally, they obediently lowered jerkily, to watch the Governor's hands, which clamped down over Jennifer's breasts. They began squeezing her breasts, jiggling them.

Jennifer's head was thrown back and she was staring up at the ceiling, a look of helpless agony on her face, her mouth open. She tried to blank out her mind, but the feel of the sweating hands upon her sensitive breasts was impossible to blank out. She heard Matthew's halting, asthmatic breathing, which sounded so fitful now that it seemed he might have a stroke.

"Excellency, *please!*" Matthew blurted, "I can't *stand* it!"

"You know," the Governor said, ignoring Matthew's remark, "you really did astound me, Matthew. Never did I expect you might actually accomplish such a feat." His hands swept down to Jennifer's legs and began rubbing the insides of her thighs. Jennifer inhaled sharply.

"But ah, Matthew, you sly devil, you knew something I didn't know. You knew that you were supplying information to the Minister of Colonial Affairs behind my back. You knew *I* wasn't the only one receiving the benefit of your diligent efforts. The Minister was too, and in writing no less! So, even though the information you gave me might not have been sufficient to achieve your ends, the favors you've done for both of us, duly reported by both of us, neither knowing about the other, *was* sufficient. How clever of you, Matthew! Playing both ends against the middle! You filthy, little swine."

"Excellency, if you'll let me ex—"

"Shut up." The Governor began unbuttoning his britches. Suddenly Jennifer felt his hands on her waist, sliding her body toward him as he stood at the side of the desk. When her hips reached the edge of the desk, she felt the Governor's hands grasp the underside of her legs and then felt him pressing against her. "No!" she gasped in terror.

"Yes, my dear. And you'd better not struggle."

He plunged into her and she screamed. Matthew screamed also, his voice a higher pitch than Jennifer's. The Governor began driving hard into her and it hurt, it *hurt*. She put the knuckle of her index finger between her teeth to keep herself from crying out again. The worst of it—the true torture—was that she could not fight him. She had to submit to this almost voluntarily.

"Uncover your eyes!" the Governor yelled at Matthew, who had pressed his palms over his eyes. "You're not in England yet! You're here, in my Colony, and my word is law!"

"I'm going to be sick," Matthew choked.

"You squeamish, fastidious fop," the Governor said, driving into Jennifer almost absent-mindedly, causing her to moan and writhe with each thrust. "You're not even half a man. You're a clever fox, though. You planted an informer within the Sons of Liberty, and instead of giving the information he gathered to me, you gave it to the Minister behind my back. Making me look absolutely foolish. Here, stand up, come over here."

When Matthew came close, the Governor, without

breaking stride, grasped Matthew's lace-cuffed wrists and placed his hands on Jennifer's breasts. Matthew jerked his hands back as if he had touched burning coals. *"Oh my God, no! I can't—"*

"Go ahead," shouted the Governor, "lay them on! You deserve her as much as I. It's you who set me up with her, you who suggested I could have her if I made the concession regarding the pirate. Lay them on, I say!"

Jennifer was in agony, feeling the burning, thrusting, piercing sensation between her legs that was tearing her apart, and now feeling Matthew's cold trembling hands press down on her breasts. She closed her eyes.

"Squeeze them, ye daffodil!" ordered the Governor. And when Matthew complied, his face registering a sickened scowl, the Governor sneered, "Little does she know, eh, that her teats are being pinched by the man who turned in the alarm on her precious pirate, and on her grandfather Silas to boot."

Jennifer's eyes opened and she stared up wide-eyed at Matthew's sickened red face.

The Governor suddenly began shuddering and he thrust once more into her, remaining in, not pulling out. He issued a long, guttural grunt. Then he was out and buttoning up his britches.

Matthew turned away, staggered off several paces, and retched.

"At least ye did it into the waste container," the Governor commented. "A man of proper manners to the very last. All right, now out of my sight. I was ordered to inform you of your appointment, and you're duly informed. The *Hominy* sails for England on the morrow after next. Be on it."

Matthew said nothing. He staggered off toward the doors, holding a silk handkerchief in front of his mouth. His face was sheathed in sweat.

"Unlock the doors!" the Governor shouted to the guards in the outer office. "Leave me rid myself of this vermin."

Jennifer got down from the desktop, picked up her

154

clothes with hands that would not stop trembling, and began dressing. She felt bruised and sensitive and soiled. Beyond the physical sensations, though, there was a veil of numbness. A single thought ran through her mind, over and over, the same thought that had been in her mind ever since leaving the prison: *Twenty-eight days and he'll be free. Twenty-eight days and this will all be over. Twenty-eight days, just twenty-eight days more to live this through.*

She did not ask herself whether she could endure another twenty-eight days of such punishment. She was afraid to know the answer.

Chapter 10

Matthew Armitage left the Governor's mansion and went directly to Haverhill prison. He wanted to tell Captain Trevor the news of his attaining a title, and to bid him farewell.

Though he and Trevor saw each other often—they were friends through a shared secret hatred of the Governor—up till now they had always met at Matthew's home or in the tavern. Matthew had never visited the prison. Now, though, Matthew felt vile revulsion and disgust, and he needed to take the sting away from the feeling by viewing the suffering of the prisoners. Seeing others in misery always made Matthew feel better.

When he entered Captain Trevor's cramped, low-ceilinged quarters, the Captain was surprised to see him. He was even more surprised when Matthew told him the good news of his accomplishment.

"You don't say?" said Captain Trevor quietly, in awe, not quite believing it. But then, scrutinizing his visitor's humorless features, he realized there was no joke or deceit involved. "You do say!" he boomed, smiling joyously, slapping Matthew on the back in a gesture of congratulations that sent him stumbling several paces forward.

"Armitage, you scoundrel, you're a man after me own heart! A title, you say? In London? What a *coup*, what a bloody bloomin' triumph over that ass the Governor! And how's he taking it, his grand Excellency, knowing you're going back to position and reward whilst he stays out here in this godforsaken Colony, being forgotten about more with each passing day?"

"He . . . was not overly pleased."

"Aha ha ha ha!" exclaimed Trevor, bursting into roaring laughter, slapping Matthew on the back again. "Not pleased, 'e says! Not pleased! You bet your britches he wasn't pleased! Having you triumph in your scheme right behind his back. Here, Armitage, set yourself down and have a swig o' the spirits." He began uncorking a jug of rum with his one arm and then pouring the golden liquid into a mug.

"Actually, I'd prefer brandy, if you have any."

"Ah, Armitage, don't be a dandy. Rum's the thing for celebrating between men."

"Well be that as it may, I'd still prefer a touch of—"

"Enough said!" the Captain exclaimed, raising his hand. "The man wants brandy, and brandy it'll be. Ye deserve whatever's to yer likin' after a coup like this." He uncorked a bottle of brandy and poured some into a fresh mug. He handed it to Matthew, then picking up his own mug of rum, he touched it against Matthew's drink, causing both drinks to slosh up and spill partly over the sides. "To yer health, 'Lord' Armitage."

Matthew grinned. "I hardly think the title I receive will be that exalted."

"Drink up, lad!"

Matthew took a few swallows of the sweet liquor and allowed himself to smile slightly. He was feeling better now that he was with someone who could appreciate the magnitude of his accomplishment. He glanced about the office at the walls of rough-cut wood and at the functional but not at all comfortable or esthetic furnishings. It was a shame he had to find his appreciation from such a coarse man. But then, one took one's rewards where one found them.

Captain Trevor sank heavily into a straight-back wooden chair and slouched way down in it, his legs extended straight forward. "And look at me," he said wearily, "still stuck out here too, high and dry like a

157

landlubber. With nothing of the sea anywhere near me exceptin' the salt of it what's still in me blood. So what am I laughing about?"

"You're laughing, my dear Captain, because I'm going to do everything in my power to get you back your command. Or at the very least to get you back into a maritime pursuit of one sort or another."

The Captain looked at him skeptically. "Are you now."

"Oh, it'll take me a while to build up my position and influence, to be sure. But once I reach the point where my word carries weight, you can rest assured I'll say the right things to the right people. In your behalf."

"That's right friendly of you, Armitage. And since it don't do me no good to be doubting you, let me say: I believe you and thank you for it."

"Don't slap me on the back!" Matthew said quickly, holding up a palm.

The thought was not in the Captain's mind. Instead, he was intent upon his drink. He raised the mug to his lips and drank the rum down in huge swallows. Then he lowered the cup and let his arm dangle over the side of the chair, the mug touching the wooden plank floor. His eyes stared moodily and unfocused at the far wall.

"I say," said Matthew, "you wouldn't be about to make your rounds, would you?"

"Rounds?" asked the Captain quizzically.

"Certainly. Don't you make rounds of the prison to be sure everything's in order and——"

"Hell no. I've guards for doin' that."

"But don't you occasionally want to check to see that everything is functioning properly?"

"The less I see of this stinking prison and these stinking guards and prisoners, the more I like it." He looked at him with wary, squinting eyes. "Why do you ask that?"

"Well . . ." He fidgeted, looked down at his brandy mug, looked over at an old ship's compass standing in the corner. "I was thinking that if you did go on your

158

rounds, perhaps I could accompany you. To see the prisoners. Just for something to do, you understand. I've never seen prisoners and I thought it might be amusing to—"

"Sure, you can see the buggers. C'mon, I'll take you on a grand tour." He pulled himself up out of the chair, picked up a riding crop and slapped it against his leg, making a whistling and then cracking sound.

It was crisp and chilly outside and the sky had become overcast with dark gray clouds. "Going to break loose any minute now," said the Captain, looking up at the rain clouds.

Matthew pulled up the collar of his greatcoat, but said nothing. His mind was not on the weather, but on the wooden structures they were passing and the fact that no prisoners were in sight.

"This be the garrison side," explained the Captain. "This here is the armsroom and here be the tool shed. Over there to the left is the guards' mess and then their quarters." They reached a wooden gate with double fortress doors and a horizontal plank running several feet above the stakes of the palisades. "On the other side is the main yard and the prisoners' bungalows."

The Captain began climbing a steep set of wooden stairs up to the tower bastion built at the far end of the gate, which overlooked both sides of the gate. Matthew followed him. The two guards in the tower saluted the Captain when he arrived, and then, when the Captain answered by touching his riding crop to his temple, they stood back out of the way.

Matthew joined the Captain at the front of the bastion, peering over the side to look down on the prison yard below. The breeze up here was much stronger and the chill air bit into Matthew's skin, making his nose and ears red and his face numb. The whistling of the wind sounded in his ears.

"There's the bungalows and over there are the dungeon cells," said the Captain pointing, squinting his eyes against the wind. "And there, Armitage, there be all the prisoners you're likely to ever want to see."

Down in the yard below, the prisoners were working. They wore all manner of britches and blouses, since uniforms were in scarce supply. Many of the men were bare-chested, despite the biting cold.

"They have saws and hatchets!" remarked Matthew, surprised.

"Of course. How do you expect them to be barking the logs and planking them without tools? But never you fret. The tools all go back in the shed when the workday's done, and it's all of it accounted for."

Matthew watched the men as they bent over their work, chopping off branches, peeling the bark off the tree trunks, then sawing the trunks with big double-handled metal saws to slice them into planks.

"The loggers chop down the trees from the forest outside," explained the Captain, "and then slide them down here by mule team. We take them in, turn them into planks and beams for export to the West Indies. The Crown makes a goodly penny off the final lot, I'll tell ye that."

Matthew was not interested in the economics of the situation. He was interested only in how hard the men were working and how much they seemed to be suffering. And he was sorely disappointed in this particular interest, for though they were working very hard, the prisoners did not seem to be noticebly suffering at all. There were no signs of misery or torture. Matthew felt cheated. He was still nauseous in the pit of his stomach from the ordeal the Governor had put him through. He wanted the cleansing relief of seeing others suffer, to make his own misery seem less vivid. But these men were not in misery! Matthew felt bile rise up in himself and he found himself wishing to inflict pain somehow, to *make* them hurt, the bastards, the insensitive louts.

The Captain's eyes were scanning the yard below. Finally he found what he was looking for. "You there!" he shouted to one of the guards in the yard below. The guard looked up. "Strike that man!" The Captain pointed to Lancelot Savage, who was bending over a thick log, skinning down its bark. He was bare-chested and his lean body was hard and bronzed.

The guard responded quickly, smashing the butt of his musket into Savage's shoulder, knocking him clear over the log onto the rocky ground. Savage lay still for a moment, clutching his shoulder, his face a mask of pain. But then, slowly, he began to get up. He was used to this treatment by now. Every time the Captain laid eyes on him, it was the same. He returned to the log, grasped the bark hide he had been stripping, and began peeling it down.

Matthew's eyes lit up when Savage walked back to the log, for Matthew could now see his face clearly for the first time. "I know that man!" he declared.

"Sure you do. The pirate. You must of seen him in the courtroom. Everyone in town did it seems."

The bile in Matthew's gut rose through his system into his throat. He was feeling very cruel and bitter now. "May I . . . speak to him?" he asked.

"What could you have to say to a pirate? But hell, never the matter, say whatever ye like."

"You!" Matthew shouted down into the prison yard, his voice sounding slightly effeminate as he raised it to shout. "Lancelot Savage!"

Savage looked up at him. The other prisoners stopped work and looked up also, anxious for any diversion from their monotonous labor, curious at the unfamiliar high-pitched voice.

"I know where you were staying when you were apprehended!" Matthew shouted. "The official word is that you arrived at the cabin just minutes before the troopers came to arrest you. But I know better, Savage!"

Savage put his hands on his hips and watched the little man high up in the tower bastion. Sweat dripped down from Savage's forehead and he wiped it out of his eyes with the back of his forearm. His entire body was

161

drenched in sweat from the hard physical labor. His muscles glistened in the sunlight that intermittently broke through the layer of dark rainclouds.

"I know you were living with that strumpet," shouted the little man up in the tower, his face becoming even redder. "I know you weren't just 'strangers' to each other!"

Savage turned his back on the man and returned to the tree bark. He grabbed hold of the peeled-back piece with both his hands, put his back into the effort in the direction he was pulling, and began ripping the bark down the trunk.

"You pretend you don't care!" shouted Matthew, enraged. "But you know where she is now? You know where your pretty little trollop is now? I'll tell you! I'll tell you!" He was leaning so far over the side now, carried away with his rage and enthusiasm, that the Captain had to put a restraining hand on his shoulder to hold him back.

"She's with the Governor!" Matthew shouted. "Yes! She's with him, I say! I just came from there and I saw her, I saw her *naked*, I saw her on her back, on the . . . on the . . ."

Savage ceased pulling down the bark, but he did not turn around to face the tower. He stood frozen, his body tense and rigid. All eyes in the compound were on him.

"I saw her being carnally satisfied by the Governor, Savage! Laying there naked on the *desk*top. How do you like that, Savage, how do you like that?! And in fact *I*—that's right, yours truly, I—I myself had my hands upon her firm b . . . br . . . (he practically choked on the word) . . . *breasts*."

In a lightning move, Savage whirled around, grasped the hatchet out of the hand of a prisoner standing near a half-chopped branch, and heaved it with all his might at Matthew's head. The hatchet sang through the air, and only due to Matthew's quick jerking-to-the-side re-

162

flex, did he manage to escape it. It sank into a post at the rear of the tower with a loud *ka-chunk*.

"Flail that man!" screamed the Captain, galvanized into action, pointing a shaking finger. "Give him fifteen lashes! Nay, twenty! Twenty lashes, Sergeant, and see that they bite!"

Savage tried to resist as the guards closed in on him, but it was no use. There were too many of them. . . .

He lost consciousness at the whipping post after counting only ten of the lashes, and when he awakened he was on the straw matting of the barracks and it was the next day. When he tried to move, streaks of pain shot through his back.

"Careful, lad," said a man next to him. "You're still bleeding."

Slowly, Savage made himself sit up. It was a major effort and he sat still for a moment afterward, listening to the loud sound of the rain as it crashed down on the barracks roof. A stream of icy cold water trickled down from a leak in the roof, catching him on his cheek. He turned his head up and moved his full face under it to let the water splash down on his forehead and eyes and cheeks and chin. Then he moved away from the leak.

There was a violent compulsion burning within him. He was so emotionally inflamed that he was actually seeing red as he stared out murderously through his bloodshot eyes.

He got to his feet, wincing against the pain, and walked over to where Mighty Mike Mulligan stood gazing out the window at the sheets of pouring rain. "I want to know," Savage said thickly. "Was it true what you told me two months ago about the VanDerLind girl?"

Mulligan looked at him with compassion and respect. No man had ever bested Mighty Mike Mulligan in a fight without winning his respect ever afterward. And now Mulligan seemed amazed that Savage was even on his feet after the brutal whipping he had received. "Ye'll not be hearing 'bout her from the lips o' the

Mighty Mulligan, laddie. Ye taught me me lesson, thankee, and once is good enough fer me."

Savage grasped his shirt front with both fists and slammed him back against the wall. He stared into his eyes from under a lowered brow. His teeth were bared, his eyes murderously intense.

"Careful, laddie," said Mulligan warningly. "Ye're in no state now to be takin' on Mighty Mike Mulligan again. After ye rest a mite and heal some, then maybe."

"Was it true?" Savage shouted. "Was it true what you said?"

Mulligan said nothing, just looked at him sternly.

"Because if it wasn't true," Savage said, his voice choking with emotion, "then how in *hell* did that bastard in the tower know to say the same thing? The same goddam thing!" He released Mulligan's shirtfront, and turned to a bald, young man nearby, who had lost his hair through disease. The man had entered the prison only a week ago. "Is it true?" Savage demanded of him, standing menacingly over him, his fists clenched tightly at his waist.

"Please, mister," the young man said nervously, "I'm just a farmer. I don't mean no hurt to no one. I'm just a far—"

Savage hit him in the temple with his fist. "Where's she staying?" he demanded. "The truth!"

The man put his hand to his forehead where he had been hit. "She's with the Governor," he said. Then he added very quickly, "The whole town knows it, it ain't just me. It's the whole town that knows it. Her cabin she was living in, she got evicted from it. She was out in the cold, homeless, and the next thing that happens, she moved in with the Governor."

Savage jerked his head back sharply and stifled an animal outcry.

"Don't blame Ephram here for tellin' you," said another frightened voice. " 'Tain't his doing, Lord knows. Everyone knows 'bout her bein' evicted, and moving in with the Governor, not just Ephram. It's just that, well, the way you thrashed the Mulligan that day, no one in his right head would say a thing to you about the lady's—"

"Shut up!" yelled Savage.

The man became silent. The entire barracks was hushed and expectant. Savage's eyes were closed tightly and he was seeing vivid red against his closed eyelids. He was breathing through widely flaring nostrils, listening to the sound of the crashing rain. A voice in his head was telling him *No, don't do this crazy, suicidal thing you're thinking.* But there was no hope of him heeding the voice in his head. He would do it, he would do the thing that he was thinking about, no matter how crazy, no matter how suicidal.

When he spoke, his voice was low and in control. "Mulligan," he said. "Now's the time to make your move. Your second chance to escape."

The sudden jumble of voices that raised in protest told him that there was little support for such an idea, if it was to be another massacre like the last one.

"This time it'll be different," Savage said, looking at the men around him. "I'll climb on the high plank and make a rush at the tower. If I make it, you won't have buck 'n' ball raining down on you while you scale the gate."

"Ye said it'd be suicide making such a rush at the tower," said Mighty Mike Mulligan.

"You're with me or you're not. I make the rush at the tower either way."

A slow smile broke across Mulligan's broad Irish face. He clapped his hands together merrily. He had been waiting for another opportunity to escape for some time. "Up and at 'em, laddies, we're bustin' out!" He began stomping up and down the barracks, kicking and bullying those who didn't rally to his cry . . . which was the majority. It took a lot of kicking and threatening and bullying, and a lot of yelling about how it would be different this time, now that a man was going to be making an attempt on the tower—but finally a ragged band of prisoners began to assemble.

Savage ignored Mulligan's shouting of instructions to his men and went to the front of the barracks. He pushed open the barn-style doors, which had never been fitted with a new latch, and looked out at the gate and the tower bastion. The chill wind beat against his face and naked chest and arms. When Mulligan and the others were ready, Savage nodded and pushed the doors open all the way. The men rushed out past him, toward the gate. There was no shouting this time.

Savage grabbed Mulligan's arm as the man rushed past him. "You stay with me," he said. "I need a boost up to the beam."

"My pleasure, laddie."

They rushed out into the cold rain. Instead of following the main body of prisoners, they veered off to the side and ran toward the far end of the gate, away from the end that the tower was on. Shots were already being fired now at the mob of prisoners, who were swarming in front of the gate, scooping up rocks from the field and pelting the guards in the tower with them.

None of the prisoners were trying to clamber over the top of the gate this time. They knew from their previous experience that this would be suicidal until someone succeeded in eliminating the two guards. They were waiting for Savage to do this before attempting to scale the gates. The air was filled with furious screams and yells and the crackling sound of gunfire. Scores of prisoners were running about at the base of the gate in a flurry of wild motion.

The stinging scent of gunfire wafted into Savage's nostrils as he climbed up on the shoulders of Mike Mulligan, who was squatted down at the base of the gate. Mulligan rose slowly to a standing position, as Savage kept his balance by leaning forward against the wall of palisades and walking his palms up the rain-soaked wooden logs as he rose. Mulligan reached his full height and strained even higher on his tiptoes. "Can ye reach it, laddie?" he yelled.

Savage was looking up at the flat beam above the gate. It was just out of reach of his upraised hand. Rain got in his eyes as he looked up. "I'm going to jump," Savage said. "Hold steady."

"Ye're a crazy bastard, laddie."

Savage bent his knees, fixed the horizontal beam in his vision, then jumped up with all his might, his arms reaching high. He caught the beam. Both hands were on it. His muscles strained and bulged as he pulled himself fully up onto it. Soon he lay flat on his stomach on the wet beam, his eyes directed at the tower. On the ground below, Mighty Mike Mulligan ran off to join the screaming, rock-throwing mob.

This is it, Savage thought. Every ounce of his concentration was focused on the tower bastion, which was dead ahead of him along the beam. The plank he lay on ran parallel to the ground, straight out to the bastion, connecting at the level of the bastion's elevated bottom. All he had to do was run straight along the beam and he would reach the guards in the tower, shoulder level to shoulder level, and he could leap inside. All *they* had to do was look in his direction. It would be impossible not to see him. And once spotted, he would be an easy straight-on target, with nowhere to hide.

He slowly got to his feet, balancing precariously on the narrow six-inch beam. He had to start his charge now, right away. Already the off-duty guards had come out of their quarters and were besieging the armsroom to secure their weapons. The armsroom attendant was struggling to get his key into the padlock to open the door. In another instant the door would be opened, the guards would be armed, and they would be rushing up to reinforce the bastion.

He began moving forward, quickening his pace. He broke into a run. From the ground below, he was outlined clearly against the dark gray sky.

The two guards in the tower had not yet seen him. They were busy firing down on the mob below. He continued running forward, balancing himself on the beam. Still they did not see him. He continued on, excitement surging through him.

Then, one of the guards caught a glimpse of movement to his side, and turned his head to look. His mouth dropped open in surprise as he saw Savage rushing toward him. Already past the halfway point, Savage poured on the power now, running as fast as he could, paying no heed at all to his balance. The guard raised his musket and fired.

He had not taken time to aim carefully and the ball hit Savage on the outside of his leg, tearing out a chunk of his calf as it whizzed by. The impact of the passing ball made Savage trip and he fell forward. Shooting his hands out desperately, he caught the beam in a fierce grip and for a moment hung with his torso and feet dangling down above the top of the gate, his arms around the beam. Swinging furiously, knowing each second was crucial, he managed to clasp his legs around the beam and pull himself back up on it. He crouched, raised to a standing position, began trotting forward again.

The guard was waiting for him with a fresh, loaded musket which he had picked up from the rack and which he now held steady, aimed at Savage's naked stomach. The other guard was firing down at the yelling mob of prisoners below.

Savage looked down the muzzle of the guard's musket as he ran right toward it, and he thought to himself: I won't make it.

The guard cocked the musket with his thumb. He waited until the wild-eyed, charging prisoner was only two yards away; he did not want to repeat his mistake of not aiming carefully. Then, when the muzzle was practically touching the man's belly, the guard fired.

The flint in the firelock, wet by the rain, did not spark. Horrified, the guard recocked. But the instant he lost to the misfire was decisive. Savage had leapt into the air and was now flying forward, screaming like a crazed wild animal. He slammed against the guard, the forward momentum of his body knocking the guard down to the wooden tower floor. Savage's hips came down on the man's head, smashing his head into the floor with such concussive force that it instantly knocked him out.

The second guard, alerted by the motion and the scream, turned around and swung the butt of his rifle at Savage's head. Savage ducked, and when he came up from a squatting position, his arms were clasped around the guard's knees. In a single swift motion, he rose to his full height—lifting the guard off his feet—backed him to the bastion wall, and shoved him over. The men on the ground below let out a wild cheer as the screaming guard came crashing down into the dirt, still gripping his musket. Men began climbing up on the shoulders of their fellows, clambering over the gate now.

Savage lost no time at all in picking up a loaded musket and firing at the throng of guards swarming around the armsroom entrance, now that it was open. His first shot struck a Redcoat guard in the forehead and the man crumpled. Savage threw down the weapon and took a new one from the rack. His next shot struck an armed man in the chest, dropping him to his knees, his eyes bugging out.

This was enough to make the cluster of guards at the entrance scatter for cover, rather than waiting to receive their weapons. Several had already obtained their muskets, though, and one of them, Savage noticed too late, was perched at the base of the tower stairs, aiming up at Savage. Just as the man's fingers squeezed the trigger, a shot rang out from the right, knocking the man over, throwing off his aim so that the ball meant for Savage's chest whistled harmlessly past his ear instead. Savage looked slightly down and to the right and saw Mighty Mike Mulligan sitting on top of the palisade wall, straddling the wall at a place between two sharpened stakes. He was holding the musket he had taken from the guard Savage had thrown over the side and was grinning up at him.

Several of the prisoners had succeeded in climbing over the wall by now, and they pushed back the bolt to the gate. Then the doors swung open and in a wild, screaming onslaught, the prisoners from outside rushed into the privileged guards' compound. They swarmed all over the area.

Though the guards were armed with swords and knives and a few with muskets, the ferocious energy of the onrushing prisoners was more than a match for them. A fierce battle raged.

Savage tore the white shirt off the unconscious guard in the tower and wrapped it tightly around his bleeding calf, as a bandage. Then he picked up a fresh musket—the very last one—and descended the tower stairs.

He skirted the main battleground, staying on the fringes, as he made his way to the stable at the far end of the compound. Just as he approached it, he saw a Redcoat ride out the opposite end, galloping at full speed on a fast stallion. It would be impossible to catch him before he reached the main garrison to alert the British troops. Savage raised the musket to shoulder level, but decided against wasting the shot. The man was too far out of range.

He heard a loud cursing in a familiar voice coming from inside the stable. He went in and saw Captain Trevor dancing around an active horse, cursing bitterly as he tried to mount her with his one arm. Finally he managed to climb into the saddle. He grabbed the reins and kneed the horse, but as she started for the exit gate, Savage grabbed her bridle and held her back.

Captain Trevor saw who his antagonist was and shouted, "You! Are you my personal nemesis? First my ship, then my arm, now my prison. Get out of my life, damn you!" He unsheathed his sword and began slicing fiercely at Savage. Savage moved to the Captain's bad side, keeping the horse's great neck and head between himself and the slashing sword. He waited for his moment and when it came, he raised the muzzle of his musket to the Captain's good shoulder and blasted away.

The Captain's scream was shrill and loud and sustained. The sword dropped away from his useless dead limb and the horse suddenly sprinted forward. Savage released the bridle and stood back. He watched the horse and rider gallop away into the darkening nightfall, the Captain's unending scream fading as the distance became greater.

Savage went back to the prison's side opening and looked out at the continuing ferocious melee. The prisoners were prevailing, there was no question of it. In just moments they would be completely victorious. Savage picked up the Captain's heavy sword and sheathed it through his trouser belt. He put on a loose-fitting gray blouse he found in the stable, mounted a sleek black stallion and then, with a slap on the stallion's flank and a loud yell, he galloped out of the stable toward the forest.

It was horrible the way it happened . . . Jennifer would never get the burning image of it out of her mind.

She was in the Governor's bedchambers, late at night. She was on her knees in the bed, facing the heavy velvet drapes of the veranda windows. She wore a long white nightgown, but it was bunched up all the way to her shoulders. The Governor was behind her on the bed with one hand over her shoulder, fondling her breast, the other hand down between her thighs.

Suddenly there was a loud crashing sound and the veranda windows flew open with a wild splintering of glass, as if violently kicked. Jennifer's face registered absolute shock as she looked and saw, standing there on the veranda, tall and rigidly straight like an avenging deity . . . Lancelot Savage.

For a split second, the scene remained frozen: Jennifer kneeling on the bed . . . the Governor behind her, his hands violating her in the most intimate places . . . Savage standing there gaunt and wild-eyed, a blood-

171

soaked bandage on his leg, a look of unbelieving agony on his face. A chilly gust of rain and wind swept into the room from the shattered veranda windows.

Then, all at once, Jennifer screamed . . . the Governor shrieked, "Guards, *guards!*" . . . and Savage moved murderously forward. The shock of the scene seemed to make him forget his sword entirely, for instead of drawing it from his belt, he advanced on the Governor with his bare hands.

The Governor made a frightened dash for the doors, but Savage was too quick for him, and for an instant Savage's fingers closed around the Governor's flabby throat and squeezed it in an iron grip. The Governor's face turned red.

Within seconds, though, the Governor's Redcoat guards were in the room, unsheathing their swords. Savage was forced to release the Governor, who sank back toward the bed and onto it, gasping. His throat was a bloodless white, with clearly defined pink marks where Savage's fingers had been. "Kill him," the Governor wheezed at the guards, in words so quiet they were barely audible. "Kill him, kill him!" he wheezed again, bouncing up and down on the bed in frustration at not being able to make the words come out.

Savage drew his sword, but instead of moving forward to meet the guards, he retreated back to the veranda windows. He had no reason to fight these men now; he had seen what he had come to see. Two additional guards entered the room: Barczic and another blue-coated Hessian. Now the first two guards, younger men who had been holding back cautiously, began advancing with confidence.

Savage was about to leap over the side of the balcony and make his escape, but before he did so, he turned his eyes full on Jennifer. She was standing against the wall now, looking shaken and guilty. She had been watching his every move since he entered the room and now, as he looked at her, Jennifer saw in his eyes the most hateful, tortured look she had ever seen.

When he spoke, his lips turned down into a snarl. "So you'll wait for me, will you?" he said bitterly, recalling the words she had said to him during her visit to the prison. His eyes were feverish. "So you'll never be anyone's woman but mine?"

Jennifer was so shocked by his venom, and by her own piercing shame, she could not respond. She stared at him, speechless.

Barczic reached Savage and lunged with his sword. Savage parried with his own sword and kicked the man hard in the stomach, doubling him over. Then Savage glanced a last time at Jennifer. She wanted to cry out against the look of pure hatred in his eyes. But before she could find her voice, he was over the side of the balcony and gone.

The guards rushed onto the balcony after him, but did not follow him to the ground below. They shouted to other guards who were already at the base of the building: "Stop that man! Stop him! He tried to kill the Governor!"

From inside the bedchamber, Jennifer could hear the sound of hooves and then panicked shouts from the guards outside: "That's him on the black stallion!" "Don't let him by, don't let him by!" There was the sound of a man's scream—Jennifer could tell it was not Savage's—then the sound of hooves again, retreating into the distance. Seconds later, there was the sound of many horses passing under the window.

The guards came in from the balcony. "They didn't catch him, Excellency, but they're right on top o' the bastard."

"Aye, they'll get him, Sir. He's only a lead of a few seconds."

The Governor was sitting on the edge of the bed, rubbing his throat. "You cowardly fools," he said.

Barczic raised himself up from the floor, rump first, holding his stomach. He had been on the floor ever since being kicked.

Jennifer looked at everyone in the room, then started for the doors.

"Where are you going?" the Governor asked.

"That's not your concern any longer."

"Stop her," he said quietly.

Two of the guards rushed after her and caught her just as she was going through the doorway. They pulled her back inside. "Let me go!" she screamed, clawing at them until they grasped hold of her wrists. They brought her over to the Governor, then released her.

"You've no hold on me any longer," she declared to the Governor, raising her chin.

He looked at her through cruel eyes, rubbing his sore throat. "No I haven't, have I?" He stared at her a moment, then said philosophically, "You were getting to be more trouble than you were worth anyway." He stood up and started to leave the room. At the doorway he turned back and said, "I don't know why I should reward incompetence, but nonetheless: You, guards . . . you can have her." He walked out and shut the doors after him.

Jennifer's eyes darted from one man to the next. Barczic smiled at her in malevolent glee. She glanced at the doorway. There was a narrow opening between the two young Redcoats, giving her a slim chance of reaching it.

The instant she started to bolt for the door, Barczic grabbed the back of her long, loose-flowing nightgown. She stopped sharply, almost before she had started—if she rushed forward now, the gown would rip right off her.

Barczic laughed coarsely at the way she stopped in mid-motion to avoid having her gown torn away . He began reeling her back toward him by pulling on the gown. She grasped a clump of the loose material herself, where the tension of his pulling was the greatest, to try to prevent herself from being reeled in like a prize catch. With nervous, abrupt eye movements, she looked at all four of the men: at the younger Redcoats, and at the more mature, more brutal-looking Hessian mercenaries.

"You men," she said breathlessly, failing in her attempt to hide her fright, "you can't do this. The Governor's word isn't law. You can't—"

One of the Redcoats, the blond one, put his hand down low on her hip. She swiveled to face him, shoved his hand away. "Listen to me!" she pleaded, panting with fright. "You—"

Barczic reached over her shoulder from behind and briefly squeezed her breast, making her swivel back to him. The other Hessian slapped her stingingly on the buttocks, forcing her to swivel back around, her eyes wide. The Redcoat on the other side now joined the game, moving his hand up swiftly from behind and stabbing her high up between her thighs. A sharp whimper burst from her lips. She turned around again, then *again* and *again* . . .

The guards laughed merrily. They had her surrounded, turning in a frenzied circle at each new provocation, her eyes wide like those of a terrified animal set upon by hunters. She tried to fend off the hands, but there were too many of them. "Stop it!" she cried frenziedly, on the verge of becoming hysterical. "Don't touch me, don't touch me!"

Two men grabbed the hem of her long nightgown, one in back, one in front, and began raising it. The other two saw the situation and laughingly grabbed hold of the hem too. From all four sides they began raising it up. Jennifer pressed her arms down to keep the loose garment from rising, but her strength was no match for the four pairs of male hands. The gown rose higher and higher, billowing outward. "Noooo," she moaned, half bending her knees, her face a mask of tortured agony.

The men's hands were at their waist level. Laughing gleefully they raised their hands in unison up to their shoulders. The gown now became like a flat round sheet held between them, with Jennifer's head and arms flailing about above it, the rest of her body writhing nakedly below it. Then Barczic dove down under the raised sheet, grasped Jennifer's ankles and jerked them up in the air. Her body, unsupported, crashed down to the floor, ripping away from the taut gown.

She was on the carpet naked, desperately trying to cover herself with her hands. The guards threw away the torn gown and stared down at her, their gazes feverish with lust, their breathing loud and raspy. Jennifer watched in horror as they stripped off their clothes. Suddenly the sweating male bodies were pressing tightly against her, rubbing against her, all at once, from all sides . . . hands were everywhere on her, squeezing, pinching, probing . . . she couldn't escape them! She became hysterical. She lost all sense. She began making gurgling noises with her mouth. When Barczic's leering face pressed down on her from above, his lips on hers, she bit him hard, saw the bright red blood spurt from his wounded mouth . . . she felt his hands close around her throat, choking her. She was reeling into blackness, thinking, *Thank you, God, yes, let me die now, please, let me die. . . .*

When she regained consciousness, she did not open her eyes. She knew she was outside and that it was daylight from the brightness pressing against her closed eyelids.

She knew she was naked from the feel of the warm sunshine on her skin.

She knew it was early morning; the dew was still on the grass, and she felt the blades of wet grass pressing against her breasts and stomach and ear.

She kept hearing a voice in her head, and she thought it was her imagination, that she was still not fully awake. Then she realized the voice was real, and that it was this voice that had awakened her. It was a pleasant, old woman's voice, full of concern and sympathy. "Are you all right, dear?" it kept saying. "Oh merciful heavens, you poor darling. What have they done to you?"

Jennifer opened her eyes. She saw a kindly face,

176

lined with age, and gray hair done up in a loose bun.

The old woman brightened at seeing Jennifer open her eyes. "You'll be all right now," she said gently. "Don't you fret, I'll take care of you. Merciful heavens, you poor child." She removed her raggedy crocheted shawl and put it around Jennifer's back and shoulders. "Here now, you have to stand. Come, you can lie in the back of my wagon, there's a blanket there. Come now, you'll be all right, I'll take care of you."

Jennifer got up slowly from the far end of the lawn fronting the mansion. Every bone and muscle in her body ached. Looking down at herself, she saw several purple bruises and bright red welts. She climbed into the back of the rickety covered carriage and lay down on a blanket. The old woman put another blanket over her, then climbed in front and snapped the reins. The mare started moving lazily down the road. The wagon creaked and shook as Jennifer lay in the back. It was a pleasant motion, a calming motion. A very fat black cat sat at her side, gazing at her with bored eyes.

"You'll be fine, dear," the old woman kept saying. "I'll take good care of you." Jennifer recognized her as Widow Barker, a kindly, eccentric old woman who lived on the outskirts of town.

Jennifer pulled the soft wool blanket tighter around herself and put the edge of it next to her face, pressing it against her lips. As they meandered down the road, she saw the Governor's mansion through the rear of the wagon, growing smaller and smaller as they drove away from it.

It's over now, she thought. She was free from that wicked place. Lancelot was free from his prison and she was free from hers. There was still the pain of the way he had looked at her. There was still the problem of making him understand, of regaining his love. But the worst of it was over. *And she had succeeded; she had saved his life and gained him his freedom.* It had not been for naught.

She fell into a deep, dreamless sleep, lulled by the rocking of the wagon.

Chapter 11

As Savage crashed through the forest, the Redcoats still in hot pursuit, he was thinking: *How could she do this to me? How could I have been so taken in by her! Oh, she put on a grand act, such a fine act, seeming so faithful, so true. . . .* The memory of how she had seemed to him, and how deeply he loved her, flared up vividly in his mind, making him wince with the agony of it. *And all the while,* he thought, *she had not really been like that at all, she had really been a . . . a common tramp, just waiting for her moment.*

God, how it pained him to think of her this way! But he had to. He had ignored reality long enough. First Mulligan had said it of her, then that short man in the tower had said it, then that other prisoner had said it, and then . . . *then! . . .* he had actually seen it for himself with his own eyes! God, he'd have rather ripped out his eyes than behold that sight!

"Hyahh!" he yelled at his mount, though it was already panting from exhaustion and lathered with sweat. When he reached the top of the knoll, he let the horse slow and brought it to a stop. He turned in the saddle and gazed out over the countryside. From his commanding viewpoint he could now see his Redcoat pursuers in the sparse forest below. They were riding off on a diagonal, he could see, taking a wrong direction. Good. He had lost them.

He dismounted and let his horse rest. He had been riding him hard for far too long. He walked the stallion to a small trickle of a stream that had formed during last night's heavy rainfall and let him drink. He patted him on the neck, trying to make up for what he had put him through. Then he lowered himself to the ground and drank from the icy rushing water.

He removed the bandage from his leg and looked at his wound. It was not bad. The blood had congealed, so there was no danger of his becoming faint from further blood loss. From the look of the wound he could tell that no bone had been shot away and that the wound would not leave him a cripple. He soaked the bandage in the stream and washed around the wound with it, being careful not to disturb the clot of hardened blood. Then he wound the bandage back around his leg. He let the stallion rest a few minutes more before remounting and heading down the north side of the knoll.

It was late evening when he arrived. He watched the trading post long enough to know that D'Arcy was not inside. Then he rode off and hid in the bushes alongside the road D'Arcy would have to travel to return to the trading post. He hoped D'Arcy had not moved since that day he and Dr. Kirby had visited Savage and D'Arcy had told him about this trading post where he was staying.

Several mounted riders and one man on foot passed along the road before Savage saw D'Arcy, off in the distance. Even before he could make out the man's features, he recognized the broad-shouldered figure and the unmistakable long blond hair. He was wearing buckskin with fringe, and moccasins.

When D'Arcy came abreast of the spot where he was hiding, Savage yelled out in a disguised gruff voice, "Halt! You're under the gun. Your money or your life."

"Aiiieee," moaned D'Arcy, bringing his horse to a halt, raising his hands in the air. He looked in the direction of the voice, but saw only a thick clump of bushes and trees.

"Please, *monsieur le* highwayman," D'Arcy pleaded, "I am only ze poor peasant in your country. I have no money. And my life, of what value is zat to you? Eet

179

has been of no value even to me. *Mon dieu*, what a hard life! Take eet, eet eez yours!" He continued staring into the bushes, squinting to see his antagonist. "But if eet's ze money you are after, well I do know ze place where *beaucoup* treasure is hidden, many cases of gold and silver. And for only ze small fee—a mere pittance—I weel tell you ze location of—"

"You'd fast-talk a baby out of its porridge if you had half a chance," said Savage in his normal voice.

"Lancelot?" said D'Arcy in amazement, squinting even harder into the bushes. "Eez zat you?"

Savage stepped forward out of the bushes, a grin on his lips, though not in his eyes.

"Ah, *mon ami!*" shouted D'Arcy, jumping down from his horse, crushing Savage in an enormous bearhug. "You are free! How did you do eet? Does Jennyfair know? She is—"

Savage lost his grin. "We won't talk about her," he said coldly.

"Not talk of her? But she eez in *love* with you! And what she eez doing for you . . . ach, ze sacrifice! At theez very moment she eez—"

"I said we won't talk about her," Savage snarled.

D'Arcy looked at his friend very closely now, noticing the set of his face and especially the look in his eyes. "Come," he said, "we go to ze outpost. You need food. You need rest. You are not yourself, I can see zat. You have a horse?"

"In the bushes. But wait—whomever you're lodging with, it could be bad if they see me. Word will be out soon that I've escaped. The bounty on my head will be twice as high this time."

"Do not fear. These people, zay are patriots. Zay know of me, know I am not really Pierre la Crêpe du Suzette, as I say I am. But zer mouths zay are like tripped beartraps. Come, get your horse, we go."

Savage retrieved his stallion from the bushes and they rode off down the road. D'Arcy kept glancing over at him sidelong, his expression one of deep concern, as

Savage told him of his escape, and as he answered Savage's questions about how many of their men were nearby and how long before they could launch a raid to retake the ship.

After they stopped talking, he continued staring at Savage, a tortured look in his eyes. Finally, he broke his silence. "Lancelot, I know you say not to speak of Jennyfair. But I must."

Savage glared at him fiercely.

"We weel speak of her now and zen not again eef you say so. But we *must* speak of her now. I am your friend. I have to tell you zat you are wrong in whatever bad thing you think about her. She eez brave and true and has sacrificed so much for you zat—"

"—That she ends up in the lap of luxury, on silken sheets, in a giant mansion, surrounded by the best and most expensive of everything in the Colony." His voice was full of bile, his red eyes burning with intensity. "And all she had to do for all of this was lay with the Governor. What a small price to pay for—"

"You are wrong! How dare you think zat! She lay weeth heem not for ze luxuries, but for you! To save you from ze hangman!"

"You stupid Frenchie."

D'Arcy's eyes narrowed. Savage had never insulted him before, ever, in all the years they had been together. This thing that was eating at his friend, he knew, must be like acid in his gut to affect him this way.

"What kind of fairy tales they teach you in that country" Savage raged, his eyes full of fury, but also full of deep racking pain. "You believe in Saint Nick too? I'll wager you do!"

"Lancelot—"

"For *me*, you say, she did it for *me*? It was just coincidence, was it, that this chance to save me came *just* when she was evicted from her cabin and had to move somewhere else? Like in with some boarding family where she'd be uncomfortable and have no privacy. But instead of making such a move, she had a chance to save my life—how grand! And all she has to do is move into the plushest residence in the land!"

"I do not know about zis eviction from ze cabin. I only know zat—"

"I'll tell you why I wasn't hanged! It wasn't a secret. The Captain wanted to keep me alive for a year so he could beat me until I wished I *had* been hanged. I'd never have lasted out that year."

He stopped speaking and they rode on in silence. Then he said, less ferociously and with a stronger undercurrent of pure pain, "You know what she told me when she came to the prison? She told me she would wait for me, no matter how long it took." His voice cracked. "And then I made an unexpected entrance into the Governor's bedchambers and saw just *how* she was waiting. Lies, she told me! Lies about her still living in the cabin! Lies about her loving me! Lies!"

"Lancelot—"

"What a fool I was! Trusting her. Believing her. She'll be my woman only, she said. Mine and the bloody Governor's is what she meant! And God knows who else's. Every salt blood rummy from the gutters of the world, probably!"

D'Arcy waited till Savage finished venting his rage. Then, when he had stopped speaking, D'Arcy said, "Lancelot, you are not a well man. You do not realize thees, but you suffer now under ze fatigue. You cannot think clearly. And I see you have a wound. You are suffering under ze fatigue and ze shock and ze lack of food. You are not yourself. We get you some food now, and ale, and you sleep for ze long time. And zen, when you are yourself again, zen we talk about Jennyfair and how—"

Savage reined in his horse sharply and halted. D'Arcy continued on several lengths before he realized what was happening. He stopped and turned to face Savage.

"We won't talk of her again," Savage said.

"But we must! I am your friend, and—"

"*Not* if you mention her name again. You are never to say that name to me again, understand! That person does not exist! She is out of my life forever!"

D'Arcy said nothing, just stared at him. Then he gestured with a nod of his head for Savage to ride up even with him. "Come," he said, "we get you some food and—"

"We'll settle this right now! If you intend to speak to me about her ever again, say so. And we part company. I don't need your blasted food or ale or . . . friendship."

D'Arcy took a deep breath and let it out slowly. He looked at his friend through sad, weary eyes. "All right, Lancelot. Nevair do we say her name again. Ze lady she eez . . . dead. She does not exeest."

Jennifer was deeply distressed. Why hadn't she heard from him? It had been over a month since his escape from the prison, yet she had received no word from him at all. She knew he had not been killed or recaptured—the British would have celebrated such an event with posted proclamations in every public square. No, he was still free, that was certain. So why had he made no effort to contact her?

His expression when last he saw her was venomously hateful. But surely he'd had time to look at the situation objectively since then, away from the passions of the moment. He must have realized by now the reason she had been sharing the Governor's bed that night. Surely he knew there was no power on earth that could have made her do what she had done . . . other than her love of him. He had to be aware of that. So why hadn't she heard from him?

She frowned in furious frustration as she thrust the pitchfork into the steaming cauldron of blue indigo dye and fished out the flaxen thread at its base. She raised the fibers up to the hanger arm above the pot, then draped them over, leaving them to drip their excess dye back into the cauldron.

She wiped her forehead with a cloth. It was hard work toiling over the steaming cauldron. The Widow Barker had told her not to do it; there was a boy from the village who did all her chores for her. But Jennifer had insisted. Now that she was finished, she told Widow Barker that she was going back in the house.

"There's a good girl," said Widow Barker from her wicker chair in the front yard. "You go rest yourself before dinner. I'll be in shortly."

Jennifer went inside, took off her sticky dress, and washed herself with cool water from the basin. She tried to take her mind off the question of why Savage had not contacted her, but it was impossible. She had thought of almost nothing else for the past month.

She could think of no reason for his not contacting her . . . at least no reason she would admit to herself. It would not be hard getting a message to her, she knew. Dr. Kirby knew she was staying here, and so did others in town. And the house was not even under surveillance! The Governor had figured, after seeing Savage's parting look at Jennifer, that she would be the last person in the world he would risk his life to see again.

She dried herself with a soft, fluffy towel, then changed into a light, yellow print dress with billowing sleeves and white lace cuffs and collar. She had just begun brushing her hair when Widow Barker rushed into the house and closed the door dramatically behind her, an excited look on her face. "Jennifer, my goodness!" she said delightedly.

"What? What is it, Mrs. Barker?"

"You have a gentleman caller! And a very nice one too, not a rotten apple like the others. Oh my, he's so handsome! He's outside right now. Here, you get dressed real fancy now, Jennifer, you have to—"

"Who is he, Mrs. Barker?" Several men had made attempts to call on Jennifer in the past weeks. The reputation she gained as the Governor's mistress resulted in her receiving unwanted attention from the worst dregs of mankind the Colony had to offer. Usually, though,

Mrs. Barker recognized the men and shooed them away without even bothering to announce their presence to Jennifer. This time, the old woman was excited.

"He's tall and strong and a mariner of some sort. He says he made your acquaintance on a ship called the *Liberty*."

"Lancelot? . . ." she breathed.

"I told him you were—"

Jennifer threw down her brush and ran to the door, flinging it open. "Lancelot!"

"No, *cherie*. A thousand regrets, but eet eez only I." D'Arcy stood on the doorstep, looking saddened by the fact of his own identity.

She was startled for a moment and her disappointment showed. "I thought . . ." Then she regained her bearings. "Hello, D'Arcy, I'm so glad you came. I haven't had anyone to talk to since—Here, come in, please."

D'Arcy entered the house. He nodded and smiled shyly at Widow Barker.

"How nice," said Widow Barker, beaming at him. "You're a foreigner. Foreigners are so exciting."

"*Merci, mademoiselle*," said D'Arcy. "But it is I who am excited at meeting such a gracious lady." He took her hand and touched it to his lips. Widow Barker blushed happily. "And what is your name, sir?"

"I am known as Pierre La Crêpe du Suzette."

"My, what a romantic name."

D'Arcy smiled.

Widow Barker seated herself in her rocker and looked contentedly at Jennifer and D'Arcy. Her fat black cat came up to her and brushed against her legs, meowing, signalling that he wanted to be picked up and put in her lap. The cat was so heavy it could not make the short leap by itself. Widow Barker lifted him onto her lap and began stroking him. She continued to smile out at D'Arcy and Jennifer.

D'Arcy looked helplessly at Jennifer. It was clear that they could not talk here.

"Um, Mrs. Barker, D'Ar—I mean *Pierre*—is an old friend. We're going to go outside for a short walk in the woods."

"Jennifer!" exclaimed Widow Barker. "Without a chaperone?"

Jennifer frowned. She looked at D'Arcy, helplessly.

"Madam," said D'Arcy, "I can see you are ze high-minded woman of ze old school. What a privilege to meet such a sophisticated personage in thees backward land. You are absolutely right." He turned to Jennifer. "No, no, *non*, Jennyfair. Etiquette must be respected. And as ze *mademoiselle* here knows—" he looked at Widow Barker "—ze proper course eez for us to take our walk on *thees* side of ze road, rather than ze far side near ze woods. Zat way we need no chaperone, as ze dear lady knows, *n'est-ce pas?*"

Widow Barker frowned in confusion. "No chaperone?"

"Ze 'near-side-of-ze-road' style, as I am sure ze *mademoiselle* knows, is in ze highest tradition of continental etiquette."

Widow Barker's confusion changed to a beaming smile. "Why, of course it is!" She was delighted to be recognized as a fellow connoisseur of continental manners. "Now you two run along, but stay on the near side of the road."

The instant they were out the door, as they were walking, Jennifer asked D'Arcy urgently, "Where is he? Have you seen him? Is he all right?"

"He eez all right, Jennyfair. Zay treated heem very badly, but he eez healing. He becomes stronger and healthier weeth each day."

"Why hasn't he contacted me?"

"Jennyfair, ze way he thinks of you . . . he does not see things clearly." When he saw that she did not understand, he added, "He does not believe ze truth about why you stay weeth ze Governor."

"He has to believe it!"

D'Arcy said nothing.

"He *has* to! Why else would he think I—" She stopped in mid-sentence, a horrified look coming on her face.

"Jennyfair, listen to me. He eez getting better now, gaining back his strength. But he was in a very weak way when you saw him last, you understand? He was not thinking weeth ze healthy mind. You understand? A lesser man would not even have survived ze torture zay put heem through. He did survive, but he was so weakened and unhealthy when he saw you zat ze shock of eet stayed in heez mind."

"But you must have told him the truth! About why he found me in the Governor's . . . mansion."

"I did, yes, of course I did."

"He didn't believe that I did it to save his life? But . . . but he has to!" A sudden inspiration came to her. "Dr. Kirby! He can tell him the truth too. Then he'll have to listen."

D'Arcy shook his head sadly. "No, Jennyfair. He will not listen. He knows ze doctor eez your friend and he would suspect zat—"

"Then you must take me to him. Right now. This instant. I don't have a horse, I'll have to ride with you. Just let me get my shawl and—"

"Eet eez no good, Jennyfair! Do you not see? He would ride away ze instant he saw you. He would nevair return. Eef zat happens I would not be near him to look after him. At least zis way I can keep my eye on heem."

She made a frustrated gesture with both her hands, shaking them, and turned sharply, so her back was to D'Arcy. She began walking along the road, stomping almost, a determined, thoughtful expression on her face. D'Arcy followed her, several paces behind.

Jennifer's brow was furled in bitter concentration. It wasn't fair! she thought. But what could she do? There had to be something. This couldn't be the end of it. What was she supposed to do, accept it graciously? Resign herself to never seeing him again, never being with him again? Was she supposed to resign herself to letting him carry in his mind's eye the image of the way he had seen her last, without him knowing the truth? No! Never! She would find a way to make him see, to make him understand.

"I am not supposed to be here," D'Arcy said. "Eef Lancelot know I come see you, eet be very bad. But we are leaving soon. We attack ze sheep soon, and we take her back and sail weeth her. I had to come tell you ze news before we go. So you are not wondering and not knowing why thees eez happening."

She looked at him as she turned to stomp down the road in the opposite direction, but she said nothing. D'Arcy saw the look of furious concentration on her face and said nothing also, simply stepped aside as she passed and followed behind her again. After several minutes, and several more reversals of direction, Jennifer stopped and turned to face him. "I have a plan," she said.

"You do?"

"He won't listen to me, and he won't believe what you or Dr. Kirby tell him. But he'll *have* to believe someone who has everything to lose by talking about what really happened."

"How do you mean? I don't understand."

Jennifer's eyes narrowed. "You and Dr. Kirby aren't the only ones who know about my agreement with the Governor. Someone else knows too. The man who arranged it. Matthew Armitage."

"Ze same Matthew Armitage who sailed for London to receive a title?"

"That's the one."

"But . . . he weel nevair tell ze truth to Lancelot! Eef he tells about ze agreement, weech he arranged, Lancelot would run heem through!"

"That's why he'd have to believe him. He'd know he's not lying. Why would he lie if it would mean his death?"

D'Arcy slapped the heels of his hands to his forehead in frustration. "Jennyfair, I despair of understanding you. You are right: eef he tells ze truth to Lancelot, Lancelot weel believe heem. But he weel *not* tell ze truth to Lancelot, because Lancelot *weel* believe heem. And keel heem. So now how does thees help us?"

"He'll tell the truth because I'll trick him into it."

D'Arcy raised an eyebrow.

"And Lancelot will hear it, because he'll be right there in hiding, listening. Thanks to you."

"I don't theenk I'm going to like thees plan."

"Here's how we'll do it," she said, her eyes brightening. "I'll go to Mr. Matthew Armitage—"

"But he's in London!"

"—and I'll pretend that I've changed my mind and want to marry him. It may take some time to convince him I mean it and to gain his confidence. When I do, I'll send a message to you. You'll bring Lancelot. You'll stay in hiding at a prearranged place, outside somewhere. Then, at a prearranged hour, I'll make sure Mr. Armitage comes outdoors with me, close enough to where you and Lancelot are hiding so you can hear. I'll get him to talk about the agreement. He won't hesitate—he won't know he's being overheard."

D'Arcy seemed flabbergasted.

Jennifer watched him expectantly, waiting for him to reply.

"How will you get to England?" D'Arcy said. "You have no money."

"I'll get there."

"But . . . how do I get Lancelot to go to thees place? He weel not go eef he knows you weel be there."

"You'll find some way to bring him."

"Eet weel not be easy."

"Please, D'Arcy."

"Eet weel be very hard."

"Please?"

"I theenk eet weel be impossible."

She reached out and touched his palms, putting her hands into his. She came up close to him and looked up into his eyes. "Please," she said. She knew she was

189

using her femininity in a way she had not used it before—it seemed harmless enough to use it this way, though, and it was in a good cause. She did not realize that she was playing with fire until she saw the way D'Arcy responded to her closeness and her wide-eyed, damsel-in-distress look.

His face became suddenly serious. Jennifer saw all the boyishness and humor in his manner vanish, and now for the first time she could see how this man had managed to survive so many dangerous years as a fugitive and pirate. There was a burning intensity in his eyes now. Here was the man of strength who lay hidden beneath the veneer of charming boyishness. Looking at him, Jennifer felt almost that she had to step backward, in reaction to the forcefulness emanating from him.

When he spoke, his voice was steady and deep and quiet, "Jennyfair, I weel do eet. I do not know how, but yes, I weel bring him to whatever place you say, when you say." His blue eyes became piercing, and the look in them was very personal and intimate—no longer disguised by his humor and boyish charm. "I weel do eet," he said pointedly, ". . . for you."

She had to look away. What had she unleashed here? This was a powerful weapon, this femininity she had never deliberately used to her advantage before. She lowered her gaze to the collar of his rough workshirt. There was silence between them now and it was an intimate silence. She had to end it, she could not allow D'Arcy to get the wrong impression from her clumsy attempt at feminine wiles. "Thank you," she said, trying to make it sound not very personal. "You're . . . sweet."

"I am not so sweet, Jennyfair."

She started to remove her hands from his. There was an instant when he did not release them. It was only an instant; when it was past and her hands were again at her sides, Jennifer was not certain there had really been any hesitation at all.

They started back toward the house. D'Arcy began

telling her the name of a ship chandler in London who could be trusted to relay messages to him secretly. As he talked, Jennifer glanced at him from the corner of her eye. The intimate, intense way he had looked at her a moment ago made her feel differently toward him now. She felt a strange sensation of . . . No, she told herself suddenly, she would not analyze it. She did not want to know what the sensation was or what it meant.

One thing was certain, though: from now on, she would have to be very cautious about the way she behaved around this man.

D'Arcy was still speaking about the ship chandler in London. He removed a gold, intricately designed signet ring from his finger and handed it to her. "Show thees to ze chandler," he said, "when first you meet heem. Zat way he weel know you are a friend of mine and Lancelot's. Otherwize, he may theenk of you as a Briteesh spy, and your messages zay weel not be delivered."

"I've never seen a ring like this before," Jennifer said, looking at it closely.

"Eet eez ze family seal of ze Calhouns. For many generations eet has been een my family, since ze time so long ago when ze Calhoun name was one of power and wealth." He shrugged, grinning. "Now eet eez one of ne'er-do-well roguishness and poverty."

He began telling her about the importance of arranging the meeting between Savage and Armitage somewhere on the coast, since it would be too dangerous for D'Arcy and Savage to travel as far inland as London itself. Jennifer listened closely.

Late that night, Jennifer lay awake in bed, staring at the dark ceiling, thinking of many things: the image Savage had of her now . . . the strange, intimate manner in which D'Arcy looked at her this afternoon . . . the way she would put her plan into action beginning tomorrow . . . the giant problems that would have to be overcome, and the uncertainties.

Tomorrow morning would be a new beginning for

her. She had a definite purpose in life now, something she had never really had before. She would find a way to get to England. She would find a way to survive once she got there. She would put her plan into action to regain Savage's love. She would succeed or . . . was it possible she might fail?

She closed her eyes, but could not fall asleep. Her mind was racing.

Chapter 12

Jennifer stood under the eaves of the building, bundled up in her coat against the wind and cold, watching the Boar's Head Inn across the street. In the distance, past the Inn, she could see the ocean, dotted with giant sailing ships coming into port and leaving it. She had been in Boston since yesterday noon, when she had arrived by coach.

Dr. Kirby had paid her coach fare and had given her the name of his cousin's family, whom he insisted she stay with. Jennifer had not wanted to accept the money for the coach and had asked instead only for the loan of his carriage. But Dr. Kirby had told her that she would either accept his offer to pay her fare by coach—or he would tie her to a post in his home and not let her go at all, rather than allow her to travel the unpoliced roads by herself.

He had been greatly opposed to her plan to go to England. But when he saw that she was just as headstrong and stubborn as he always knew she was, and that he could not talk her out of it, he offered to raise money himself to pay for her ocean passage. That, however, was too much to accept. Jennifer thanked him but declined his offer. When he asked how she intended to raise the money on her own, she said she did not know. She did know, though, that the first step of her plan was to get to Boston, the port from which her sea voyage would begin once she did raise the money. Dr. Kirby had wished her well, told her she was an utter fool for doing what she was doing, threatened once more to tie her to a post in his home and finally kissed her on the forehead and let her go.

Boston was an awesome city. It was busy and bustling, and much larger and more diverse and colorful than her own hometown. Even so, though, there did not seem to be any greater number of opportunities for a young girl to earn a decent wage. And Jennifer needed much more than just a decent wage. She had checked with the passage office yesterday and found out what it cost to book sail to England. She would have to find work that paid very well indeed if she intended to earn the amount in any reasonable length of time.

A gust of wind mussed her hair now and made her shiver. A few drops of rain began to fall. She pulled her coat tighter around herself. The Boar's Head Inn across the street was a high, red-brick building, with smoke curling up from twin chimneys at each end of the roof. The establishment was very busy. Horses and carriages kept coming by down the cobbled road and stopping in front of it. Patrons were coming in or going out through its doors every few minutes. Jennifer had always heard it said, with contempt, that one way for a pretty girl to earn money quickly was to waitress in a tavern—if the girl was the sort who gave no mind to her reputation. She crossed the roadway and went inside.

It was like entering another world. The giant room was very warm, almost to the point of being hot, and the air was thick with tobacco smoke. It was very boisterous and noisy, with loud laughter and talking and arguing. All the customers at the bar and the tables were male.

As she stood in the doorway, people began to notice her, and very quickly all the talking and laughing stopped. Everyone was watching her. A buxom, blonde serving girl in a low-bodiced dress came up to her and said urgently, " 'Ere now, you can't come in here." Though her words were strict, her eyes seemed friendly enough, and Jennifer thought she could talk to her. "I'm looking for work," she said quietly.

"You?" said the girl, arching her eyebrows in surprise, looking Jennifer up and down. "You're not the type, honey. Out ye go now, I'm afraid. Ladies ain't allowed in here."

"But I'm—"

"What's the trouble here?" said a loud male voice. A man who seemed to be the owner of the establishment—a powerfully built older man—was coming toward them. "You're disturbing our guests."

"She's wanting a job," said the blonde girl. "I told 'er—"

"*You?*" said the innkeep in good-natured surprise.

"I—I've been a serving girl before," Jennifer lied. "I work hard and I'm honest and . . ."

As Jennifer spoke, the owner was noticing that his guests were watching the girl appreciatively. Nothing pleased the owner more than pleasing his guests. His hands suddenly went around Jennifer's waist and before she knew what was happening, she was being swung up and onto a table top. She nearly stumbled, but managed to right herself. The customers seated at the tables around her looked up at her, smiling delightedly.

"She wants a job as a serving wench, mates," the owner shouted to his customers. "What d'yer think?"

A loud cheer went up from the crowd, as glasses were raised high in the air. Several men whistled and there was the sound of hands clapping.

"Maybe I should tell her no?" shouted the owner, toying with his guests.

The audience responded with loud boos and hisses and catcalls.

"I should tell her yes?"

More cheers and wild applause and whistling.

"Yes it is, then!" The owner smiled, grasped Jennifer about the waist, and swung her down from the table. "You've a loyal following right from the start. Prove true and ye'll be rollin' in the tips. Prove false, and it'll be a pauper's life for ye. Since there ain't no wages to speak of." He turned to the blonde girl. "Betsy, take

195

her off into the kitchen and get her fixed up, will ye?" He looked at Jennifer. "She's got the basic equipment but she's needing the duds to show it off properly."

"Come on with me, honey," said Betsy in a friendly voice. "I'll take care of you."

As Betsy led her through the crowded, smoke-filled room, Jennifer heard wisecracks and whistles from the smiling, drunken men she passed at the tables. One man tried to grab her and she backed away quickly and went around to the other side of the table. As they were passing into the kitchen, Jennifer said to Betsy, "No wages? I thought there were wages and that they were high?"

Betsy looked at her appraisingly. "You'll get on famously, honey, don't worry. 'Tis a good crowd we get here, and appreciative too."

The kitchen was spacious and bright. Huge animal carcasses hung on spits in the fireplace. Copper utensils and servingware lined the brick wall. Betsy took Jennifer to the back pantry and pulled a folded garment from the shelf, handing it to her. Jennifer unfolded it. It was a short orange dress—far too short in the hemline and with a bodice that would cover less than half her bustline. Violet-colored threads were laced throughout the fabric of the garment, giving it a gawdy, garish look. The ruffles bordering the bodice and at the hem were violet also.

"Don't you have anything more modest?" Jennifer asked.

Betsy laughed.

Jennifer saw that the kitchen help was watching her, some from the corners of their eyes, others more openly. The heavyset, stubble-bearded cook, standing with a wooden ladle in his hand, was looking at her with undisguised interest, smiling, exposing a huge gap between his front teeth. Betsy guided Jennifer further back into the pantryroom and pulled the curtain shut. "You can change in here," she said. She watched with amusement and a touch of sympathy as Jennifer changed into the outfit and then tried to tug the top of the bodice up higher, unsuccessfully.

"Tell the truth now," Betsy said, "why's a sheltered one like you going in for wench's work? You can't fool me, honey. I know you never been in this line before."

Jennifer did not know whether she could trust the girl. But she did seem friendly and, besides, Jennifer needed someone to talk to. She might need this girl's help to learn the ins and outs of the job, too. "I have to earn a lot of money," she said.

"Surely not for a life of luxury. You're not the type for that either. I know my intuitions."

"I have to book passage to London. It's complicated. I can't tell you all of it. But . . . I have to get there soon, and if I only earn money from sewing and house chores it will take me years."

Betsy shook her head sadly. "Darlin', let me tell you. No matter how bad you're in need, if you're not cut out for this line o' work, you won't last. It takes a special feeling for . . . uh . . . for not giving a damn. You, honey, you've got too strong a sense of your self-respect, that's clear as the day. Least, it is to me."

"Well," said Jennifer, looking down at herself, trying again to pull the bodice higher, "I hope it's not so clear to the owner. I *have* to make this work."

"Suit yourself." Betsy gave Jennifer an apron, which she put on, and then led the way back into the kitchen. Jennifer nodded and tried to smile as she was introduced to the kitchen staff, including the heavyset cook.

"Here we go now," said Betsy, as she led Jennifer through the open doorway into the main room, "onto the battlefield." She patted Jennifer's arm reassuringly and gave a small smile.

Learning her new trade was not hard. Jennifer simply circulated among the tables that were assigned to her, listened closely to the orders for food or brew that she was given, then fetched the items to the table. She worked hard and was constantly busy. The men made lewd comments about her, but after she lost her keen self-consciousness, she managed to bear it without flinching. She could see that it was all in good humor. No one really meant to insult her. In fact, the various comments were intended as compliments. Still, she could not help being shocked at some of the more colorful ones.

After several hours, she began thinking that she might actually become accustomed to this kind of work. There were quite a few drawbacks to it, such as the constant clamor of voices—shouting, cursing, singing—and the smell of stale air and tobacco and liquor. But there were positive aspects too: the change of pace from everything she was used to, for instance, and the chance to gain an education about a side of life she had never been exposed to before. And her customers truly did seem to appreciate her. Many gave her pennies and even a shilling or two when she fetched their orders quickly.

During a moment when she and Betsy were both at the bar at the same time, waiting while the owner poured the drinks, Jennifer said to Betsy above the din, "I think you were wrong. I'm doing fine. I can do this."

Betsy just smiled at her tolerantly, as if she knew something that Jennifer did not. "Luck to you, then," she said.

It was after the dinner hour when Jennifer made her first—and final—misstep. The crowd was much rowdier, now that they were more sodden with rum and ale and whiskey. Their comments were more obscene too, and by now they were definitely affecting Jennifer. The men no longer seemed good-natured to her, but simply slobbering and drunken and disgusting.

She was bringing a round of drinks to the table when one particularly boisterous man—a young, handsome, green-eyed man who had a lantern jaw and curly brown hair—reached behind her as she set the drinks on the table, and laughing to his friends, exclaimed "What a fine piece of fluff!" He pinched her hard on the buttocks—and did not let go. Jennifer jolted upright, her eyes wide with shocked surprise. The young man and all the others at the table laughed rowdily. He still did not remove his hand! Jennifer took a mug of ale and upended it over the man's curly hair.

The laughter died instantly, except for one fat man who began laughing even more uproariously at the sight of the golden sticky liquid dripping down the man's face and neck. The curly-haired man shot out his fist and smashed the fat man in the face, bloodying his mouth and dislodging several teeth. The fat man put a napkin to his mouth and rushed away making a moaning sound.

The curly-haired man was sitting very stone-faced now. Slowly he got up from the table. He turned to Jennifer, cold fury in his eyes, his fists clenching.

Jennifer stood still, frightened. Just when she was certain that the man would strike her in the face so hard it would scar her for life, the owner reached them and rushed between the two of them, shouting at her, "Out! Out! Out of here! You're through, you stupid bitch!" He swiveled to face the curly-haired man. "I'm *terribly* sorry, Cap'n Garrett! She's a new girl, you know, a damn fool lass in from the country." He turned back to Jennifer. "Out of my sight I said, before I thrash the daylights out of you!"

Jennifer started toward the kitchen, but the owner grasped her by both shoulders from behind and proceeded to push her ahead of him toward the front exit instead. Then, at the doorway, he shoved her through it, so hard she fell to the ground outside, scraping her palms which she thrust in front of her to break her fall. The owner did not stay to issue further words of parting, but turned back inside to continue his profuse apologizing to the man he called Captain Garrett.

Jennifer picked herself up from the road. It was raining hard now. She felt cold and her body ached from the exhaustion and hard work of the past nine hours. People on the street were staring at her. She remembered that she was wearing the low-bodiced serving dress and crossed her hands over herself. She shrank back against the facade of the building. She had to get her clothes back. She could not walk halfway through Boston looking like this . . . she would be arrested as a harlot. Surely, though, she could not go back into the main room of the tavern.

She went around to the side of the building, stepping in mud up to her ankles, and then to the back. She hesitated at the rear doorway which led into the kitchen. Finally she opened it and went in. The owner was there, speaking to his cook. He spied her, picked up a copper pot and heaved it at her. She barely managed to duck back outside as it smashed into the side of the doorway. Through the doorway, she saw him coming forward, a furious look on his face, and she decided that now was not the time to reason with him for the return of her coat and clothing. She shrank back around the corner and ran halfway down the side of the building.

She waited there, breathing quickly, watching the corner of the building. When she saw that he was not pursuing her, she leaned back against the wall, hugging herself against the chill and the rain. Her hair was drenched and stringy now, her blouse almost transparent with the wetness. The naked skin of the upper part of her bustline glistened with wetness. She felt like crying.

"Hey there," said a girl's voice.

Jennifer looked and saw Betsy coming toward her from the distant corner. She was carrying a package under her arm, protecting her hair from the rain by holding a rectangular, tin baking tray above her head. She looked down at the mud she was wading through as she came toward Jennifer. "Hello," she said, coming close, looking up at Jennifer. "I told you. Didn't I tell you?" She handed Jennifer the bundle, which was Jennifer's clothing wrapped in her coat, and shared the marginal protection of the small baking tin.

"Thank you," Jennifer said. She looked around. People on the street at the front of the tavern were passing by the corridor between the two buildings where Jennifer now stood. "I can't change here," she said.

"Do you have a choice, darlin'?"

Jennifer brushed her stringy hair out of her face. She removed her coat from around the clothing and put it on over her wet dress. She belted it tightly, then put the rest of her clothes inside the coat next to her stomach. "I'll return the dress to you later," she said.

"Don't bother. I wouldn't be showing my face around here if I were you." She laughed gaily. "You've a real eye for trouble, ain't you? You couldn't pick one of the irregulars for spillin' ale on, or one of the poorly payin' ones. No, you hadda pick none other than young Cap'n Pauly Garrett hisself, the best customer the Boar's Head ever seen, what with his whole crew that he brings in every time he's in port."

"I didn't pick him! He's the one who—"

"I know, I saw." She laughed again. "Didn't Betsy tell you you weren't made for this sort o' work?"

Jennifer said nothing. She felt horrible.

Betsy seemed in no hurry to return to work. She seemed happy to have someone to talk to. She lowered the heavy baking tin and held it loosely in front of her. Both of them stood against the side of the building, getting wet.

"Don't feel bad," Betsy said. "Some of us were made for laborin' around drunken louts, and some ain't. It comes easy to me. Even so, though, tonight is my last one at the job." She tried to look happy, but instead a shadow of guilt crossed her face as she said, "I'm headed right where you want to be goin'. England!"

"You are?" Jennifer said, surprised.

Betsy nodded. "Tomorrow most likely. And with none other than Cap'n Pauly hisself, if you please."

"How long did it take you to save enough for your passage?"

"Well, I didn't save enough, exactly."

Jennifer looked puzzled. "Then how? . . ."

"Pauly Garrett's ship is famous here in Boston," said Betsy, giving a roundabout answer. "You never heard of it? The *Not A Lady*?"

"No."

Betsy lowered her eyes. "His main cargo on the eastward voyage is . . . girls. Colonial girls for English sportin' houses."

"Oh Betsy! Why!? Why would you do such a thing?"

She shrugged. "The adventure, maybe. And"—she looked at Jennifer with a hint of bitterness—"and not all of us are cut out to be *ladies*, who can marry into a fortune if the need be." She seemed to be accusing Jennifer of being such a person. But then her expression became pleasant and friendly again. "You hear all sorts of tales too, you know, about girls shippin' over to England to work in the houses and then comin' back home as wealthy women of position. After your two year's indenture period is up, half of all the money you make, you keep."

Jennifer said nothing. But her expression must have betrayed her skepticism, for Betsy added:

"Anyways, it's the one chance I've got and I'm taking it. I don't care so much what people think about me. I don't think so highly about most people, so it's even. I'm not so prim and proper. I've no aversion to sportin' a bit, if truth be told. And if I can make life maybe easier on myself this way, why I'll give it a crack, you bet I will." She paused. "I'm not sayin' such a thing is for everyone, mind you, but I know my own self, and life here ain't so all-fired wonderful that I'll be sad to leave it for what may be better."

When Jennifer still said nothing, Betsy took her silence for disapproval. She raised her chin high and turned to leave. "You stick to your sewin' and house chores," she said huffily, "like you're best cut out for."

Jennifer touched her elbow. "I want to go on the ship, too," she said.

Betsy turned back, astonished. "You?" She laughed merrily, as if at a joke.

"No, really! I *must*. It'll take me forever to save enough for a paid passage. But this way—Look, is there any reason I can't sign myself into indenture as a . . . um . . . 'sporting girl'?"

"Whore is the word you're lookin' for, darlin'."

"And then when we dock in England, I'll just run away, before they can put me in one of those houses."

"As easy as that, is it?"

"Isn't it? They don't put you in chains or anything, do they?"

"Well, no, that they don't do." She looked at Jennifer curiously. "Why is it you're so desperate about getting to England?"

Jennifer hesitated. "I love a man. And—"

"He's an Englishman?"

"No. He's a Naval officer, one of our own. But I have to get to England because—" She stopped speaking and looked at Betsy very carefully. Could she trust this girl? Betsy was watching her with eyes that had become very sympathetic the instant Jennifer had said that she loved someone. Betsy seemed to have a soft spot for women who had problems with the men they loved.

Jennifer did not want to tell anyone her plan, but she did need to have someone on her side, to help her. And Betsy seemed to have information that Jennifer could use to help accomplish her plan. And besides, she was beginning to like the girl. She took a deep breath, then began telling a slightly altered, but basically true, story about Lancelot Savage and the newly titled man in England who held the key to regaining his love.

It seemed very strange to be talking about this to a stranger, especially under these circumstances: standing here in the rain, ankle deep in mud, both of them getting drenched and seeming not to care. When Jennifer finished her story, Betsy smiled at her.

"That's beautiful," she said. "I wish't I was loved like your pirate loved you." She stuck out her chin determinedly and nodded her head. "Well, I'll aid you in your plan, you bet I will. But know this in advance, honey: it'll be dangerous. When you sign on as an indentured woman, you become the same as any other cargo on a bill of lading. You know what that means?"

"Well..."

"It means Cap'n Garrett'll be accountable for seeing to it that the full cargo is delivered. He won't be getting his payment for any goods that ain't delivered. So he'll be more than careful, don't you know it, to make sure he don't lose any of his precious cargo."

"I still want to go," Jennifer said. She was frightened and excited at the idea. "I have to go, Betsy, there isn't any other way I can do it."

"So be it, then! Well, tomorrow in the afternoon they do the inspectin' at dockside. They don't take everyone that shows up. Only the most pleasin'. But those they do pick have to be ready to board right then and there. The *Not A Lady* sails right after the choosing."

Jennifer listened closely as Betsy told her all the details. Then she nodded when Betsy said to meet her at the dockside tomorrow, so they could arrive for the inspection together.

"Thank you for helping me," she said to Betsy when she finished speaking. "I couldn't do this without you."

Betsy smiled at her and squeezed her hand. Then she turned and began walking back to the rear-door entrance to the Boar's Head.

Jennifer trudged through the mud back to the cobbled street, then started back toward Dr. Kirby's cousin's home, where she was staying. She knew she was embarking on something that could prove as bad, if not worse, than her situation with the Governor. But, strangely, she did not feel faint-hearted at the prospect. She had a strong sense of determination. Come what may, she was a woman now—no longer a girl—who was taking her first tentative steps toward shaping her own destiny, gaining back the man she loved. Now if only fortune would shine on her just a little bit....

* * *

"I see you're wearin' your dress from the Boar's Head," said Betsy, when Jennifer met her at the dock the next day. "Good idea. You'd look too prim and proper in your high-buttoned clothes."

Jennifer finished removing her coat. She had worn it not for warmth—it was bright and sunny today—but to cover up the scantiness of her attire. Now that they were at the place along the dock where the *Not A Lady* was docked, she put it into the bag she carried.

Betsy looked her over critically. "Can't you look less ... serious? You know, more cheery, more the kind of girl men would feel happy and relaxed with? Here, let me see you smile."

Jennifer smiled.

"That's *awful*."

"I know it. I'm nervous. I can't help it." She tried to smile again.

"That's a little better. You best hope your figure carries it, though. You won't make it on personality."

Jennifer felt like laughing at the remark. But she looked at the *Not A Lady* and suddenly nothing seemed funny at all. Several girls were in line ahead of them, each holding her own bag of belongings so she would be ready to sail if chosen. A wide, high-railed boarding plank extended from the dock to the ship's hold and every so often a tall, hard-looking woman wearing a black eyepatch came into view at the hold's entranceway, saying, "Three more. Step lively." Then the next three girls in line would cross the boarding plank and disappear into the hold. One or two or all three of them usually came out a few minutes later, walked back down the plank and then away. "Those are the ones who haven't made it," Betsy explained quietly to Jennifer.

Jennifer was very tense and tight inside by the time they reached the head of the line. The whole situation seemed crazy. Her on a whore ship? Bound for the brothels of England? Impossible! What would Silas have thought? But then there was no more time to think of the strangeness of the situation, for the black-eyepatched woman appeared in the hold entranceway and called for the next three girls. A thin, dark-haired girl went first, followed by Betsy, and then Jennifer herself walked bouncingly on the unsteady wooden plank, thinking of nothing but the fact that she *had* to reach England.

They were ushered into a corner of the high-beamed hold, where two men leaned comfortably against a pile of flour sacks in front of a slightly raised platform. One of the men was a clerk, wore bifocals, and held a clipboard and a quill. The other man, sloppily attired in the odds and ends of a merchantman's sailing outfit, was Captain Pauly Garrett.

"Up on the platform," said the eyepatched woman in a manly, no-nonsense voice.

The dark-haired girl led the way again. Once they were all on the platform, facing the two men, the woman said, "Off with it. Strip down to your waists."

Jennifer froze for a moment. But seeing how casually Betsy and the other girl obeyed the order made it a little easier. She put down her bag and started taking off her clothes, trying to seem casual about it. She was the last one to finish. She stood there with her hands at her sides, looking straight ahead, above the faces of the two men. Captain Garrett had said nothing upon noticing her. Even without looking directly at him, though, she could tell that he was smirking.

The tall woman came onto the platform and went up to the dark-haired girl. She glanced at her for only a second before turning to the Captain. "Too skinny," she said.

Pauly Garrett nodded.

"Off the platform," said the woman. The dark-haired girl started to say something, but the woman cut her short with a curt "*Off* the platform. Now." The girl stepped down angrily, put on her clothes, picked up her bag, and hurried away toward the boarding plank.

The woman now went up to Betsy and inspected her

206

carefully. "Let's hear your sounds for when you're with a man who thinks he's the best there is."

Without hesitation, Betsy began moaning softly, working her way up to quite loud and enthusiastic moaning. Jennifer listened with a combination of awe and disbelief. She hoped she would not be called on to fake a similar performance.

"A girl of experience, eh Betsy?" said Pauly Garrett pleasantly. "Ye'll be a prize in England. But what a pity for me, not havin' ye around at the Boar's Head no more. Who'll I have to whack on the behind, eh? I'll be missin' you, damned if I won't."

Betsy curtseyed, smiling happily at the attention she was being given by the handsome young merchantman captain. "You'll see plenty of me on the voyage over, Cap'n Pauly. I know of your tricks. I've heard word."

Pauly Garrett laughed.

"Tell your name to the clerk," instructed the tall woman curtly. "He'll give you your papers. Mark your X on all three copies, or sign your name if you can do that."

Betsy stepped down and pranced merrily over to the bespectacled clerk.

The tall woman went to Jennifer now, who stood so tensely that she was almost rigid. The woman looked her up and down. When she put her hand to Jennifer's breast, Jennifer jerked back.

"Too jittery and unrelaxed," said the woman, walking away. "Off the platform."

"Wait," said Jennifer, "I—"

"*Off* the platform!"

"Oh now, Nicole," said Pauly Garrett, "why be so hard on the little darlin'? She does have the looks, after all."

The woman glared hatefully at him. "I say she's jittery and unrelaxed. That's my judgment. And I'm the company's portside agent."

"That ye are, Nicole. But I'm the master of my own ship. And I say we take her along or we don't take *any*

207

of 'em—leastwise not for a week or so. Whilst I attend to unforeseen repairs." He looked at her with one eye narrowed. "I'd hate for you to have to explain to your company why you couldn't get the cargo off in time to arrive within a week of its schedule. Me, they wouldn't blame. Me and your London agent Jack, we're drinkin' mates as close as brothers."

The woman glared at him an instant longer, but then turned away to fetch three more girls. Apparently she had had run-ins with him before and had learned to give in—if not gracefully, then at least quickly. "Tell your name to the clerk," she said to Jennifer as she walked away. "Mark your X on all three copies."

Jennifer looked at Garrett. He was grinning at her, one eye still narrowed. She pulled her dress up in front of her breasts, quickly. Pauly Garrett laughed.

Chapter 13

The *Not A Lady* was smaller than the other two vessels Jennifer had sailed on and, along with the other girls, she was seasick during the first few weeks of the voyage. It was horrible. She felt nauseous and weak and headachy, and her head kept spinning round and round.

Instead of a cabin, the girls were lodged in the ship's hold. Hammocks had been strung from interior beams. Most of the girls were too seasick at first, though, to appreciate the amenity, and preferred to sleep on the various sacks of provisions on the floor of the hold. The sacks were less comfortable, but also less swinging and dizzying; that was what really mattered. Food was served in the ship's galley and the girls were given the freedom to roam the topdeck whenever they liked, except during inclement weather when it would be dangerous or during sailing operations that demanded the crew's undistracted attention.

The crew was constantly pinching the girls and joking with them in a vulgar way. Most of the girls were fun-loving and did not mind at all. Jennifer hated it. Her only consolation was that the crew sensed her aloof attitude and generally left her alone. Why waste one's efforts on a cold fish when there were so many more responsive, appreciative ladies around?

The crew's recreation was limited to pinching and joking, rather than anything more intimate, due to Pauly Garrett's standing order that no seaman tamper with the merchandise—at least not until the final day of the voyage, when the cargo would be safely in port and ready for delivery. This rule was intended to keep the crew's mind on their sailing and was strictly enforced. Though Pauly Garrett was a man of sloppy dress and manner, the way he ran his ship was not sloppy at all. He was known throughout the trade routes not only for his youth, but also for his skill at running a tight, disciplined ship whenever he was under sail. Once the ship put into port, however, the crew was always rewarded for its abstinence by a solid day and night of free-for-all partying, drinking, and carousing.

Jennifer dreaded the day they would pull into port and tried frantically to concoct some scheme that would let her escape what was being referred to as "Party Day." She also needed to devise a plan to escape from the ship itself, before the masters of the brothels arrived to take the girls into their charge.

Next to the problem of finding such workable escape plans, Jennifer's most worrisome problem was the threat of being attacked by Pauly Garrett. The fact that he forbade his crewmen from sporting with the cargo did not mean that the girls were left alone. Garrett allowed himself a privileged exemption from his rule, which he took full advantage of. In fact, he even had a regular pattern of behavior, which had become notorious and legendary.

Betsy explained it to Jennifer thusly: "It's like a game with him and he sticks right closely to his own rules. He never lays with any girl on his ship more than just one time. But he never lays with them less than one time, either. He makes it a point of pride, y'see, to bed every girl he transports. And they're all to his liking, o' course, since he nay-says any that ain't during the portside inspections."

Jennifer was soon exposed to the way Pauly Garrett took his women, and she was appalled and repulsed by his coarseness and insensitivity. The idea of inviting a lady into his cabin did not seem to occur to him. Instead, he came down into the hold whenever he wanted a woman, and took her right there, paying no heed of the others around.

The very first night at sea, Garrett had taken Betsy, who had not minded at all; she had been proud, in fact, to be the first one of his choosing. Over the course of the next several weeks, he had come down into the hold at irregular intervals, whenever the mood struck him. By the time they were within a fortnight of reaching their destination, he had lain with every girl on the ship—except Jennifer.

Jennifer knew she was next and the terror mounted with each passing day. What could she do? How could she keep him away? She still had not come up with a workable plan when, during the last week of the voyage, Pauly Garrett came up to her as she stood in the open air on the topdeck and said "Tonight, beauty. Tonight it'll be."

It was Betsy who came up with a plan to handle the situation, at the last possible minute. But she would not explain it to Jennifer.

"You just act lovey dovey," she told Jennifer. "Act like you crave it and love it. Don't let him catch on that you don't really want it, that's the main thing, or he'll know he's been tricked when it's over."

"But I don't understand! You're not telling me how it'll help for me to act so . . . romantic."

"It's part of the plan for me not to tell you," she said stubbornly. "You just do as I say. When he comes for you, just let your natural feelings rise up in you and make real nice to him."

"If I let my natural feelings rise, I'll end up biting his ear off."

"Oh." She hesitated, perplexed. "Well, forget your natural feelings then. Just act instead. Put on a show. Act like he's the only one for you and you're wantin' him so badly you're meltin' for it inside."

"But Betsy, what's your *plan*?" she pleaded in frustration. "Why won't you tell me?"

"If I tell you, you'll be expecting it and it'll show in your eyes. You have to do it my way, that's all I can say, or you'll ruin it for sure."

211

The idea of following a plan she knew hardly anything about was stomach-tightening horror for Jennifer. But she had no choice. She had to trust Betsy. She could not possibly try to resist Captain Garrett. If she did so, he would know she was not whorehouse material and immediately become suspicious about why she had signed on for the voyage. He would have her under lock and key then, probably, to make sure she was delivered to the brothel company without any complications.

When Pauly Garrett came down into the hold that night, carrying a ship's candle-lantern, he was staggering drunk and singing a nautical ballad in a horribly off-key voice. He stumbled over to the red-haired girl, Jennifer's friend, and fell onto the pile of sacks next to her, his face on her stomach. Even in his drunken disarray, he maintained the mariner's presence of mind to hold his lantern steady.

The red-haired girl put her arms around him happily. The captain raised his head and looked at the girl, holding the lantern close, squinting through his stupor. "You're not the one I want," he drawled drunkenly. "I remember you. I already had you."

"Aw, come on, Pauly," the girl joked. "You can't expect a girl to get by with only one time from a salt-blood seaman like yourself."

"I'm afraid," he said, rising laboriously as the girl tried to hold him, "you'll just have to make do. Cap'n Pauly Garrett has his duly appointed rounds, y'know, and nothing shall stay a seafaring man from his . . ." He caught sight of Jennifer and smiled wolfishly.

There was fear in Jennifer's heart, but in keeping with Betsy's clear instructions, she disguised her fear by her actions: she went over to the Captain, even before he came to her, and put her arms around him and kissed him. "I've waited so long for you," she said, drawing back her head.

Pauly Garrett's mouth dropped open and he gaped at her moronically. "I don't under—. . . that is, I thought you . . . I mean . . . *uhhh.*"

212

"I was only playing with you, with that ale I poured on your head. You thought I didn't want you?" She kissed him again. "I craved you the minute I saw you."

"Yes, well, that's . . . uh . . . quite understandable." He was still surprised, but the slow grin creeping across his face showed that this would not keep him from enjoying the situation. He put his free hand to the back of her neck and forced her head forward, kissing her very hard. She tasted the rum that was on his lips and in his breath.

When his hand moved to her shoulder and began a trip downward, she backed away from him, took his hand and led him over to the spot on one of the rolled-up emergency sails which she had made her bed. Garrett grinned. The candlelight flickered across his features, casting dark-angled shadows on his face. He set the lantern down.

Jennifer felt the anxiety well up in her. When was Betsy going to make her move? If this progressed much farther, it could be too late! She glanced desperately around the hold when Pauly Garrett turned his eyes down to busy himself undoing his britches. In the dim, candle-lit darkness, Jennifer saw that all the girls were watching her and the Captain with bated breath. Betsy was watching too—and *smiling*.

Oh God! thought Jennifer. Was it possible Betsy had deceived her? Could her resentment at Jennifer's being what Betsy called "a lady" be so great that she had deliberately set Jennifer up for this situation, under the guise of helping her? The thought shocked her. There was nothing she could do now, though, but continue following Betsy's instructions and pray that the girl had been truthful with her.

She unlaced her dress and slipped it off, as Pauly Garrett watched with hungry eyes. She began removing her underclothes, slowly, hoping for something to happen that would stop her.

Pauly Garrett licked his lower lip with his tongue. "I been lookin' forward to this, beauty." He rubbed his

213

palm over his stomach. His naked body was lean and well muscled. The thought of having that body pressing against her own naked skin made Jennifer tense. "You're better than the others," he said to her, smiling to himself. "A real classy piece, yes indeed, I been saving you 'til last. It's going to be fine, beauty, it is indeed." He came toward her.

She froze as his hands went around her waist to her behind and touched her there. His palms gripped tightly and pulled her against him. God no! she screamed in her mind. Stop him, please stop him! Had Betsy deserted her?

Garrett pushed forward, dropping her onto her back on the loosely rolled canvas sail. Just as the bulk of his body began coming down on her, Jennifer saw a flash of motion, heard a crash, and felt Pauly Garrett's body drop like a dead weight off to the side of her, partially covering her arm and breast. The man remained in this position, unmoving.

Betsy looked down at Jennifer, still holding the cloth-wrapped clay cistern—now in shattered pieces—which she had smashed over Garrett's head.

"You didn't . . . *kill* him?" Jennifer asked fearfully.

"Nah. These sea dogs, their heads are like iron spittoons." She grasped Garrett's wrist and tugged him off to the side, away from Jennifer. "You did real good," Betsy said, smiling. "This'll work fine now. You just wait and see."

Jennifer looked at Pauly Garrett. He was breathing regularly, his face calm and peaceful and still retaining the hint of a smile. His cheek was against the canvas sail. She got up and began dressing hurriedly.

"You'll just have to undress again in the morning," Betsy advised, watching her with curiosity.

"I don't care!" Her words were too sharp. She touched Betsy's wrist. "I'm sorry. I'm still . . . this was hard for me."

Betsy nodded. "I understand, honey." Her eyes were sympathetic.

Jennifer finished dressing and then pulled a blanket over her shoulders and hugged it tightly around herself. She needed the feel of clothing against her skin. She would go mad without it. She sat down and listened closely as Betsy began detailing the next phase of the plan. . . .

At the first break of dawn, when the hatch covers above the hold were lifted open to let in fresh air and sunlight, Pauly Garrett roused himself awake. He had a seaman's instinct for waking at first light. He sat up, put his hands to his head and groaned. He closed his eyes tightly, opened them, closed them tightly again, opened them. When he looked to his side, he saw Jennifer laying right next to him, her back toward him, under the blanket.

Jennifer turned over to face him, holding the blanket tight against her. She faked an expression of having just come out of a deep sleep, even though she had been lying wide-eyed and alert for the past several hours. She made herself smile at him with a look of deep contentment.

"What the hell happened?" he said in a groggy voice, rubbing his head.

Jennifer's voice was soft and throaty, "You were wonderful . . . Pauly."

"I was?"

She made a soft moan of satisfaction in her throat and looked at him with admiring eyes.

"Aye, I was at that, wasn't I?" he said proudly. He still seemed confused. He reached down for the blanket covering Jennifer and jerked it away. She was naked underneath. He stared for a moment, not seeming to notice the way Jennifer's entire body had tensed. He appeared to be satisfied with the evidence. "That damn rum," he mumbled, rubbing his head. There was no bump to belie the true cause of his headache; Betsy had seen to that by wrapping the cistern in thick layers of cloth to dull the blow.

Pauly Garrett looked at Jennifer again, with eyes that suddenly became hungry. "Pity it's time to be risin'," he said. "I could do with more." He looked regretful. Then his eyes brightened. "Well, actually now, it's not all that late yet . . ." He put his hand on Jennifer's hip.

Suddenly he heard Betsy yelling at him irately, "You didn't give *me* no seconds! Why does she rate? Tell me now, eh, eh? That's not fair at all, now is it!"

The other girls in the hold took up the protest. "I want more too!" "Seconds for me, seconds over here!" "You said it was against your rules!" "Unfair, Pauly, unfair, unfair, unfair!"

He looked out at the multitude of somewhat-angry, somewhat-playful faces, and listened to the protesting, demanding voices that assailed him, and he seemed stunned. Finally, he had enough. "Shut yer yaps!" he shouted. "Blast the lot o' ya! Shut up now, I'm telling ya!"

The girls quieted down quickly, seeing that he was genuinely angered.

"No one tells me what's fair and ain't fair," he declared. "*I* make the rules here." He scowled at them a moment longer, then turned back to Jennifer.

She stared up at him wide-eyed, lying naked on her back. Her hands were at her sides, palms down, nails digging tensely into the canvas sail. She watched him grin lewdly at her and she thought to herself desperately: I must act like I like it, it's going to happen regardless. If I don't act like I like it, he'll know I'm not what I seem. Then I'll be watched so closely, I'll *never* be able to escape.

He put his hand to her breasts and began rubbing and caressing them. She made herself moan softly. He continued stroking and squeezing her until her nipples stood up erectly. Then he began rubbing them between his fingers. Jennifer made herself whimper softly. His hand went down to her loins and began rubbing and caressing her there. Soon Jennifer was moaning repeatedly and she realized with a start that she was no

216

longer forcing herself to do this, but was doing it naturally. She stopped, but when Pauly Garrett frowned at her curiously, she quickly resumed.

His hand at her loins became more active and now he moved his other hand there to join it. Both hands began playing up and down her, in and out of her. She swallowed hard and tried to fight down the feeling. She heard herself breathing in shallow gasps. She would not have to pretend that she was excited anymore, she knew. Garrett's hands were down there, he could tell she was responding, the evidence was clear enough.

Her loins were burning up with sensation as his two hands, his ten fingers, moved all over her. She began squirming and writhing, arching her back. She stared up at him, frowning in torment. The pinpricks of pleasure stinging her loins were becoming unbearable!

Suddenly he maneuvered her onto her back and suspended himself above her on his knees and straightened arms. From his expression, he seemed to be waiting for her to do something. She had no idea what. She began to panic, thinking she was somehow giving herself away. Was there something she was supposed to *do*? Desperately, she tried everything she could think of. She moved her legs farther out to the side and raised up her hips to greet him, feeling utter humiliation sweep over her as she did so. She licked her lips vulgarly. She stroked his chest with her hands. *What in heaven's name was there to do?* What was he waiting for?

He lowered himself down and pressed into her. She jolted rigid with the sensation. He remained inside her, not moving, staring down at her. She clasped her legs around his waist, loosely. He began thrusting deeply, rapidly. She shuddered, feeling herself burning up with passion and pleasure. She turned her head to the side and saw that the girls were all watching her, raptly. She shut her eyes, not wanting to see their staring faces. She tried to make herself stop being so loud, but she was past the point of control. No wonder so many of the

217

girls were enamored of him—the things the man was making her *feel*!

She was shamelessly thrusting her hips against him now, moving with him, rubbing her hands all along his chest and flanks, gazing at his handsome face. *I'm only doing this because I have to,* she told herself, *so he doesn't get suspicious. Only bec . . . only . . . because I . . .* "Aaahhhh!" She cried out as a startling wave of pleasure washed over her. Soon she was sobbing and shuddering, on the verge of bursting apart. Then, all at once, her lower body began to explode with searing ecstasy, sending streaks of pleasure flashing through her. The sensation continued on and on . . .

Then he cried out too and thrust deeply into her. An instant later, he jumped up to his feet. Now that he was satisfied, he did not linger. He dressed quickly, winked down at her, and started away, whistling gaily. Jennifer was left on her back, feeling guilty and soiled, as if she had been used and discarded.

The rest of the voyage was uneventful until one of the girls—a petite, delicate-featured girl—took ill and began burning up with fever. The others took turns tending her as best they could. There was little that could be done, though, until they reached port and a doctor could be summoned. They put wet cloths on her forehead and tried to feed her the freshest of the not-very-fresh rations.

As the day of arrival in port came near, Jennifer began feeling a sharp sense of dread. She had considered many plans for avoiding the "Party Day," and for escaping from the ship before she could be turned over to the brothel masters. The plan that struck her as most practical was so simple, it seemed impossible it could actually work: when the crewmen rushed down to the hold for their recreation, after tying up in port, Jennifer would go topside, slip over the side of the ship, and swim to the wharf. She was not a very good swimmer, but it would only be a few short yards between the ship

218

and the wharf. Once on dry land, she would either escape inland, or hide somewhere on the wharf until the danger of discovery was past.

When the fateful day finally arrived, she was so tense and nervous she could not eat. "Land ho!" the spotter in the crow's nest had called early that morning. Excitement had surged throughout the ship. None of the girls had ever been in England before. There was a keen sense of anticipation about what their new life would hold. Everyone wanted to go up on deck during the actual docking, but Pauly Garrett forbade it. He did not want his crew distracted during the complicated procedure.

From inside the hold, Jennifer heard Garrett and his mate barking orders to the crew, then heard an urgent "Easy now, easy I say!", and finally she felt the jolt as the ship touched lightly against the wharf. The *Not A Lady* was small enough so that she did not have to drop anchor half-a-league out at sea to conduct unloading via longboat.

Jennifer said an emotional goodbye to Betsy, very quietly. Betsy hugged her and smiled and wished her luck. Jennifer wanted to bid goodbye to the other girls, too, whom she had become friendly with . . . but she could not risk letting them know her plan. So she simply walked over to the rear hatchway ladder and when Betsy called everyone's attention to the front—under the guise of making a small speech about how everyone should keep in touch with each other once they were farmed out to the various houses—Jennifer climbed up the ladder and stuck her head out the hatchway.

It was a clear, breezy day. She glanced quickly around to see that no one was nearby to notice her, then scampered onto the deck and ran over to the nearby rigging locker which she had set as her target earlier. She raised the hinged lid, climbed inside, and lowered the lid back in place.

She waited in fearful anticipation in the darkness for the sound of loud footsteps, the vision of brightness that would come as the lid was jerked open and some angry

219

seaman would stare down malevolently at her, shouting at her to get out.

But the footsteps and the angry face did not come. And the only shout she heard was Captain Garrett's voice yelling to someone on the shore to fetch a doctor because they had a feverish girl aboard.

It was cramped and uncomfortable in the wooden rigging locker. She lay on her side on coils of hard rope and netting, and felt them press unyieldingly against her body. The air was stale and filled with a pungent salt-sea odor. She waited tensely. It was only a few minutes before she heard whoops and wild happy yells, and quick footsteps as the seamen rushed over to the hold hatch she had just come out of and climbed down inside. When the last of the excited male voices faded away and the sound of the footsteps ceased, she lifted the lid a tiny bit and peered out. No one else was coming. She waited a minute longer. Still no one.

Her heart was beating so fast she heard its pounding in her ears. She lowered the lid and then maneuvered around inside the locker to pull the hem of her yellow, floral print dress up to her waist and secure it with a long ribbon she had brought. This would keep the dress from clinging to her legs in the water, making swimming impossible. She raised the lid again, saw that no one was coming, then raised the lid up further, stepped out, shut it after her, and without an instant's hesitation rushed to the side of the ship and climbed over.

She held onto the railing before dropping down. She looked to see if she had been noticed. The only person in her vision was the one crewman who had been assigned the thankless task of standing guard at the boarding plank, which had been extended out from the wharf. His back was toward her. He was at the forward section of the ship on the side away from Jennifer, the side that faced the wharf. This was good fortune; he would not hear the splash when Jennifer hit the water.

She took a deep breath, let go of the railing, and

dropped down to the ocean below. The drop was greater than she thought. When she hit the water, she sank far down into it before bobbing back up to the surface. The icy coldness was a shock to her body. When she was on the surface again, she treaded water as best she could while taking deep breaths. She tried to hold onto the side of the ship, but there was nothing to grab hold of, only smooth wood. She started swimming around the stern of the ship to the starboard side which faced the wharf. She had not jumped off this side originally for fear the crewman near the plank would spot her.

She was dangerously out of breath by the time she reached the starboard side and saw with fright that the journey would be longer than she had thought. She could not swim directly to the wharf as she had planned. Looking at it, she could see that it was a solid, vertical-walled embankment, with nothing to grab onto to raise herself up or even steady herself with while she caught her breath. Desperately, she scanned the area. Jutting out perpendicularly from the wharf, was a wooden fishing pier on wooden log stilts. This was two shiplengths away. If she could reach the wooden stilts she could hold on to one while resting and catching her breath. The wharf embankment also turned into a sloped surface there, where it connected to the pier. This would make it easy to climb.

But could she reach the pier? Could she swim that far? Already she was gasping for breath. If only she could grasp onto something now, for just a moment, to catch her breath! But there was nothing. Visions of her drowned, lifeless body crept into her mind as she eyed the wooden pier, deciding what to do. Swim for it? . . . or call out to the crewman on deck so that she could be rescued—and then held prisoner in a whorehouse for a score and four months. There was no choice. Taking a huge draft of air into her lungs, she began swimming for the pier. No one on the wharf was standing close enough to the edge to be able to see her now. She swam almost parallel to the wharf and in close to it. Her muscles felt weak. Her entire body felt fatigued from the monumental effort of swimming and treading water without respite.

She was halfway to the wooden stilts supporting the pier when she realized she was not getting enough air. She was gasping and drawing in as much as she could, but it was not enough, she was growing faint and dizzy. She focused her water-blurred vision on one particular stilt-log of the pier and concentrated every ounce of her energy on reaching it. An eternity passed, with the dizziness seeming to overwhelm her. She lost all sense of time. Nothing mattered but continuing the strokes of her arms, the kicking of her legs, even though her mind no longer seemed to be with her.

Then, mercifully, her outstretched hand touched the water-swollen wood piling. She wrapped her arms around it, hugging it for dear life as she filled her lungs with air, and more air, and more air still. Her breathing seemed so loud she thought surely someone must hear it. But to anyone on the pier above her, the constant sound of the sea drowned out all other noises. Jennifer looked back at the ship. The watchman was looking off to the side away from her, whittling a block of wood with his dagger to amuse himself. He had not noticed her as she swam away from the starboard side.

She took a long time catching her breath. Then she began swimming toward the end of the pier, that joined onto the wharf embankment, stopping ever so often at a piling to catch her breath some more. Each piling was completely encrusted below the waterline with barnacles, which scratched her legs when she brushed against them. Finally she felt solid ground beneath her feet. She walked up the gradual rise of it until the water level moved down from her shoulders to her waist, and then to her knees. Then she was out of the water entirely, on the sloping surface of the wharf embankment.

She lay on her stomach and breathed deeply, allowing herself a moment to rest and gather her strength. It was cool under the pier. The waterline rose and fell with the crest of each mild wave, touching her ankles, then moving up her bare legs to her waist, then down again to her ankles. She lay with her eyes closed, wishing she could stay there like that forever. But she knew she could not. Her absence would be discovered soon. And this would be the first place they would look for her. She could climb up the sloping embankment to the wharf, but then what? She could not travel inland like this, walking along the road in her soaking-wet clothing and bare feet. The sight would surely attract attention and give her away. No, the only answer was to find someplace to hide on the wharf itself.

Forcing herself back into action, she made herself sit up. She untied the ribbon that held her dress hem up around her waist, and pushed the dress back down around her legs. She stood up and walked along the sloping embankment to the side of the pier, then climbed up the embankment as high as she could go without leaving the protection of the pier. She looked out. The wharf was busy with people. On the other side of the pier she saw stacked crates of cargo, which had recently been unloaded from a merchant vessel. The vessel was probably just in from the Indies, she imagined, for each crate was painted with the word SPICES in large letters. The crates were near enough to the edge of the wharf so that she could run to them, if only the dock were not so crowded. The stacked crates would be only a temporary refuge, she knew, but at least they would allow her to leave the underside of the pier where they would surely look for her. Once she reached the crates, she could search for a new hiding place further away.

As she watched the scene on the wharf, a horse and open carriage came speeding down the wharf road near her. She had to duck back under the pier quickly to avoid being seen. The carriage continued down the road past where she was hidden and then stopped just beyond the crates. Jennifer looked out again, once the carriage was past her. She saw a tall man in a gray coat

223

with a black fur collar climb out of the carriage, carrying a black bag. He rushed to the boarding ramp connecting to the *Not A Lady* and crossed over to the ship. Probably the doctor that had been summoned for the feverish girl, Jennifer thought. She went back to scouting the area for a place to hide. They would be coming for her any moment now, as soon as they discovered she was missing.

The very moment she thought this, a commotion suddenly broke out aboard the *Not A Lady*. Crewmen appeared on deck and began rushing around frantically, looking everywhere on deck—in the longboats, up in the rigging, in the supply lockers. Pauly Garrett appeared near the boarding ramp, shouting at the watchman who had been guarding the ramp. The watchman seemed amazed and dumbfounded by his captain's loud shouting and wild gestures. As Jennifer watched, Garrett hit the man in the jaw, and in a fit of rage shoved him up over the side and down into the ocean below. Then he began rushing down the ramp toward the wharf, shouting for his crewmen to follow, his face furious.

Jennifer had to get out of there, now, this very instant. All the people on the wharf were watching the commotion on the *Not A Lady*. Jennifer scooted out from under the pier and ran across the dock road toward the crates of spices. As soon as she reached them, she realized with a shock that she was worse off now than ever before. The crates were stacked not in an unordered jumble of nooks and crannies as they had appeared from her vantage point, but in neat rows, with open aisles facing out toward the *Not A Lady*. There was no place to hide!

"You, search there," came Pauly Garrett's voice. "And you, over there. The rest of you spread out, look everywhere. Mr. Kamins, take a detail out under the pier. She swam for it, I'll wager, and there's the only place she could climb up at."

Jennifer swiveled in all directions looking for a place to hide. Her eyes lit upon the doctor's carriage, and she ran to it and dived inside, into the front boot. There were no blankets or other articles to cover herself with. Anyone looking into the boot would see her.

Two crewmen rushed by, on their way to the underside of the pier. "The bloody bloomin' whore," said one, his voice filled with bitterness. "The whole bloody voyage I been waiting for today, Party Day, and now instead of enjoyin' our pleasures, we got to be chasin' around the damn dock a-searchin' out a runaway!"

"I'll stomp her royally if'n I'm the one to find her," said the second crewman.

"*You'll* stomp her royally? *You'll* stomp her royally? *I'm* the one what was just startin' in on that bouncy blonde, at long last, when Pauly calls us out to . . ." The words faded as the men moved away from the carriage.

Jennifer knew they would find her. Each minute that passed as she lay on her side in the boot brought added certainty. She could hear the sounds of the search: the curses, the shouts to one another about where to look. It was not only the crew that was searching for her now, but others on the dock as well. Pauly Garrett kept shouting "Twenty pounds reward to the bloke who finds her! Twenty pounds in gold to the one who brings her back to me!"

Suddenly a head thrust forward into the carriage, looking into the back seat. The head was so close, Jennifer could see the hairs sprouting from a mole on the back of the man's neck. If he looked in her direction, he would see her. Instead of doing so, though, he spied a spice crate several feet away with a suspiciously ajar lid, and rushed over to investigate.

"Twenty pounds!" shouted Pauly Garrett. "Twenty pounds and the right to be first to lay into her!"

There was the sound of more running feet and more shouting voices. After a minute, Jennifer heard Pauly Garrett again, but this time he was closer and was shouting about an entirely different matter.

"Don't tell me how to run me bloody ship! I don't

need no quacksalver medicine man telling Pauly Garrett about runnin' his bloody ship!"

The doctor's sophisticated, cultured voice was equally loud and angry: "I'm telling you to sail with decent rations, that's what I'm telling you! That girl is fevered thanks to your salt pork and hardtack! Human beings need freshness in their victuals. It's a wonder you didn't lose her *entirely* to the fever, and others along with her."

The voices were moving even closer. "Pork and tack is fine enough for my crew!" protested Pauly Garrett. "If my crew can get by on it, then so can—"

"Your crew, Sir, is not made up of frail women."

"Blast it now, they're not so frail!"

"I don't care to discuss it further. Just see that you do as I say. Get some decent fresh food into the girl, along with spirits mixed with water. And you get her out of that stinking hold into the fresh open air."

They were at the carriage. The doctor came into Jennifer's view as he began climbing into the carriage. He looked to be in his mid-thirties, very straight-backed and aristocratic, with a strong nose and jaw and a thick gray wig.

"I'm not a nursemaid!" yelled Pauly Garrett, who was still out of sight.

"Well blast it, man, you're also not a—" The doctor stopped. His eyes fell on Jennifer in the boot.

"Eh?" said Pauly Garrett.

The doctor looked back at him. His expression was disturbed and perplexed. For a moment he said nothing. Then he said, "You're also not a very decent soul, as I was saying." -

Pauly Garrett's profile came into view now, his lantern-jawed face leaning menacingly close to the doctor. "Decent enough to feed fresh-tasting doctor meat to a sea full o' hungry sharks."

As Jennifer watched, the doctor again seemed to hesitate, unsure of his actions. Then his expression became resolute, as if he had made a decision. He set his black bag down in the right side of the boot, hiding

Jennifer's curled-up legs from view. He climbed into the seat and put his legs into the left side of the boot, practically touching Jennifer's face with them in the small compartment. He took off his gray coat and draped it over his knees, hiding her face and upper torso from view.

"You're like an old lady," mocked Garrett, "putting a muffler over your toesies."

"And you, Sir, are like the scum of the earth. Transporting human 'cargo', since that's the only way you can gain a captaincy at your young age. And then skimping on the fresh rations to pad your pocket with more profit."

Jennifer heard the sound of Garrett hitting the doctor hard, and felt the doctor's legs jerk slightly. There was a moment of silence. Then Pauly Garrett said disgustedly, "Ah, what for am I wasting my energy on *you*? I've a runaway on my hands to track down here." His footsteps moved off. Jennifer heard him shouting to a group of men further down the wharf.

The horse began moving forward at the doctor's command. Jennifer felt the jolting and bouncing of the carriage as the horse was maneuvered around in an arc. Then the carriage was facing the direction from which it had come, and the horse began clopping down the wharfside road, away from the pier.

After several minutes, the coat was removed from the doctor's knees, and the man raised his legs up onto the top rim of the boot. "Come sit beside me," he said sternly. "You're safe now."

Jennifer stuck her head out of the boot and looked around cautiously. They were on a pleasant country road, passing small cottages at intervals along the rolling green plains. No one was in sight. She climbed out of the boot and sat down on the seat beside the doctor. "Thank you," she said, "for saving me."

He lowered his legs back down to the boot. His eyes were directed straight ahead. "Young lady, I'll have you know that I don't take kindly to women of loose morals."

227

"I'm not like that!"

"You came over on the *Not A Lady*, did you not? That speaks for itself."

"But I ran away from them! That's why you found me hiding with all of them after me."

He looked at her for the first time now, his expression not at all as stern as his words. "I know. That's what makes it so strange. If you're not a woman of that ilk, then why in heaven's name did you indenture yourself for the voyage?"

"I . . . I had to get here. And I couldn't afford passage. It's important for me to be here. I can't say more than that to you, though I am grateful to you, Sir." She shivered. Her clothes were still soaking wet.

The doctor reached into the back, where he had thrown his gray coat, and fetched it forward. "Here, put this around you. I've no desire to have a pneumonia patient on my hands."

She put the jacket over her shoulders. "You're angry," she said, looking at his face.

"Well of course I'm angry! What a fine situation you've put me in. You know it's the height of illegality for me to be aiding you this way. That rude young captain has a bona fide claim to your services."

"You won't take me back?" she asked, horrified.

He looked at her. "No," he said, "I won't do that." He sighed wearily and seemed to lose some of his tenseness. "But, I swear, I don't know what I will do with you. I can't very well just drop you off along the road somewhere. You haven't any money, of course?"

"No," she lied. She did have a few pounds, sewn into the seam of her dress. It was money she had earned weaving for the women of the Colony, which she had kept hidden during the time she had stayed with the Governor and during the ocean voyage. If she told the doctor she had the money, though, he would not feel as obligated to help her. And at this point, Jennifer knew, she needed all the help she could muster.

228

"So here I am," the doctor lamented, "transporting an indentured fugitive, who has no money and no place to stay." He turned to her. "Well, you certainly can't stay with me!"

"I wasn't thinking of doing so."

"What were you thinking of doing, pray tell?"

She hesitated. "There's a man, a Colonial, who shipped over here recently. Matthew Armitage is his name. Have you heard of him?"

"Nay. But there's many Colonials that ship over these days, what with the threat of rebellion being so great."

"If you could help me find him, I'd soon be off your hands. He'd take me in, I'm sure of it."

The doctor looked at her. "You must think I'm quite a soft touch, eh, asking me to go out of my way like this to help you?"

"No," she said with sincerity in her voice. "I think you're a kind man. Even though you're angry at me, and you're acting coldly, I can see through that. You saved me, when the easy course would have been to give me over to Pauly Garrett. And you offered me your coat just now to keep me from catching a chill. I know it was out of kindness, though you say it was to spare yourself having another patient."

He dismissed her words with a snort. "What's your name? he asked.

"Jennifer VanDerLind."

"Well, Jennifer VanDerLind, you seem to have found yourself a soft touch after all. Yes, I'll help you to find this Matthew Armitage fellow. I'll do it just to get you out of my hair. First, though, let's go to my home where you can dry yourself and rest. We'll start making inquiries about him on the morrow."

Jennifer thanked him, and then turned her eyes away to the gently rolling fields of England, covered in lush tall grass. She wondered how soon it would be before she could relay a message to D'Arcy, telling him that the plan was working, and asking him to bring Lancelot Savage for the prearranged meeting.

Chapter 14

When Jennifer viewed the exterior of Matthew Armitage's home the next day, she was very surprised. It was not as opulent or impressive as she expected. The rumors she heard indicated that he had gone triumphantly to England to claim a substantial titled position and all the trappings that went with it. This two-story masonry home she was viewing now, though it did look impressive, was certainly not what one would expect from a titled aristocrat.

She thanked the doctor for bringing her all the way to London and for his other kindnesses toward her. Then, as his carriage disappeared down the street, she walked up to the door of the house, and rapped on it with the mounted demon's head knocker. After a moment, a liveried servant answered.

"I'm here to see Mr. Armitage, My name is Jennifer VanDerLind."

The servant invited her into the antechamber, bowed, then went through the high-ceilinged, colorfully decorated living room into the open doors of the study. Within seconds, she heard Matthew's voice, quite loudly: "Jennifer VanDerLind you say? Here? You're mad, you silly fool!" Then she saw Matthew marching through the doors of the study toward her, appearing shorter than she had remembered him. He wore a lace-front white shirt, yellow vest and tight pink silk pants. He stopped in his tracks when he saw her and gaped.

"Hello, Mr. Armitage," she said.

"What the hell are you doing here?"

She was still standing in the antechamber, where the servant had left her. "May I come in?"

"What the *hell* are you doing here I say!"

She looked him square in the eyes, across the distance between them. "I've come to accept your proposal of marriage."

He paused, his eyebrows arching. "It's just as I thought," he said. "You've lost your mind." He turned to his servant. "Fetch me a brandy." He turned his eyes back to Jennifer. "*Do* forgive me if I don't offer you the hospitality of the household. But you are, after all, a filthy *slut*. You recall, of course, the circumstances of our last meeting? You were on top of a desk at the time, I believe, *un*clothed, in the midst of the most dis*gust*ing act of animal copulation." His face contorted in revulsion.

Jennifer lowered her eyes. The memory and the image it called up were extremely painful. "That was not my doing," she said.

"No, no, of course not, you were simply a disinterested bystander. How *fool*ish of me to think you were somehow in*volve*d in the affair." He pulled a kerchief from his sleeve and began wiping the palm of his hands with it. His face looked as if he might become sick. "You even managed to sully *me* with the feel of your disgusting br—br—*fe*maleness."

The servant handed him the goblet of brandy on a silver platter. Matthew lurched for it and drank the liquor down in quick, desperate swallows. "Another," he said, replacing the glass.

Jennifer came forward now, into the living room. She stopped several feet from him, when he began backing away nervously. "Mr. Armitage, you once told me I would do you much good as your wife. You said I could help advance your career. I was naive then and I foolishly said no. I'm a wiser woman now. I would like to change that answer to yes."

231

He laughed derisively. "You think I *need* you now, is that it?"

"I didn't say that."

His voice took on a tone of cynicism as he talked, but it seemed to Jennifer to be entirely defensive, motivated by a need to justify himself. "Oh, of course, you see these grand surroundings," he said, gesturing at the furnishings and the room itself in flamboyant sarcasm, "and you think gloatingly: Whatever happened to the titled po*sition* he was supposed to have? It never materialized, did it, so maybe he needs me now, to help advance his career."

He glared at her bitterly. "Well I've no *need* for you, you . . . you . . . you *woman*. So they *did* overstate their promise to me! So instead of the knighthood I was expecting, I find myself with a portfolio position assisting the Minister of Trade. It's a *high* position, nonetheless! And I'm full well capable of making it higher, by God, you bet I am!"

The servant appeared with the second brandy and Matthew gulped it down greedily. Then he went over to a big button-quilted, tan leather chair near the hearth and sank down into it, looking glum.

"I didn't come to gloat about any setbacks in your career," Jennifer said quietly, preparing to tell him the lie she had carefully fabricated. She went to the chair he sat in and she knelt before him, trying to make herself seem humble. "I came here because I've come around in my thinking and I want the things you promised I could have as your wife. Fame, wealth, position. I now believe what you told me when you proposed, Mr. Armitage: together, we can do much good for each other."

He looked at her suspiciously. "And *what,* might I ask, brought about this change of heart?"

"I may be naive, Mr. Armitage, but I'm not a fool. I have eyes. I can see where my 'virtue' led me . . . and where your ambition led you. Here you are in London itself, the center of the world, with a high position in

232

government. And with your ambition and talent you'll go far, there's no doubt of it."

His expression was still suspicious, but Jennifer could tell that he was not unreceptive to what she was saying; he clearly liked being told he had talent and would go far.

"That's where my ambition has led me, yes," he said. "And you, you're dis*sat*isfied, are you, with where your *virtue*, as you call it, has taken you?"

She made her voice sound bitter, with the bitterness directed at herself. "It's taken me to the Governor's mansion, as you well know, where I was treated like a slave. It's cost me almost a year of my life and all of my friends. And now, what do I have to show for it? Nothing at all." She lowered her head. "I'm tired of being poor and of being used as a bootrag by men of power and position."

Matthew Armitage sneered at her and a grin of malevolent enjoyment crept across his face as he watched her appearing humbled before him. His expression was smugly superior, as if he knew some secret which she was unaware that he knew. "You're quite neg*lect*ing to mention the *main* part of it, aren't you dearest? Not that it's of any significance, oh no, but nonetheless: the fact that your precious pirate virtually *spat* upon you for your efforts?"

He laughed when Jennifer looked at him in surprise. "Yes, I'm quite aware of the details of his escape, and of your little *rend*ezvous in the Governor's bedchambers. I make it a point to keep informed. I know also that he and his men managed to retake their ship in a bloodbath of a raid. Now they're back making a nuisance of themselves on the high seas, disrupting His Majesty's shipping. But that's of little concern to you, is it not? All you care about is that you *sacrificed* yourself for him—you silly romantic!—and the heathen scum returns your gesture by grinding you underfoot."

"Yes," she said painfully.

"No wonder you've come round to thinking in terms of what's best for Miss Jennifer VanDerLind."

She looked at him with a hint of pleading in her eyes and when she spoke, she could not hide the true desperation in her voice, which betrayed how important this really was to her. "Will you still have me as your wife?"

He stood up from the chair quickly, in a lurch, and moved away from her. He walked halfway across the room, his hands clasped behind his back, and then he turned sharply and faced her. "I don't trust you!" he declared whiningly.

She stood up. She was feeling distressed and frightened. This was not working as she had planned. He was offering too much resistance. What if she could not convince him? What if she could not work her way into his confidence? There would be no prearranged meeting then, at which Savage could overhear Matthew's confession and learn the truth. She would never have his love again then . . . he would go through life thinking of her with hatred, carrying in his mind's eye the vile, debased image of the way he had seen her last. . . .

"Please," she said. "I only want what's best for—"

"I don't trust you, I say! You know it was *I* who informed on your grandfather! You know it was *I* who informed on your pirate! The Governor told you all that. And now you ask me to be*lieve*, do you, that you suddenly wish to be my *wife* and aid my car*eer*?"

"All I care about now is improving my lot. What you did to others, for the sake of your ambition, is—"

"And how did you get here anyway?" he said, his eyes narrowing suspiciously. "I know what it costs to book passage across the ocean. You certainly couldn't pay it."

She tried to bring him back to the subject of marriage, and to turn him away from his panicky suspiciousness, by making her own voice calm and reasoned. "Mr. Armitage, if you'll have me as your

234

wife, I'll make my goal in life the advancement of your career. I'll stop at nothing to—"

"No," he said suddenly, coming to an abrupt decision.

"But—"

"No." He was resolute. "There's too much here that's suspect. I distrust your motives. And I can see you truly *have* lost your girlish naiveté, as you say; sophistication is a treacherous trait in a woman. No, you're as beauteous as ever, but I think I prefer to manage my career on my own, thank you. Good day Jennifer. Oscar, show the lady to the door." He turned away from her, went back into his study, and closed the doors.

She stood for a moment, not knowing what to do. The servant was holding the front door open for her. "Madam?" he said.

She went in the other direction, to the study, opened the doors and walked in.

"Get out of here!" shouted Matthew. "I'm through with you! I'm finished with you!" He stood near a table that was littered with maps in front of a wall that was completely covered with maps of various sizes and colorings. "Go help someone *else* further their career. Go find some cockney pimp; that should suit you well enough I *dare*say. Go further *his* career, go peddle your wares in the *street* for all I care."

"I'm leaving," she said. "But I want to tell you something first: I'll find a way to prove that I can help you. And then I'll come back. You'll have to believe me then."

"Oscar! Oscar!" When the servant appeared, Matthew said in a whining, high-pitched voice: "Get her out of here!"

The servant's hand went around Jennifer's upper arm.

"You think I have *time* for you and your silly 'proof,'" Matthew exploded. "Look!" he said, running around the room, pointing at the maps. "I have to *study* these stupid things. My ignorance of foreign trade affairs is what's holding back my career, that's what they're saying. I need a *coup* in the area of foreign trade, that's what I need. And how am I supposed to engineer *that* little miracle when my concentration is disrupted by you running around annoying me with your presence? *Will you get the hell out of my life, damn you!*" He threw a cartographer's chartbook at her, barely missing.

The servant was tugging her out of the room. Jennifer turned and left. The servant walked with her across the main room and ushered her out the front door. Then Jennifer found herself outside on the porchstep, blinking against the bright sunshine with absolutely nowhere to go.

As the front door was being shut firmly behind her, she heard Matthew yell from his study, *"Oscaaar!"* But then the door was closed and she could not hear the words that followed.

She did not hear Matthew order his servant, when he reappeared in the study, to hire a man im*med*iately to investigate how Jennifer had managed to pay her fare across the ocean. Something unusual—and hopefully exploitable—had taken place, Matthew suspected. And with quick action . . . why, the matter *just* might be turned to his financial advantage.

Chapter 15

Savage could not get her out of his mind. Even high up here, in the crow's nest, where the magnificent panorama of blue sea and white sky almost always absorbed him completely, he still was thinking of her. Why had she done this to him? If only he could let himself believe the fairy-tale answer D'Arcy had told him. But no, he was through lying to himself. And besides, there was no need to lie to himself anymore. She was no longer part of his life. He had put her out of his life for good.

He frowned. Now if only he could get her out of his *mind* as well! But no, the images lingered, eating away at him.

He scanned the sharp line of the horizon. The pinpoint that was the ship he had been watching for twenty minutes was now changing course. Savage looked down past the billowing mainsail to D'Arcy on the deck below, who was squinting up at him, appearing very small with the distance. "She's coming about to nor' by nor'west," Savage shouted, cupping his hands to his mouth.

"Nor' by nor'west, Harlan," D'Arcy shouted to the man at the helm.

Savage grasped hold of the mast more tightly as the ship pitched about to take the wind from the new direction, putting him at a very sharp angle out over the sea. The swinging and swaying was at its wildest this high up, and the wind was at its fiercest. When they were settled into the new course, Savage pulled his telescope from his belt and focused it on the dot that was the unidentified ship. "I can make her out now," he called down.

"A frigate?" D'Arcy shouted.

"She's a merchantman, flying the King's colors. And she's low in the water with cargo."

D'Arcy shouted something else to him, but the wind was whistling so loudly in Savage's ears that he could not hear. He began his descent down the rigging. Too bad she was a merchantman, he thought. He was sorely in need of a good battle.

Savage knew he was more and more in need of violent satisfaction of late. D'Arcy noticed it too and worried over it. He worried over the fact that Savage had taken to drinking and getting blazing drunk in waterfront bars, when they were in friendly ports. He worried over Savage's recent inclination to pick fights when he was drunk—fights that often ended with the crippling of the man or men foolish enough to oppose him.

The main thing D'Arcy worried over, Savage knew, was his belief that Savage could not see the effect some of his new self-destructive acts were having on the crew—such as his reckless new habit of attacking ships that were much stronger than the *Liberty*. He was alienating the crew, D'Arcy said, to the point where there might soon be a challenge to his right to captain the vessel.

But hell, Savage thought now, as he climbed down the swaying rope rigging, D'Arcy was just a mother hen, that was all. He worried too much. Savage felt stronger and healthier now, and more attuned to his men and ship, than he had felt ever since taking that belly wound so long ago that laid him flat on his back in Jennifer's cabin.

The thought of her, now, again, was like a wedge of pain driven into his mind. He grimaced bitterly. He wondered where she was. Probably with the Governor still, he told himself. Or with some Redcoat general by now.

238

He reached the bottom of the rigging and dropped down to the deck below. D'Arcy was at the railing, looking out. "She eez fooleesh to run from us," he said. "With ze full cargo, she has no chance."

Savage waited till they were close enough and on line with her, then yelled to his forward cannon: "Fire across her bow!" The cannon fired, filling the air with the stench of burnt powder. The vessel did not come to or strike her colors. "Once more," Savage ordered, "and this time, tickle her good." The second shot came so close to the ship's bow that it looked as if it would knock off the tip of it. The merchantman struck her colors and slowly came about. When the lines and grapple hooks had secured the vessels together, Savage led the boarding party over the side.

"We're none of us resisting," said the merchantman captain grimly, approaching Savage. He was a stout old sea dog with a curly, black and gray beard. "Take what you come for and leave us in peace."

"That's how I prefer it," Savage said. He watched his boarding party put the ship's crew up against the railing, while D'Arcy led a few men below decks to search the ship.

"What's your cargo?" Savage asked.

"Tea. For the port o' Boston."

Savage told the captain he could either dump his cargo over the side . . . or abandon ship while Savage scuttled his vessel with a broadside. The captain, being a reasonable man, ordered his crew to jettison the cargo.

Savage instructed his men to let the English crew do as they were bid, but to keep them under close watch. He was in the midst of directing the rope-and-tackle transport of the merchantman's four cannons over to the *Liberty*, several minutes later, when D'Arcy appeared on deck again, grinning.

"Lancelot," he said, "tea eez not all zay carry." He moved aside and out from the passageway behind him stepped a full-bodied, blonde young girl. She was very pretty in a sophisticated, refined way, and had classic

239

aristocratic English features. The expensive formal white gown she wore was frilly and ribbony and covered an abundance of billowing petticoats beneath. Her hair was done up in a fashionable stacked style. Savage looked at her in bewilderment; it was crazy for a woman to dress so elaborately when she was at sea, among seamen.

"I found her in ze corridor, walking along as eef nothing unusual was happening. She loves me, Lancelot, I can see eet in her eyes. Eez zat not so, *cherie*?"

The girl raised her chin and half-lowered her eyelids, in a gesture of haughty aloofness. D'Arcy laughed. There was no fear at all in the girl's eyes.

"Damn it, Madam!" cursed the English captain, "I told you to stay hidden in the mattress locker in your cabin! They'd never have searched for you there, not knowing you were even aboard!"

"Really, Captain," said the girl in an elegant drawl, "you can't expect me to hide beneath that stuffy old mattress. Why, think what it would do to my hair."

Savage grinned. Several of the crewmen nearby laughed.

The girl looked at Savage with the haughty unruffled eyes of an aristocrat. "So you're the barbarian who waylaid us from our route?"

He bowed. "At your service, Madam."

She acknowledged his bow with a slight nod. "Well I hope you'll be quick about whatever it is you're doing. My fiancé is awaiting my arrival in Boston and I'd hate for us to be *too* very late."

"Damn it, milady!" exploded the captain. "Don't tease around with these pirates, I tell ya! They're vicious! Leave them do as they will with the cargo, stay out of their sight, and let them be off!"

She sighed, showing great disdain for his dramatics, and rolled her eyes heavenward. Then she looked at Savage. "You *will* allow me a spot of tea before casting me out to the sharks, won't you? When your streak of viciousness overcomes you, that is."

240

"I'll make a point of it."

"Don't believe heem," D'Arcy interjected, stepping forward. "He eez a cad and a liar. I am ze one who you should beg for mercy. I am ze one who loves and adores you. Lancelot, he lies even about ze tea. Look!" He pointed to the sacks of tea being dumped over the side by the ship's crew. "He orders zat done. Ze tea, overboard."

She looked at Savage with a feigned expression of alarm. "But why?"

"Tea is bad for you," Savage said. "It stains your teeth brown."

"I know why," the girl said, smiling coyly. "It's that wicked tea tax, isn't it?" She pouted. "Well, I suppose I'll just have to make do with water and lime juice for the rest of the voyage. You really *should* be ashamed of yourself," she said to Savage, "inconveniencing me this way. You are a barbarian after all, I see."

Savage turned away to watch the progress of the tea sacks being slashed open and dumped into the sea. The cannons had already been safely transported to the *Liberty*. They would be casting off soon. He looked back at the girl.

She seemed to be enjoying the excitement of being boarded by an outlaw vessel of the Colonial Navy. She pouted exaggeratedly, sticking her pursed lips out at the merchantman captain, who was eyeing her with a frustrated and burning temperment.

"Zis fiancé you have," D'Arcy said, "he eez a cad and a liar, too. You should leave heem. You should marry me, I am ze true nobleman of ze spirit. I weel make you so happy."

"I'm sure you will, Sir. But I really must meet my Major Perry in Boston. He's expecting me."

"The swine," joked D'Arcy, putting on a serious face. "I see heem, I run heem through. Then I console you, ze poor widow."

The girl smiled at D'Arcy. Then she looked at the captain, who was still scowling at her. She leaned close to Savage and said, "I daresay *he* actually accused *you* of being barbarians. But you should *see* the atrocious accommodations he's put me up in. Why, it's positively sadistic of him to expect a lady to get by in so small a space. Come, let me show you, you be the judge of who's the proper barbarian."

"I'll take your word for it," Savage said.

"No, really, come on, let me show you. You won't bel*ieve* how unaccommodating it is."

"I'll go look weeth you!" D'Arcy volunteered.

Joking shouts came from half a dozen of Savage's crew, who joined in the chorus. The crewmen were taken with the girl, delighted by the way she refused to think badly of them. It made them feel good to know she did not look at them as evil men who should be feared and run from. The girl seemed to be having the time of her life, flirting with the pirate captain. When she arrived at her destination, she could tell all her new girl friends about the exciting, dangerous episode, and make them envious.

Savage let himself be drawn forward toward the stairway that led down to the row of cabins. He was grinning slightly as he entered the corridor, but then as he walked behind her, he noticed something that made him lose the grin; the girl had the same way of walking that Jennifer had. It was a loose-limbed, prideful, unconscious-of-her-body way of walking, with her shoulders thrown back and her head held high. Savage didn't like seeing this similarity now.

"My fiancé, Major Perry, was transferred over to the Colonies last year," she said as they moved down the corridor. "That's why we decided to delay our wedding." She stopped at a cabin and looked at Savage. "I told him I'd wait forever for him. But he's impatient, and—"

"Stop talking," said Savage. He suddenly had a throbbing headache. He didn't like being in this corridor. He didn't like being reminded of Jennifer. He felt tense and hot all over.

242

"Oh, don't be like that," the girl teased, not sensing the darkness settling over his features. "We're such love birds, my major and I, I'm just *dying* to tell someone about it. Why, he even has the very cutest way of pecking me on the cheek. He—"

"Shut up," Savage said, very quietly but intensely, the words coming from deep in his throat. His head throbbed violently. It was dark in the corridor, and cramped. He realized now that, though he had joked with her abovedecks, it had been mostly for his crew's sake, to prove to them he was not so deathly tense as he had been recently. The truth, he realized, was that he did not like this pretentious English girl, to whom everything was a game and nothing was serious. He turned and started back down the corridor.

"Oh but wait," she said, grabbing his arm. She pointed out the cabin she had brought him down to see. "Here it is. Look." She stepped inside and twirled around. "Isn't it just the *tiniest* thing you've ever seen? My daddy, he'd just *die* if he saw me in this little hole. I'm accustomed to our estate in Covington you see, and—"

She stopped talking when she saw that Savage was not looking at the room, but directly at her. He stood in the doorway with an intense, brooding expression. "Oh, you're no fun at all," she said sharply. "It's just like they say back home. You Colonials take yourselves too seriously. At least my Perry is mature. When I said I'd wait for him, no matter how long it took—"

Savage entered the cramped room, grasped the girl's skirt in his fist and jerked it sharply. It tore at the seam where it was joined to the upper shirtwaist. The girl's mouth went wide in disbelief. Savage jerked the skirt hard all along the seam, spinning her around, until it separated completely from the rest of the dress.

Now the girl screamed "You animal!", and hit him on the shoulders with her small fists. But it was not until Savage ripped off her billowing petticoats—exposing her from waist to kneesocks, save for her silk underdrawers—that the impact of what was happening fully dawned on her.

"Oh, my God," she whispered, her eyes filling with terror. She cowered back. Then she yelled "You filthy Colonial, get away from me!", and tried to run. Savage put his hand to her underdrawers as she rushed past him and ripped them away. He grasped her wrist before she could get out the door. She shrieked loudly as he flung her back into the room, onto the bunk. Everyone on the ship would hear the scream, Savage knew. He didn't care.

"Keep away from me, you animal, keep away," the girl said terrified, raising up her hand to ward him off. Her eyes went wide and her mouth dropped open as she watched Savage strip off all his clothing. She began crying in fright, looking at his deeply tanned, hard, lean body and at his murderously intense face. She glanced down with fearful, reluctant eyes at his throbbing, rigid sex and her sobs suddenly became filled with frenzied panic.

Running footsteps sounded in the corridor. Savage turned to see D'Arcy appearing in the doorway, having come to investigate the girl's scream. D'Arcy's expression became deeply pained when he saw what was happening. Savage kicked the door shut in his face viciously.

He turned back to the girl, who was cowering wide-eyed in fear, covering her naked sex with her hand, shaking her head pleadingly from side to side. Savage's lower lip turned down, baring his teeth. He advanced on her . . .

When he reappeared on the deck several minutes later, stepping out from the darkness of the corridor into the daylight and the open air, he also stepped into a semicircle of hateful, accusing eyes. Even his own men were looking at him with deep scorn and violent resentment.

"Maggot," said the merchantman captain.

Without even looking at him, Savage grabbed the

man's curly, salt-and-pepper beard and yanked him along with him to the side of the ship, then heaved him over. The captain went crashing down into the ocean between the two ships. He started yelling for help, chokingly, the instant he bobbed back up to the surface from underwater. He would be crushed if the ships came together in the water. A young seaman rushed forward to throw him a line, but Savage shoved the man away hard, his hand against his chest.

"Is the operation complete, Mr. Calhoun?" he said to D'Arcy, not looking at him.

"Aye. Ze cargo has been dumped and ze cannons transferred."

"Order the men back."

"Back to ze ship!" D'Arcy yelled to the boarding party. Grappling hooks were unfastened, men swung back across on boarding lines. Savage looked the deck of the British ship up and down a final time, then he too swung back aboard the *Liberty*.

D'Arcy was the only one from the *Liberty* still aboard the merchantman. He took a lifeline and threw it down to the bearded captain floating in the sea between the ships, who grasped it desperately. Then D'Arcy crossed over, at the last minute, as the ships were drifting away from each other.

Savage was at the bridge. He stared out to sea unwaveringly, a granite look on his face, as the ship turned into the tradewinds.

Later in the day, D'Arcy went down to his cabin, sat at the small table, and wrote a letter on a piece of paper he had torn from the back of the ship's log.

Cherie—

> If your plan it is to work, you must do it soon right away. If you delay, it will be too late to matter. He is breaking apart very fast now.

> D'Arcy

He looked at the letter, which he intended to give to the chandler when they arrived in the secret cove in England, so the man could relay it to Jennifer. But now, rereading it, he realized he could not send her such a hopelessly bleak message.

He crumpled it up in his hand, went to the porthole, and threw it out. Then he leaned against the bulkhead, thinking. There was only one acceptable way of getting the information to her, he knew. But it was to be used only as a desperate last resort. . . .

Chapter 16

Jennifer handed the crumpled wad of small denomination bills over to the lanky, unpleasant-looking Frenchman, and waited while he counted the money. She glanced around nervously at the muddy, garbage-strewn back alley she was in, which was bordered on each side by the back doors of various seedy waterfront establishments.

She had been searching the port city of Southampton all afternoon, looking for a Frenchman who would help her in the scheme she'd concocted to win Matthew Armitage's confidence.

So Mr. Armitage needed a triumph in the area of foreign trade, did he? To impress his superior? If Jennifer's scheme worked well, he would *have* that triumph—and know that she was responsible for it. The triumph would not be a real one, of course, but by the time he realized he'd been tricked, it would be too late for him to do anything about it—hopefully. If she was wrong, it could mean her life.

"The money it is all here," said the Frenchman, looking up. "I thank you and bid you *au revoir*." He started to go.

"Wait!" Jennifer said, grasping the back of his fashionable brown coat, making him turn back to her. "You're sure you understand my instructions?"

"Madam," he said impatiently, "you've explained them to me twice already. For so small a fee as you pay me, you should leave me go immediately, not keep me here listening to your instructions."

"Could you repeat them to me just once more? Please, it's very important."

He sighed, but shrugged his acquiescence. He held up the sealed letter Jennifer had given him. "This, I take to the Minister of Trade in London. I present myself as an official courier of the House of the Marquis de Calhoun, and say that I have just arrived from Paris. I deliver the letter to the Minister personally, beg my leave, and make sure I am not followed. Yes? I have it right?"

She nodded, but was still unhappy about his anxiousness to get the matter over with. If he did not act out the role properly, her scheme would fail. Then her chances of winning Matthew Armitage's confidence would be lost forever. She bit her lower lip.

The Frenchman's manner was only passably that of a courier, she knew. But he did have decent clothing at least—he was a dealer in stolen goods—and he was willing to undertake the mission for the small amount she could afford to pay him. It was almost all the money she had left after paying for her boarding in London.

"Well then," said the wiry Frenchman, bowing, "I am off. I bid you good day. I hope your deceit is successful." He turned and sauntered down the alley, holding Jennifer's sealed envelope carelessly.

Jennifer felt great anxiety as she watched him leave. If only there were some way to make sure he did as he was paid to do! So much depended on it! But of course there was no way. He could easily throw the letter away as soon as he was out of her sight, and save himself the ride to London. He did seem basically reliable, though.

She returned to London by public coach, arriving by nightfall, and went to her room. She was hungry, but was too late for dinner at the home where she was boarding and she had no money left to buy dinner outside. She huddled under her thin blanket in the small, cold attic room and tried to fall asleep.

In the morning, she dressed in her yellow floral-print dress, which had a modest bodice and puffed-out shoulders, and left for Matthew Armitage's home on foot. She had to advise him about the letter that would soon arrive, so he could be prepared to take credit for it. Otherwise, he would act so ignorant about it in the Minister's presence, it would be clear he had no knowledge of the event he was supposed to have engineered. One thing Jennifer would not tell him was that she had forged the letter.

An elegant blue and silver coach was in front of his house when she arrived, with a red-jacketed driver on top and a liveried footman waiting at the door. She was passing the coach and starting up the walk just as Matthew came rushing out of the house, ostentatiously attired for a business function. He wore tails, high hat and a frilly white shirt, and carried a leather binder of documents in his hand.

When he saw Jennifer, his face registered surprise. Jennifer thought he would yell angrily at her and continue right past. But instead of acting nasty, as he had the last time she had seen him, he composed his features into a smile.

"Well, Jennifer!" he said brightly, seemingly determined to appear pleased to see her. "I'm *so* happy you decided to honor me with a repeat visit. How *rude* of me to treat you so poorly last time. But, you see, well I can only plead that I was in a*troc*ious fettle that day. The rigors of the job, you know."

He had stopped in front of her on the walkway, instead of passing her by.

He glanced at the coach nervously now, as if he were in a hurry. "Give me just a moment!" he shouted to the driver, who nodded, sitting straight in the seat, in his red jacket and cap, looking straight ahead.

"Mr. Armitage," Jennifer said, "you don't have to apologize for the way you behaved toward me. I didn't come here for that. I came to give you the proof I said I would give you last time. Remember? Proof of my

249

desire to work for the furtherance of your career. I—"

"Wait, wait, wait," he said hurriedly, glancing quickly at the coach, then back to her. "I'd love to hear your story, truly I would, but the Minister is waiting. And I assure you, the Minister *detests* waiting. Tardiness is equivalent to treason in his book. So if your explanation could perhaps wait until I return—"

"You're going to meet the Minister?" she said surprised. "Already?"

His eyes narrowed. "Whatever do you mean 'already?' "

"Well I didn't know he'd summon you so quickly."

He looked at her with growing interest. "Explain yourself. How, pray tell, did you know he was going to summon me at *all*? This isn't the sort of information every common tram— that is, it isn't generally known when a Minister summons his assistant. I myself wasn't aware of the fact an appointment was desired until the coach arrived just minutes ago."

"It's quite close to the hour, Sir!" the driver called out to Matthew.

"I'm coming, I'm coming!" he shouted, starting to edge forward down the path.

"Mr. Armitage, wait!" Jennifer said. "I must tell you this before you go!"

"No, *you* wait. I want you to do exactly that: wait for me in the house. Will you? It's important that you not leave this house till I return. You *will* do that, won't you?" He smiled with a sly fox's smile that made Jennifer go on her guard. "I'll be back just *ever* so quickly, these appointments never last, but in the meantime—"

"Wait, Mr. Armitage! Listen!"

"Can't, have to go!"

She grabbed his arm to stop him. "Just listen to this, it's important!" If he left without hearing her out, he would destroy the plan she had set up, and then there would be no chance at all of wheedling her way into his confidence. "If you hear the name Marquis de

250

Calhoun mentioned, say that you are an acquaintance of his, and know the family."

"What's this? What nonsense, I know of no—"

"But say you do! They're a wealthy family of traders in Paris, and they have enough influence to—"

"Mr. Armitage, Sir!" said the driver.

"Coming, coming!" He rushed toward the coach, holding his hat on his head with one hand, and his brief in the other. "Now you stay in the house!" he called back to Jennifer. "Until I return. It's imperative that you do. If you wish for me to consider even the remotest possibility of marrying you, you'll do as I say!"

But instead of leaving it as an order, he smiled at her before climbing into the coach, in what appeared to be an attempt to show that he was friendly and not a person to be afraid of. This was enough to confirm her fears that something was seriously wrong. His being cordial to her in the first place, and seemingly happy to see her . . . and now this attempt to not scare her off . . . all of it pointed to the fact that treachery was afoot. She knew she should leave immediately. But how could she, when the main thing she was trying to show him was that he could depend on her to do as he asked, and to work in his behalf?

"Oscar!" Matthew shouted out of the coach window, as the coach started forward. "This is Jennifer Van-DerLind! She's staying until I return! You hear me, Oscar, this is Jennifer VanDerLind, and she's staying!" The coach was far off down the street by now, but Matthew's head and shoulders were still sticking out of the window, looking back.

Jennifer turned and saw the servant standing in the doorway to the house, nodding his acknowledgment. Then he turned his eyes to Jennifer, bowed impersonally, and motioned her inside. "Madam," he said cordially. He seemed completely oblivious to the fact that his last meeting with her had been unfriendly.

Jennifer entered the house. The servant followed her

in and shut the door. "Would Madam care to remove her bonnet?" he said.

Jennifer took off the cloth bonnet and handed it to him. He put it in a pantry near the door. Then he led her into the main room and bade her to sit down. "A spot of tea, perhaps?" he asked in a formal manner.

"Yes, thank you."

He bowed and left the room. Jennifer remained sitting for a few minutes, but she was too restless to sit. Too much was at stake! She hoped he would hurry back from the meeting with the Minister, so she could find out if her plan had succeeded—or failed. She walked about the big room, looking at the paintings on the walls and at the clavichord in the corner, which she suspected was only for show, since she doubted if Matthew Armitage played.

What a grand house he had acquired for himself, she thought, even if it wasn't the home of a nobleman. She wandered into the study. The colorful cartographic displays were still on the walls, lining almost every inch of spare space next to the shelves. In the shelves themselves were all manner of intricate artworks, from sculpted statues and painted ceramics to crystal displays and even a few leatherbound books. Matthew Armitage did indeed have cultured taste, she could see.

After several minutes of wandering around, she began to wonder what was happening with her tea. Something warm would be very welcome after her long walk in the chilly air. And even though she had had breakfast a few hours before, some scones would be well appreciated. When the butler did not reappear after a few moments more, she wandered off through the door by which he had exited. She walked down a long corridor which appeared to be a service hall, and then into the kitchen at the far end of it. A cook was preparing food for the evening's meal, bending over a pot in the hearth, stirring it. But no one else was in the room.

The cook did not see her at first, his back being toward her as he stirred the pot. Jennifer looked around at the kitchen, which seemed even more complete in its equipment and accessories then even the kitchen of the Boar's Head had been. Condiments filled trays to overflowing. Utensils adorned the walls. The smell of rich foods and tangy spices filled the air. Well of course, she thought. It stood to reason that a man like Matthew Armitage would have a taste only for gourmet cuisine.

The cook turned around, saw her, and practically fell back into his pot with surprise. "Blimey, lass, you bloody well give me a start, you did. Here now, what you doing in my kitchen? And who are you anyway?"

"I was invited into the house," she said. "To wait for Mr. Armitage."

The cook blinked and stared at her blankly.

"The butler," she said, "Oscar? He said he would fetch me some tea."

The cook scratched his head and frowned. Then he shrugged, as if the matter were too weighty for anyone of less than the greatest intellect to puzzle out. "He said nothing to me 'bout no tea. But if it's tea ye be wanting, and if you're a guest of the Master's—" He looked at her uncomprehendingly. "You sure, are you, it's Master Armitage's home you're supposed to be in? He don't often entertain young women such as you. Oh, a nobleman's daughter once, that he did, but I can see from your looks and attire you're not of that station. Not hardly."

Jennifer was becoming suspicious and worried. "Where is Oscar?" she asked.

"That one? He left through the back door here not a quarter hour ago. Just whizzed right on by, as if he had a tardy appointment with the King himself." He laughed, appreciating his joke. "A likely happening, eh, Oscar and King George?" He chuckled and shook his head.

Jennifer turned and left the kitchen. She went back down the service passageway, quickly. She had to get out of here. Matthew had been too anxious to have

her stay. And Oscar apparently wished to advise someone of her whereabouts so urgently, he could not even
spare a moment to order the cook to brew a kettle of
tea. She came out of the service passageway into the
main room just in time to see the front door opening
and Oscar stepping through—and right behind him:
Pauly Garrett.

She turned and ran back into the passageway, but
not before they had seen her. She heard the sound of
running boots behind her, loud in the narrow passageway. She rushed out through the doorway into the
kitchen, and bolted past the cook toward the open
back door. The running bootfalls sounded close behind
her, but she knew she could make it, once she was outside. She had never met any man who was as speedy
on his feet as she was. She rushed to the door and ran
through it toward the outside sunlight.

Then she was tripped by an outstretched boot and
fell headlong into the dirt, breaking her fall only partially by thrusting out her hands, scraping her hands
and knees and cheek. She stumbled back to her feet,
but by now there was an arm around her waist, holding
her back.

"Let me go, let me go!" she screamed, trying to
wrestle free of the restraining arm.

"Not very likely," said a gruff voice. Then her arm
was caught behind her, and in an instant both her arms
were locked behind her, held tightly by the man who
was standing to her rear.

Pauly Garrett burst upon them now, and just behind
him came the servant Oscar, looking winded from the
unaccustomed exertion. Garrett looked at Jennifer
closely, raised her chin in his hand, scrutinizing her.
Then he removed his hand as she tried to bite him, and
he spoke to the man holding Jennifer, "Right smart job,
there, Constable. Thanks for the aid."

"Constable?" Jennifer asked in astonishment.

"She's the one for sure?" said the constable, still
holding her arms locked back.

Pauly Garrett pulled a rolled piece of yellowed, cracking paper from inside his shirt, removed the ribbon securing it, and held it, unrolled, up to the constable's eyes. "That's her name and her signature. And even if they be of an alias, as many of 'em are, I still have my witnesses."

"You don't need witnesses, Captain," said the constable. "These indenture papers look proper to me. And the way she come running out like the devil hisself was givin' chase, well it's quite enough evidence."

"Are you a constable?" Jennifer said in a panic, trying to twist around to look at the man. "If you're a constable, then help me! He wants to drag me off to a . . . a sport house! He wants to make a whore of me."

"Here ye go now," the constable said to Garrett, shifting his position so that he could let the captain slip his arm under Jennifer's shoulders while the constable removed his own arm.

"Are you listening to me!" Jennifer shouted, terrified. "You can't just give me over to him!"

The man ignored her completely. "A real hellcat she is," he commented to Pauly Garrett, who smiled in acknowledgment. Garrett was busy tying Jennifer's hands behind her with a leather strap.

"Please!" Jennifer yelled. "Help me!"

"Which house she be signed over to?" the constable asked Garrett. "I've a goodly urge, on occasion, to lay into one o' these Colonial tarts."

"The Bultaco. That's where she was destined afore she slipped off the ship . . ." He jerked her wrists, which were now lashed together behind her, high up in the air. Jennifer groaned with the pain. ". . . Making me *shy* of my promised cargo," he said bitterly, jerking her wrists up higher, forcing her to bend forward. ". . . Making me forfeit my monetary commission," he said, jerking her wrists still higher, doubling her over at the waist, forcing a scream from her lips. ". . . And losing face on a non-fulfilled bill o' lading for the *first* time in my whole bloody career!"

He jerked her wrists up so high this time that she shrieked in pain, and begged him, "Stop it, you're breaking my arms!"

"You don't need arms for what you'll be doin'," Garrett said angrily.

The constable thought this was funny and began laughing a rumbling laugh. "These Colonials," he said. "They instigate trouble enough to make us keep a full garrison over the ocean, raising tax dollars here to maintain them. And then they expect sympathy from us."

The constable came around in front of Jennifer now, as she stood doubled over at the waist with her wrists raised high behind her. Her head was on the level of the man's belt, her brown hair hanging down into her face. The constable grasped her hair and jerked her head up so that he could see her face. The strain caused a sharp pain in Jennifer's neck.

"Not a bad piece," the constable said, looking at Jennifer appraisingly. "Though a bit too spirited, if ye want me honest opinion."

"A temporary condition," said Pauly Garrett. "The Bultaco has a fine way of beating out any excesses of that damnable trait." He started moving Jennifer forward, guiding her from behind by her raised wrists. He moved her past the servant, who looked perturbed by this unseemly incident. "Be sure to come visit," Garrett said to the constable over his shoulder.

"Ye sure she'll still be there?" he laughed, "and not runnin' away once more?"

"She'll be there," said Pauly Garrett confidently, as he moved off down the path. "Unless she can carry the whole bed and frame with her, down the stairs and out the door. She'll have to, as that's what she'll be chained to. For the next two years and another on top of it to pay me back the reward I'm having to give this Armitage dandy for arranging her capture."

He guided her around the house to his horse in front and then lifted her up at the waist and draped her over the horse in front of the saddle. He climbed up into the saddle, put his hand firmly on her behind to keep her from sliding off the horse—his fingers digging in tightly—and kneed the steed forward in the direction of the Bultaco House.

The Bultaco House was run by a hard-looking, short blonde woman named Emily, who wore such large quantities of gaudy heavy jewelry—brooches, bracelets, pins—that she seemed weighted down by it. Though she ran the establishment, she was only part owner.

The other owner, Jennifer discovered to her surprise, was Pauly Garrett himself. This was generally kept a secret, since if the other brothel owners knew he had a vested interest in seeing that the Bultaco received the loveliest of the Colonial girls he transported, they would find someone else to supply their houses. They already suspected the Bultaco got more than its fair share of the best girls, but had no way of proving that this was the result of foul play or favoritism.

After being marched through a red velvet entry lounge, where she was displayed to Emily, Jennifer was led by Pauly Garrett up to a windowless, small, second-floor room, where she was manacled with heavy metal braces at both wrists. She was put onto the bed and the braces were then connected to short chains, which hung down from the top of the bed's metal-frame headboard.

"You'll be released for your meals," Pauly Garrett said, "and to wash, exercise, that sort of thing. Yes, don't look astounded, you'll be properly exercised. It's important for ye to keep in good shape, understand. The rest of the time you'll stay chained here to the bed." He grinned, starting to leave the room. "Having a grand time, I'm sure."

"Please let me go," Jennifer begged, watching him with horrified, pleading eyes as she lay on her back on the bed, her hands chained up over her head to the top

257

of the headboard. "I'll pay you back every shilling it cost for the voyage."

"And how are you going to do that?" he asked snidely. "Sell off part o' your vast land holdings? Part with a few trinkets of your diamond jewelry?" He sneered at her. "You'd be lucky, I'll wager, if you had a tuppence to your name."

"Please," she said desperately, "I'll find some way! But don't leave me here! Not to this! I couldn't stand it!"

"Oh there, there," he said, his voice suddenly becoming almost gentle as he watched her fearful desperation. He came away from the doorway and sat on the edge of the bed next to her. "Don't worry so much. I know you'll be able to pay me back what's due me, as you say you will. I don't doubt it."

"Yes," she said, uncertain of his meaning but anxious to have him believe her. "I'll find a way to get you your money. So if you'll just let me go—"

"And you know how you'll do it," he said pleasantly, "how you'll pay me it all back?" He smiled. "With *these*," he exclaimed in sudden fierceness, grasping her legs, pushing the hem of her dress and petticoats all the way up to her waist so that her long shapely legs were exposed. She tried to kick, but he had her legs locked together under his arm. "And with *this* precious little beauty *here*," he said, jerking her undergarment so hard that it ripped away from her skin, leaving her loins completely exposed.

She buckled her back and jerked her arms wildly within the confines of the chains, but no escape was possible. "You animal!" she screamed at him, on the verge of tears. "You vile despicable beast! Get away from me, get away!"

Pauly Garrett grinned down at her in scornful glee. "That's very good," he said appreciatively. "You'll go over just fine with some of our more 'sophisticated' clients. One gentleman in particular comes to mind, who has a great fondness for lovelies like yourself all manacled up in chains."

"You scum!" she screamed at him, struggling wildly. "How could you do this? You're the lowest, the lowest of the low! Oh, you——"

Garrett was laughing. "Wonderful!" he roared through his laughter. "They'll love it! Not only is she in chains, but she struggles and fights like a she-demon! Oh, you'll be the prize of the house, beauty, I can see it already. 'Course, you may not last out your whole three years in such good shape. Pity, but those what appreciates the chains and struggling also have unfortunate fondnesses for slapping around the merchandise. We do try to discourage it, o' course, but . . ." he held his palm out to his side and shrugged, ". . . well, gentlemen do get carried away at times. And so long as they pay properly fer their pleasure, that's what really counts."

He stood up from the bed, and now that her legs were free, she kicked viciously, managing to strike him hard in his side before he could scramble out of the way.

"Ow! Damn you, you fiery bitch, that hurt, by God!"

"And I'll give you more like it!" she screamed, trying to kick out further, though he was beyond her reach by now. Her wild kicks finally made her slide off the bed onto the floor, so that she now lay with her naked bottom on the faded, brown throw rug, her arms stretched tautly to where they were chained at the headboard.

"Here," said Garrett, coming forward to take advantage of her practically immobile position, "let me aid you there in doffing them uncomfortable garments, eh?" He stood over her, one leg on each side of her hips, grasped her petticoats and jerked them violently, hearing them rip. He tugged hard until they came completely off of her. He flung them across the room. Then he reached down to the hem of her dress, which was

259

now around her waist. He pulled it up over her breasts, about to take it all the way up over her head so her full voluptuous body would be exposed.

But when Jennifer cried out, in her panic, "I'll kill you for this!", he stopped. The dress was completely covering her upraised arms and head, from her armpits to her wrists now, blocking all vision. Garrett ceased pulling it up. Jennifer felt the sides of his boots leave her hips, where they had been touching, and knew he had stepped back away from her.

"I can tell when my presence is not wanted," Pauly Garrett said with a touch of malicious humor. "All right, beauty, I'll bid you good day then. And I'll certainly not help you off with your garment if you don't wish it. But—" She felt his hands grasping her ankles, then pulling her body taut. Suddenly she was being raised high into the air. The hands released her ankles and she felt herself bouncing down onto the mattress of the bed once again. "—do let me help you onto your bed," Garrett said. "Our clients aren't high-class and all, true, but they do prefer beds to floorboards."

"Oh God," she cried, "don't leave me like this!"

But without a further word, he left the room. She heard the door slamming shut behind him. She was manacled, stretched out on the bed with her entire body from her collarbone down nakedly exposed. Her face and arms were completely enveloped in the bunched up dress that made vision impossible. Jennifer began shaking with a fear and terror that was worse than anything she had ever known. *Never* had she been so helpless before, so much at the mercy of merciless souls.

For a moment, she was so fearful it paralyzed her into immobility. Then she began to collect her wits about her as best she could. The first thing to do, she realized, was to try to force the dress back down over her body, so she at least could see. She moved around as best she could on the bed, at first trying to shake the dress down from about her arms and head by shimmying her body wildly. This proved of no avail. Next she tried to scrape the dress down into place by pressing her face and lower arms against the mattress and moving herself forward along the mattress by pushing with her knees. She was in this position—her face and breasts pressed down on the mattress, her behind raised in the air, knees parted, trying to push herself forward—when the doorlatch jiggled and she heard the door come open.

She caught her breath in terrified anticipation. The voice she heard, almost instantly, surprised her with its whining familiarity. "Jennifer, *please*! How dis*gust*ingly brazen must you *be*? Will you *kindly* cover yourself? Have you no *shame*?"

"Mr. Armitage," she screamed, "help me!" Relief welled up in her. It did not matter at this instant that Matthew Armitage, so he could have the reward, was the one who had contacted Garrett and set up her capture. All that mattered right now was that, for the moment, she knew she was safe. Matthew Armitage would certainly not molest her sexually. And possibly, just possibly, he could be persuaded to help her.

"Please help me," she pleaded.

"Well, I *may*. As a matter of fact, I've come to discuss exactly that, but . . ." whining and screaming at once "will you *cover* yourself, blast it woman, my *God* but you look re*volt*ingly vulgar!"

"I can't!" she cried. "Can't you see that I'm—"

"Here, allow me," said a strong, masculine voice, then Jennifer felt Pauly Garrett's hands at the level of her manacled wrists, grasping the hem of her dress, jerking it away from her arms and face, then pulling it down over her body. He stopped when the dress was at her waist, and instead of pulling it all the way down so it covered her completely, he merely bunched up several folds of the garment and tucked it between Jennifer's thighs.

This covered her for Matthew's benefit, but at the same time it left her shapely legs completely exposed.

261

She pressed her legs tightly together and curled her knees up, as she lay on her side looking at Matthew Armitage and Pauly Garrett. Both men were standing, Garrett with his fists at his hips, smirking, Matthew with his palms and fingers pressed together in front of him, touching his lips. He was clearly uncomfortable, somewhat cowering, very conniving looking.

"Jennifer, you mentioned . . . um . . . a certain Marquis de Calhoun was . . . uh . . . had a trading house in Paris which . . . ah . . ." He turned to Garrett. "I do so hate to trouble you, but would you be so good as to leave us in private for just the *scantest* moment. We have business to discuss, you see, and it's of *rather* a confidential nature. It—"

Garrett held up a hand. "Aye, aye, don't bother me with your explainin'. Just remember you've got business to attend to with *me*, too, regarding this matter of the girl here, which you come about." He started to leave, but turned back halfway through the doorway and said to Matthew, grinning, "And don't be sneakin' no free titty rubs now, in me absence."

"I *beg* your pardon," Matthew said, flushing pinkly.

Garrett chuckled and left the room. Matthew Armitage checked the door to make certain it was completely closed, then turned to Jennifer. He carefully arranged his face into a smile. "Well, Jennifer!" he said in a falsely joyful voice, "how *are* you?"

"I'm exactly as I appear, Mr. Armitage. Chained, brutalized, aching, and captive. All of which I have you to thank for."

"Umm . . . yes . . . well, let us not dwell on recriminations." He shook his head quickly, as if to dismiss the subject. Then he returned to the matter he had come about. "Jennifer, that House of Calhoun you spoke to me of earlier! Well, it seems that the Marquis de Calhoun, evidently the patriarch of the trading family, has sent a communique to my superior, the Minister, commending me for bringing to the Marquis's attention the excellent quality of British textiles. And for persuading him to purchase a very sizable quantity of various items for his financial and commercial clients on the continent, beginning the quarter after next." He looked at Jennifer and frowned. "I must confess to you, I've never even *heard* of this Marquis, much less held a buying conference with the man."

"You didn't confess that to the Minister, though, did you?" Jennifer asked.

"Goodness *gracious* no! Your foresight in warning me about the name put me sufficiently on guard. And while I didn't exactly fib to the Minister that I *had* arranged the trade—at least not in so many words—I also did not go so far as to *deny* it. All in all, this promissory trade communique from the Marquis Calhoun has put me in quite good stead. Uh . . . how did you arrange it, may I ask?"

"I know the Marquis through grandfather Silas. They were close friends. When you refused to believe that I'd changed, and that I truly wanted to marry you to further both our lives, I got in touch with the Marquis. I arranged for this purchase, to show you I was sincere. To show that I *could* help your career. The Marquis did it as a favor to me."

"That's quite a favor. Several hundred thousand metric tons worth, as a matter of fact."

"A purchase of that size is nothing to him. His trading family controls most of the commerce on the continent. Secretly, of course."

"Well . . . I *am* grateful to you Jennifer."

"Then get me out of here!"

"Please," Matthew said, stepping back, "let us not raise our voices."

"Mr. Armitage," she said, beginning in a quieter, more sedate tone, "get me out of here. Will you please *get me out of here*!"

"Silence!"

When she became quiet, he began pacing the small room, his palms and fingers pressed together again, head lowered, fingertips against his lips. "You know," he said, "at first I was not inclined to believe the veracity of the communique. But the Minister pointed out to me the official seal of the House of Calhoun, stamped in wax upon the document. And also, though I myself have not heard of the family, the French courier who delivered the Marquis's missive explained that the Calhouns are one of the great trading families of the continent and pride themselves on their anonymity."

"Secrecy is a way of life to them," Jennifer said, hoping she sounded convincing. "They have so many enemies, they must do everything by stealth and through proxies."

"Yes, I can understand that," said Matthew thoughtfully. "The governments of the continent would frown on any organization that wielded so much power within their boundaries, which was not subject to their control." He paced some more. Then he suddenly stopped and looked at Jennifer enthusiastically. "By God, this really *is* a legitimate transaction, isn't it? And I, I myself, will receive credit for its arrangement!"

"Yes, Mr. Armitage," she said, relieved that he believed her ploy. By the time her scheme was discovered to be false, two quarters from now, her plan to have Savage hear Matthew Armitage's confession would be completed, and she would not be around to suffer the consequences of the discovery—at least it would have worked that way had she not been captured.

"I can do more for you, too," Jennifer said to Matthew Armitage, trying to make her voice sound tantalizing with promise. "This is only the start. You do see now, don't you, that I'm sincere in wanting to aid you? You'll rescue me from this horrible place?"

"Well . . . that latter request may be a bit difficult," he said, hedging. When he saw her angry expression, though, he added hastily: "But I'll *cer*tainly do my best, Jennifer. I'll do my very *ut*most, I assure you, in your behalf."

He went to the door to call Pauly Garrett back into the room, but before he opened it, he said, "You know, I do appreciate this. And I am impressed by it. But I must say, as far as trusting you completely . . . as yet I can't bring myself *quite* to do it. I did inform on your grandfather, after all. Yes, yes, I know, you told me that's water under the bridge and all that. But nonetheless . . ."

"If you need more proof, I'll give it to you! Give me another chance and I'll prove myself all over again. But you must get me out of here first!"

"There's no need to be repetitious. I heard you the first . . . *three* . . . times." He opened the door and looked out into the hall. "Ah. If you will, please, my good Captain?"

He came back into the room, Pauly Garrett behind him. "Finished your little talk, eh?" said Garrett playfully. "Now we get down to business. Good." He clapped his hands together, obviously happy at the prospect of entering a business discussion where he was certain he would get the better of the deal. "Now I suppose you're anxious to buy back the girl from me. That's what you come for, after all."

"Well," said Matthew, his brows rising in feigned disinterest, "It *was* an item I was con*sid*ering. Casually considering, that is." He plucked at the ends of his frilly lace cuffs and sighed wearily. Watching him, Jennifer knew the man vainly thought of himself as a master of negotiations.

Pauly Garrett did not seem impressed in the least. He had a thick brown cigar in his hand and he put it between his teeth and puffed at it strongly, sending clouds of odorous white smoke wafting toward Matthew, enveloping his face.

Matthew coughed and stepped back, waving the smoke away with his hands. "Do you *mind*?" he said, perturbed, his eyes watering.

"Not the least," said Garrett, grinning, puffing on the cigar between his teeth.

"I'll give you forty pounds for her," said Matthew.
Garrett laughed loudly.

"Well . . . perhaps I *could* go to sixty."

"Ye'll go to a thousand if you want the wench back," said Garrett, "that's what ye'll go to."

"A *thousand*?" repeated Matthew disbelievingly. "*Pounds*?"

"What'd ya think I was speakin' of, eggs?"

"But that's—why, that's preposterous! *You* only paid *me* twenty pounds for her return. And even when you add to that the cost of the *voy*age, which, yes, I suppose it *might* be fair to include . . . why, even then it comes to less than three hundred pounds."

"This here is a piece o' merchandise what is in great demand," declared Pauly Garrett with sudden enthusiasm, rushing up to Jennifer, pulling her hair back so that her chin was raised up. "Look at the line o' that chin. Look at those meaty lips." He grasped her knees and flipped her over on the bed, onto her stomach. "Look at the beauty here," he said, slapping her naked behind, making Jennifer scream, then gripping her cheek tightly and vibrating it. "Look at the firmness!"

"Stop it!" Jennifer cried.

"Captain, if you *please*!" whined Matthew.

"A thousand's what I'm askin'. And I can make that back many times over in the next three years, what with the fees my clients will be payin' for the pleasure of the lady's company."

"I'll give you three hundred pounds," said Matthew.

"A thousand."

"Four hundred pounds."

"A thousand, I say!" He jerked the hem of Jennifer's dress up to her wrists again, enclosing her head and arms once more, blinding her. He jerked her over onto her side on the bed and his arms went around her from behind, cupping her breasts, squeezing them as he held them toward Matthew as if they were on display. Jennifer screamed. "Just look at these beauties," Garrett declared. "Big and juicy. A thousand's a mere pittance for what she'll bring in to me!"

"Five hundred then, damn you! Five hundred En-

266

glish pounds!" shouted Matthew, revulsion thick in his suddenly high-pitched voice. "And that's my top and final offer! You'll never get a thousand back from her services! She'll never last out the three years; none of them do, you know that! Everyone knows that!"

"Maybe so," Garrett said, releasing her and stepping away. "But I'll surely get more than only five hundred."

"I'm sorry we cannot do business," said Matthew, his voice so squeaky and sickened, he seemed about to retch.

"Mr. Armitage!" Jennifer shouted, through the cloth of her dress, terror gripping her. "Don't leave me here! Please, Mr. Armitage, give him what he wants! I'll do—"

But she heard the door slam and, with heart-sinking despair, realized that he was gone.

Chapter 17

"Well, so you'll be with us awhile after all," said Pauly Garrett. "Might as well start you earning your keep, eh beauty? Your first customer be downstairs waiting. I told him of your . . . restrained situation, shall we say? He's eager to make your acquaintance."

"Captain Garrett," she pleaded, trying another desperate ploy: to reason with the man. "Listen to me, please. If you'll just—"

"Treat him well," Garrett said, ignoring her. "He's the son of a steady client."

"I'll find some way to pay you the money! Just let me—"

The door opened and then closed shut. She wriggled and strained and pulled at her chains furiously, knowing even as she did so that there was no hope of pulling them loose. The dress still covered her eyes.

The door opened again. A second later, it closed. She stopped struggling. She lay face down on the bed, so her breasts and the front of her could be hidden as much as possible. The man who entered the room had not yet spoken. After a long moment of tense, piercing silence, Jennifer said, "Are you there? Who is it?"

She was answered not by words, but by the sound of heavy, excited breathing.

"Please, whoever you are, won't you help me? They've . . . they've kidnapped me and chained me here, against my will. Surely it's illegal what they're doing to me! I must escape. Please, if you're any sort of decent person at all, won't you help me?"

"It wasn't to help you that I came here, milady," said a young, callow voice.

"Why, you sound like only a boy! How old are you?"

"Old enough!" came the angry reply.

"Please, wait, I—I didn't mean to give you offense. It's only that I . . . you must help me. You sound young enough to still have some innocence to you. You can see how evil this is, what they're doing to me. You must be able to see it. Will you help me?"

She heard only the sound of his heavy breathing. Still, she had not yet heard the rustling of clothing being shed and he had not yet touched her. These were hopeful signs. Perhaps she might still be able to reason with him. "I . . . I think I'm older than you. It would be wrong to have a . . . a relation with a girl not your own age. How old are you? You sound not yet fifteen."

"I'm fifteen and more!" he shouted, suddenly enraged. "It's been half an annum since my fifteenth birthday! Why do you women insist on making me out to be a child? Why do you constantly insult my manhood this way!"

"I'm sorry, I only meant that—"

"Hold your tongue! I'm master of this situation and you'll do as I say!" His voice sounded so tormented and bitter, it seemed almost on the verge of lunacy. "No one heeds my word at other times, no, not the word of a 'mere boy.' But here you'll do as I command! I'm the master now! Now: turn over onto your back, I'll have a look at you."

Jennifer did not move. Her head and arms trapped within the bunched up dress, she could see nothing but the fabric of the material against her eyes. She felt incredibly exposed, lying with her breasts and stomach pressing against the rough wool cover of the mattress, her backside completely naked. But to turn over would be to reveal herself even more fully. "You mustn't do this," she said. "You're only a boy . . ."

"I'll show you what only a boy can do," he sneered.

269

She felt the bed depress at her side as he sat down on it next to her. And then, shocking her with the unexpectedness of it, she felt the sharp slap of his hand across her naked buttocks. She yelped in stunned surprise.

"Onto your back, I say, I'll see your wares, I demand it!"

"Please . . ." she moaned. Then she endured several stinging slaps across her buttocks that quickly gained fierceness and became extremely painful. He slapped her again and again with the flat of his hand, making her cringe and writhe wildly in pain. "Stop it, stop it!" she cried, "It hurts, it *hurts,* oh stop it, *stop it!*"

But he would not stop, nothing would make him stop, and the spanking hand came down again and again, searing her buttocks with burning agony, as she kicked her legs hysterically. Finally she could take no more, and groaning, she rolled over onto her back.

The hand ceased its assault. She lay on her back now, sobbing loudly, her arms manacled high above her head to the top of the headboard, her body stretched out on the bed, knees close together. She was breathing in quick gasps.

"You still think I'm a child?" he said gloatingly in his nasty voice.

She said nothing.

"Answer me!"

"No!" she cried out. "I don't think it, I don't!"

She heard him chuckle softly. "Move your knees apart," he ordered, "though keep your ankles close together as they are."

She sobbed. She could not endure more of the painful spanking. She did as he asked. She felt his hand descend on the silken-haired mound of her womanhood and she jerked. The hand moved up to her breasts. It was a very soft hand, not rough and calloused like others that had defiled her. But the way it began to abuse her body now made it as bad as any of the others. The hand squeezed and pinched her, and probed rudely

270

about. It rubbed down over her breasts and stomach and pressed down between her legs.

Soon Jennifer began to feel strong sensations, even though she tried to stop herself from feeling them. The hand did not stop. It continued its assault for five minutes at least, it seemed, and then for longer, and then she could swear that it must certainly be a quarter of an hour that his hand had continued abusing her breasts and loins—and sparking them into intense sensation.

Her body was responding with a sensual thrill that made her catch her breath. Her nipples had become hard and a ferocious quivering yearning sensation between her legs could not be ignored. She felt guilty, and perverse, and *evil* almost, responding like this to . . . to anyone other than Lancelot really, but especially to a *child*.

Each rough caress brought added pleasure to her body and a wicked sense of longing. Her breathing quickened. Then the hand stopped and the depression near her on the bed resumed its natural level as her assailant stood up. She heard the rustling sound of clothes being removed. Then she felt his hands at the hem of her dress, near her wrists, and she realized sharply that she did not really want to have the dress pulled away from her eyes now, not at this moment. She didn't want to have to *see* this person who was about to rape her. She didn't want to have to look into his eyes, to watch him as he drove into her helpless chained body. It was too late to worry the question, though. His hands pulled at the hem of her dress roughly, bringing it down around her shoulders.

She could see now. And the sight that greeted her eyes frightened her—not with fear for her safety, but with fear of the perverseness of what she was involved in. The boy was truly that: a young boy. He seemed less even than his fifteen years. He was slim and unmuscled, standing nakedly at the side of the bed. He had a rounded physique and soft skin with no hair on it at all, except down about his sex, where there were dark wisps of it.

Looking at him, Jennifer felt blushingly perverse. This was a *child* who was doing this to her, debauching her in such a manner. But the child had an arrogant, commanding look on his handsome pouting face. And down between his legs he had a blade that was so long and hard it made it difficult to think of him as anything but a full-fledged male. Such a gift of overendowment seemed *obscene* on such a young, almost hairless body.

No, Jennifer thought, she could not allow this. Not with a boy almost five years her junior. She turned over onto her stomach. Without a word, he began spanking her stingingly across the buttocks. She jerked and yelped and, after a furious barrage of unending blows, began to cry. But she did not roll back over to offer him the front of her body.

"Open your legs."

"I won't do that."

He began spanking her again, feverishly, stroke after vicious stroke, until she was weeping shudderingly, her skin sizzling with hurt. She was so close to fainting, her mind was no longer in control. Some other force seemed to be guiding her actions. It made her spread her legs apart.

"Wider!" he ordered.

"Please, no!" The degradation! To be beaten and commanded about by a mere boy!

"Shall I give you a taste of my leather belt?"

Crying with humiliation, she spread her legs wider, as wide as they would go without tearing her apart. Then she felt the length of his body lay down upon the length of hers, and felt his hard fat shaft press against the lip of her womanhood. Without hesitation, he thrust himself into her, all the way up to the hilt. She exhaled all her breath in a gutteral moan, and her eyes opened wide. Unbearable pleasure shot up from her loins. She tried to fight it down, the situation was too horrible, too obscene! Being ravaged by a young boy.

But she could not fight down the sensation; pleasure coursed all through her body.

The strangeness of her position gave added intensity to the fiery feelings spreading through her: she was on her stomach, with his body pressing down on her from behind. She could not see him, could not feel any part of him moving except the hard bolt of maleness that violated her relentlessly, lighting her loins aflame, exciting every nerve ending down there with pulsating pleasure. Then, all at once, the fire in Jennifer's loins exploded like a volcano of pleasure, sending glowing sparks of sensation throughout her. She screamed in ecstasy.

The boy continued thrusting and then finally he too reached his peak, and he began shuddering. Then he moved off her. He dressed while watching her writhing silently on the bed. His young eyes were contemptuous. "So now you've been done by a 'mere boy'," he said.

She shook her head. "You're no boy," she breathed. "No matter what your age."

"And you're certainly no 'captive woman', as you'd have me believe. Those chains are there at your own asking I'll wager."

"That's not true!"

"Isn't it?" he sneered. "You're no less than a bitch in heat. Responding to me as you did. That's all you are, milady, why lie to yourself? A bitch in heat, that's what you are, it's as simple as that."

"No!" But as she watched the slim, slight body disappear into trousers, blouse, and waistcoat, it occurred to her that his words might prove prophetic. She was not that awful thing he just called her, not now . . . but she could easily become it if she continued to be subjected to such forceful passionate assault. She had to find a way out of here! She had to, or yes, she *would* become what he was accusing her of being: a bitch in heat, a captive of her vicious primal passions, no longer faithful to Lancelot, no longer faithful even to herself.

"Help me escape!" she screamed suddenly. "I've got to get out of here!"

He laughed scornfully. "Still lying to yourself? You know you'll never leave. You'll be addicted soon enough, I can see the signs. Addicted to the stiff manly rod. You'll be addicted like a rummy to his jug, and never want to leave it. Even when they finally let you go, you won't be able to leave here, to do without it."

"It's not true!" she screamed, the force of her denial so violent that it was clear to both of them that she feared his words might easily prove true.

He shook his head, grinning in haughty amusement, and left the room. Jennifer lowered her head onto the mattress and began sobbing.

By the end of the first week, she was convinced she would remain captive here in this vile house forever— if she did not escape soon.

It seemed that there was no hope. She would never see Savage again, she thought. She would not be able to put her plan into effect, would not be able to lure Matthew to the coast where Savage would be in hiding, listening. None of this would come to pass, and instead of regaining Savage's love, she would live out her days *here*, in sordid depravity, undulating her hips for every drunken sailor and filthy lout who could pay the price.

But then, just when the situation seemed bleakest, she had an unexpected visitor. She knew it was Matthew Armitage who waited outside her door by the way Emily rushed in first and covered Jennifer's nakedness with a blanket. Then, only after she was completely covered from the neck down, was the door opened and the guest waved into the room with an inviting smile from Emily.

Jennifer was so mentally numb and dazed from the past days of torment, she could do nothing but stare at him blankly.

Matthew sat down in the room's one chair, facing

the bed. He began talking to Jennifer the instant Emily left the room, closing the door after herself. "How good to see you again!" he began enthusiastically, trying to disguise his distaste at the sordid surroundings, and his embarrassment at having to visit her again. He had clearly thought that he was through with her for good. "You're looking just . . . um . . . that is . . ." His words trailed off into oblivion and he frowned, giving up on his attempt to put on a falsely cheerful face.

"What do you want?" she said to him. She was sitting up with her back against the headboard, her arms over her head. The wool blanket covered her entirely from her neck to the tips of her toes. It was coarse and scratchy and felt very abrasive against her tender skin that had been made even more tender from the physical abuses she had suffered.

"Oh," said Matthew, trying to be casual, "I just dropped in to see how you are, and to . . . uh . . . wish you the very best, of course. And . . . uh . . ."

"Out with it! What do you want from me! You wouldn't have come if you didn't want something from me!"

"*Well*, there's no need to be *rude* with me. After *all*, I am your friend."

She would have laughed had she not been under such a fog of mental numbness.

"That is, I'm friendlier than *most* of the men you've encountered lately, shall we say?" When he saw that she would not respond to him at all, except for the hateful look in her eyes, he decided to try a new tack. "By the way, Jennifer, the Paris headquarters of the House of Calhoun, where exactly *is* it? I think I might like to visit there sometime, perhaps."

She said nothing, only looked at him in stony silence.

"Oh, yes, yes, I remember, it's a *secret*, isn't it? But nevertheless, if you could just let me have the location of the section of the city they're based in, or the street they're on, then perhaps? . . ."

She was beginning to understand. "You need to contact them," she said.

"Well, I wouldn't put it quite that way. I might someday like to . . . oh . . . exchange a polite greeting, perhaps. Or something of that nature."

"You need to contact them to confirm the purchase. Or to make arrangements for the actual delivery."

"I was thinking," he said, as if embarking on a different subject entirely, "they probably have a London agent, don't they? Why, I'm sure they do. That's how you transmitted your message to the Marquis originally, isn't it? It must be, since I've done a bit of research into the subject, and I *know* you didn't ship across the Channel during that period. So if you'd be so kind as to perhaps give me the name of the London agent?"

She closed her eyes in a slow blink, then opened them again and stared at him coldly. Her hair was disheveled. The hollows under her eyes were more pronounced now than they had ever been. Her lower lip seemed swollen. And there was a hardness in her manner that had not been there before.

If it had done nothing else of value, her experience here in the Bultaco had done one positive thing for her: it had made her harder. She had always been a woman who knew her mind, knew what she wanted. Now she was a woman who was hardened enough to make herself do what she had to to *get* what she wanted. There was no longer any naiveté or innocence in her manner. If she could somehow manage to escape from this horrid place, the rough edge of hardness would probably leave her. But she knew she would never return to the innocent way she had been before.

"Mr. Armitage," she said, "if you want to contact the Marquis, you'll have to get me out of this place."

"Well, that's *quite* impossible, you know it is. You heard that reprehensible oaf tell me it would take a thousand pounds—a thousand pounds, mind you!—to buy your freedom. Now, dear Jennifer, you do realize

I'd do *anything* to help you, but, well, some things are just out of the question. I mean, I *couldn't* spare that amount of money, even if I—"

"Then leave me," she said. "I've nothing more to say to you."

"Oh, now, now! Let's not be hasty. I'm sure we could work out an equitable arrangement. Perhaps there are things I could bring you? A nice bedgown perhaps? Some decent food?"

"Get out of here."

"But—"

"Get out! Get out, you cretin! Get the hell out of here!"

He stood up and cowered back, but made no move toward the door. She knew now the urgency of his obtaining the information he wanted from her. If he didn't desperately need it, he would not still be here, subjecting himself to her rage.

"You'll get me out of here, Matthew Armitage, or you'll never learn the way to contact the Marquis." She watched him scowl in frustration and shake his fists up and down, like a small child throwing a tantrum when it cannot have its way.

"On the other hand," she continued, "if you do rescue me from here, I'm sure I can use my influence with the Marquis to arrange further purchases and trades that will advance your career even more. But you have to decide quickly. I won't be in any condition to do your career good as your wife if I have to spend even another week in this place."

He stood looking at her angrily. But Jennifer could tell from the desperation in his eyes that he had no choice in the matter. She had saved herself from this place after all.

"Well damn, damn, *damn*!" exclaimed Matthew. "You can't do this to me! I need a letter of inquiry delivered to him. And right away! If I can't inquire about confirmation, why, the original letter will mean nothing! And look what *that* would mean to my career."

She stared at him silently.

"Oh, all *right*," he exclaimed in a whining voice. "But you'd best do as I tell you!" he scolded, waggling a finger at her. "If you don't do right by me as Lady of the Manor, the woman who represents me to polite society, why, I'll . . . I'll . . ."

She wanted to play-act her role now, to tell him that she would help his career and be dedicated to nothing but his advancement, assure him that he would never regret this decision. But as much as she wanted to begin play-acting right away, she could not bring herself to do it. She had too little strength and her mind was not working properly.

Well, she thought, there would be time enough to deceive him later. For now all she wanted to do was to get away, leave this place, go somewhere where she could lie outside in the sunshine, fully dressed, with her arms at her sides rather than chained above her head. And relax, rather than having to stare in dread at the door of the dingy room, wondering when it would open again to usher in some new barbarian to abuse her.

"Just get me out of here," she said.

Matthew Armitage sighed. "As a matter of fact, I planned to do that very thing. All along. You needn't have threatened me!" He went to the door of the room, opened it, and called out into the hall. "Emily? Oh, Madam Emily? I'd like to suggest a business proposition to you, if I may."

Within ten minutes, they were outside the house, Jennifer wearing the torn and tattered dress she had originally come in, which had been put away in a closet. She sank far down into the seat in the coach as the horses began moving forward.

She closed her eyes. Matthew was talking to her in urgent tones, but she did not want to listen now. There would be time for that later. Now the only thing in the world she wanted to do was blank her mind. Fall asleep and not awaken for a hundred years. . . .

278

Chapter 18

One of the first things Jennifer did, now that she was free of the Bultaco, was to go back to where she had been boarding before she was captured and retrieve her clothing. Hidden in her clothing was the signet ring D'Arcy had given her. She then forged a second letter, stamped the seal of the Marquis on it in wax, and made arrangements to go to Southampton to seek out the Frenchman again, in the back alley he frequented as a purveyor of stolen goods.

Matthew was leery of letting her out of his sight, in view of the amount of money he had invested in buying her back. For a time, it looked as if she would not be able to get to the Frenchman to give him the forged letter. Finally, she told Matthew that if he wished her to deliver his letter of inquiry to the London agent of the House of Calhoun, then he would have to grant her leave. Since Matthew was desperately in need of contacting the Marquis, he was forced to consent. He even relented on his insistence that she take him with her on her excursion, when she told him firmly that the agent's demand for secrecy prevented this. She was not surprised, however, once she was on her way, to find that she was being followed.

Through daring and imaginative use of backroads and paths, Jennifer managed to rid herself of the lackey whom Matthew had assigned to tail her. Then she continued on to Southampton, found the Frenchman in the same alleyway in which she had discovered him originally, and gave him the second forged letter along with her instructions on the time and manner of delivery. She paid him with the money Matthew had given her to pay the "London agent's" fee.

When she returned from the trip, Matthew Armitage was extremely relieved to see her again. He had assumed, upon learning from his lackey of Jennifer's deliberate outmaneuvering of his surveillance, that her intention was to escape from him and that he would never see her again.

"You see?" Jennifer said to him. "I told you I was honest in my desire to remain with you, as your wife. I didn't have to come back. But I did."

"Well, of course you *knew* I would have had you apprehended, had you not returned. So *nat*urally you—"

"Oh, come, Matthew! When are you going to face the truth and believe me?"

He mumbled out an evasive answer, then turned the discussion to another subject. Several days later, though, when the letter she forged was delivered to the Ministry where Matthew worked, he came home beaming and joyous and absolutely ecstatic.

"Jennifer, I am de*light*ed," he exclaimed, clapping his hands. "Your contact with the Marquis is *so* rewarding." He actually began skipping merrily about the room, singing the praises of the wonderful Marquis and of the coup that Jennifer had managed for him. He even handed her the letter itself, holding it out to her on open palms, as if the document were a piece of royal treasure.

"Just *look* what the Marquis had to say! And addressed directly to *me*! Why, you should have *seen* the surprise and respect the Minister accorded me when I brought the communique in to him. With me acting *oh* so casually, as I handed it over." He turned his head to the side and primped the hair at the back of his neck as he said this.

Jennifer read the letter she had forged, as if seeing it for the first time:

My Dearest Matthew,

So good to hear from you. In response to your missive, let me assure you our desire to purchase the aforementioned quantity of textiles is as great as ever. You may consider this an official confirmation. Payment will be rendered in French francs or English sovereigns, as you prefer.

Initial delivery and payment is to take place on the second quarter, as previously mentioned. We look forward to transacting much commerce with you in the near future. Respect for your talents is high among our directors. With warmest personal regards, I remain,

> Your humble servant,
> Marquis de Calhoun [his seal]

P.S. All correspondence must be liaisoned through our dear friend J.V., whose confidentiality we have the highest regard for.

"Very nice," Jennifer said, handing back the letter.

"Of course it's quite the pity he found it necessary to mention *you*, right in the letter itself." A small shadow of gloom fell across his features. "The Minister asked me about that."

"Naturally you told him that J.V. was someone you had the foresight to introduce to the Marquis, to gain his confidence?"

He looked astounded. "Why, yes. Yes indeed, that's exactly what I said. Jennifer, we seem to be thinking quite similarly of late, have you noticed?"

She smiled. "I'm learning to think like you more and more all the time, Matthew. So I can serve you better."

He looked at her sidelong. "How nice," he said, his voice drenched with skepticism.

It was then that Jennifer decided to broach the idea she had been holding back for several days: the idea of having Matthew throw a major ball, at which Jennifer would act as hostess, and which London's social luminaries would be invited to. The purpose of giving the ball would be to further Matthew's career.

The reason Jennifer wished to actually further his career was that she needed more evidence to show him that she really *was* interested in his welfare; so he would not be suspicious when she finally found the right moment to suggest they take a vacation together on the coast. At present he was too skeptical of her motives to agree to such a thing, even despite his momentary delight at the "Marquis Calhoun" coup she had engineered for him. She needed another example of her dedication to his career to make him lower his guard. Then she could spring the idea of a trip to the coast without arousing his suspicions.

Jennifer had held back mentioning the idea of the ball up until now because the project involved spending a large sum of money, if it was to be done right. And one thing she had learned quickly about Matthew was that he was loath to spend even a ha'penny unless absolutely forced to, regardless of the benefit that might accrue.

"Matthew," she said to him now, as he smiled gloatingly down at the Marquis's letter. When he looked up at her, she told him her idea.

"Give a ball, you say?" he responded in amazement. "For fifty couples? Lord, Jennifer, you must think I'm *made* of money! Such an event would be in*cred*ibly costly. And after negotiating your freedom from the Bultaco, plus the amount I spent buying their silence about your ever having even *ent*ered that blasted hellhole . . . why, it's unthinkable! And besides, what could I possibly *gain* from such an event, eh, answer me that?"

"You'd meet the men who could do your career good. You're not meeting them now, you told me so. The officials you are meeting through your various contacts, the ones who actually take note of you, they're not highly placed enough to matter."

"They're not so *very* minor, I can assure you," he said defensively.

"But they're not the ones you'd like to be able to

meet, are they? No, those you'd like to meet, the higher-echelon officials, they give parties . . . but you're never invited to them."

"Now see here!" he exploded, "there's no need to impugn my—"

"Let me finish, Matthew. All I'm saying is that if *you* give a party and invite *them* . . . and if you make a good impression on them, an impression of a bright, capable up-and-comer who they'd do well to have on their side . . . why, they'll start inviting you to their parties. And gladly."

He pulled in his lips in a thoughtful scowl. "I don't know," he said uncertainly. "It's not that I haven't considered the idea. But . . ." he looked up argumentatively, ". . . suppose I do give a ball, and it should go *bad*ly. I'd be in even worse of a position then."

"It won't go badly. I'll learn what to do. And I'll do it well. You'll see. It'll increase your worth a hundred times."

"Well what makes you think they'd even *come* to my party, the ones we'd want? How do you propose to entice these 'gentlemen' who scorn having me at *their* homes?"

"Something I learned from Silas, who was a diplomat as well as a printer. When you give a party, give it in honor of a highly placed man. The highly placed man will likely come, since he's the guest of honor. And those beneath him will come to honor him, for fear their absence will be viewed by him as an insult. So . . . you asked me what you should give the Minister for the anniversary of his taking office?"

"Yes, I did. And I must say, you were not in the least bit helpful. You gave me not a single suggestion for a gift."

"Don't give him a gift. Give him a party in his honor instead."

His eyebrows raised. He put a finger to his lips thoughtfully. "It could work . . ."

"It will work."

He looked at her menacingly from under lowered brows. "If it doesn't not even your contact with the Marquis will save me. My advancement will be stunted. I'll be a laughing stock, if this goes badly. In which case, *you* will no longer be of any value to me at all."

She lowered her eyes and did not ask him what the consequence of that would be. She had listened closely when he made his financial deal to buy her indenture papers away from Pauly Garrett and the madam of the Bultaco House. One condition he insisted upon was that he be able to sell her back to the House, at three-quarters what he paid for her, if she ceased to be of value to him.

Matthew had taken to introducing Jennifer as his wife, so their living together would not appear scandalous. Even so, Jennifer knew he had not introduced her to enough people as *Mrs.* Armitage that he would have to think twice about trying to explain her disappearance, should it occur.

When Matthew said nothing for a long time, simply glowered thoughtfully, Jennifer said, "You wanted me as your wife once, because you thought I could aid you in your climb to wealth and position. Because of my looks and whatever gracefulness you think I may possess."

"So?" he sneered.

"Looks and poise count for nothing if no one sees them. You can't impress your superiors with the 'prize' you've chosen, if you keep me shut out of sight."

He sighed. His upward momentum had been stopped cold recently, Jennifer knew, due to his being a stranger within the closed circle of English officialdom. All the flattering and conniving skills he had developed to aid his career in the Colonies were useless here. He was desperate to find a way to ressume his ascent. "Well, all *right*," he declared snappishly. "We'll give a ball then. But it had best be successful! *I warn you!*"

* * *

On the strength of his triumph with the House of Calhoun trade agreement, Matthew managed to gain the Minister's acceptance of his invitation to attend a party given in his honor. Matthew and Jennifer then set about deciding which men of import to include on the guest list.

When the R.S.V.P. invitations they sent out began to return, Matthew was astonished at the excellent response he was receiving. Jennifer acted nonchalantly—"Of course they accepted. Didn't I tell you they would?"—though in truth she was quite surprised also.

Once the invitations had been accepted, Jennifer went about making preparations for the ball itself. She contracted for the musicians, hired a renowned chef to prepare the evening's refreshments, purchased an abundance of various liquors, and supervised the preparation and decorating of the ballroom. She was constantly rushing about attending to details during the weeks preceding the party.

Soon she realized something that was interesting to her due to its unexpectedness: she actually enjoyed what she was doing. It was a challenge. Jennifer also found it quite exciting to enter this unfamiliar new world of elegant clothing, expensive decorations, and respectful caterers and suppliers. She seemed to fit in very well in her role as lady of the manor.

She found that she needed no instructions whatever in matters of taste and style, such as in arranging the ballroom. In other matters, though, she did need help, for they required a knowledge bred of experience, which she did not have. So, with Matthew's grudging consent ("And how much will *this* little frivolity cost me?" he asked), Jennifer hired a matron, who had once been prominent in the city's social circles, to tutor her in the areas of dress, hairstyle, etiquette, and protocol.

Now, on the eve of the ball, as Jennifer stood fretting in uncomfortable stillness while Louisa helped with her dress, the elderly matron seemed to read her mind. "Oh don't worry so, milady. All of it will turn out fine. I have a sense for these things."

"I hope you're right," Jennifer said nervously. "You don't know what it will mean if it doesn't go well. It won't be just bad. It'll be disastrous."

Louisa cinched Jennifer's corset tighter, making Jennifer lose all her breath. Then she closed up the back of Jennifer's gown and laced it up again for the second time. "You've made all the right preparations," she said, "I've seen to that. All that's left now is for you to be charming and poised. And if I do say so, you've certainly a natural flair for that. Why, your manner would make one think you were born to the high life."

"You really think so, Louisa?"

"It's not only I, milady. You saw the looks on the shopkeeps' faces when we went to make our purchases. They recognized a gracious lady when they saw one, even though your attire at that time wasn't at all appropriate to such an image. But as for your image now . . . here, let's give you a look at yourself." She stood up from her knees and, now that the elaborate grooming and gowning was complete, turned Jennifer around and let her see herself in the full-length mirror for the first time.

Jennifer was so stunned by the sight that greeted her eyes, she jerked even straighter than the tightness of her corset required. The face in the mirror was hers, yes, with the same rich full lips and big sparkling blue eyes. The shapely brows were hers, yes, and the honey brown hair. But the strikingness of the image! "Louisa," she gasped, "that isn't me!"

"Well, it's certainly not Helen of Troy, though it could easily pass for her."

Jennifer's hair had been done up high on her head with ringlets falling down and framing her modestly pinked cheeks. Her hair had not been powdered, but had been sparsely sprinkled with tiny flecks of a shiny

286

substance that made her hair glitter shimmeringly with each movement, as the flecks caught the light.

Her fine white shoulders were bare, as was her throat and a daring bit of her cleavage, exposing the soft fair skin of her swelling breasts. The high-waisted dress of pale blue taffeta, in the newest fashion, billowed out around her hips and was cut away in front, exposing her decorated petticoats. Giant folds of the taffeta were gathered together in back. The daring plunge of the gown's squared-off bodice was offset by the rise of the very pale blue chemise she wore beneath it. Her sleeves flared out boldly from the shoulders, tapering down to lacy cuffs at her wrists.

The modified polonaise gown would have seemed ostentatious and flashy on others, but as Jennifer looked at herself with growing satisfaction in the mirror, she realized that the dress and the hairstyle seemed made for her. They served to highlight the natural beauty of her fine features and well-turned-out figure, as if to declare to the world: Only a woman such as *this* could do justice to such a gown and coiffure.

Whereas only a moment ago she had been nervous and jittery, now, as Jennifer viewed herself in the mirror, she felt a warm glow of confidence sweep over her. She was not a callow young girl anymore, to be blown about by the winds of fortune. She was an elegant lady of grace and dignity, one who from the look of her could twist the world about her finger if she so desired.

What a heady sensation! Why had she never realized it before? It was not the gown and the grooming that imbued her with the fascinating sense of womanly power and charm she now felt. No! Rather, it was the raised, arrogant chin, the coolness in the eyes, the essence of a woman who suddenly knew her own worth. Why, it positively radiated from her!

"Oh, yes," said Louisa admiringly, stepping back for a fuller view, "you can see it now, can't you? I can tell from your eyes. You've a proper appreciation for your own glory now, haven't you?"

Jennifer nodded and found herself smiling. "I do, Louisa," she said softly. "I really do."

Louisa came up to her and hugged her gently, then looked at her with a sadness in her eyes. "Don't lose it," she said warningly, as if she herself had once had it, but had let it slip away. Then the matron brightened. "Now," she said triumphantly, "to the ball!"

Jennifer touched her hand. "Thank you, Louisa." Then she braced herself emotionally for the new world she was about to enter, left the room, and went to the stairs that led down into the ballroom.

The first guests had already begun to arrive. Matthew stood at the ballroom entrance, greeting a couple who had just entered, after they had been announced by Oscar at the door. Most of the guests had wandered into the main part of the ballroom and were mingling among themselves, enjoying the music of the orchestra, partaking of the wine and liquor and refreshments.

As Jennifer began descending the stairs, a few guests noticed her, and then others looked up to see what it was that these few were watching so intently. By the time she reached the ballroom floor, all eyes in the room were upon her, filled with fascination in the case of men, and envy or admiration in the case of women. All eyes, that is, except Matthew's—he was greeting another pair of guests at the ballroom entrance and had not seen her. She walked across the ballroom toward him, feeling the eyes of the guests turning to follow her.

Matthew was dressed in a baroquely embroidered square-tailed coat, flowing scarlet neck scarf, tight knickers and high-heeled buckled shoes. The distinguished looking couple he was greeting were clearly not overly pleased at being here, having come only to avoid appearing disrespectful to the guest of honor, Minister Kensington. Matthew sensed their displeasure and seemed very nervous. As Jennifer approached him, she was struck by the comical juxtaposition of his shortness against the magisterial height of the guests he was addressing.

Matthew turned to glance briefly at her as she came up to him, turned back to his guests, then did an amazed double take at Jennifer, his mouth actually dropping open. And remaining open.

"Hello, darling," she said to him, with the hint of a taunting smile at his awe-struck inability to bounce back to proper form. Then, prodding gently, "Our honored guests are? . . ."

"Ah!" he exclaimed, shaken back to reality. "Yes! Of course!" He turned to the distinguished couple, who were waiting patiently. "Lord and Lady Esterbrook, may I present my wife Jennifer."

Jennifer curtseyed politely. "An honor, Your Lordship. Milady."

The tall, white-wigged, long-faced Lord was clearly taken with Jennifer. It showed in his eyes, as he nodded in acknowledgment of the introduction. His wife recognized this and quickly put her arm through his, possessively.

"The Lord is . . . ah . . . involved in Colonial affairs and is—"

"Yes," said Jennifer, deliberately maintaining a look of false admiration in her eyes, "I'm familiar with His Lordship's reputation. The sternness with which you respond to Colonial provocations is a brilliant strategy for maintaining order in the provinces, Your Lordship.

Lord Esterbrook smirked in flattered satisfaction. "Mister Armitage, I'm delighted that my reputation has somehow come to the attention of your lovely wife. I had not flattered myself that my humble accomplishments would be at all widely known."

Matthew began stuttering in a search for words. Jennifer saved him. "Why, Your Lordship," she said, "you're too modest. You're one of Matthew's great heroes. He discusses your accomplishments with admiration so often that, well naturally I can't help but be well informed of them." She did not mention that she had quizzed Matthew for information about all the dignitaries who would be arriving tonight and had studied their accomplishments diligently.

Lady Esterbrook was regarding Jennifer with calculating eyes now, which were grudgingly appreciative. Lady Esterbrook seemed to realize what Jennifer was doing and she was not so petty as to be unable to appreciate a skillful performance.

Lord Esterbrook suddenly relaxed from his stiff, distinguished posture and slapped Matthew on the back, smiling and exclaiming, "Armitage, I've underestimated you, to be sure! So you're up on my accomplishments in the Colonies, eh? We'll have to get together soon, eh, let's make a point of it!" Then he and his wife moved off, the Lord glancing back over his shoulder at Jennifer.

Matthew turned to Jennifer, his eyes filled with gratitude. "*Darling*," he exclaimed, holding his arms open to her, as if about to embrace her.

"Please, Matthew," she said quietly, looking away, "you forget yourself."

He looked instantly guilty. "Hmm, yes, I—"

"Now listen to me," she said urgently, "you must be more charming with the women. If you don't, my making the men think well of you may not be enough. You can do it. You just have to relax and let your natural self take over. You do have a cultured manner, after all, and you can be quite—" she was about to say 'boot-licking,' "—flattering when you set your mind to it."

"I can indeed," he said coolly, clearly impressed by her concern about his utilizing his talents to create the best possible impression.

Another couple was announced at the door now and came forward to be greeted. Jennifer repeated her flirtatious performance and again succeeded in completely disarming and enchanting her guest. Matthew became less nervous now, and claimed the attention of the man's wife by commenting knowingly—and favorably—on the essence she was wearing. The woman responded delightedly. Buoyed by this success, Matthew ventured into other areas in which he could impress her by demonstrating knowledge of subjects of which most men had no inkling at all. He commented knowingly about the fabric and fashion of her dress, and on the "oh, too, *too* ravishing" style of her hair. The woman blushed with pleasure.

Soon, more and more guests began to arrive and the musicians struck up the first dance number. Jennifer had practiced daily under the instruction of Matron Louisa and was very graceful on the dance floor now. As the evening progressed, she was asked to dance by almost every one of the men present, from the stately old dignitaries to the younger, more dashing and handsome officials and members of the peerage.

She flirted with each man she met, and by a combination of admiring glances and complimentary words, she managed to elicit a smile or look of appreciation from almost everyone. The men flirted with her openly. She felt very light and heady as she swirled around the dance floor, listening to the gay laughter and the merry music, and feeling the effects of the two glasses of champagne which she had not been able to refuse without giving insult.

She looked at the glittering crystal chandeliers, the brightly colored clothing, the laughing faces. She was having a wonderful time. The evening was progressing perfectly and she was the focal point of the ball. It seemed almost certain that Matthew would benefit from her performance, which meant that soon she would be able to lure him to the coast, so she could have back what she wanted: Lancelot.

Even the need to be falsely pleasant to these Englishmen, who were the oppressors of the Colonies, did not darken her mood now. Such pleasantness and compliments were necessary if she were to achieve her purpose. But in addition to that, there was a certain glimmer of satisfaction in seeing that she, a simple Colonial girl, could so easily turn the heads of these upper-crust Englishmen who would soon be the enemies of her people in the coming revolution. What strength of resistance could they possibly offer, if they were so weak in character that they could be deceived and twisted around her finger by a mere girl?

The answer to that question—an answer which dampened her enthusiasm and optimism about success—came only a few minutes later with the arrival of the Minister himself, Lord Kensington. He entered the ballroom looking bored and displeased, showing no expression of apology for his tardiness. As he was announced at the door, a hush fell over the room. All eyes turned to view the highly placed member of government and the Royal court, who was also reputed to be a personal intimate of the King himself. Conversation soon picked up again and eyes turned back to the party, so as not to give the impression that the dignitaries were overawed. The impact of the man's glowering presence, however, continued to be felt, casting an aura of sobriety and self-consciousness over the affair.

Jennifer excused herself from the Admiralty official she was conversing with near the glimmering crystal punchbowl and moved across the floor toward where Matthew stood greeting the Minister. She walked with her head high, in a graceful sweeping motion.

When she was near, the Minister glanced over at her, and instead of turning his eyes politely away after a moment, he continued staring at her with his small beady eyes in a very ugly, beefy, glowering face. He was a squat, heavy-set man with drooping jowls and bushy black eyebrows, which clashed with the snowy whiteness of his long wig. He was dressed in proper formal attire, but with a rumpled carelessness that showed his disdain for style and fashion. And which emphasized the fact that he was powerful enough to not need abide by its canons.

He stood with his head lowered into his double chin, his shoulders hunched unattractively forward, as he watched Jennifer approach. "Jennifer," Matthew said to her, "this of course is the man I've spoken of *so* very often, one of the most *terri*bly talented men in government, my mentor, Lord Kensington."

Jennifer curtseyed. "I'm honored, my Lord."

The Minister grunted in greeting. He seemed disgruntled and unhappy. Jennifer would have taken it as a reflection on herself or her party but for the fact that Matthew had warned her he was of this mien by his very nature. That was one of the problems Matthew had been encountering in his attempts to curry the man's favor: the Minister was not appreciative of Matthew's cultured manner and style. He was a crude man who viewed Matthew as nothing more than a dandified sissy.

Jennifer did not attempt to flatter him, sensing instinctively that such a strategy would be ineffective. "Happy anniversary, Your Lordship," she said simply.

"Is it?" he said in a gruff, coarse voice. "Happier than the other anniversaries of office I've endured? It'll do, I suppose. Too much happiness, I hear, is bad for the liver anyway."

Jennifer could tell from the very slight way his mouth raised up at the corner that he had intended this as a joke. She made herself laugh and smiled brightly.

"Don't *laugh* at the Minister," complained Matthew in an appalled voice, fearful that she had given offense. "Please for*give* her, Your Lordship, she's not ac*cus*tomed to the finer points of—"

"Oh, hush up, Armitage. Your appreciation for dry wit is exceeded only by your towering physical stature."

Matthew looked insulted, but quickly subdued the look. He noticed that the Minister was staring unabashedly at the shapely fullness of Jennifer's breasts visible above her bodice. "Perhaps you'd care to dance with my wife?" he suggested with oily smoothness.

"Dancing is for fops."

"Hmmm. Yes. Well . . ." Matthew was at a loss. A footman came by with a tray of drinks. He took one and drank it down in a long, quick draught.

Jennifer did not know how to handle this man, either. She was relieved when one of the young blades to whom she had earlier promised a dance came up to her and slightly drunkenly offered his arm. She bowed and excused herself from the Minister, and let her escort lead her out onto the dance floor.

She danced to the gay music, smiling demurely, though what she really felt was a frown. Her mind was on the Minister. It was all very well to have the other high officials at the party take an interest in Matthew, but in the end, it all went for naught if the Minister himself could not be persuaded to think of him more favorably. It was the Minister who would or would not recommend Matthew for advancement out of his present position.

As she was being swirled in a wide circle during a movement of the dance, she had a chance to look through the crowd and see the Minister and Matthew again, both still standing at the door talking. Something of import had just been said, and an advantage had somehow been gained by Matthew. She knew this because Matthew was smiling broadly, with the look of self-satisfied confidence that meant he had discovered the way to achieve success with his opponent. Jennifer wondered what that way was. What was the secret to gaining the Minister's favor?

When the dance ended, Matthew came toward her and accosted her as she moved off the floor, taking her by the arm and moving her out of the room into the empty hall. "I've found a way to win him over!" he declared exultantly.

"Wonderful, Matthew. What is it?"

"Well," he said, raising an eyebrow in an animated, almost feminine gesture, "it seems that the Minister is a man who believes in reciprocating a favor. *Quid pro quo*, as it were. And he's made it *em*inently clear that while he doesn't actually *like* me," he frowned at this, but then brightened quickly, "he'll be *more* than happy to recommend me for advancement in return for a simple favor." He beamed at her.

"What favor does he desire?"

"He wants to make love to you!" he declared happily.

She regarded him in frigid silence. "Matthew, I won't do that. And you know it."

He looked taken aback. "How *dare* you spoil my chances? You pledged yourself to the advancement of my career. Now you have this *ex*cellent opportunity, and you're *balking*?" His expression turned nasty. "It's not as if you're a lilywhite virgin, after all. You've been had by the scum of the earth. You are *soiled* merchandise! How *dare* you refuse to aid me." He paused and his posture seemed to deflate. "Besides, I've already told him the answer is yes."

"The answer is no. I'll help you with your career, as I said I would. I've done so tonight, as you can see. But there is a limit to what I'll do." She looked at him sharply, her eyes flashing. "Yes, I've been raped by the scum of the earth, as you well know. But that's not the same as freely submitting to such debasement, as you're asking of me now. I was in chains at the time!"

Matthew's eyes narrowed threateningly. "And you can be *back* in chains again, too, if you fail me."

She glared at him, though there was real fear in her heart. She knew it was not an empty threat. But she also knew it was not so great a threat anymore as he made out. He may have been able to carry it off easily a few hours ago. But now he could not simply force her into a whorehouse, not after she had been introduced to polite society as his wife. Still, Jennifer felt a chill of terror creep up her spine at the thought of being held prisoner again, chained to the bed, raped repeatedly. The memory was so painful, it made beads of sweat break out all over her skin.

Even if he did not send her back to the Bultaco, as he probably could not do, there was still another consequence of her refusal to do as he asked: now it would be harder than ever to persuade him to agree to a vacation on the coast.

Oh, if only she could blank her mind, hide from herself long enough to just *do* the damnable thing he asked! That would solve her problems. But no, she could not make herself even consider the proposition. Aside from all else, the man was simply too loathsome. She could never let herself be touched by that squat ugly body and those fat hands. If she tried, she might end up losing control and slapping the man's hands away from her, or cursing at him hysterically. Where would Matthew's career be then?

Matthew glared at her with a violent fierceness, then turned and stalked away.

Jennifer stared after him, unsure what to do next. Finally she decided to go back to the ball. She would continue to woo the other influential men who were present, to influence them to think well of Matthew. Perhaps in the end that would count for something with him. . . .

She returned to dancing and mingling with the guests, though the music sounded tinny to her now and the brilliance of the ballroom seemed to have lost its sparkle. She kept glancing over at the Minister, who stood in a corner of the room, holding court. All the guests at one time or another came up to him to pay their respects, saving him from having to move about the room himself. Each time Jennifer looked at him, she saw his beady eyes staring back at her—and strangely, they were still filled with expectation. Hadn't Matthew yet told him of her refusal?

It was at one of these moments when she was glancing at the Minister that her eyes were distracted by Babette, the maid, who was standing in the threshold of the service corridor doorway, off to the side of the room. She was waving frantically at her to catch her attention. Jennifer went over to her as soon as she could.

"Milady," said Babette, urgently, "there is a man outside the kitchen door. He says he must speak to you right away!"

"At this time of night? Who is he? What does he want?"

"The man is French, milady. He has very long hair, blond it is, and he's awfully big-chested. He won't give his name, except to say—"

She did not wait to hear the rest of it. She brushed past the petite, dark-haired girl and rushed quickly down the corridor. She entered the brightly lit kitchen and walked quickly through it, saying nothing to the cook and his helpers who looked up at her in startled bewilderment as she went by. Then she rushed out the back door into the cold night.

Chapter 19

It was dark outside. Gray clouds scurried across the heavens, making it seem as if the full moon itself were racing through the clouds. After the warm stuffiness of the crowded ballroom, the outside air seemed especially crisp and clean. A chill wind blew all around her. Jennifer shuddered.

She walked forward several paces, seeing no one. She looked about, then walked a few steps further forward. Hearing a twig snap behind her, she turned quickly to see D'Arcy standing there, strong and tall, wearing black britches and a heavy blue coat over an open-chested white shirt. His long blond hair blew about in the strong wind.

"Why are you trying to hide from me?" she said.

He frowned in surprise. "Jennyfair? That eez you? *Mon dieu*, how am I to recognize you when you look so . . . so . . ." His eyes traveled from the high bun of her hair, past her lips and throat, down to the naked swell of her breasts showing above the top of her bodice. He gestured helplessly with his open palms, unable to find words. "You are lovely like a Venus," he said finally.

She glanced around hurriedly. "D'Arcy, come with me. We can't stay here, someone might come out." She led him off into the darkness toward the latticework arbor several yards away, which was situated in the midst of a shrubbery and flower garden. When they were beyond the hearing range of the lighted rectangle that was the kitchen doorway, she said, "Is everything all right? Why are you here?"

"Jennyfair, everything eet eez not all right. Everything eez very badly. I wrote a message for ze chandler, to have heem deliver eet to you. But now zat we are in ze secret cove, while we resupply, I think to myself: ze message eez not enough. I must go to her myself with ze news.

"Lancelot doesn't know you're here?"

He grinned tersely. "Lancelot theenks I am out womanizing, as I always am out womanizing when we are in port. He does not know zat, instead, I find out where thees Armitage man you told me about lives, and zat I now come to see you."

The faint trace of dance music wafted out to them on a particularly strong breeze, then faded away.

"What did you want to tell me, D'Arcy?"

He frowned. "Lancelot, he still loves you very much."

She brightened. "He does?"

"*Oui*. But do not feel hopeful, Jennyfair. He still will not allow even the mention of your name. He has ze love for you, yes, but ze bitterness eez zair too. Ze problem, ze thing zat I come to tell you: *ze love eez driving heem crazy!* He drinks ze whiskey now. Nevair before! And he does . . . other things too zat before he nevair did. Eet eez very bad.

"Ze men," he said, shaking his head, "zay begin to gripe about ze way he eeze now. Before, zay would follow heem anywhere! Now, though, he takes ze crazy chances, risks ze sheep and ze men. He fights vessels weeth so much more firepower. He snaps at ze men. Sometimes he seems like a crazyman in a trance."

Jennifer's expression was one of deep pain as she listened and imagined the suffering Lancelot must be going through.

"Two days ago when we just arrive in ze cove, we are drinking on ze beach, he and I, and suddenly like lightning he leaps up and throws ze bottle at a boulder,

299

shattering eet, screaming, 'The bitch, the goddam bitch!' And he looks at me like zair is a fire deep in his gut." He shook his head. "Jennyfair, eet cannot go on like thees."

She felt deeply saddened and pained. "If only there was something I could do," she said. "I love him so much, D'Arcy."

D'Arcy turned away from her upon hearing these words. But then he looked back. "Maybe zair is something you can do."

"What is it? Tell me. I'll do anything!"

"Your plan to have heem hear ze confession of thees Armitage man? Eef you can do eet soon, very soon, right away?"

"Soon?" She lowered her eyes. "He won't go to the coast with me just yet. I'll have to wait till he trusts me more before I can ask him. Or until he wants something badly from me, and can't refuse me a favor in return. That may not be for awhile."

"Zat ees bad. Lancelot, I theenk he does not have 'awhile.' Soon, eef he does not change, he either will kill heemself by taking ze crazy risks in battles, or ze men zay will mutiny."

"They wouldn't!"

"Jennyfair, he eez no longer ze same man. He eez not ze Lancelot zat you knew before." He came up close to her, and she saw the desperate urgency in his furled brow. "You must start ze plan soon, right away, or eet weel do heem no good at all. Eet weel be too late."

She turned away from him and stared in anguish into the night, at the white globe above, which sliced through the smoky gray clouds. What could she *do*?

"We leave soon," D'Arcy said from behind her. "To intercept a British merchantman zat eez coming in weeth tobacco from ze Colonies. We weel meet her out on ze high seas, away from ze Admiralty escorts. We seenk her. Zen, in a month, we arrive back heer to finish ze provisioning. Can you get thees Armitage to ze coast then? Een a month?"

She swiveled around quickly and said in a sharp voice, "Why must it be the coast? Why can't you bring Lancelot here? *You're* here. It can't be that unsafe."

"You forget ze important fact. I'm here, *oui,* and I weel return safely to ze sheep. But zat eez because no one eez searching for me, Jennyfair. No one knows I am here. Lancelot, if he hears thees confession, he weel kill ze Armitage man. Ze Briteesh, zay will put out ze dragnet for us zen, to find us. You see, Jennyfair? Eef we are already at ze coast, we just row out to ze *Liberty* and set sail. Eef we are here in London, though, we must travel across ze country to get back to ze coast. Weeth every soldier in ze land after us."

She nodded. She had really known this all along. She was grasping at straws now, out of desperation. She shuddered and hugged herself. In the low-bodiced, off-the-shoulder taffeta dress, she was afforded almost no protection at all against the chilly wind.

D'Arcy took off his heavy coat and put it around her shoulders.

"Thank you, D'Arcy."

His hands remained on her shoulders, where he had draped his coat over her. He gazed deeply in her eyes with a look of passionate intensity. Jennifer drew back, startled. D'Arcy removed his hands. He looked away, guiltily.

"I'll do it," she said. "I'll have him there, at the coast, in a month."

"You are certain?"

"No. Yes. I don't know!" She closed her eyes. "D'Arcy . . . yes. I'm certain. I don't know how, but I will do it. I'll have him there."

He smiled at her for the first time. "You are like me now in thees matter, Jennyfair. You ask me to bring Lancelot to ze coast, and do you remember what I say? I say to you, I do not know how I weel do eet, but *oui,* I weel bring heem there."

"You still have no idea how you'll get him there?"

He shook his head, then shrugged. "Maybe I hit heem over ze head and carry heem there."

Jennifer knew he was joking, though she could find no glimmer of humor in his eyes. She listened as D'Arcy now told her the details of where the meeting on the coast would have to take place and the signal they would use to notify each other of their arrival.

Then D'Arcy said, "Jennyfair, I have to tell you zat after thees month, we weel not be in zeez waters again for a long time. Admiral Joel eez ordering us to ze coast off Boston, to run ze supplies into ze city, away from ze blockaded harbor.

"So it's either have Matthew and Lancelot together at the coast in a month, or not at all," she said. "Is that what you're telling me?"

D'Arcy nodded.

Music from inside the ballroom again wafted out to them on a gust of wind. The wind rustled leaves in the shrubbery around them. Jennifer looked at the kitchen doorway, and saw a figure silhouetted against the rectangle of light. She recognized the short profile. It was Matthew, standing in the doorway, looking for her. Babette had obviously told him where she had gone. The young maid was in constant fear of incurring his wrath. Matthew's figure remained in the doorway a moment longer, then retreated back inside.

"D'Arcy," she said, "I have to go back." She handed him his coat.

"I understand." They looked at each other for a moment before she turned to go. "You look lovely, *cherie*," he said.

"Thank you for coming, for risking your life to come all this way inland. Lancelot doesn't know what a good friend you are to him." She wanted to take his hands and squeeze them, to show friendship and affection, to give him something more than only words. But she did not dare. His feelings toward her were unmistakable now. And though she did feel stirring of feelings that

302

were more than just affection for him, she had to make it clear there was only one true love in her life, and would always be just that one. So she did not touch his hands now, or do anything that would encourage him in his feelings.

"Goodbye," she said gently, starting back toward the house. "Goodbye, D'Arcy."

"*Au revoir, cherie.* A month from today, we meet again, on ze coast at Crespi."

She walked back to the kitchen doorway alone, then went into the house. The cook and staff looked at her with more than just casual attention, but said nothing. She went into the passageway, then back into the ballroom. People were dancing and laughing, more drunken and gay now, though tiring noticeably. The instant she reappeared in the ballroom, Matthew rushed up to her, grabbed her arm, and pulled her back into the passageway with such force that she knocked one of his fencing competition trophies off the wall where it was on display, as she went past it. Matthew slammed the door after them. His grip on her arm was tight. He was furious.

"Where *have* you been, blast you, a*band*oning our party! A hostess leaving her party unattended, why, it's unheard of! What must our guests think! And who was that Frenchman Babette told me about?"

"Calm down, Matthew. I was only gone a moment, and—"

"A quarter hour it's been, at least!"

She kept her expression unruffled as she looked at him, and said, "The Frenchmn you asked about? He's the London agent of the House of Calhoun. The Marquis sent him personally."

A look of fright leapt into Matthew's eyes, replacing the anger. His mouth dropped open. "But . . . but . . . but what did he *want*? He's not going to cancel the trade?" he asked, his voice rising in alarm.

"Lower your voice. They can hear in the ballroom if you shout."

"Is he? Is he going to cancel the trade?"

"Not at all. In fact, the agent relayed the message that he's considering increasing the amount of the purchase."

Relief flooded Matthew's features. His face relaxed.

"That's not why he came to see me tonight, though," she added quickly, hitting upon a way to protect herself from being sold back to the Bultaco. "The main reason he came was to see if I was still here. The Marquis heard rumors I'd been spirited away. He wanted to check before continuing with the trade."

"Why, how could he even im*a*gine such a thing?" Matthew said with indignation. "Why would anyone possibly wish to rid themselves of—that is, to separate me from my *dear* loving wife?" He patted her on the hand now, with false affection. "You did assure him you were *per*fectly fine, of course?" he asked with concern. "And that there's no reason in the *world* for the deal to be aborted?"

"Yes. But I think his agent will wish to check back with me occasionally."

Matthew frowned deeply. After a moment, he said, "We'd best return to our guests, don't you think? It's gauche enough to have *one* of us rudely absent, not to be placing any *blame* of course. But to have *both* of us gone . . ."

"Matthew," she said boldly, as he began guiding her by the arm back toward the ballroom. "I want to go to the coast. Just you and I. To the resort at Crespi."

"To the coast? Whatever for? Surely you can see I'm busy enough attending to the demands of my career." They walked out through the doorway, back into the ballroom. He immediately put a false smile on his face for the benefit of those who would be watching. "What a silly idea, wanting to go to the coast."

"But I do want it," she insisted. "It's important to me. And it would give us a chance to plan the next step of your career advancement together, without interruptions. So—"

"We'll speak of it later," he said. He noticed that the Minister, standing across the floor from them with his arms folded across his chest, was appearing more disgruntled than usual. "Here, why don't you go say a pleasant word to the Minister. He is looking *ra*ther unhappy, wouldn't you say? And after all, one purpose of giving this expensive ball *is* to please him."

She did not want to have to deal with the Minister, not now that the man had made clear his intentions toward her. But she did want to convince Matthew she had his best interests at heart. Reluctantly, she went over to the ghoulish Minister.

He looked her up and down, as if he owned her.

"Are you enjoying the party, Your Lordship," Jennifer asked.

"No. I hate parties." His voice was so gruff it seemed as if he were croaking the words rather than speaking them. "I'd have left hours ago, but for what I've been promised at the party's end."

"And what might that be, Your Lordship?"

He leered at her. "No need to play coy with me. I know it's all been arranged. Your dandy of a husband has at least one admirable trait. Practicality. I told him what I wanted, he told me what he wanted, and we struck a bargain. Very civilized. In the finest English tradition."

She was looking at him with astonishment and a touch of fear. So Matthew hadn't told him that the arrangement was off. How could she say it to him now without arousing a dangerous reaction? She looked in the man's beady eyes and saw that there was something lethal and frightening there. She had to be careful.

"Nice breasts you have," he said, staring unabashedly at her bodice. "Though a bit large for someone as small-shouldered as you."

Fury raced through her. He did not know her sordid past. As far as he was concerned he was addressing a refined lady of the manor. How dare he speak to her

305

this way? Her instinct was to slap him. But to do so, she knew, would mean an end to Matthew's career.

The Minister frowned uncomprehendingly at the look of fury in Jennifer's eyes. She said nothing to him, simply swiveled sharply on her heel and walked away.

As she rushed off, she saw Matthew, only a few feet distant, hurrying past her to try to soothe the Minister and somehow salvage the situation. He had been standing nearby, watching them all the while, to be ready in case of emergency. Jennifer did not even bother shooting him an icy stare as she stormed past him; it would be useless. Behind her, she heard the Minister's angry voice. "You led me on, Armitage!"

"Please, Your Lordship, you don't understand! You see—"

As many of the guests watched, the Minister stormed outside, past the butler, without bothering to retrieve his hat or cape. Matthew rushed after him still trying to save the situation.

Immediately thereafter, the guests began to leave rather hurriedly. Since London was such a geographically close-knit city, the guests would be returning to their homes this evening, rather than staying the night as they would have had the ball been held out in the country. Jennifer bid her guests goodnight at the door. She saw with relief that her performance for the evening had not been totally wasted. Several guests mentioned they'd be happy to have her and Matthew over to a party sometime in the future.

Jennifer was in the midst of dismissing the musicians, when Matthew came back into the room. He marched up to her, grasped her by the arm, and pulled her off through the doorway into the hall. She had expected that he would be furious with her. Instead, he was pleading.

"You can still save the situation!" he declared. "Won't you do it? Please?"

"How? By going to bed with that horrid creature?"

"No!" he said brightening. "That's not it at all!" He

looked about secretively to the left and right, though no one was in the hall with them. "All you have to do," he said, "is let him—now this may sound strange, but hear me out—just let him peep through the keyhole while you undress for bed."

She looked at him with an expression of distaste, but said nothing negative.

Enthused by her lack of protest, Matthew continued, speaking quickly. "He knows you won't voluntarily let him touch you, you made that clear enough. But he doesn't have to actually *touch* you, you see. He has this strange liking for viewing women without them knowing it. And he thinks you won't know it, that you won't volun*tar*ily be agreeing. He thinks I'll be letting him into the hall outside your room on the sly, without your knowledge. "You see?" he said brightly. "That's all there is to it! Just undress and get into bed, while he watches at the keyhole."

"Why are you telling me this?" she asked suspiciously. "This isn't like you. Your natural way would be to go ahead and let him stand outside the keyhole and watch, without your telling me."

"Are you accusing me of stooping to the use of unscrupulous methods?" he asked, his voice rising with indignant innocence. When he saw that she would not be swayed by his tone, though, and that she merely continued looking at him levelly, leaving the question stand, he pulled his neck scarf away from his Adam's apple and cleared his throat loudly. Then he said, "Well, actually, it *did* occur to me that if we didn't agree on this in advance, you might notice him outside the keyhole, and—"

"Throw a tumbler of water in his eye through the door."

Matthew winced at the thought. "Please don't do that," he said painfully. "And also, there's another reason I'm telling you this. You see, I was thinking that perhaps you could put on a bit of a *show* for him in

307

undressing. Perhaps be a bit slower about it than usual. It *is* my career that's at stake, after all."

She looked at him for a moment, saying nothing. The pleading look in his eyes was so acute, he seemed almost like a starving dog begging for a bone.

"Matthew," she said quietly, telling a lie, "my birthday is on the twelfth of next month. If we could go to the coast, to celebrate?"

"You're taking advantage of me!" he shouted.

She almost laughed at him. "*I*? Taking advantage of *you*?"

He clenched his fists and jerked them up and down in front of him, frustratedly. He pursed his lips. "I don't know *why* you're so anxious to go to the coast. There are *scads* of excellent resorts right here in London. But . . . well, all *right* then! You put on a show tonight—a good show, mind you! A grand show, no less! And on the twelfth, I promise to let you go to—"

"I want you there with me! It's so we can plan your career together."

"All *right*! Don't be so dem*a*nding. Well then, we're agreed." He looked at her questioningly, not quite believing it. "We'll both go to the coast on the twelfth. And you'll please the Minister tonight, in the manner of your undressing."

She nodded.

"Oh, and there's one thing more," he added, bolstered by his success. "He enjoys watching a bit of a show put on with an *ostrich* feather of all things. If you could just—"

"Absolutely not! Don't even *tell* me what it is he likes done with them, I don't want to hear it!"

He jerked his fists up and down once more in frustration, but decided not to press the issue. He already had accomplished more than he expected. "The Minister is outside," he said, "in his coach. I'll fetch him back shortly. In the meantime, you get upstairs and prepare yourself. I'll send Babette in to let you know when it's time." He walked away from her, out of the hall.

Jennifer waited upstairs in her room, feeling that she had come out quite well in their exchange. Undressing while that creature watched her through a keyhole was not so bad. At least she would not have to endure the man's hands upon her body—and worse. She would not even have to see him. And in return for her concession, she had gained Matthew's promise to go to the coast with her. All in all, she had done quite well for herself. Especially considering that she might have been willing to agree to much more than that—if she could force herself to!—in order to get Matthew to the coast.

Still, as she sat on the edge of the large canopied bed, she felt nervous and tense at the thought of having that man watch her undress. She was very appreciative when Babette came into the room, a moment later, bearing a tray on which was a flask of champagne and a glass.

"The Master said you'd be a bit tensed up, Madam, and that this would calm your nerves some."

"Thank you, Babette," Jennifer said. She almost never drank wine or spirits, but tonight, she felt, was a special occasion. Besides, she needed it. She glanced at the keyhole, and yes, there he was, the hideous brute, his beady eye straining through the large vertical keyhole. Jennifer poured a glassful of the sweet bubbly champagne. She drank it down. It felt good in her mouth and going down her throat.

Well, she thought, it's time to begin. I'll do it quickly and get it over with.

She stood up. And instantly she sank back down again to the edge of the bed. My, but she was suddenly so *dizzy*.

"Here, let me help you, Madam," said Babette. "You've had a real night of it, haven't you? Running about as you have, playing the perfect hostess."

With Babette's aid she stood up again, feeling very

shaky on her feet. Babette started undressing her, first removing her shoes, then unlacing her gown at the back. Jennifer's mouth was very dry and she felt extremely weak. It must be the champagne, she thought. This drink, on top of the two she had earlier, that was what did it. She certainly was not one who got along well with liquor, that was for sure. She blinked her eyes shut, then opened them after a long minute. The beady eye was still staring at her through the keyhole. Jennifer looked away. For some reason, she felt very dry-mouthed.

Babette slipped the gown off Jennifer's shoulders and helped Jennifer pull her arms out of the billowing taffeta sleeves. Then she removed the pannier and pushed the gown down past Jennifer's hips. Jennifer stepped out of it. Babette unlaced the tight corset and removed it. Immediately Jennifer felt much better, much freer and lighter. She took a deep breath of air and was surprised when it nearly made her swoon. For a moment stars danced dazzlingly before her eyes. She grasped the canopy post for support.

Babette spent a few moments on Jennifer's elaborate hairstyle, and when she was finished, Jennifer's long hair fell naturally about her shoulders. Then Babette helped her out of her fluffy petticoats.

Jennifer was wearing only the linen slip that covered her from midway down her breasts to her ankles now. Thank God, she thought, it will soon be over. I'll be out of this slip, the Minister will see his fill, and then I'll be under the covers and *asleep*. Sleep seemed so greatly desirable now, as if nothing in the world mattered so much as lying down and letting all the tension ease away from her as she drifted silently off . . .

But this maddening dry-mouthed thirst was irritating her. "Babette," she said, and was surprised at the way her voice slurred. She almost could not control her vocal chords enough to speak properly. "Another gloss . . . gluss . . . *glass* of champagne plizzz." She shook her head sharply to clear it.

310

Babette filled the glass to the brim with champagne and handed it to her. Jennifer drank only two swallows of it before her arm suddenly went slack and the glass fell out of her hand onto the rug. She bent to retrieve it, when her knees suddenly went weak and she started to collapse. Babette was too slight of a girl to hold her up, and instead of even trying, she simply pushed Jennifer hard in the direction of the bed when Jennifer began to crumble.

Jennifer ended up half on and half off the bed. Babette grabbed hold of her wrists and tugged her fully up onto the bed. The golden satin bedcover felt smooth and cool beneath Jennifer's skin. She tried to say "Thank you" to Babette, but the words came out slurred.

Babette finished undressing her, untying the bow cord at the top of Jennifer's slip, then pulling the slip off of her. Then, rather than leave Jennifer crumpled uncomfortably on the bed in the haphazard position she was in, she arranged Jennifer's weak arms and legs so they pointed out to the four bedposts.

Well, Jennifer thought, blushing pinkly over her entire body, this is a fine show for the Minister's peeping eye. Much finer than she had ever intended to give him. Surely he won't be disappointed with *this*. Babette gently slipped a pillow under her head, raising her head so that Jennifer could look down past her naked body to see the eye of the Minister still at the keyhole, gazing directly up between her spread legs.

All right now, Jennifer thought. *Enough of this!* He's had his show. Now if Babette will just pull the sides of the bedcover over me and cover me up. And then snuff the candles so I can get some sleep . . .

But instead of covering her up, Babette did something very strange. She bent down and reached for an object hidden under the bed, and when she came up again she had it in her hand: a long, thick-spined ostrich feather.

Jennifer's eyes went wide. "What are you doing!"

she tried to say, but the words would not come out. She tried to rise off the bed, but she could not move. Her muscles would not respond to her mind's commands.

Now she understood. It was not the champagne that had done this to her. It was what Matthew had undoubtedly put into the champagne before giving Babette her instructions and sending her into the room with it. *She had been drugged!* And now what could she do about it? She was immobile.

Babette looked nervous and guilty and could not look Jennifer in the eyes as she began following Matthew's instructions. She kept her eyes focused on the various parts of Jennifer's body where the thick bushy feather now began passing over.

Jennifer watched the feather touch down on her shoulders and throat, and she surprised herself by almost moaning with the sensation. It was too unbearably intense! What strange drug was in that drink? It made her skin a thousand times more sensitive than it had ever been.

The feather skimmed softly over her arms and shoulders and then over her breasts. It moved in a circular motion, touching her full breasts, passing over her rosy pink nipples repeatedly with the light, maddeningly tantalizing motion. Her breasts seemed to swell with the exquisiteness of the sensation and her nipples felt as if they were exploding with pleasure at each slow pass of the bushy thick feather.

Jennifer tried to raise up her arms and kick with her legs, but she only succeeded in moving her limbs slightly, making it appear as though she were wriggling in a seductive manner. She tried to speak, but all that came out was a long moan.

The feather moved down her stomach, over her legs, then crept up the inside of her thighs. When it touched at her sex, her mind went wild with the shocking pleasure of the sensation. The feather rubbed her repeatedly, up and down, in small circles, never leaving the excruciatingly sensitive area, driving her insane with the tickling, tingling, teasing motion. Damn that drug! she cursed. Whatever it was, it had turned her body into a single quivering raw nerve of sensitivity.

Jennifer was feeling that she could not take the sensual torture a moment longer when, at last Babette put the feather away and closed Jennifer's legs. Suddenly the maid broke into tears. "I'm so sorry," she sobbed, "so sorry! Forgive me, milady, he made me do it! The Master said he'd turn me out if I didn't. I'd be a pauper, no money, nowhere to go. Master Armitage would see to it I wasn't hired anywhere again. Please forgive me, I'm so sorry, milady!"

Gently, she pulled the golden bedcover up over her exhausted body, sniffling and sobbing all the while. "I'm sorry," she sobbed once more, snuffed out the candles, and left the room, rushing past the surprised Minister.

When Jennifer awakened in the morning she was still weak from the effects of the drug, but she washed and dressed, then went downstairs. Matthew was at the dining table, eating breakfast. When he saw her enter, he leapt up and rushed around to the far side of the long table, so that the table was between them.

"Darling, it all worked out for the best!" he protested.

She tried to come around the table toward him, but he scooted over to the side, keeping the expanse of polished teak between them. "The Minister was su*perbly* pleased!" he exclaimed.

Jennifer picked up a dish of porridge and flung it at him. He ducked, and it shattered against the wall. She threw a pitcher of cider at him. It hit the table in front of him and ricochetted up into his stomach, wetting his brown waistcoat thoroughly.

"Please, will you lis*ten* to me! I'm telling you it was for both of us, dearest! It's a team effort we're putting forth, isn't that right? To advance my career, and thereby better *both* of our lives?" He ran quickly

313

around the end of the table as she came rushing at him from the opposite end. "And not only that, but listen to this: I've made reservations at Crespi! That's right! Just as you wanted! The bungalow is already booked for the twelfth, and, why we're practically there already, dearest!"

She slowed down. She stopped, standing there, out of breath, out of energy, her posture slackened from the lingering effects of last night's drugging.

"There now," said Matthew, tentatively regaining his composure and dignity, now that the storm seemed to be past. "Isn't that *just* what we both wanted? *I* get the Minister's assurance of speedy promotion, and *you* get a birthday celebration on the coast." He smiled at her brightly, and spread his arms wide. "Isn't it simply de-*light*ful the way it all worked out?"

She pulled a chair out from the table and sat down.

"I told you, Jennifer, I have only your best interests at heart. And *nat*urally what's best for me is best for you too, under the circumstances." He frowned. "You do see that, of course?"

She did not answer. She hardly talked to him at all for the rest of that day or during the remaining days of that month. Then, during the first week of the following month, she began packing their trunks for the trip to the coast. The main thought she had to console her, as she filled the trunks with assorted clothing, was that Matthew Armitage would soon be dead. He would be dead and gone, preferably sliced to ribbons. Dead and gone and out of her life forever. And in only a few days!

Chapter 20

Now that the date for the meeting on the coast was definitely set, the problem for D'Arcy was how to get Savage to it. He could not tell him the true reason he wanted him to go to the coast. He had mentioned Jennifer's name a short time before, testingly, when Savage had been in a good mood. They had been laughing and joking in the captain's cabin. When D'Arcy mentioned her name, as if in a passing, casual remark, Savage's face suddenly became hard and his eyes icy. He stood up, kicking back his chair, and stalked out of the room.

So, D'Arcy thought now, as he stood at the helm directing the *Liberty,* a subterfuge would be necessary. He hated the idea of having to lie to Savage. Of having to trick him. But there was no other way.

When Second Mate Harlan came to relieve him at the helm, he went to search out Savage. He found him at the stern, taking readings with his instruments. D'Arcy leaned against the railing, squinting against the salty ocean breeze, as he waited for Savage to finish.

"We'll be sighting her soon now," Savage said, folding up a metal instrument he had been holding at eye level. "Maybe this afternoon even." He grinned at D'Arcy. "I hope you've a taste for good Virginia tobacco. We'll have enough to give the whooping cough to a whole army, once we find this merchantman."

"Tobacco, she eez not my favorite," D'Arcy said. "Rum and women, zay are my favorites. Though not in zat order, perhaps."

"No rum or women on this trip. We'll be back in port soon enough, though. You'll have your fill of both then."

He looked amazingly good, thought D'Arcy, considering his emotional state. He was stronger and more dashing than ever. He stood with his back straight now, the thick curls of his black hair framing his strong cheekbones and forehead, the V-neck of his maroon shirt showing his chest. In port, he practically had to fight off the wenches—a thing he no longer bothered to do. But the way he looked at the moment, D'Arcy knew, was only part of the story. D'Arcy had also seen him lately in his unguarded moments: brooding self-pityingly in his cabin late at night, or filled with such teeth-clenching, nostril-flaring self-hatred that he shouted at his men and seemed on the verge of smashing things.

"Lancelot, when last we were in ze cove for ze provisions, and I went ashore?"

"To do your usual whoring around," he grinned, with an undercurrent of scolding. "To do it in an area where they're so panicked with pirate fever you're lucky you didn't get recognized and shot on the spot."

"I did more zan only ze whoring. I went on a secret mission."

Savage looked at him curiously. "Secret even from me?"

"I weel tell you about eet, so eet eez not secret from you. But only part of eet can I tell you now. Ze rest you must see for yourself."

"This is sounding melodramatic. You sure you're not just using me to practice your tall tales on while we're at sea, so you'll be in good form for the ladies when we dock?"

"Ze life of a first-rate sea captain eez at stake," D'Arcy said, his tone deadly serious. "Eef something eez not done to save heem, eet will be too late. He will bury heemself with his death wish, which he does not know zat he even has."

316

"Who is this man?" he asked with concern. "And don't give me this 'secret mission' malarky, either. I want to know what this is all about. Is it Captain Ambrewster you're talking about of the *McCarty*? He seemed quite a bit worse for wear when last we saw him, after that disastrous engagement up north."

"Not Captain Ambrewster. Another captain. And I cannot tell you heez name for ze simple reason zat you would not believe me."

Savage grinned, but furled his brow, too. "I don't know whether to laugh at you or take you seriously. If I take you seriously, I'm liable to have you sent down to sickbay and tied to the cot till you come to your senses. What do you mean I wouldn't believe you if you told me the man's name? You're my closest friend and my First Mate. I'd believe anything you tell me, within reason."

"Lancelot, I must ask you theese: trust me."

He frowned. He began pacing up and down the deck, glancing at D'Arcy, then out to sea. "All right. What do you want me to do?"

"When we dock again, for ze provisions, you and I must go ashore, and travel down ze coast. To ze resort of Crespi. Zair we weel go to a secret meeting, where a matter of great import weel be discusssed."

Savage said nothing, just looked at him sidelong.

"Eet eez important, Lancelot. Otherwise I nevair ask you to do thees thing."

Savage nodded. "If you say you want me to do it, I'll do it. Though I'll tell you frankly, my strong temptation really *is* to send you down to sickbay. It's dangerous for us to be roaming around the coast. We've been harassing the seaports there so long, every mother's son has seen drawings of us by now, and knows our looks. And they're all bounty crazy in that area." He paused, and then shrugged. "But if you want it, then all right, I'll travel to Crespi with you. Overland, of all things, since we can't bring the ship in that close to that patrolled area." He grinned. "Anyway, what better cause to die for than to humor a friend's insanity, eh?"

"Also," said D'Arcy, "I should tell you of—"

"Ship ahoy!" shouted the watchman in the crow's nest. "Ship ahoy! Ship ahoy! A league to Sou/SouWest!"

D'Arcy squinted in the direction of the sighting. He could make out only a tiny dot. Savage put the telescope to his eye and said, "That's her. She's the proper make and flying the King's colors. But . . . strange."

"What eez strange?"

"She's not low in the water as she should be with a hold full of tobacco. She's far too light and swift."

D'Arcy took the scope when it was handed to him and confirmed Savage's observation. "Something eez wrong, Lancelot," he said, looking. "Her draft, eet eez too shallow."

"Call battle stations," Savage said quietly.

D'Arcy gave the command and within seconds men were scrambling about the deck rushing to prepare the cannons and adjust the sails for combat. Savage and D'Arcy went to the helm. When they were close enough to fire a salvo across the bow of the enemy ship, Savage again looked through his scope. Then, as D'Arcy watched, he lowered the telescope, grinning. "I understand," he said.

"What eez eet? Tell me."

Savage slammed the heel of his hand down on the railing, happily. "They've set a trap for us! Look at her sides," he said, pointing, "look closely. That's no merchantman! There are cannon ports there, only they're closed up so we can't see them!"

D'Arcy looked and could see that he was right, even without the telescope. "Lancelot, she's a three-masted first-rater. She's too mighty for ze *Liberty*."

"Nonsense. We've the advantage they thought *they* had. They expected to take us by surprise. But now we're the ones who'll surprise *her*. She doesn't realize she's been spotted for what she is." He shouted to his cannoneers. "Prepare to rake her with a broadside! Forward section to rake her decks. Aft section, fire at her waterline."

D'Arcy watched the ship grow larger as they swiftly approached. The strategy was sound: move in close and let the enemy think a shot was going to be fired across their bow in warning. But instead, cut to the side at the last minute and let loose with a devastating barrage. Still, D'Arcy was not happy at the idea. The enemy ship was a full class larger than the *Liberty*. She would be heavily armed. The old Lancelot would never have taken a risk such as this. Even though his strategy, if successful, would lessen the odds against them, they still were at a strong disadvantage.

Savage was silently counting off the seconds now, his face taut with excitement. It was a daring, deadly gambler's game. He wanted to get in as close to the enemy as he could, and then turn at the very last second before the enemy opened her cannon ports and fired. The enemy ship would be waiting till the last instant also, not wanting to betray that she carried cannons until the *Liberty* was too close to avoid taking major damage.

"Almost," said Savage in a low, steady voice. His cannoneers were waiting in sweating tension for the signal to fire, each man frozen like a coiled spring, waiting for the signal to snap into action. "Almost . . . almost . . ."

D'Arcy could read the name on the enemy now: the *Forrette*. He recognized the ship. She had a skillful captain who had built his reputation as a stalker-hunter.

"Almost . . ." said Savage, raising his palm. "*Hard to starboard, Harlan!*" he shouted, then within seconds of the ship's coming around into the wind: "*Open fire!*"

The maneuver was brilliantly timed. The *Forrette*'s cannon ports were flying open the instant the *Liberty*

319

cut hard to starboard, when the British captain realized the true nature of his ship had been discovered. It was too late, though. Savage's cannons let loose a broadside barrage that splintered and shattered the open upper deck of the *Forrette,* and blasted holes in her lower line cannon ports.

"Hard to port!" shouted Savage, bringing the *Liberty* around stern-forward, showing only her lean bow to minimize the damage of the answering fusillade. The fusillade came quickly, shattering much of the upper deck, and bringing down two cannon stations.

The battle was underway and for the next twenty minutes the two ships fired and maneuvered for position wildly. The *Liberty* held even against the mightier British vessel, thanks to the effect of Savage's surprise opening salvo. But as the cannons continued to roar, the *Liberty* was rocked with barrage after barrage of fiery metal.

Small fires broke out on the deck and black smoke billowed up thick in the air. Wood splintered, bulkheads shattered, as the cannonballs kept crashing in. The crackling sound of the fires and the blasting of the cannons blended into an unending wall of noise, punctuated by the screams of the dying and Savage's shouting of commands. The stench of gunfire and burnt wood made breathing difficult. Many men started to choke. D'Arcy saw an enemy ball crash into the upper crossbeam of the crucial mainsail, and he rushed up the rigging with two other men to fasten a splint into place so the canvas would not lose its wind. To lose the mainsail in the midst of battle would mean certain death.

The rocking of the ship, and the sharp turning maneuvers in response to Savage's battle commands, made it almost impossible to hold an even footing on the mast. One of the men reached too far forward to grab a bracing line D'Arcy had thrown, fell off the crossbeam, and plummeted down screaming to his death on the deck below.

Just when D'Arcy and the other seaman were completing their tenuous brace, sweating and straining their muscles to the limit, D'Arcy looked down and saw a gut-wrenching scene: the ammo detail, in the midst of bringing two kegs of powder up from the magazine, was felled by a shrapnel ball that burst apart near the hatchway they had just come out of. The four men in the detail slammed back against the cabin decking, and then dropped dead and motionless near the powder kegs. The heavy powder kegs themselves began sliding and rolling with the motion of the ship, toward a fire that was raging near the helm.

Savage saw the lethal situation also. He himself was the nearest man to the rolling, sliding kegs. He leapt over the railing of the bridge and rushed down the deck toward them. He stopped one keg with both his hands, getting in front of it and bracing his legs back. He managed to halt it before it reached the fire. The second keg, though, curved in a circular motion as the ship rocked under a new barrage, slammed right into the back of Savage's knees, then rolled onto his legs. Savage writhed and twisted, trying to push the keg off of him, but his legs were trapped under it, and it was too heavy for him to push off by himself. Making the situation even more volatile, the raging fire now leapt across the deck, blocking off access to Savage, trapping him inside a ring of fire that threatened to blow the powder kegs at any instant.

Several men stood shouting and moving about frantically beyond the ring of fire, trying to find an opening in the ring so they could rush in and help Savage. The circle of fire, though, widened rather than narrowed, making it impossible to burst through it. The men raised their palms to protect their faces from the intense heat and kept circling looking for an opening. Pails of water were being brought up, but they clearly would arrive too late to be of any use. The powder would blow at any second. Realizing this, the men began to rush for cover.

D'Arcy, high above the scene in the rocking, swaying mast, could see Savage very clearly. He was inside the circle of fire, as yet untouched by the flames, struggling and straining to shove the heavy keg off his legs. D'Arcy grasped hold of a boarding line and prepared to move off to the side of the crossbeam, so he could swing down into the circle of fire. Savage looked up, saw him, and waved him away. "You fool!" he shouted up, his glistening wet face animated, his words barely audible through the crackling fire. "You crazy maniac! Stay back! She'll blow any second!"

D'Arcy rushed down the crossbeam to its end, balancing precariously, so that he would have a great enough angle to swing into. Then, grasping the coarse hemp boarding line tightly in both hands, he swung down from the crossbeam in a steep arc and careened through the wall of fire into its center.

The back of his blouse was on fire. There was no time to try to snuff it, though. He bent over Savage's legs, and straining with all his might, shoved the heavy keg off to the side. Then he helped Savage up and instantly, without a word, the two of them leapt through the wall of fire at the side of the ship, over the side railing, and plummeted down to the ocean below, D'Arcy's shirtback blazing.

They were under the sea when the powder kegs exploded. The noise of the explosion was so fearsome, Savage heard it beneath the yards of water that covered him. He bobbed back up to the surface. He looked around frantically, but could not find D'Arcy. He ducked under the water again and began swimming in a circle, his eyes wide open and stinging with saltwater. He kicked hard with his good left leg and less hard with his right leg, which was weakened and barely mobile.

He found D'Arcy, still underwater, his eyes and mouth wide open. He grabbed his shirtfront and kicked wildly to bring them both back up to the surface. When they reached the air, D'Arcy began coughing and choking. Savage held him tightly about the chest and kicked with all his strength to keep both their heads above water. Suddenly the air was filled with diving bodies, then the water around them was crowded with men grasping hold of them, keeping them afloat.

Savage was stunned. Even though he and D'Arcy were in danger of drowning, how could so many men leave their stations in the midst of combat? No matter what the peril to him and D'Arcy, two men's lives did not justify abandoning battle stations when each active cannon could mean the difference between victory or defeat.

He was preparing to yell at the men surrounding him, just as soon as he could clear his throat of the water that was making him cough and choke . . . when he looked off to the south and saw the reason why so many men felt they could turn their attention away from the battle: the battle was over. The three-masted *Forrette* was angled bow up in the water, gurgling and churning the sea around her as she sank slowly down into it, her stern section already deep under. The big ship had taken too many balls at her water line, flooding her bilges and hold.

Savage thrashed around in the water for a moment more, and then—he felt it creeping up on him all along—he slowly lost consciousness. He came back awake hours later, after he had been raised by a rope cradle back aboard the ship. He was in his cabin now, on his own bed, wearing his sopping wet clothing. He jerked upright in the bed.

Richards was there, standing over D'Arcy who lay stomach down on the second bunk, waving a stiff square of canvas like a fan over D'Arcy's back. Savage got to his feet quickly and fell back down to the bed again instantly.

"Careful, Sir," said Richards, looking at him, "you're—"

"How is he?" Savage said. He stood up more slowly

this time and kept his balance while he walked over to where D'Arcy lay. Neither of Savage's legs were broken, he could see, though his right leg was still painful and weakened from the weight of the keg.

"Mr. Calhoun's not doing so very well. The Doc, he's been up to look him and you over, but had to rush back down to sickbay again. There's lots o' wounded down there."

Savage stood over D'Arcy. D'Arcy lay with his head to the side. His eyes were closed, his long hair stringy and disheveled. His back, covered with salve, was red and swollen—but not badly burned. It had been only seconds between the time his shirt had caught fire and he had plunged down to the ocean, quenching it. D'Arcy's face was dripping wet with sweat. Savage grabbed a cloth and wiped it. He looked at him closely. "Why does he seem to be doing so poorly, when the burns on his back aren't all that bad?"

"It's the shock to his body, the Doc says. He be in a shocked state. The burns'll heal, no problem there. But unless he comes quickly out o' the shock, he may not make it."

Richards had ceased fanning D'Arcy's back with the canvas while he answered Savage. Now his hands hung loosely at his sides.

"Fan him, damn you!" Savage shouted, "or I'll smash your blasted head in!"

Richards recoiled at the shout, as if slapped. He raised the fan and began furiously beating the air over D'Arcy's oiled back.

Savage pressed the heels of his palms to his eyes and took a deep breath to calm himself. After a minute, he squeezed Richards' shoulder in a gesture of apology. "I'm sorry, Richards." Richards was still too shaken, though, to respond. He kept beating the air furiously with the canvas fan.

Savage left the cabin and went up on deck. There was the strange stillness and quiet now that always followed after a battle, once the fires had been extinguished and the wounded evacuated belowdecks. The shattered bulwarks were the only testament to the fact that a battle had ever taken place. The noise of the cannons and the shouting of the men were gone. The stench of the gunpowder had dissipated to the wind. Even the blood that had stained the decks, and the coarse sand strewn about to make the decks less slippery, had been washed away, leaving the decks clean and drying in the baking sunlight.

He nodded to the men he passed and traded comments. He looked the ship over from stem to stern, pleased to see that the damage, while extensive, was not irreparable. Down in the sickbay he walked among the wounded, talking to them, trying to keep spirits high. His mind was not with him as he did these things. He was not paying attention to what he was doing. He was thinking of D'Arcy. Would he live?

During the next few days, life on the ship returned to normal. Repairs were made. The lightly wounded returned to their stations. And Savage set the ship back on its course for the secret cove on the English coast where they could continue their reprovisioning.

The only thing that did not change was D'Arcy's condition. He remained in a coma. The ship's surgeon had instructed two men to take him down to sickbay, but when they arrived at the Captain's cabin, Savage ordered them away angrily, telling them that First Mate Calhoun would remain in his cabin . . . until he was either healed—or dead. It would be one or the other, and according to the ship's surgeon, they would know which it was to be within a matter of days. If D'Arcy did not come out of his coma by then, he would die. It was as simple as that.

D'Arcy had taken to speaking deliriously at times. Savage had stood over him and heard him say many indecipherable words and sounds. Some of the words were understandable, though. D'Arcy often spoke the phrase, "Adreana, my dearest darling." And "Adreana, zay weel nevair part us. I love you, Adreana. I weel

325

love you always." Then one day, D'Arcy stunned Savage by mumbling a different phrase: "I love you, Jennyfair. I always weel love you, Jennyfair. Jennyfair, my dearest darling."

Savage stared at him. Then he shook his head and thought to himself how strange it was the way delirium could warp one's mind, confuse things.

"I always weel love you, Jennyfair," D'Arcy mumbled, tossing and turning in his delirium. "For the rest of my days." The rest of his mumbling was in French. Savage heard Jennifer's name spoken in the midst of an indecipherable French sentence.

Then one day, after tossing and turning wildly in his coma, D'Arcy shot bolt upright in his bed screaming, in the middle of the night. Savage lit a lantern and went over to him. The Frenchman was drenched in sweat, breathing heavily, his eyes wide open. "Eye-yi-yi," said D'Arcy, "such a nightmare I have, nevair do I want to have eet again."

Savage looked at him.

"Thees giant green monster," D'Arcy explained, gesturing animatedly, "he comes running after me on hees three legs, shouting at me as I flee from heem: 'Dinner!' he shouts. 'Dinner! Come back here, dinner!'" He shook his head and rubbed his hand through the golden hairs on his sweat-soaked chest.

"You know you've been in a coma for four days," Savage said to him quietly.

"Who? Me?"

And that was the end of his coma. He was perfectly healthy after that, and only in minor pain from the burns on his back. He asked what he had been babbling about while delirious, but Savage only shrugged and said he had not been listening. At various times afterward, though, D'Arcy would turn sharply and notice Savage staring at him with a strangely pensive look. Savage always looked away at these times and said nothing.

On the third day of the new month, they arrived in

the waters off the secret cove, where they lay at anchor while resupplying. On the tenth day of the month, D'Arcy and Savage set out on foot toward the resort of Crespi, several miles down the coast. Savage still had no idea what their expedition was about, but he had promised he would attend this secret rendezvous D'Arcy had arranged, and now that it was time, he went.

He kept wondering, as they hiked along the coast, what was behind this mysterious trip. He felt very curious, and as he looked at D'Arcy he also felt the slightest bit resentful, without knowing why.

Chapter 21

On the morning they were to leave for the resort, Matthew tried to back out of his promise to go. "I've got far, *far* too much work to do at the Ministry," he whined, "and besides, how does it *look*, did you ever give a thought to that? How does it *look* to have an assistant to the Minister go gallivanting off for a vacation when it's not even a holiday? Why, I'll be scorned as a work-shirker for sure if I do such a thing." He thrust with his sword at an imaginary enemy, then danced back a few paces, practicing his fencing moves for an upcoming competition.

"Matthew," Jennifer answered calmly, "you promised to go, and you will go." She was not perturbed by his last-minute resistance. She knew him well enough so that she had been expecting it, and had devised a means to counter his resistance. "And you needn't worry about the Minister thinking of you as a work-shirker, either."

"Needn't I?" His expression became sarcastic. "Why, pray tell," he said, his sword-hand on his hip, the other flitting about in the air, "need I not worry about a very legi*ti*mate concern, which will *cer*tainly be uppermost in the Minister's mind?"

"Because I've decided to stop letting my inhibitions prevent me from helping your career to the fullest measure possible."

"Meaning?"

"Meaning I'll go to bed with the Minister and with anyone else, if it'll advance you. I'll let nothing stand

328

in the way of your ascent through the upper ranks of government."

He was dumbfounded with delight. "Why, that's . . . why that's *won*derful!" he exclaimed. "Oh, Jennifer, you've finally seen the light! Oh, my goodness, *noth*ing can stop us now. Now we'll truly forge ahead, past all the others." He sheathed his blade and sat down on a footstool, an enthusiastic dreamy look in his eyes. He began laying plans to take immediate advantage of this new turn of events. "There's Lord Jensen who can do me much good, and then there's Towers in the Exchequer. And of course, Bryon Downsworth has been hungering to get into your skirt for God knows how long, ever since he saw you at the ball really. *He* can do me incredible good, with his enormous influence and connections."

He stood up, and clapped his hands, as if having reached a momentous decision. "That's it! Bryon Downsworth, we'll start with him, this very night! I'll go and arrange it."

"Wait," she said, stopping him with her hand on his arm as he began to leave the room. "Tonight we won't be here. Tonight we'll be in Crespi."

"Oh, but *dar*ling, surely we can put that off just the *short*est while? Till next week perhaps, or maybe in the spring."

She stood in the center of the high-ceilinged living room, shaking her head. "Matthew, you promised me this trip, and you promised it to celebrate my birthday, which is tomorrow. It's too important to me for you to put it off."

"Well, I don't see *why*," he complained disappointedly. "I mean, there really isn't all *that* much to *do* at the blasted place. Except look at the ocean. And I get seasick looking at the ocean anyway. Wouldn't you rather spend a fine thrilling night at the theatre?" he said, trying to persuade her with false enthusiasm. "And then afterward the three of us could come back here, and you and Bryon Downsworth could go to the bedchamber and—"

"There'll be time for that, Matthew," she said, coming up to him and putting her hands on his shoulders. It was important to keep him at ease and not irritate him. He had to be at ease when they were at the coast, or he would never speak freely of the subject she needed him to talk about. "I'll tell you what," she said, forcing herself to smile at him pleasantly. "The night after we return from the resort, then you can bring Downsworth in. And the Minister himself, if you like, on the night following. And after that, why anyone else you wish."

"I say, Jennifer, you *are* being quite accommodating. Well, in view of this, the very *least* I can do is help you celebrate your birthday on the coast as planned. After all, you didn't *really* think I'd renege, did you, after giving you my word?"

She said nothing. The butler appeared on his way into the study. "Oscar," she said to him, "please put our bags in the coach. They're packed and waiting upstairs."

Oscar looked at Matthew questioningly. Matthew sighed and then nodded. Oscar turned and went upstairs for the bags. Matthew said to Jennifer, in the manner of extracting an iron-clad promise, "You *will* spend the first night back with Downsworth, though? Or with the Minister, if he seems at that time to be more in a position to aid me?"

"Yes, Matthew, I will."

He withdrew his sword and began thrusting and lunging with it joyously, prancing about the room as if he were in a duel with a shadow figure. When the bags were loaded into the carriage, Matthew went up to dress in his most ostentatious sporting outfit—high-brimmed tri-corner hat, sporting coat with long tails, britches and knickers, and boots with polished buckles. Then they climbed into the carriage and began their trek to the coast.

The resort at Crespi consisted of several luxuriously appointed bungalows built closely together on a promontory overlooking the sea. Surrounding each bungalow were lush, thick bushes, shrubs, trees, and undergrowth spilling out from the forest at the rear of the cabins. The cabins formed a rough semicircle, at the center of which was a two-story lodge which provided dining and socializing facilities for the high officials and members of the nobility who frequented the resort.

Jennifer and Matthew arrived late the next morning, having spent a night at a roadside inn during their journey. While Matthew flung himself upon the giant goose-down bed, after instructing the resort servants on where to put their bags, Jennifer went out onto the patio veranda. Her scarlet and black, ankle-length cape caught the breeze and billowed slightly out from her body. Beneath the cape she wore a light travel dress of mint green muslin, with white lace cuffs at her three-quarters sleeves and a white lace collar that extended out to her shoulders. Her hair was done up in a bun.

"Jennifer, what the *devil* are you doing out there?" asked Matthew, with great weariness in his voice. She knew that inside he would be flat on his back on the bed, dabbing at his face with his silken kerchief. Ever since spending last night at the low-class inn, he had become increasingly irritable with each passing hour. "How can you have so much energy? I should think you'd want nothing more than to rest yourself before you collapse."

"In a minute, Matthew," she called to him from the veranda. "I want to see the view."

"Well *do* take care, darling. After all, your lovely body is quite important to us, you know, you must look after it properly."

She wanted to reply sarcastically to him, but she held her tongue. She could not risk showing her ire now. All her efforts had to be geared toward putting him completely at ease and not stirring up any suspicions of her antagonism toward him.

It was extremely hard for her to be even commonly civil to him now, much less pleasant. Now that she was so close to being rid of him, the full measure of her hatred and revulsion for the man rose up in her, threatening to suffocate her. His conniving, deceitful manner . . . his nasty way of pushing himself forward while trampling those who stood in his way . . . his hypocrisy . . . his *mean*ness . . . all these things which she had been forced to bear up under silently while living with him now made her want to retch. She detested the man. And it took all of her effort to not show it.

"Jennifer," Matthew scolded, "come in here right away. You'll catch your *death* of cold."

"It's hot out, Matthew."

"Well, you'll catch heat prostration then! Don't argue with me! Come back in here and rest yourself."

She made certain he could not see her. She took a red piece of ribbon from her pocket and tied it in a bow knot to the base of one of the railing posts which ran waist-high around the veranda. Then she went back inside.

Savage was still keenly curious about the nature of their secret mission. D'Arcy had not told him any more about it during the past night and day of their overland trek to Crespi. The resort now lay directly before them as they squatted down in the forest undergrowth looking out at the semicircle of bungalows. They had traveled through woods and back roads to get here, hiding from sight whenever anyone came near.

"Well," Savage said quietly, "so we're here. Now what?"

"We go around to ze front of ze bungalows," D'Arcy answered in the same quiet tone. "Where ze verandas face onto ze sea."

They crouched low as they made their way around to the front of the cabins, and as they then traveled through the dense green brush and shrubbery, which hid them from view. As they moved along from bungalow to bungalow, D'Arcy inspected their verandas. Finally he found what he was looking for and they stopped. "Wait here," D'Arcy said.

Savage looked at the veranda of the bungalow they had stopped in front of and saw the piece of red ribbon tied around one of the railing posts. He watched D'Arcy pull a similar piece of red ribbon from inside his shirt as he looked around to see which tree nearest them was the thickest and most conspicuous. The counter-signal to show that they had arrived, Savage figured, was to tie the ribbon to the tree. Whoever was in the bungalow would see it when they came onto the veranda.

D'Arcy moved off toward the tallest, thickest tree and stopped. He began to stand to his full height, so he could tie the ribbon in a conspicuous place, when suddenly someone came out from the cabin. D'Arcy ducked back down quickly.

Savage looked at the man who came out from the bungalow bedroom onto the veranda and his face registered a look of disbelieving shock. This was the short man who had taunted him from the guard tower at the prison! What was he doing here? What secret mission could possibly involve this man with D'Arcy and himself?

Before he had time to wonder further, the man turned around and shouted back into the bungalow: "Jennifer, you brought me all this distance just to see an *ocean*? My God, Jennifer, we could as easily have celebrated your birthday at *home,* putting a seascape over the mantel to lend the exact same effect." He went back into the cabin.

Savage looked at D'Arcy with an expression that was at first quizzical, but which quickly became furious when he saw D'Arcy's answering look of worry over Savage's reaction. So Jennifer really was here. D'Arcy had brought him out here to meet with Jennifer.

Savage began tromping angrily through the under-growth, back in the direction from which he had come. D'Arcy started after him. Savage made no attempt to stay hidden from view. As D'Arcy rushed after him, he kept glancing nervously over at the bungalows, and all around them, to make sure they were not being watched.

"Lancelot!" D'Arcy called under his breath, grasping his shoulder when he was near enough.

Savage shoved the hand off his shoulder angrily, and continued stalking away. D'Arcy looked quickly around them, and followed. When they were in the tall trees of the forest, far enough away from the bungalows to allow talking, D'Arcy caught up with him again, grabbed his arm, and spun him around to face him. "Lancelot, you must listen to me."

"Listen to a turncoat?" Savage said bitterly, his eyes fierce. "So you can lie to me some more? So you can trick me again?"

"Lancelot, what I did, I did for you. You do not understand ze situation. You do not know ze truth of why Jennyfair lived weeth ze Governor."

"I told you never to mention that name to me again!" His face was contorted in fury, his teeth bared, his hands clenched into fists.

D'Arcy realized he had to tread lightly now. Savage was like a wounded animal. He was in such pain and torment over his feelings for Jennifer, he might lash out wildly at any moment. "You love her so much you are crazy weeth eet," D'Arcy said, trying to make him see. "Can you not give just a few moments to hear ze truth?"

"I'll not give a second to help that bitch!"

"To help *you,* Lancelot. Eet eez you who are crazy with ze pain, thinking zat she turn against you."

Savage slugged him hard in the face, knocking his head to the side.

D'Arcy turned back to face him, his eyes raging. But he did not strike him back. "Lancelot," he said, his voice filled with determination, "you will have to come back weeth me and listen to what zay say to each other. I have given my word zat I will take you zair. And, because I love you and cannot let you slowly keel yourself zis way, I *weel* take you zair. I am bigger zan you. I weel take you zair even if I have to peek you up and carry you."

Savage's eyes narrowed. He drew his sword from its sheath and stepped back a pace to give himself room to swing.

D'Arcy did not draw his sword. He moved a step forward, putting himself within range of Savage's weapon. Savage's hand raised up high, ready to slash down with the sword. His teeth were bared, his eyes murderous. D'Arcy took a step closer. "Stand fast," Savage commanded. D'Arcy could hear Savage's angry breathing and see his nostrils flaring. He moved a step closer, putting himself chest to chest with Savage and eye to eye. "Lancelot," he said softly, "you owe thees thing to me."

Savage looked at him piercingly for a long moment, his raised sword trembling with the tension of his grip, then he thrust the weapon back into its sheath.

"I'll go back," Savage said. "I'll listen to what you want me to. As you say, I owe it to you for saving my life. But then after I do this, we're through, you and I. I don't want to have to see you again." His voice was coldly metallic, his eyes ruthlessly intense. "You can return to the ship before I get there. Take a boat and go to the cove where Ambrewster reprovisions the *McCarty*. Join his crew. Or join the bloody Redcoats for all I give a damn. Just stay out of my sight. We're enemies. If I see you after this, there's a good chance I'll kill you."

D'Arcy's head was lowered as he listened to this. He felt great pain, hearing these words from his dearest friend. But there was nothing he could do, nothing he could say in response. Finally, he nodded. Then he turned and started back through the forest, toward the bungalows. Savage followed.

They crouched and went back to the spot where they had originally stationed themselves, in front of the cabin with the red ribbon on the veranda post. Then D'Arcy went to the thickest tree nearby and tied his piece of red ribbon to a prominent branch. He returned in a low crouch.

Savage was sitting with his back against the trunk of a tree now, his legs stretched out before him, facing away from the bungalow. He stared moodily out at the great expanse of blue ocean off in the distance and at the white gulls dotting the air above it. He said nothing to D'Arcy and refused even to glance in his direction. D'Arcy sat down also, facing the patio of the bungalow. He too said nothing. He waited, grimly.

Inside the cabin, Jennifer was feeling very tense. Her stomach was in knots. Would D'Arcy succeed in bringing Savage? she wondered. If he did, then she would soon have to go outside to the veranda, with Matthew, and begin the conversation she hoped would set straight the true facts and regain Savage's love for her.

What if something should go wrong? she thought in horror. What if she could not make him speak of it, or worse, if he spoke of it but in such a way as to distort the facts? This was her last chance. If she did not succeed in convincing Savage of the truth now, she never would.

She looked at Matthew, who was practicing his fencing exercises again, parrying and thrusting with his sword, dancing swiftly to and fro. He glanced at her and frowned.

"A birthday celebration indeed," he said nastily. "We could have done as much celebrating at home and with far less inconvenience." He thrust at an imaginary foe, his free hand on his hip, his sword arm raised up with the wrist lowered to aim the swordpoint downward.

"I told you, Matthew, the main reason we're here is so we can talk about the next step in advancing your career. We could never do it at home. You never gave me your full attention."

"Well? So talk," he said, not looking at her. He lunged at the air, going down on one knee.

Jennifer walked out onto the veranda and looked searchingly at the brush and trees and undergrowth before her. She was almost startled when she saw the red ribbon tied around the branch of a big tree several yards away. She scanned the forest floor, but saw nothing.

She was extremely tense. Calm down, she said to herself. Don't ruin it by showing how nervous you are. She took several deep breaths, smoothed down the pleats of her skirt, raised her chin, and went back inside.

"Matthew," she said, in a casual, almost gay voice, "I *have* helped your career, haven't I?"

He glanced at her. "Oh, I sup*pose* you've been a bit of a boon. It's debatable, though, whether you've been boon enough to be worth the thousand pounds I paid for you."

"But haven't I been? I arranged the trade with the House of Calhoun. And I—" she lowered her eyes "I put you into the good graces of the Minister."

He laughed sneeringly. "Yes, you were *so* cooperative in that venture."

"I've promised to be cooperative in the future, though. With the Minister and any others you wish. Don't forget that."

"What are you getting at?" he asked suspiciously. "What's the point of all this self-congratulation?"

"I just want there to be a truce between us for awhile. I'm tired of always bickering and fighting. I'm on your side, surely you can see it. Can't we stop fighting, and relax with each other for awhile, so we can discuss your career in peace? Just ease off on the . . . the hostility you always have toward me."

337

He smirked. And then he sighed. "*Well,* dearest, it's not as if you're the essence of pristine purity, who deserves to be ad*mired.* But yes, I sup*pose* I can be big enough to treat you with a bit of mildness. Though I really don't know why—"

"Here," she said, backing toward the veranda, "let's go outside while we talk. It's so much nicer."

He sighed again in an exaggerated, tolerant manner. Then, with a great show of magnanimity, he put his sword away in the sheath on the bed and came out to the veranda. He leaned over the railing and gazed out at the greenery and at the sea beyond.

Jennifer sat down on one of the wicker porch chairs. "Maybe we can best figure out where to go from here with your career if we backtrack a bit and looked at your past accomplishments."

"That's a *mar*velous idea," he said, suddenly elated. The prospect of reliving the glory of his past coups pleased him greatly. He turned to face her, leaning back against the railing. "Well, I suppose my most *note*worthy achievement," he said, smiling at the recollection, "was placing that informant within the ranks of the Sons of Liberty. *My,* but that was a stroke of brilliance! You see, what I did was—"

"Wait, Matthew. I was thinking of . . . maybe we should look at more recent accomplishments." Her voice was becoming high and taut. *Calm down,* she ordered herself. "Maybe we should talk about how you arranged to have me . . . move in with the Governor."

"Ah yes, that little coup." He shook his head happily, smiling wistfully, obviously pleased with himself. "The trick to that one," he recalled, "was in not letting you know what you were getting into. Not coming out and actually *saying* it. You see, I knew you'd never consent to the arrangement if I spelled it out for you, no matter *how* much you loved your pirate. If I said, 'You must live with the Governor for a year as his mistress, to spare your pirate from the gallows,' why, you'd have thrown me out. Wouldn't you have?"

Jennifer lowered her eyes and said nothing.

"So I knew I had to *finesse* the situation. That's when the idea came to me: have the pirate right outside the window, being beaten to a bloody pulp, when the Governor put the offer to you! A stroke of *gen*ius, eh? You'd actually *see* him being beaten. *Then* you couldn't refuse the Governor's offer, could you? Knowing the price of your precious *virtue*"—he spat out the word—"would be the agonizing death of your lover. You couldn't refuse the arrangement then, could you, eh?"

"No," she said quietly. "I couldn't refuse it."

He laughed, pleased with himself. "You see? I arranged it *per*fectly. And not only that, but I *al*most managed to do him in anyway, in spite of the agreement. What I did was, I went to the prison and when I saw him, I *told* him about your little dalliance with His Excellency!" He clapped his hands together in delighted appreciation of his maneuver. "I *knew* it would drive him berserk, and well, of course it *did*. It drove him to attempt an escape, which *surely* should have resulted in his death." He scowled. "But alas, he somehow managed to bring it off, the bugger. Pity."

He grinned mischievously at Jennifer. "*You* knew, too, that the knowlege of your living with the Governor would drive him to attempt a probably fatal escape. That's why you lied to him when you went to visit him at the prison, isn't it?"

She looked up, surprised. "How did you know about that?"

He chuckled. "My good friend the captain told me of your visit. But as for how I knew that you *lied* to your pirate . . . *well*, it's *merely* the application of logic, dearest. I mean, it stands to reason, doesn't it? You knew if you told him the truth, he wouldn't stand for it. He'd order you to cease the arrangement with the Governor, in which case he'd be hung immediately. If you complied. But since you would *not* comply, he'd attempt an escape so that you'd no longer have *reason* to sacrifice yourself for him, since he'd be dead. So . . . to save his life, you did the only thing you could do. You lied to him."

"Yes," she said. "To save his life."

Matthew yawned. "I'm becoming bored with this tale. Let me tell you about another coup, about how I knew your grandfather Silas was printing documents. Now *there* was *real* treachery and cunning. What I'm about to tell you—"

"Will be the last words you'll ever tell anyone." The strong male voice came from down beneath them.

Matthew jerked about frantically and looked down. There, in front of the raised veranda, stood Lancelot Savage, his face grim, his fists on his hips.

Matthew's jaw dropped open. He turned to Jennifer and for a split second glared at her. Then he slapped her across the face and ran for the front door of the bungalow. Savage jumped up to grab hold of the veranda railing, then pulled himself onto the veranda. Matthew was at the front door by now. He jerked it open and started to rush through it, only to bump into the chest of D'Arcy Calhoun, who stood outside the doorway, blocking it. Matthew backed into the room. D'Arcy came in after him, closing the door.

Matthew saw Savage unsheath his blade and hold it down at his side. He looked at D'Arcy, who made no move to arm himself. Then he looked at his own sheathed blade lying nearby on the bed. He lunged at it, but fumbled trying to draw it out from its scabbard. Looking around feverishly, though, he saw that there was no hurry. No one was making any move to prevent him from drawing his weapon. In fact, Savage was standing still, patiently waiting for him to do so. D'Arcy was standing with his hands folded across his chest.

"So," said Matthew, a tight grin creeping over his thin lips. "It's to be a fair fight, is it? A duel of honor?" He bowed formally, mockingly, and yanked the blade free of its scabbard.

"Lancelot," Jennifer warned, "he's a master swords-man!"

"*En garde!*" shouted Matthew, raising his sword into the air with a flourish, then advancing on Savage so swiftly and expertly that Savage had no time to execute an effective parry. The blade sliced into Savage's forearm, cutting through his blouse and into his skin.

Savage began fighting back. They dueled furiously for several minutes, Savage standing mostly in place, retreating back occasionally, while Matthew danced about the room, hither and yon, clearly enjoying the advantage. Savage was busy fending off the adroitly executed thrusts and feints and lunges.

Jennifer went over to D'Arcy and stood near him as she watched the vicious combat, frightened for Savage's life. D'Arcy's arm went around her shoulders protectively. "Lancelot," Jennifer breathed, "kill him."

"True loyalty," laughed Matthew, lunging quickly, scraping the flesh on Savage's hip. "Your allegiance to me knows no bounds, does it, *dear*est?"

Jennifer watched Savage fending off Matthew's advances, occasionally making a strike of his own. She watched his taut, purposeful face, which was even more handsome than she had remembered it. She became deathly frightened as each new thrust of Matthew's sword landed nearer to his torso.

Matthew began talking continuously as he dueled, believing that if he could incite his adversary to blind anger, the man's rage would overcome his skill. "Your precious *Jen*nifer is a soiled article, pirate. How un-dis*crim*inating of you to still want her. I believe I mentioned to you that I *pers*onally have laid my own hands on her."

"Kill him, Lancelot," Jennifer said, through clenched teeth.

"And of course, His Excellency the Governor has laid various parts of his anatomy on her. Or in her, as the case may be."

"Kill him," she breathed, feeling the bile and hatred

341

rise up into her throat. Oh *God,* she hated this man! She *detested* him. The horrid, wretched tortures she had gone through these past months had all been his doing. He had engineered every bit of it! And she had had to keep her silence, pretend to be his ally. She had been forced to silently swallow her hatred of him, all the while smiling so he would not suspect her true feelings. Now it all was coming back to her, the utter loathing she felt for this cretin who had killed her grandfather, who had despoiled her body and tortured her soul.

"Then too," taunted Matthew, "there was Minister Kensington. Oh, I *must* tell you about that one."

"Kill him!" she shouted, insane with rage. She started forward toward Matthew. D'Arcy had to hold her back. "Kill the scum, Lancelot. Slice him to pieces!"

But Savage was in no position to kill Matthew Armitage. His opponent's fancy swordplay was easily keeping him at bay. His only chance lay in gaining an opportunity to use his street-fighting savvy, which the dandy would not be able to counter. He kept looking for an opening. He knew it would come soon; Matthew was enjoying himself too much, grinning and mockingly play-acting with his sword. He was becoming overconfident.

"And now, Mr. Pirate," said Matthew, executing a flurry of thrusts that made Savage retreat backward, "if I may be permitted the *coup de grace.*" He was about to lunge forward a final, fatal time, when Savage withdrew the scarf from around his neck, wrapped it about the blade end of his sword, and grasped the sword-blade with both hands.

Matthew looked stunned. Exploiting Matthew's surprise, Savage began advancing forward, swirling the sword in a circle over his head and at his side, forcing Matthew to retreat backward to avoid being smashed by the heavy swinging hilt. Matthew looked fearful and confused. No one had ever attacked him this way before. How did one respond to such an attack? Desperate to halt Savage's advance, he made a rash move, thrusting in under the swing of the sword. Savage lowered the angle of his circle, bringing the hilt smashing down on Matthew's blade, snapping it in two. Then Savage stepped in with his boot and kicked Matthew sharply in the groin.

Matthew shrieked and doubled over, grasping himself. Savage took the scarf away from his blade and grasped the sword properly by the hilt.

"Spare me!" cried Matthew, still bent over, clutching himself. "Oh, spare me, spare me, I beg you!" He began crying. Savage lowered the point of his blade toward the man's chest, and without hesitation, ran him through. Matthew Armitage collapsed to the floor, silent and unmoving.

Savage wiped his blade clean on the man's silken shirt, then resheathed it. He looked at Jennifer.

She looked back at him, uncertainty in her eyes, desperate hope in her heart. "Lancelot?" she said.

He stood looking at her, unmoving, his face expressionless. Then the hard features of his face relaxed. His eyes became gentle. "My love," he said softly.

She rushed into his arms. He squeezed her tightly to him. One hand moved to her head and began stroking her hair. "Oh, Lancelot," she said, the words sounding like a sob. Tears welled up in her eyes.

"I love you, Jennifer," he said, in the deep manly voice that had once been so familiar. How long had it been since she had heard these words from him? How many torturous, agonizing months had she gone not knowing if she would ever hear them again?

"I love you," he said, squeezing her tightly. "Forgive me for doubting you. I could kill myself for the pain I've put you through."

She hugged him and let her head rest against his chest for a long while. Then he was grasping her shoulders and pushing her back so he could look in her eyes. His bright slate gray eyes were filled with emotion. She looked at the strong mouth, the prominent

343

cheekbones, the hollows under his eyes. God, how long it had been! How long since she had seen this face close to hers, looking at her lovingly. Deep stirrings of yearning spread through her.

He put his hand to the back of her head, clutching her hair, and brought her face close to his. His lips descended on hers, pressing hard against them, forcing her lips wide apart. Her head was bent backward, his mouth searingly on hers. His hand at the small of her back pressed her body tightly against his. She felt his throbbing manhood pressing against her loins, spreading languorous, sensuous feelings all through her. She would have gasped from the thrill of the sensation, but his mouth was still on hers, his tongue probing inside.

The frustration she felt was so sharp it was almost painful when she heard D'Arcy say gently, from the veranda where he now stood, "Lancelot. We must go."

Savage pulled his head back and looked at her again. He grinned his mocking, loving grin, which taunted and excited her. She stuck her tongue out and licked his lips. He grinned more broadly and then, with great reluctance, released her and stepped back.

Savage went to D'Arcy, who was outside on the veranda, looking around at the two other bungalows—one on either side—which were within viewing distance of them.

"I see no activity," D'Arcy said. "I believe no one watched as we came into ze cabin."

"I wish there was a way we could make sure no one's watching when we leave."

"I weesh zat also. But we cannot wait for ze nightfall."

"Can't we?" asked Jennifer.

"No," said Savage. "They'll wonder why your swordsman here didn't come to the main lodge for dinner, and send someone out to check. Besides, the longer the *Liberty* stays at anchor in the cove, the better the chances of her being discovered. We can't wait seven or eight hours here until it's dark."

344

Savage and D'Arcy discussed the best way to handle the situation, and decided that Matthew's body would have to be dragged out into the forest. If they left it in the bungalow, it would be discovered as soon as the proprietors of the resort became suspicious and started looking around. If they hid it in the forest, it would give them extra time before a report went out to the authorities. Especially since Jennifer would go to the lodge and tell them that she and Matthew were about to stroll down to the beach and not to worry if they were not back early.

There was a danger of being seen by the guests in the two neighboring bungalows as they dropped Matthew's body over the edge of the veranda and then climbed down themselves. But the danger existed whether they carried Matthew with them or not. Either way, Savage and D'Arcy had to leave the cabin secretively and they ran the risk of being seen and reported while doing so.

Matthew's body was wrapped in a blanket and the plan was put into action. Savage checked the neighboring verandas to make sure no one was out there watching, then he and D'Arcy shoved the blanket-wrapped corpse over the side. Then they jumped down together into the undergrowth and quickly carried the corpse off deep into the forest, crouching low to avoid being seen as they traveled.

Jennifer cleaned the blood off the floor and off Matthew's sword, resheathed the sword, then went out the front door to the lodge office. Part of her task was to see if the people there were calm, or if they were agitated due to a report of someone having seen men dropping off a balcony and rushing through the forest carrying a blanket-wrapped bundle.

The clerk she talked to was calm, businesslike and impersonal. He nodded when she told him that she and Matthew were going to take a stroll down to the beach and were bringing a blanket to sit on. "Very good, Madam," he said, smiling in an impersonal, officious way.

She went back to her bungalow, but instead of going inside, she walked around the side of it to the veranda facing the sea, acting very casual in case she was being observed. Then, when she was out of sight of the lodge, she went into the high undergrowth and rushed forward in a bent-over crouch toward the forest. Savage spotted her when she was near, before she spotted him. "Over here," he called. She came over just as they were putting the finishing touches to a mound of branches, brush and leaves, under which they had hidden the corpse from sight.

"Well," said D'Arcy, standing up. He had been on his knees, arranging branches. "We go now, eh?"

"D'Arcy," Savage said.

D'Arcy looked at him.

"Those things I said before. About your being a turncoat and my not wanting to have you around anymore . . ."

D'Arcy grinned and dismissed his comment with a wave of his hand. "Eef I believe all ze crazy things you say to me, I become as crazy as you."

Jennifer watched as Savage slapped D'Arcy hard on the upper arm, affectionately, and kept his hand there, looking his friend straight in the eye. D'Arcy reciprocated by slapping Savage hard on the arm also and squeezing his shoulder. Then they released each other, and without a further word the three of them began the overland trek back toward the cove where the *Liberty* was anchored.

They traveled for seven hours with hardly any rest stops at all. By the time Savage finally decided it was too dark to travel and that it was time to make camp for the night, Jennifer was completely exhausted. She collapsed on the forest floor, leaned back against a tree, and breathed the crisp night air, letting her muscles relax. She listened to the chirping sounds of the crickets and the other night creatures. She looked up through the tops of the trees at the bright stars twinkling in the dark blue sky. There was a pleasant fragrance of moisture and greenness in the woods.

After a few minutes, D'Arcy built a fire. The woods were so dense at the place where they were encamped, there was no danger of the fire being spotted from a distance. Dinner consisted of dried provisions and a *bota* bag of water D'Arcy and Savage had brought from the ship, along with an unfamiliar sweet nectar fruit Savage had found in the forest.

After dinner, D'Arcy stood up and said, in a voice that sounded very awkward and self-conscious, "Well, I think I go for a walk in ze woods now."

Jennifer was astonished. "You're going for a *walk*? After half a day of tramping through the woods, wearing your feet down to the bone?"

D'Arcy just stood there, looking awkward and embarrassed. He glanced at Savage. Savage did not return his look; his eyes were directed at the fire, which he was busying himself feeding with fresh wood, as he crouched before it. Then D'Arcy glanced at Jennifer. Finally she understood and lowered her eyes. D'Arcy walked away from the small clearing they were in and disappeared into the forest.

After a minute, Savage stood up. He came over to Jennifer and stood gazing down at her. She looked up at the handsome strong face of the man she loved, and suddenly all the fatigue and weariness miraculously left her body. In its place she felt a sensation of lightness and a thrill of expectation. It's been so long, she thought. She let her eyes travel down his body to the swelling bulge straining at his britches. . . .

Chapter 22

Savage bent forward and took her hands, then raised her to her feet. She felt his arms go around her as she put her hands on his broad shoulders. She looked in his slate gray eyes, feeling the slightest bit fearful and uncertain. How long had it been since they were last together? Well over a year. That same old mocking, taunting look was still in his eyes.

He pulled her against him and she felt the hard roll-shaped bulge pressing against the thin material of her dress. His hands clutched her buttocks and squeezed. For a moment he squeezed too tightly and it hurt her. Then he relaxed his grip.

She cocked her head to the side and parted her moist lips. She tried to kiss him and was surprised when he held his head back, not letting her. He continued looking at her with that smug, slightly superior grin, while pulling her hips so tightly against him. She could feel the heat of his sex directly against her loins. A warm, languorous feeling flowed through her.

Savage put his hands to the buttons of her dress and began unfastening them. He opened the front of her dress and pushed the dress down her shoulders, then freed her arms from the sleeves. He pushed the dress down to her waist, along with the slip she wore beneath it. She clasped her arms tightly about his neck, her cheek against his chest. She felt the linen of his shirt against her naked breasts. Savage's hands stroked her up and down her flanks, along the sides of her breasts. His fingers crept in between their two bodies and began fondling and kneading her breasts. She closed her eyes and let out a soft moan, as the tingling thrill of pleasure began to wash over her. He pushed the dress and slip down past her hips, his fingers hooking into the top of her underdrawers as he did so and pulling them down also. He pushed the bunched up garments down past her knees and made her step out of them.

He stepped back to look at her firm, full body as it was illuminated by the orange yellow glow of the flickering campfire. Jennifer stood with her hands clasped in front of her, touching her lips, her elbows close together over her breasts, partially hiding them. Savage pushed away her hands. Then he stepped back again to gaze at her as she stood nakedly, her hands at her sides, her breasts rising and falling with her excited breathing. Her lips were parted, her eyes half closed.

He pulled off his shirt and then his boots. He made her stand there watching him as he slowly undid his britches, slid them down his legs, and stepped out of them. His body was harder and straighter than she had remembered it. And more scarred. Bruises and welts were everywhere on his skin. Still, as the glow from the campfire flickered across him, it made him appear like a golden statue, the bruises and scars making him seem, strangely, even more sensual and exciting.

Her eyes traveled down across his flat stomach to the thick, strong jutting shaft of his manhood. He seemed to have planned this, the direction her eyes would take. He stood with his legs braced apart, hands away from his sides, grinning at the way her eyes were fixated upon him. She tried to smile back at him, but the expression that passed over her face was not a grin, she knew. It was a look of deep, agonizing love for this man, whom she felt so intensely about that she thought she would cry. "I love you, Lancelot," she said.

He lowered her onto the moist forest floor. She felt the coolness of the grass against her shoulder blades and buttocks. He nudged her knees apart and came down on top of her, slowly pressing into her. He began to move in and out of her with a wildness that galvanized her with sensation. Her love for him, and the physical intensity of the pleasure sweeping over her, mixed together to make her feel she was losing her mind. Her mind seemed to evaporate as her body took over completely and soon she was writhing and moaning and whimpering like a helpless animal.

Stop it, she ordered herself, D'Arcy will hear! But she was beyond self-control now, she was nothing but a volcano of wildly sensitive nerve endings, inflamed with passion. Soon Savage's body began to tense rigidly, and she heard a groan of pleasure that she knew he tried to suppress but could not. She locked her legs tightly about his hips and squeezed with all her might.

After an eternity of bliss, the shuddering of their bodies ceased. Savage raised his head up and looked at her. "My love," he said. His eyes were filled with emoion.

But then, suddenly, it seemed as if the love in his eyes somehow clouded over and, for a moment, it looked as if his eyes became dark with bitterness as he gazed at her. She could not tell for sure, for he rolled off her almost instantly when the bitterness seemed to appear and he began dressing. She watched him dress. No, she thought, it must have been her imagination. . . .

She looked at his face as he turned toward her, and she cast her doubts aside. There was certainly no bitterness there now. Love welled up in her like a blossoming flower. Savage lay back down beside her and put his hands on her naked back. She laid her head against his chest and let herself be hugged. Soon she began to feel the chill of the night air on her skin. Goosebumps arose. She stood and began dressing. She watched Savage watching her. Her feelings for him, and her happiness, were so strong, she felt as if she might cry from the fullness of the emotions.

She was lying with her head against Savage's chest, his arm around her, when D'Arcy reentered the clearing. He had preceded his entrance by a noisy thrashing about in the bushes that would have done justice to a herd of wild stallions. When he came into the clearing, he squatted down in front of the fire and rubbed his hands together, then held his palms out toward the warmth.

Jennifer expected him to make some joke about the wilderness he had just come from, or about anything else—joking was his usual manner. But his face, as he now glanced at her sharply, was serious and forbidding. She had wanted to smile at him, but now she did not dare. There was too much tension in his manner. Without a word, D'Arcy lay down on the ground, where the grass matting was particularly thick, and closed his eyes.

Jennifer frowned. She was glad they would reach the cove and the *Liberty* sometime tomorrow. This situation of her and Savage being together, with D'Arcy being the odd man out, was having a bad effect on D'Arcy. Clearly such a situation could not last for more than a day or so without becoming explosive. It would be easier once they were on the ship. There would be other distractions to take D'Arcy's mind off of her. And more important, they would no longer be a group of only three, with D'Arcy's outsider status painfully blown up out of proportion.

Yes, she thought, she was glad they would reach the *Liberty* tomorrow. Things could not continue this way for much longer than that.

She looked at Savage. His eyes were closed, his face relaxed. He was breathing evenly. She snuggled up against him warmly, her face in the crook of his shoulder and neck. She felt satisfied and fulfilled. There was a tinge of irritating bewilderment about the bitterness she thought she saw in his eyes, but she dismissed this from her mind. She closed her eyes, and slowly, with a smile playing across her lips, drifted off to sleep.

With the first rays of sunlight, they awoke and continued their journey. Early in the afternoon, they crested a grassy knoll that looked down on the sea and on the cove where Savage had left the *Liberty* anchored offshore.

The *Liberty* was gone. The sea beyond the cove was filled with English ships, combing the water in obvious search of something. The beach where the dingy had been hidden was bristling with Redcoats, rushing to and fro, checking the surrounding area. The dingy had been discovered, and Redcoats were inside and all around it, looking it over. Jennifer put her wrist to her mouth in shock.

Savage jerked her down with him to the ground. The three of them lay in the grass, peering over the crest of the knoll.

"They're fanning out from the beach," Savage said to D'Arcy.

"Zay must have arrived in only ze last few minutes."

Savage watched a moment longer, his expression grim. "Let's get out of here," he said. "Back into the woods."

Jennifer was so astounded by the sight below, she did not move. She just lay on the knoll, looking down, watching with alarm and fascination. Savage grasped her hand and jerked her to her feet. The three of them ran back toward the woods from which they had just come.

They ran into the woods, through thickets and briars, rushing to get away from the Redcoat troops who already were fanning out, preparing to search in their direction.

Jennifer kept tripping over the hem of her long dress as she ran. After she did this twice, with Savage and D'Arcy helping her back to her feet each time, Savage said to her, "Tie the hem up around your waist." She did not want to do that. Instead, she grasped her skirt about midway down its length and raised it up so that the hem was higher, coming to about the level of her knees.

This did not work well, though. She could not run as quickly through the woods with her hands down at her sides holding her skirt. Savage turned his head back to see why she was still running slowly. When he saw, he dropped back to her and in a swift, unhesitant motion, put his hands to her dress and *yanked* it hard just below the waist.

The seam holding the waist to the upper portion split. He yanked again, tearing the skirt completely down. They stopped running so Jennifer would not trip, now that her legs were impeded by the loose material. Savage made her step out of it, then he bunched it up into a ball and stuck it inside his open shirt. He grabbed her hand and they began running again.

Jennifer was wearing only a half-slip, which came down to several inches above her knees. It was meant to be worn with pantaloons, but she had not worn pantaloons today. She wished she had. As they ran, the bushes and shrubs nicked at her bare legs, scratching them. That was not the worst of it, though. Even more unsettling was the fact that D'Arcy was behind her as they ran along in a single file. Jennifer felt terribly exposed. Her long legs were bare, her hips and lower body were covered only by the thin linen slip that kept riding up to her scanty underdrawers as she ran.

She was so embarrassed by fears that he was staring at her that she turned her head back to look, to assure herself she was just imagining it . . . that he had far more urgent matters to be concerned with at the moment than the shape of her derriere. But when she looked, she saw that her fears were justified. He was staring fixedly at the place where the hem of her slip kept riding up to her undergarment.

She shot him an angry glare. He looked up and grinned. "I am *français*," he said, as if this explained his behavior.

353

"Well, stop it!" she ordered, blushing angrily.

Savage glanced back to see what the commotion was about. He saw nothing worthy of his attention, turned his eyes forward again, and continued running and pulling her with him deeper into the woods.

After a long period of nonstop running, Jennifer thought she could go no further. She was panting and gasping for breath, and the muscles in her legs seemed unable to continue pushing her forward. Savage and D'Arcy were panting also and their bodies were sweating, but neither of them seemed even close to slackening their pace.

She did not want to say anything. She continued running as long as her legs would carry her forward, keeping her silence, hoping that Savage would call a stop so they could rest and catch their breaths. Finally, her legs caved in and she stumbled to the ground, unable to force herself back to her feet. Savage, holding her hand, knew instantly that she had fallen. He turned quickly, scooped her up in his arms and continued moving deeper into the forest.

"I can keep running," she said to him, gasping for breath, "I just need . . . just a rest. Only a few minutes . . ."

"We don't have a few minutes," he panted. "They'll be combing the woods for us. The deeper we get into it now, the better our chances."

She tightened her arms about his shoulders.

"All those troopers on the beach," Savage said. "What a response to a simple killing! Who was that dwarf anyway? Back in the Colony, I never even heard of him."

"He was in the government here," she said. "They made him assistant to a minister."

Savage hiked her up higher in his arms, readjusting her weight to keep his arms from weakening. "Jennifer, my love," he panted, "next time you save me from the hangman, please, make the arrangements with a low-level lackey? Someone they won't send half a regiment to avenge."

After several more minutes of running, when Savage's muscles were weakening so much under the strain of carrying her that she began sagging in his arms, D'Arcy came up even with Savage and said, "Shall I take her from you?"

Jennifer instantly felt a sharp sense of foreboding. Don't let him do it! she thought. She knew through her intuition that it would cause problems later. She wanted to warn Savage, but there was nothing she could say without offending D'Arcy.

Savage did not even bother to reply. Instead, he swiveled to the side D'Arcy had come up on and pressed her against the Frenchman's chest. D'Arcy's arms went under her back and beneath her bare upper legs. To keep from falling during the transfer, she had to put her arms around his neck.

The Frenchman smiled at her. Jennifer looked away. She knew right then, for certain, there would be trouble among the three of them during the trek that lay ahead. D'Arcy's smile was not one of only sexual interest. That she could have handled, safe in the knowledge that he never would force himself on her. He was too gentle and cared for her too much. *That* was the problem and it showed in his smile: he did care for her. He had feelings of protectiveness and warmth for her, and—but she did not want to think of this now. She turned her eyes to the front and watched the branches and leaves of the trees go by as they rushed forward.

Finally, when Savage and D'Arcy both reached the point where they could run no further, they collapsed onto the forest floor and lay there panting and gasping for breath. D'Arcy had set Jennifer down on a heap of dead leaves near a tree. She sat up, her legs curled under her, watching Savage anxiously.

Savage was on his stomach, his hands near his head. When his body stopped heaving with the violent intake of air into his lungs, when he was relaxed enough to breath normally, he turned over onto his back. She had been waiting for this. She crawled over to him and reached inside his shirt. She withdrew the torn material that was her skirt, pulled it over her head, and pushed it down to cover her legs.

"We're safe from zem now you think?" D'Arcy asked.

"For a while. We're deep enough in here that they'll have to spread their men thin, as they fan out in a semi-circle from the beach. If any of them come across us, they'll just be scouts, not a full patrol."

D'Arcy stood up. He took his knife from its scabbard, went to a young sapling, and began slicing at its springy green bark. "So now we go north, eh?"

Savage nodded. "That's probably where Harlan would sail to. To the inlet cove near the border with the Scots. The one we used to hide in two, maybe three years back. You remember it?"

"I remember eet well. Zair was zat Scotch *fille* who found us on ze beach ze last day we stay zair." He turned to Jennifer and grinned. "She fall in love weeth me. I cannot help eet! I try to fight her off, but no, she fall een love weeth me and zen, right on ze beach, I lose my . . . how you say? . . . my virtue."

"Yes," said Savage. "For only the hundredth time."

D'Arcy continued slicing at the tree's pliant green bark. Finally he managed to strip back a long cord of it. He hacked it off at the base of the tree, grasped it in both hands, and pulled at the ends to show its strength. Then he walked to Jennifer and handed it to her. "To tie ze skirt back into place."

"Thank you, D'Arcy." She wrapped the cord around her waist and tied it into place with a knot. Then she raised the skirtwaist high enough over it so that the hem came up to her knees, where it would not hinder her from running.

"It's a three week journey, I'd say," said Savage, "from here to the old cove. Keeping to the woods as

356

much as we can, moving along back roads when we're out of the woods. Judging from the strength of troops they sent out to the beach when the longboat was discovered, they'll be looking for us long and hard. We'll have to stick to untraveled territory as much as we can."

D'Arcy agreed. He pulled off the sack that was lashed to his back by a strap, which cut diagonally across his torso. He looked at the meager remains of the provisions they had brought and sighed. He took out the *bota* bag of water and handed it to Jennifer. She drank a few swallows from it greedily, soothing her parched throat. She wanted to drink more, but there was not enough for her to do so. She handed it to Savage. Savage drank sparingly also, then gave it to D'Arcy, who finished it off.

Savage rose to his feet. He reached his hand out to Jennifer, and helped her up. Then the three of them resumed their trek through the forest.

That night, D'Arcy again went for a convenient "walk in the woods," though this time more grudgingly. When he was gone, Savage came over to where Jennifer stood by the campfire, put his arms around her, and began undressing her.

She was taken aback by the suddeness and by the lack of prelude. He did not kiss her, did not hug her. He simply began undressing her. His expression was not friendly. It was cold and businesslike. She put her hands on his cheeks and moved her head forward to kiss him, so that she could feel the warmth and affection she knew was there, to prove to herself that this coldness she detected was just her imagination. But Savage drew his head back.

"What is it?" she asked, concerned.

"Nothing," he said. "I just want this instead." And he pulled her slip away, baring her breasts. He put his hands to her breasts and began caressing them roughly.

Jennifer was deeply disturbed. There was no gentleness in his manner. He was treating her more like

357

a whore than like the woman he loved. Still, his roughness did not stop her from becoming quickly aroused. Nothing, it seemed, could keep her from becoming aroused and thrilled by the feel of his hands roaming all over her and the sight of his naked body. Even looking at his face excited her, but there was no warmth or affection in his expression to make this an act of love, that's what troubled her. He was looking at her with the coldness of a man taking possession of a harlot. Surely he could see how she felt about this! she thought. He must be able to see the way she needed affection from him now, any small sign of caring, to make it right. But if he did see it, he did not respond.

Instead, he lowered her quickly to the ground and entered her with a violence that made her gasp. Despite the wild pleasure that shot through her loins, the only expression that came to her face was one of distressed puzzlement. "Why are you treating me this way?" she finally blurted out, unable to contain the question.

"You don't like it?" he said. But then—whether deliberately or not, she did not know—he began thrusting so furiously into her that she became lost in the flood of sensation and was unable to answer his question.

Afterward, she lay with her head against his chest. Judging from the way he had just treated her, she expected that he would not hold her or touch her now, or give any sign of caring. But she was wrong. His arms went around her and he held her tightly. So tightly, suddenly, that it seemed as if a violent battle was raging within him and that he needed to hold onto her desperately, for dear life.

He shifted position and looked into her eyes. There was an expression of tortured agony in his eyes and of deep love. His lips parted, and he was on the verge of giving voice to his feelings, explaining himself. But he was having a hard time making the words come out. His mouth was open, he was frowning—in silence.

"What *is* it?" she asked, her voice filled with fear.

But his lips closed tightly and he just shook his head. His eyes glowed with infinite sadness and pain. He hugged her tightly, desperately.

The next morning, he said nothing about the episode. But his attitude toward her, as they broke camp and began the day's journey, was one of cold, unfeeling harshness. Jennifer was in torment, not knowing why he was acting this way toward her. She thought about it all day, as they moved out of the woods and onto level plains, sticking to paths and backroads, keeping the coast close by on their left.

D'Arcy noticed the strange way Savage was behaving toward her, too, Jennifer saw. He said nothing about it. But he did give her sympathetic glances occasionally, when Savage was not looking.

That evening Savage again treated her roughly and without affection when they were alone together, and afterward seemed very angry with himself, as if he hated treating her this way, but for some reason could not stop himself.

She tried to speak to him about it. "Lancelot . . . you seem so . . . so *hard* lately. Are you all right? What is it? Is it me. Is there something I'm doing that—"

"It's nothing!" he snapped. He stood up and moved away from her.

"You can tell me," she said softly, a hint of pleading in her voice. "I want to help."

"I said it's nothing! Now will you leave it be!" He glared at her fiercely.

Jennifer said nothing further. Whatever this mysterious thing was that was disturbing him, he was far too sensitive about it to discuss it. Jennifer remembered something D'Arcy had told her earlier, when he came to visit the night of the ball. He said that Lancelot was different. That he had changed and was not the same man. She had not thought about it then, but now she knew what he meant. The question that tormented her was: did this new person that he had become still . . . love her?

Savage tossed and turned all that night, groaning in his sleep. His expression was tortured and sweat broke out over his face and body. Jennifer watched him, uncertain whether to wake him. Finally, she did so, nudging his shoulder gently.

He came awake with a start, jerking upright, his eyes opening wide with torment. She watched him, but—even though she wanted to—she did not touch him or try to comfort him. She did not know if he ever wanted her to touch him again.

He remained sitting up, breathing heavily, for a long time. Then, after a while, he lay back down again and closed his eyes, taut and unrelaxed.

Jennifer watched him for a long time. A strong impulse overtook her and she leaned forward and kissed him on the lips. He made no response. It won't change things if he doesn't love me, she thought, feeling wounded inside. I'll still love him. I can't stop.

In the morning, when they resumed their journey, Savage was brusque with her again. They were traveling along an uphill grade in a field overlooking the coast when Savage turned to her, as she walked along several feet behind him, and said, "Stop lagging behind! You're holding us up." He turned his eyes forward again, without a further word.

Jennifer looked down at her legs and at the ground and tried to make her legs push more forcefully against the rising hillside. It was hard, damn it! She was not used to trudging along for hours on end, day after day. Just as she felt that she was on the verge of falling back even farther, due to her weak, fatigued legs, she felt a strong arm go around her waist.

She looked up and there was D'Arcy, smiling softly at her, his eyes gentle. He had come up to help her. He took her arm and put it over his shoulders. As they walked together now, it was far easier, for D'Arcy was supporting much of her weight. And though she did not want to be walking with him this way, she knew she could not continue on without his aid; her legs were too weak.

When Savage reached the crest of the hill, he glanced back and saw them walking together, D'Arcy's arm around her waist. He stared in stony silence for a moment, then turned his back on them and continued on.

After Jennifer and D'Arcy crested the hill also, Jennifer pushed herself away from him. She could manage the downhill part by herself. She smiled at him—a very slight smile, as little as possible—to thank him for his help. Then she stepped off to the side and began walking down the hill by herself.

The days passed quickly. Soon a week was gone, and then two weeks. They had traveled through woods, across plains, on the outskirts of villages, along the coast. Twice they had seen Redcoat troops actively searching for them. Both times they had hidden until the troops passed.

Food turned out to be no problem. D'Arcy proved skillful at catching small game. And when passing farmhouses or isolated cabins, Savage or D'Arcy would sometimes sneak up to the window, and if finding that no one was home, would enter the cabin and come out with an armload of provisions.

Jennifer had become more able to take the long distance walks each day without as much fatigue, though she still was not able to keep pace with Savage.

If not for the growing tension between Savage and D'Arcy over the harsh way Savage was treating her, the journey would have seemed like an exciting adventure: traveling across a foreign land in the company of two strong handsome men, living by their wits, camping under the stars. Often they were so close to the coast, Jennifer could watch it at her left as they traveled. The sea was deep blue, with bubbling white foam lapping up on the rocky shoreline. White gulls circled overhead, squawking. Several times they walked along the beach itself, to avoid an overland route that would have taken them through a major township. Jennifer had felt the cold wet sand on the bottom of her feet.

The trip really *could* have been fun and exciting, she knew, if only Savage weren't treating her so badly . . . and if only D'Arcy weren't reacting to this in a way that threatened to explode into violence between the two men at any moment.

She thought of this now as she stood at the bank of a shallow backwoods stream, looking into the surrounding foliage to make sure she would not be seen. D'Arcy was off hunting for game. Savage was a few yards distant, out of sight, busy fashioning a new hunting spear from his knife and a tree branch to replace the one he had broken last night.

Jennifer stripped off her clothing, laid it on the bank, then waded out into the center of the shallow stream. Even at the center, the deepest point, the water only came up to a few inches above her knees. She bent forward and began washing herself with her hands. She had been feeling filthy lately, from several days of not being able to bathe. The cool, sparkling water felt wonderful as she washed it over herself, cleansing from her skin the dirt and grime that had accumulated from days on the trail. The sunlight filtering through the treetops felt good too, as it warmed her skin.

If only she could let herself enjoy it! If only she could rid her mind of this nagging problem that refused to leave her: the problem of D'Arcy's growing affection for her and the explosion she knew it would cause.

His feelings for her had become more intense with each passing day. She could see it in the way he looked at her and in the way he acted toward her. She knew it was painfully hard for him to keep his silence while watching Savage treating her so roughly. He did so in the name of their friendship.

That friendship, though, was showing signs of strain. The rigors of the dangerous journey were wearing down both of the men. The need to be constantly alert to avoid capture, the physical strain of the endless hiking, the worrying doubts about whether the *Liberty* would actually be there in the cove when they arrived . . . all these things were eating away at their resistance and making them irritable.

One sign of the growing tension between them was the way D'Arcy had stopped disappearing for a walk in the evenings, so Savage and Jennifer could be left in privacy. Instead, he just lay there in whatever encampment they found themselves, looking surly. Savage and Jennifer had begun leaving the encampment themselves. Always when they returned, D'Arcy would act sullen and hostile for the rest of the night.

His natural good-naturedness had left him long ago. Now Jennifer would often catch him staring at her broodingly, with keen longing in his eyes. It was not only a physical longing, she knew. It was a yearning for her to show some sign that she felt affection and warmth toward him, similar to that which he felt for her. Sometimes he even—

Her train of thought snapped.

D'Arcy was standing there on the bank, staring at her.

How long had he been there? She had just this instant looked up. Quickly, she tried to cover herself with her hands, but there was no way of hiding the fullness of her body. She bent her knees slightly. She wished she could sink from sight into the water. The stream was far too shallow, though, to offer any protection from D'Arcy's burning gaze.

Go away! she wanted to scream at him. But she dared not. Savage was only a few yards away. He would hear her. He would come and see D'Arcy standing here, unabashedly staring at her nakedness. D'Arcy would look up at him, but would not leave. It would surely spark off the explosion Jennifer knew was coming.

So she could not scream at him to leave. She could not order him away. She could only stand here cower-

363

ing in the stream, looking with pleading helplessness at him. Her feet were braced apart for balance, her knees pressed tightly together. One hand covered her below the waist, the other hand and arm was pressed over her large breasts, failing miserably in an effort to cover them. The rounded curvature of her breasts at the bottoms and sides was fully exposed.

D'Arcy did not move. He did not grin. His expression was similar to hers in one way: along with his fierce gaze, which burned into her, there was also a look of helplessness in his eyes. As if he himself were no more in control of the situation than she was.

A full minute went by without his leaving or taking his eyes off her. Desperately she silently mouthed the word "please" to him, begging him to turn and go away. He remained on the bank, standing over the spot where she had left her clothing, looking her up and down. His expression was that of a parched man, dying of thirst, gazing at a glass of cool water. There was a long hardness pressing against his britches, its shape and thickness clearly outlined against the tightly stretched fabric.

She heard a rustling sound on the bank to D'Arcy's side. She jerked her eyes to the spot. Lancelot? No, she saw, it was only a forest creature scooting up a tree. But it could have been Lancelot. And it would be, if she remained here much longer. He would come to see if she was all right. She had to do something. She could not let Savage stumble onto this scene.

She began wading through the water toward the bank, to where her clothes lay—and to where D'Arcy stood. His gaze became more feverish as she approached him. She saw the corner of his mouth twitch and his upper lip break out in beads of sweat.

She was only a few feet away now. She kept moving forward, tensely, dry-mouthed with anticipation. She knew from the focus of his eyes what a pitiful job her forearm was doing trying to stop her breasts from bobbing up and down as she waded toward him. She was on the bank now, next to him. She looked in his eyes, their faces only inches apart. Slowly, she bent down and grasped her garments, leaving her breasts nakedly exposed as she did so. She began to move off to the side.

His fingers closed over her forearm. He held her. She closed her eyes in anguish and her mouth came open. His grip on her arm was gentle, not tight. She opened her eyes, looked at him, and said in a very quiet voice, "Please, D'Arcy. You're too decent to do this. It'll ruin everything. You know that. It'll destroy all of us if you do it. You. Me. Lancelot."

His voice was choked with emotion: "You know how I feel about you?"

She hesitated. "Yes."

"How do I feel about you?"

"Please, D'Arcy. Let me go."

"Say eet. I want to be sure zat you know. How do I feel about you?"

She lowered her head. "You love me," she said.

"Zat eez right, Jennyfair. I love you. And now you tell me thees . . . and do not lie to me: do you love me?"

Her head was still lowered. She arched her eyebrows in a frown of pure agony. A wellspring of emotion flooded up in her. She pressed her lips tightly together to seal them.

D'Arcy continued looking at her, saying nothing, waiting.

It wasn't fair! she thought. Why did life play with her like this? Why couldn't life be simple? Why did it have to torture her this way? Why did it suddenly force her to realize the soul-wrenching truth. "Yes," she said. "I love you."

He released her arm. She started away. His big hand moved gently down her shoulder blades, down her spine, over her firm buttocks. Then she was past him. She hurriedly got dressed, not caring that she was still dripping wet and that the clothes would stick to her.

Then she started back toward the encampment to rejoin Savage, not permitting herself even an instant's backward glance at—oh dear God!—at the second man she loved.

Chapter 23

That night, Savage had a dream—the same dream he had had every night for the past two weeks. Only tonight it was worse than ever. His body squirmed and twisted and thrashed about wildly, drenched in cold sweat. His muscles were tense and rigid, his lips parted in a tortured snarl. The nightmare vision ran in ragged, disjointed images through his sleeping mind:

He was dueling Matthew Armitage, parrying his unexpected expert thrusts, losing ground. Off to the side, Jennifer stood near D'Arcy. D'Arcy's arm was around her. Savage could not spare a glance to look at them. What expression was on their faces? Were they smiling? . . .

They were rushing along the trail, the British close behind. He was alone in the lead. Where were the others? He turned his head back to look. Jennifer and D'Arcy were together, behind him, D'Arcy's arm around her waist. He jerked his eyes away.

"I love you, Jennyfair," D'Arcy said in his delirium.

Suddenly a streak of blinding white lightning flashed through Savage's mind, rebounding back and forth within his skull. The images began to jumble.

Savage was in the prison dungeon, straining at the whipping post, the cat-o'-nine rawhides slashing across his naked back . . . D'Arcy was in the corner, lying on his stomach on the bunk. His body jerked spastically, making the salve on his back glisten. "I weel always love you." Savage stared at him. "Jennyfair, my dearest darling. . . . Beneath him, Jennifer lay looking up at him, the sweat on her naked body glistening as it caught the light . . . Savage could not turn his head to glance at their expressions. Were they smiling? . . . The whips slashed down, the pain was excruciating. He opened his mouth to scream. . . .

He jerked upright, his eyes opened wide and staring. He was awake. His mouth was gaping wide open. Silent. His body was shuddering and sticky with cold, clammy sweat. He closed his mouth. He looked around him. He was still at the beach where they had made their encampment for the night. D'Arcy was several feet away, still sleeping soundly. Jennifer was at his side, staring up at him with pain in her eyes, her lips parted. Her eyes were wet.

Savage threw his head back and breathed deep lungfuls of cold air. His body would not stop shuddering.

"You're in such torment," Jennifer said softly. "Won't you let me help? I love you. I can't bear seeing you suffer like this." Tears streamed down her cheeks. She looked as if she wanted to touch him, but did not dare, not knowing if he would allow it.

Savage watched her crying softly and silently. Slowly, he moved his hand near her face. He was about to touch her, to brush away a teardrop that streamed down her fair, pale skin from the corner of her eye . . . to make the first tender gesture toward her since they had been reunited. But then, just as his knuckles gently came near her skin, the image flashed through his mind again, blindingly: *Jennifer and D'Arcy in a lovers' embrace.*

He jerked his hand away.

"What *is* it?" she cried.

He stood up quickly and staggered far off down to the beach. He stood at the waterline, his head thrown back, breathing in gasps. The surf crashed deafeningly in front of him. His head throbbed. His body shuddered. He knew Jennifer's eyes were on him, desperate for some sign of affection, some hint that he still loved her. But he did not dare turn around to give her the reassuring look she needed so badly. *How could he? He could barely fight down these images enough to just be civil to her!*

Oh, if only he could *ask* her, voice it openly, get the tormenting question out of his mind! "Were you and D'Arcy lovers while I was rotting in Haverhill?" But no, he could never get that damnable question past his lips. To ask the question was to open the way for the answer. And what if the answer should be yes? He couldn't stand it. God, *why* did he have to love her so dearly! The agony of it!

He rushed far forward into the crashing surf and plunged into it. He remained underwater in the freezing coldness until his lungs were about to burst. Then he stood up, gasping, his hair slicked back. The riptide pulled at him strongly, nearly drawing him backward with it. He stood his ground, freezing and shivering wet in the moonlight. The roar of the surf was thunderous. No one could hear him. He opened his mouth and screamed.

The blow-up came the next day. Jennifer had seen it coming. Savage's mood, ever since last night's nightmare, had been ugly. Whatever it was he had dreamed, the effect it was having on him was devastating.

D'Arcy had not acted any differently toward her since telling her he loved her at the stream yesterday. He had been holding back his feelings. Now, though, as Savage's harshness toward Jennifer became even more severe—as though he were trying to exorcise some demon from himself by treating her roughly— D'Arcy's face began to flush with red and his lower jaw jut out far forward.

Jennifer wanted to say to him: It's all right. Don't say anything. Only a few more days and we'll reach the ship and this flashfire situation will be over.

She dared not say this to him, though, for Savage, in his presently overwrought state, would surely fly into a

369

rage over it. He would view it as an accusation that he was not fully in control of himself and had to be coddled like a child. So Jennifer said nothing. Instead, she tried her hardest to keep up with Savage's giant strides, so as to give him no reason to speak harshly to her—so D'Arcy would have no reason to feel provoked into springing to her defense.

Her strategy did not work. As Savage crashed forward through the woods, which they had reentered this morning, he called over his shoulder to her, "Bring me the *bota*, I want a drink."

He did not stop walking forward, just held his hand out to his side, open. Jennifer unslung the *bota* bag of water she carried across her shoulder, and started to move up to Savage to give it to him. But Savage did not slow his pace and Jennifer's weary legs would not carry her any faster forward than she was already going. D'Arcy, bringing up the rear, started forward to take the bag from her and . . . give it to Savage? Throw it at the back of his head? Jennifer did not know.

Before she could find out, Savage stopped, turned, and yelled "I said I want the water!"

"Lancelot!" D'Arcy yelled.

Savage glared at him.

"Do not treat her zis way!"

"D'Arcy, no!" Jennifer pleaded.

Savage strode up to D'Arcy and stood before him, hands on hips, glaring furiously. "What business is it of yours?"

"For ze long time now I say nothing to you of ze way you treat her. I know ze tortures zat zay do to you at Haverhill, zay steel are weeth you. I know you are not yourself now, not yet. But Lancelot, *mon ami,* you cannot treat Jennyfair in zis cruel way! She eez so good, so wonderful—"

"Stop it, D'Arcy!" cried Jennifer.

"You're defending her to *me*?" said Savage enraged.

"Someone must make you see ze light! How can you

treat her so horeebly after all zat she do for you? Living with ze Governor to save your life. Traveling all ze way to England and living weeth zat despicable toad, just to show you ze truth and gain back your love."

"Yes, all of that," exclaimed Savage. "And maybe more too? Maybe laying with *you*, '*mon ami*'," he said cuttingly, "while I rotted in stinking Haverhill?"

D'Arcy raised his hand and slapped him hard across the face. Jennifer screamed. "How dare you speak of her zis way!"

Savage slugged him in the mouth, leaving a trickle of blood at the left corner. They stood face to face, glaring at each other with mindless fury. Then, both at once, they came together. Fists swung so wildly and swiftly, Jennifer could see only a blur. Blood spouted from the faces of both of them. Then they were on the ground, rolling, tumbling, slugging it out. Jennifer, screaming for them to stop, tried to force them apart. It was impossible. She ended up sprawled breathlessly on her back in a tangle of vines, after being struck violently away by a stray fist that accidentally caught her in the stomach. She thought the fist was D'Arcy's, but could not be sure.

She staggered to her feet. The wind had gone out of her and she could no longer scream at them to stop. But she could not stand idly by either. From the fierceness of the battle it seemed clear that there was a chance it might end with only one of them still alive. No matter what their present intentions, their fury was so great that, in the passion of the moment, fists could easily escalate to either strangleholds or swords.

She looked around in desperation. There! She went to it, picked it up from the ground where Savage had dropped it. Then she held it, the makeshift throwing spear, clutching it in both hands at the point where the knife was joined to the branch . . . holding the blade against her chest. Slowly she raised the knife up and then stopped, holding it ready to plunge.

"Jennifer!" came Savage's frantic shout.

She held the knife poised above her breasts, her hands tense and trembling. She heard scurrying movement and then Savage came rushing against her, up from a crouch, putting his body between her and the spear. The knife dropped away from her hands.

Savage was crushing her in his arms, holding her with such force—even now that the threat was over—that she knew his hungry embrace was caused by his desperate need of her. He hugged her as if he were afraid to ever let her go. Her hands went to his head and she ran her fingers through his tousled, thick, sweat-soaked hair. "It's all right, Lancelot," she said softly.

He released his grip so that she could draw back, but he kept his arms around her. She saw the look in his eyes. He did not have to say the words. She knew now. He loved her.

D'Arcy was standing next to them, a worried look on his face. "You would not have done eet?" he asked. "Eet was just a threat, yes? You would not really have plunged ze knife into? . . ."

"I don't know," she said and realized suddenly that it was true. "I couldn't have beared to see either of you die at the hands of the other." She looked at D'Arcy, and at Savage, and she saw from the partially subdued rage still in their eyes that this interruption in their battle might prove to be only a temporary one. She had to do something further, right this instant, while the fires of anger were momentarily banked. Or they would roar back ablaze and the combat would resume.

"D'Arcy," she said, "go away."

He looked at her, pierced with hurt.

"Till your temper, and Lancelot's, cools down," she added quickly. "Go away until both of you are men again, instead of animals."

The wounded look was still in his eyes, but now there was also anger at not being able to finish what had been started. He glared at Savage for a moment, and Savage returned his look. Then D'Arcy turned sharply on his heel and started away. He pointed to the single hill visible through the treetops. "Zair!" he exclaimed. "Zair eez where I wait, at ze dry lakebed near ze hill." Then he disappeared through the bushes and was gone.

She turned her eyes to Savage. He gazed at her tenderly. She slapped him stingingly. His eyes went wide with disbelief and fury. It was a bold move and it was a gamble, but, Jennifer thought, the time had come. Being a captive to passivity had almost lost her everything she held dear. Now it was time—long past time!—to bend fate to her own will, rather than letting fate direct her life in its own capricious way.

"You should be ashamed," she said angrily. "Accusing me of being unfaithful to you with D'Arcy."

He released her from the circle of his arms and regarded her with a blend of anger, curiosity, and faint approval.

"Why do you insult me like this?" she said. "I've never done anything to hurt you. I've never wavered in my love for you."

"The cat bares her claws at last," said Savage.

"It's *you* who've been unfaithful to *me*," she said, feeling real rage well up in her. It had been suppressed for far too long. "It's you who doubted me. It's you who lost faith and believed I became the Governor's mistress of my own choosing." Her blue eyes were flaming. "And now, even after we have that settled, you *still* think gutter thoughts about me. The nerve! Accusing me of . . . of . . . and accusing D'Arcy too! You don't know what a true friend he is to you!"

Savage was staring at her intensely. "Do you love D'Arcy?" he said suddenly.

"I love *you*, you fool! That's all that matters. I'll always be your woman, and *only your* woman. I've always loved you, and I always will love you. Nothing will change that, Lancelot, not even your not loving me."

His eyes became softer. "But I do."

"You have a strange way of showing it!"

He looked at her with deep anguish. She could see that he was about to tell her how hard it was for him. She stood silently, waiting.

His words came out slowly and agonizingly. "You don't know how . . . bad . . . Haverhill really was. I don't want you to know how bad it was. But I want to tell you this: for a long time I thought it destroyed some important part of me. The part of me that's sensitive and gentle. You have to be hard to survive in there. You have to be so hard, there's no room for anything *but* hardness. When I escaped, I thought I'd be able to bring back the sensitive part that I'd shoved aside. The germ of it was still alive. But—"

His lips compressed tightly and his eyes became hard. "When I broke into the Governor's chambers that night, and saw you there, with his—when I saw you like that, I knew the sensitive part was gone for good. I couldn't let myself be sensitive again. Because I had a shred of sensitivity left to me then, and what did it gain me? It drove me mad! Seeing you like that! After the horror of all those months, when it was only the thought of you that kept me alive!"

"Lancelot—"

"Wait. I want to tell you this. D'Arcy, he tried to make me see the truth, but I wouldn't listen. I couldn't listen. The shock of it was too much. Then, when I lay outside your veranda at Crespi, and heard the way it really was, I thought the pain was all over. The need to bludgeon to death all signs of sensitivity in me. I thought I'd become my normal self again, at last."

He suddenly kicked violently at a dry, low-hanging branch, snapping it off. "I was wrong." His voice was bitter. "The gentle part wasn't there. The sensitivity. It could have been there, I could have brought it back. But I kept it buried. Deliberately."

"Deliberately?" she asked, shocked. She had not thought his behavior toward her was deliberate.

"Can't you see? I was afraid that if I let myself *feel* again, let myself love you . . . I might find that I

374

didn't have your love in return. Then it would be the scene at the Governor's mansion all over again. The same horrible pain. Opening myself up to your love and finding that it wasn't really there."

"But you knew it was there! You heard what Matthew said! You knew the truth then, knew how much I loved you!"

He shook his head and now his eyes peered at her with an even deeper intensity. He seemed as if he were, being torn apart over the thing he was about to say. He hesitated. The air was thick with anguish.

"It wasn't your living with the Governor, by then, that made me think I didn't have your love. It was something else." He gritted his teeth. The words seemed to rip right from his very heart. "*It was thinking you had an affair with D'Arcy!* Thinking the two of you . . ." He let the words trail off.

"But I didn't, Lancelot," she said softly.

"I know that now." He shut his eyes. "And you think, it would have been so simple if I only could have asked you. But I couldn't. I couldn't ask it."

She went to him. He put his arms around her and hugged her tightly.

"Is it over now?" she asked, after a moment.

"Yes." There was still a residue of bitterness in his voice, though, and pain. "I'll tell you this. It drove me crazy, seeing the way I was treating you. It tore me apart."

"I could see that."

He kissed her. At first his lips were hard and tense against hers. Then, slowly, they relaxed. The kiss became gentle, the way it had been so long ago, in the days before his capture and trial. Things would be better now. She knew they would.

She remained in his arms for a long moment, feeling his love surround her. Then she drew her head back. There was still a loose end to be attended to. "We have to go get D'Arcy," she said.

"*You* have to go get D'Arcy," he corrected.

"Me?"

"It's the only way. Think about it. He's obviously in love with you. Someone has to set him straight about the way things stand between us. Someone has to tell him that no matter how much you might care for him—and I know you must care for him some; I care for him a great deal myself—but no matter how much you care for him, he has to understand you're my woman, and mine alone."

"Yes," she said, knowing it was true. D'Arcy would have to be told just exactly that.

"And this 'someone' who has to tell him this," Savage said, grinning for the first time in a long time, "is not going to be me. You're the one he's in love with."

She lowered her eyes.

"You have to go to him and talk to him. Then after you tell him all of this, bring him back here." He paused. "And if you don't come back, I'll know you left me and went over to him."

She looked up at him sharply. He was grinning. It was a joke, she thought. But looking deep into his eyes, into the circles of slate gray, she wondered: was it a joke? He intended it as one, but was there really more to it than that?

"And tell him I'm sorry I almost killed him." He grinned. "You'll have to tell it to him at least three times. He's a stubborn Frenchman, and would rather finish a fight than accept an apology over the matter that started it."

"You're joking now. This isn't something to joke over. It's serious."

"I know it." His expression became somber. "It's hard not to make a joke of it when the feelings are so strong. But all right, tell it to him straight. I love him like a brother. He was right to do as he did and I was wrong. If he hadn't called me on the way I was acting, I might still be treating you badly. And hating myself for it every minute."

"That's better." She kissed him once more, briefly,

376

then started through the bushes in the direction D'Arcy had gone. She glanced back once and saw him staring after her, grim and stony-faced. Then she turned forward again and walked off toward the dry lake near the hill. There was a natural pathway that led to the dry lake, and she walked along it, brushing aside low-hanging vines and leafy branches. This area was fertile with game, she knew. The pathway had probably been worn into the undergrowth by trappers who treaded it regularly.

As she walked toward the hill, her thoughts became dark and unhappy, and her expression was one of pouting. True, she was happy over Lancelot's words to her, and the fact that he would be gentle and loving to her again, from this day on. That was wonderful news and it made her joyous. The sadness she felt came not from that, but from her present mission. Here she was, going to the man she loved—the other man she loved—who was gentle and good, and who loved her dearly, and she was going to have to tell him that his hopes for her ever returning his affection were doomed. His love for her could never be fulfilled. He would have to give her up. She knew it would pain him deeply to hear her say this. But it did have to be said. No matter how much she cared for D'Arcy she would never leave Lancelot or do anything to hurt him.

Well, she thought resignedly, as she neared the dry lakebed at the base of the hill, D'Arcy would understand. It would be hard for him, and painful. But he would understand. And he would accept. He had to. There was no other choice. . . .

Chapter 24

"No!" he declared. "I refuse! I absolutely refuse! I love you and I weel *have* you, and zat eez all zair is to eet!"

"But D'Arcy, I love him! And I'm—"

"And you love me too, no?"

She lowered her eyes. "Yes. But—"

"No buts, Jennyfair! We are two lovers, and at last we have found each other." He kneeled down before her, as she sat on the boulder in the midst of the dry, cracked lakebed. "You think eet has been easy, holding my silence, pretending to not care for you so deeply? All ze while watching Lancelot show no love to you at all? Eet was torture, Jennyfair! And you know how I feel about eet now? About holding silent of my love for you, in ze name of friendship for Lancelot?"

"You—"

"I feel like ze fool! And ze coward! Ach, how *stu*peed I have been!" He slapped his palms to his forehead. His entire face and body were highly spirited and energetic as he stomped around, gesturing sharply, swiveling in his tracks, emotionally expressing his feelings to her. "I should nevair have waited so long! I should have spoken of zis days ago! But my love for Lancelot, you see, eet made me pause, for I know he too loves you truly, deep inside. But Jennyfair, what I should have done, ze true course for me, I should have brought my love out into ze open! And zen we talk of eet, he and I, man to man!"

"No, D'Arcy," she managed to interject, "you

378

shouldn't have done that! You did right by not saying anything at all. It was a bad time for Lancelot. There were problems he had that—"

"And for me eet was *not* ze bad time?" he asked, kneeling before her again, grasping her hands. "*Cherie,* nevair in my life have I had so bad a time as when I love you and cannot say eet."

"D'Arcy that's past! That's over with!"

He looked at her dumbly.

"Oooooooh!" she cried in frustration. She stood up and walked away from him, to gain some distance so she could act more in control, more objectively. Calm yourself! she thought. Don't get as excited as he is.

"Listen to me, D'Arcy," she said quietly, gesturing with out-stretched hands. "What I'm trying to tell you is that what you should have done *before* doesn't matter. We have to deal with the situation at hand, the way things stand now. And the way things stand now is that, no matter how much I care for you . . . and I do, D'Arcy, I do care for you . . . but no matter how much I care for you, I can have only one true love in my life and that has to be Lancelot."

"Why?"

"Why?" she repeated. He stunned her with the simplicity of the question. "Well, because . . . because . . ."

"Ah ha!" he declared triumphantly. "You have no 'why'!"

"Of course I do!" she declared, forgetting about her resolve to stay calm and even tempered.

"No, Jennyfair, you do not!" he declared, leaping to his feet. "And I prove eet to you. Answer me thees: do you love me?"

"I told you I do!"

"And you love Lancelot?"

"Yes!"

"And do you love Lancelot more zan you love me?"

That caught her short. She paused. "That isn't fair, D'Arcy."

"Eef you do not, zan ze only reason you have for

379

saying I must no longer love you, while Lancelot he can love you, eez zat Lancelot eez ze *first* one to love you, and me, I do not declare my love until ze long time later."

"Being first or second has nothing to do with it, damn it! You're twisting things!"

"Zan what has to do weeth eet, Jennyfair? What is ze reason zat you say to me I must stop loving you?"

She felt like throwing her hands up in the air in exasperation. What else could she say to him? Why couldn't it be simple? Why couldn't he just accept what she said, and leave it go at that?

"D'Arcy, you're playing games with me, aren't you? Oh, I don't mean you're lying to me. I know you're not. But all of this gesturing and running around and this heated emotion . . . it's all to confuse me, isn't it? To make *me* get emotional too, so I can't think straight?"

He smiled at her warmly. He came up to her and stood in front of her, looking down into her pale blue eyes. "Jennyfair," he said calmly, "eet eez not false, none of eet. I feel ze emotion and I show eet. For too long I have not shown eet, zat ees what caused ze problem. But . . . I know you weesh me to speak to you weeth ze calmness, so I do eet. I speak weeth ze calmness. And I know too zat you want me to not argue weeth you. You want me to say yes, I love you so much, I do as you say. But Jennyfair I love you so much, I can *nevair* do as you ask me. I can nevair give you up."

He put his hands on her upper arms now and looked at her with kind, loving, faintly smiling eyes.

"I tell thees to you as simply and calmly as I can. Weeth no pointing and shouting and like zat. Weel you leesten to eet?"

"I'll listen," she said. She did not want to hear what he was going to say, though. It could only make things more difficult for her. And things were already far too difficult. His words, his actions, his mannerisms . . . all of it was pure D'Arcy. Seeing him, listening to him, made her aware of how strongly she felt toward him. She bit her lower lip. She looked away so that she would not have to see the loving kindness in his eyes, which made her feel weak when she looked at it.

D'Arcy put his finger to her chin and turned her head back toward him. "Thees eez eet. I say eet to you once, and zen you do not have to hear me make with ze wild shouting and like zat, for you weel know what I have to say in ze most baseec, simple way. Eet eez thees: I love you more zan I ever love any woman. My life means nothing to me eef I must live eet weethout you."

"Please, D'Arcy," she begged, "don't—"

"No, no," he scolded gently, raising a finger. "You asked for eet weethout ze 'wild emotion,' and now you must listen to eet." He continued, "I think ze honorable thing eez for me to say 'farewell, I bow out now,' and leave you to Lancelot. But ze honor eez no consolation for me eef I must lose you. I tell you now, Jennyfair: I nevair will give you up. Eet has taken all of my life to find you, and now zat I have found you, I weel not let you go."

He stopped speaking and just looked at her. His expression was slightly amused. He obviously knew, she thought, that this straightforward, simple way of stating his love for her was more devastating than the wildly emotion charged way she had made him forsake. Now, as she looked up at him, he bent his face down and started to kiss her.

She jerked her head back. "D'Arcy, no!"

"*Cherie*," he said softly, "I take no more zan only zis: a small kees. But zis thing, *cherie,* zis thing I do take." He bent her head back. His mouth lowered on hers. She tried to resist, but her arms were trapped by his arm, which went around her body, holding her tightly.

His lips were thick and firm, and they pressed against hers with a surprising gentleness. They moved about on her lips, his mouth opening and closing slightly. His tongue probed about inside, his thick lips pressing harder against her mouth. She tried to cry out, but the sound surprised her and came out like a soft moan.

He released her suddenly and stepped back.

She almost stumbled backward with the unexpectedness of being suddenly unsupported. She knew her lips were still parted and the expression on her face was the farthest thing from a look of anger or resistance. That was why he had released her so suddenly, she thought. So he could see the look on her face before she had a chance to compose it into suitable indignation . . . and so he could let her *know* that he had seen it.

He was grinning at her, with a mischievousness that seemed to say: You see? You cannot fool me or your emotions.

Jennifer took a deep breath to clear her head and to restore strength to her suddenly weak body. Then she said, "That proves nothing."

D'Arcy shrugged, still grinning.

Suddenly, Jennifer found herself wanting to cry. What could she *do*? How could she solve this problem of the other man that she loved, who refused to gracefully fade into the sunset and out of her life? She could not let the situation continue like this. Think what it would do to her relationship with Lancelot!

When it occurred to her that there really was *nothing* she could do, that she was stuck with this problem and that it would not go away, she exploded. "Damn you!" she shouted at D'Arcy. "You . . . you . . . you're selfish! And you're ruining my life!"

He said nothing. His eyes looked saddened, but still resolute and determined.

"Now you listen to me, D'Arcy Calhoun! If you can't do as I say, if you can't accept that all my love is for Lancelot, then . . . then . . . well then you stay away from me, do you hear! Don't even come back to the encampment! Just . . . just you go your way, you go to the cove on your own. And we'll go our way. And then we'll meet you there. And you stay away from me, you hear!"

"You're crying, Jennyfair," he said softly.

"Oh shut up, you!" She turned and ran away from him, into the woods, back down the natural path in the undergrowth. After several minutes, she slowed to a walk. She looked behind her and listened and knew that he was not following her. She continued down the path toward Savage, drying her eyes and cheeks on the sleeve of her dress, so Savage would not see that she had been crying.

She was halfway back to the encampment, when a filthy, hairy hand with dirty black fingernails clamped itself over her mouth, the thumb and index finger of the hand pinching her nostrils shut. She tried to scratch the hand and pull it away, but her right arm was gripped and held behind her. She scratched and flailed about with her one free hand, panic stricken, struggling to free herself from the filthy hand at her mouth and nose. She tried to scream. She tried to bite. She could not breathe.

Soon she was swooning into a void of blackness. Her last thought as she plunged into the bottomless depths of the void was that now she would never see Lancelot again.

Savage waited an hour for her to return, which stretched to two hours. When the sun began setting, casting long shadows through the forest, he started off along the trapper's path toward the riverbed at the base of the hill. When he arrived, he saw that D'Arcy was gone. Jennifer was gone too.

He stood motionless for a long time, the blood draining from his features. Then he started off in the direction of the cove, where the *Liberty* would hopefully be waiting.

* * *

Jennifer came awake slowly, languorously. She did not immediately remember what had caused her to black out. In her groggy state, her eyes still closed, it seemed as if she were merely awakening from another night on the trail and would find herself still in the company of Lancelot and D'Arcy, about to begin another day's journey.

Then she opened her eyes.

She saw two men sitting at a table in a corner, eating. One was thin and gangling and wiry. The other was heavyset like a bull. Both were dressed completely in animal skins and hides, except for the bullish one, whose extremely hairy chest was bare. Both men were grimy and dirty and had stringy long hair. They were eating hunks of roasted meat, tearing it off the bones with their teeth. They were not looking at her, and had not noticed that she had come awake.

Jennifer's lips hurt. The memory came back to her: the hand closing over her mouth and nostrils, suffocating her into unconsciousness. She looked around. She was in a small, single-room wooden cabin, with a dirt floor, and a rock hearth that had a fire blazing in it under a roasting spit.

The door to the ramshackle cabin was wide open and through it she could see the woods, brightening with the first rays of morning sunlight. She glanced back at the men at the table. Then she bolted for the door, running with all her might.

She was almost to it when suddenly she tripped and fell to the dirt ground, though there was nothing in her path to trip her. The men at the table noticed her now. She scrambled to her feet and rushed forward again, only to trip once more.

"Well, she's awake, Lemuel," said the thin one, in a backwoodsman's drawl.

Jennifer looked to see what was preventing her from rushing forward. She saw a loop of rough-strand rope tied to her right ankle. The rope was draped over the main ceiling beam of the cabin and tied at the other

384

end to a hook protruding from the wall. There were other hooks on the wall, most of them holding up animal skins and pelts.

She tried to untie the knot binding her ankle, struggling feverishly. The two men sat at the table looking at her, casually munching on their breakfast. "She shorely is a looker, ain't she?" said the hairy-chested one.

"That she be, Lemuel. Best I laid eyes on since last fall in Coventry, when we went to sell the hides."

"You pigs! You beasts!" Jennifer screamed at them, struggling wildly to untie the knot, breaking the top of one of her fingernails in the process.

The men watched her with interest, slowly biting off and chewing their food. After a minute, Lemuel said to the skinny one, "Ye best raise her up, Adam Semple. She'll have that knot busted soon, otherwise."

The skinny one stood up from the table and untied the rope from the hook. He began pulling on the rope, which was draped over the ceiling beam. He pulled at it arm over arm, dragging Jennifer backwards away from the door. She clawed at the dirt beneath her to resist the backward movement, but in vain. The skinny one kept tugging at the rope, arm over arm, until Jennifer was hoisted into the air by her ankle. She cried out.

Adam Semple ceased pulling on the rope once Jennifer was high enough in the air, upside down, so that her head was an inch off the ground, her long hair dangling into the dirt. He retied the rope around the hook in the wall and sat back down at the table.

"Let me down!" Jennifer screamed. "You filthy pigs!"

The hem of her skirt and her slip were down around her neck and she raised her hands to push them back in place, to hold them so they at least covered her underdrawers. At the same time, she raised her free leg and tried to hold it locked together at the ankle with her tied leg, so her legs would not be so brazenly spread apart. The effort was hopeless. The two men at the table ignored her. She was undisturbed while she struggled to maintain the painful, awkward position, but after a few moments, her muscles were aching and rapidly weakening.

Her hands were the first to drop away, when utter fatigue drained them of strength. She released the skirt and slip, letting them fall back down about her neck. Her hands dangled down into the dirt. Soon she could no longer command the great strength required to hold her legs locked together and her free leg dangled off to the side.

Humiliation at her shameful, wide-open position spread over her, but the main feeling she experienced was stark terror. These two in the corner looked and smelled more like animals than like men. "What are you going to do with me?" she asked fearfully.

"What do yuh think?" said Lemuel, taking a bite from his bone, then wiping his greasy, stubble-bearded face with the back of his hand.

A desperate idea flashed into Jennifer's mind. "You'd better not hurt me!" she warned. "You'd better release me right now. Do you know who I am? I'm the wife of the assistant to Minister Kensington! If you don't let me go right now—"

Adam Semple slapped his palm down on the tabletop and let out a whoop of joy. "You were right, Lemuel! That be her, all right, she be the one!"

"I knowed it," said Lemuel, beaming with pride. "Didn't I tell ya? When those soldiers searching out the north quadrant says they's looking fer the wife of a murdered member of His Majesty's court, and then I seen this one here, I knowed it was her.

"You'd best hightail it into Coventry, huh, Lemuel, to bring 'em back here so's we can git the reward?"

"*Me* hightail it?" the hairy-chested one said angrily, grasping the thin one from across the table and shoving him backwards so that he fell over in his chair. "You're the one to go hightail it. Whilst I stick it out here, standing guard."

386

"Shucks, Lemuel."

"And be quick about it, yuh mangy goat. There's another bounty out for those what were with her, who helped her in her crime. If the soldiers git here quick enough, they might catch 'em. With us bein' the ones gettin' the bounty."

Adam Semple scowled as he stood up from the dirt, but did as he was told. He grabbed his musket and started for the door. He stopped near Jennifer, gazing down at her fair-skinned legs and at the scanty undergarment that was her sole protection. Jennifer tried to raise her free leg again, back next to the roped one, but could not muster the strength. A groan escaped her lips.

"Don't you even think it," Lemuel said from the table. "She's got to be in tip-top shape to git us the bounty."

"You wouldn't be cheatin' on me?" said the thin one, his eyes narrowing suspiciously. "Waitin' fer me to be gone so's you c'n have her all t'yourself?"

Lemuel threw a meaty bone at the man, hitting him in the chest. "Git outa here. Accusin' me of such a thing."

Adam Semple turned and left through the open doorway.

Once he was gone, Jennifer tried to think of some way to trick the hairy-chested one into releasing her. Now that there was only one of them instead of two, it might be easier.

"Lemuel," she said to the man, as he sat at the table continuing his meal. "That's your name, isn't it? Lemuel, I have something important to tell you."

He looked at her without interest, munching his food open-mouthed.

"My husband was very wealthy. He had a treasure in gold sovereigns, and he brought it here to bury it. That's why he came to the resort at Crespi, to hide his treasure. I can take you to it. I know where it is." Her voice was desperate and she knew it, but she could not make it less so. "Just let me down? Please? I can make you rich, you'll see I can!"

Lemuel stood up and came over to her, his boots next to her face. She looked up at him, straining her neck. The image of the man was upside down, due to her position.

"Yer going to take me into the woods and show me this 'treasure'?" he said.

"I promise I will! Thousands and thousands of golden sovereigns!"

"You're going to go into the woods lookin' like that? Why you're not fit to be seen by man or beast in them scruffy rags yer wearin'." He put his hand between her legs and ripped away her underdrawers, leaving her bare. She screamed and tried to kick him. He grasped her free leg at the ankle, and held it tightly. He gazed down at her loins.

"Let me go!"

He continued staring at her loins and soon started to drool. He ripped away the upper part of her dress, and her slip, and then the skirt part which had been separated at the waist by Savage so many days ago. She was naked now, with only the strip of green treebark, which had been holding up her skirt, still in place around her waist. She watched the trapper throw her clothing into the fireplace. It shriveled into wisps of smoke almost instantly, as it caught the flames.

The trapper put his rough hand on the inside of her leg and rubbed it up and down her thigh, moving from one leg to the other, pressing over her loins. Then without warning he grasped her at her bare loins, *clutching* her.

Suddenly there was a sound at the doorway, behind her where she could not see. Lemuel looked there, startled. A fist caught him in the chin, knocking him backward.

"Lancelot!" she cried, wild with relief and gratitude.

But the visitor came into view and she saw with heart-sinking despair that it was not Lancelot at all.

"Yew liar!" the skinny trapper yelled at Lemuel. "Cheat!"

"Aw, now Adam Semple, damn it, I was only—"

"Backstabber! Sham! Yeah, 'keep her in tip-top shape', 'e says! You just wanted her all fer yerself!"

"Aw, now Adam Semple. All right, all right, ye caught me. So I took advantage a wee mite? They's plenty a' her fer both of us. Let's lower her down now and I tell you what . . . you gits her first. Right?"

The thin one contemplated this a moment, then nodded.

Jennifer screamed at the top of her lungs as they began lowering her down into the dirt. She knew it was futile to scream and to fight them, but she could not help herself, could not stop herself from twisting and kicking and lashing out with all her might.

Both trappers stripped themselves naked. The hairy-chested one pulled her to her feet. He grabbed her from behind, forcing her arms up into the air while his hands locked together behind her neck, pushing her head down on her chest. The tall gangling one came up in front of her and stared at her, bouncing back and forth from one foot to the other in uncontrollable glee, laughing at her like a lunatic. "Heee he *heeee*," he laughed, bouncing from foot to foot.

He put his arms back behind him, slightly out to the side, and pressed himself up against Jennifer, his skinny chest and stomach rubbing against her breasts, his maleness prodding her just above her navel.

He flung his arms around her torso and pulled her tightly against him. She tried to kick him or knee him, but he was too close against her and too tall. He began jumping up and down, laughing his maniacal "heee he *heeee*!" His body was filthy and began to sweat profusely. Soon he was drenched in a sticky, oillike substance, which covered Jennifer's skin too as he bounced, sliding his body up and down along the length of her.

"You filthy, dirty *scum*," Jennifer screamed at him, wincing tightly in torment.

"Heeee he *heee*!" He grabbed her breasts in the "V" of his thumbs and forefingers, lowered himself down so his chest was on line with her, and began rubbing her breasts against himself, pushing them from side to side against his thin sunken chest. Jennifer groaned and moaned and cursed him. Her head was pressed down forward, so there was no way she could bite him—until he bent over low and tried to kiss her on the lips. Then she did bite him, hard. He leapt back with a look of wounded surprise.

Lemuel, behind her, laughed raucously. "I guess she showed you, Adam Semple! I guess she shore showed you!"

The gangly thin one stalked over to the wall, pulled down a three-strap harness that looked like it was used to muzzle hunting dogs, and shoved it over Jennifer's face. "Noooo!" she screamed. He adjusted the straps until her scream died away because her jaw was strapped tightly shut by the muzzle. Then he stepped back to admire his handiwork.

Lemuel, behind her, lowered his arms to around her waist, raised her up into the air, and began thrusting his hard shaft in between her legs, so it pressed up against the bottom of her. Jennifer's hands were free now and she scratched and clawed fiercely at the hairy hands locked together in front of her. Lemuel thrust against the bottom of her loins several seconds more, then shoved her away from him, cursing angrily. He held up his bleeding, shredded arms and looked at them.

Jennifer was panting loudly, half-crouched forward. Her nails were bared, her eyes murderous. Neither of them risked coming at her. Then she made a mistake. She moved her hands to the muzzle biting into her face, to try to unstrap it. The two trappers charged at her from opposite sides, their bodies slamming against her, sandwiching her between them. The thin one, behind her, grasped her in the same armlock the other had used on her, forcing her head forward, her arms up into the air. Lemuel grabbed her ankles. They moved her over to the pile of thick furs in the corner. The thin one lay down on his back with her on top of him, her back to his chest. Lemuel held her struggling ankles tightly, allowing the thin one to hook his own legs over Jennifer's, then spread Jennifer's legs apart. Jennifer tried to cry out, but the muzzle made any sound other than the groaning coming from her throat impossible.

She struggled wildly, but it did no good at all. The assault on her body gained rather than lost momentum, until Jennifer's strength drained away completely and she could struggle no more. She lay there passively between them as they degraded and defiled her. Finally, after an eternity, both men rolled away from her, satiated.

They left her limp and sweat-covered and aching on the bed of furs. The skinny one got dressed in his animal hide clothing, retrieved his musket, and left the cabin. Lemuel bound her wrists behind her with a leather strap, pulled a large fur pelt over her, and removed the muzzle. He went over to the table and ignored her.

It was a long while before Jennifer could think clearly again. When she could, she wondered, through a fog of pain and despair, where's Lancelot? Where's D'Arcy? Why hadn't they come to save her? D'Arcy was an excellent woodsman. Surely they'd have no trouble tracking her to this cabin. Why hadn't they come for her?

There was still hope, she thought desperately. They could still arrive in time to rescue her. But they had to hurry. They had to get here before the Redcoats arrived to take her back to London. *Where were they? Where in damnation were they?*

She half expected them to appear at any moment . . . to come bursting into the cabin, run this vile trapper through at swordpoint, then whisk her up into strong arms and carry her off to safety. She kept hoping this to happen all through the afternoon and into the evening, until finally, just after sundown, the Redcoats came for her and it was too late.

Adam Semple was the first one through the door, and after him came a Redcoat lieutenant and a sergeant. The main body of the detail was ordered by the sergeant to wait outside, since the single-room cabin was far too small to accommodate them all. The lieutenant looked at Jennifer, as she lay in a corner, covering her nakedness with the large fur pelt. Then he looked at Lemuel and all around the cabin, as if inspecting the premises to make sure they were safe.

"It's quite all right, Sir," the lieutenant called through the doorway. "And aye, the girl is here."

Jennifer watched the doorway. She saw the ugly, bulky figure in rumpled well-to-do clothing enter and recognized him immediately: Minister Kensington.

The Minister looked around the small cabin distastefully, his eyes finally settling on Jennifer. "So it is you after all," he said. His voice was even gruffer and more croaky than it had been the last time she had heard it. There was still the complete lack of humorlessness about him. He was grim, serious. He went up to her and inspected her as she lay huddled in the corner.

"What's this . . . *thing* you're wearing?" he asked, reaching down to touch the pelt, lifting it off of her. When he saw that she was naked beneath it—when everyone in the room saw it—he dropped the fur pelt back over her and turned to Lemuel. He hit him across the mouth with the back of his hand. "You swine," he cursed. "What'd you do to her? Assault her?"

Lemuel cowered back, protecting his face with his hands. "No Sir, Your—Your Lordship, Sir," he protested, frightened. "I never laid a finger on her! Not even—"

"And you?" said the Minister, turning to Adam Semple.

Semple was blanching white, also fearful of what

this powerful, highly placed official might do to him. "I wasn't here!" he pleaded. "I was . . . I was fetching the soldiers, that's where I was! Please, Your Lordship, Sir—"

"Shut up." He looked down at Jennifer. Her contemptuous expression showed that she remembered the circumstances under which they had last seen each other. He sneered at her scornfully. "I recall seeing you wearing quite different attire, Madam Armitage. At the ball you hosted? You were very stunning. Fancy gown. Hairstyle. Quite the lady you were then. Now you look like just another wild animal."

"Get me some clothing, then," she said, "so I can dress myself."

He looked around the room for the clothing she had been captured in. He shrugged, not finding it.

"They burned it," she said.

"Uh, Your Lordship, Sir," said Lemuel, diffidently, "about the reward? The bounty for her capture?"

The Minister was thinking about some other matter though, his beady eyes focused on Jennifer. "Get them out of here," he said to the lieutenant. "You and the sergeant go too. And shut the door."

"Aye, Sir," said the lieutenant.

Once they all had gone, the Minister sat down heavily in one of the room's two chairs, near the table, and dropped his hands loosely in his lap. He looked at Jennifer for a moment without saying anything. Then he said, "You're sought after by the authorities for your husband's murder, did you know that?"

"I didn't murder him."

"You told a clerk at the central lodge you and Armitage were going off for a walk at the seashore. Then his body's found in the underbrush, run through with a blade. And you being nowhere in sight."

"I don't fence," said Jennifer, tossing back her head.

"Being an accomplice is enough to get you hanged, in a murder."

"I wasn't an accomplice to anyone!" she declared. "I

393

was . . . kidnaped! By the hoodlums who killed my husband. There were three of them—short, buck-teethed Spanish brigands—and after they killed Matthew, they—"

"Spare me the details," said the Minister wearily, waving his hand in the air. "I've no desire to play magistrate." He looked around the room, bored. "I only mention all this to let you know your situation. It's this: if the soldiers take you back to stand trial, you'll be hanged. The first female hanged in Britian in ages, but make no mistake of it, hanged ye *will* be. Armitage was a damnable bugger, to be sure, but still, he was an official of His Majesty's court. While you . . . you're no more than a once-indentured whore."

"How did you know that?" she asked sharply. Matthew had paid large sums of money to keep that information secret.

"I went through his effects soon as I heard of his death. And I found this." He pulled a rolled, cracking piece of yellowed paper from an inside pocket, opened it and held it out to Jennifer. The bold black lettering at the top of the paper declared CONTRACT OF IN-DENTURE, and at the bottom was her signature. At the side were the signatures of previous owners: Pauly Garrett for the Bultaco House, and Matthew Armitage.

The Minister rolled the paper back up and put it into his pocket.

Jennifer stared at him uncertainly, not knowing what he wanted.

"Armitage owed me a sizable debt. Did you know that?"

"No."

"Well he did," the Minister said bitterly. "And his estate, such as it is, isn't worth a farthing. He owed money everywhere. Borrowed to buy you back from the Bultaco. Borrowed to finance your expensive ball. And for all sorts o' crazy schemes he had his thumb into. Which weren't so crazy, probably. Would've turned him a nice profit, I'd say, if he'd lived long enough to—"

"What do you want from me?" Jennifer blurted fiercely. She was tired, sore, and filthy. She wanted to have this over and done with, no matter what the outcome. "If you're to take me in to be hanged, then take me! But at least be quick about it! Take me where I can have a bath and some clothing . . . and . . . and . . ." Her words petered out as she viewed his beady-eyed, blank-faced countenance. It was like talking to a wall.

"Here's what I want from you, Mrs. Armitage: my investment back. That's why I came all the way out here—out to Crespi—soon as I heard of your husband's murder. So's I'd be here when they found you, and get to you before they took you in for trial." He stood up and came over to her. "Ye think I come here for my health, ye stupid bitch? I come because you're the only collateral left in the estate that's worth anything! And so long as I hold your indenture papers, you belong to me, to sell to whomever I please!"

For a moment, she was terrified. The thought of being sold back to the Bultaco and chained to the bed loomed up in her mind's eye. But then she realized something. "You can't sell me to a sporting house," she said. "If I'm a wanted fugitive, then—"

"Don't be a fool. I can do anything I please. What do you think, I'm a third-rate administrator of some kind? I'm Francis Kensington, ye bloomin' moron!"

Matthew *had* told her how powerful this man was. Now the true horror of her situation began to sink in. She must have reflected it in her face, for the Minister suddenly laughed at her arrogantly and said, "There, that idea knocked you off your high horse, didn't it, *Lady* Armitage? Yer thinkin now that I really *can* sell you back to a sportin' house if I desire it. And indeed I can! And may! But the decision isn't up to me. It's up to you."

She looked at him in astonishment.

"You see, I have other plans for you. If ye cooperate, you're spared the whorehouse. If ye don't, then you're not. Simple as pudding."

"Cooperate with what?" she asked warily.

He squatted down on his knees before her and stared at her with his beady eyes, which suddenly became excited with greed. "I'll hold an auction. You'll be the main and only attraction."

"You're selling me off to be some man's slave? Why, that's no different than selling me back to the sporting house!"

"Isn't it? If I auction you, you'll be bought by a man of wealth and position. Those are the only sort I'll invite to the auction. My contacts in the world of finance and commerce are the highest. Noblemen from France. Gentry from Spain and Italy. Even a sheik or two from the Arabias. And of course, a few discerning brother Englishmen would gladly join in the bidding.

"You see your choice? You can refuse to cooperate, in which case I sell you back to the Bultaco or some similar establishment . . . where you can be prodded by every filthy gutter-crawler owning the price of admission. Or, you can cooperate with me. In which case you find yourself the well prized possession of a gentleman of refinement."

"What sort of cooperation did you have in mind?"

"Act like the lady you are. That's all." He grasped her hair just above her forehead and bent her head back, so her face was raised up. Jennifer grimaced at the sudden pain. The Minister regarded her features carefully. "Aye, you're a lady. You've the looks and the carriage. Though you seem to belie it as often as not. But what I want from you is to act the part. I'll have you fitted out in the best finery, have your hair done up that crazy way you had it afore."

He released her. She snapped her head to the side, then looked back at him and thrust her chin forward petulantly.

"You see why I'm needin' your cooperation? These

396

fine men o' the world I invite to the auction, they're the sort who appreciates a true lady. And are willing to pay dearly for one. Oh, not just *any* lady, mind. But one with the looks of you? . . ."

His eyes wandered down to her naked shoulders. He grasped the fur pelt and pulled it down to her navel, baring her breasts. Jennifer closed her eyes but said nothing.

"Aye, a true lady possessed of such beauty as you have is rare indeed. Most ladies are frumpy and that's puttin' it mildly. But you, you'll fetch me a fine penny. *If* you act out the role for me, with the grace that comes so natural to ye. If you don't, then you're only another looker of a tart. And gentlemen do not bid fortunes for tarts."

He stood over her now, waiting for her to say something. "Well, which'll it be?" he demanded.

She looked him in the eyes, her own eyes flaring. "Neither. Arrest me instead. Your influence can save me from trial if the facts are in doubt, but I'll bet it won't be so weighty if I'm a confessed murderer! Well, will it?"

She could read the answer from the look in his eyes. "Just as I thought. You're powerless to stop my hanging if I admit to the crime. And I'll do it, I'll confess! I'll say I stabbed him with his own sword, if that's the only choice other than being dragged off to a brothel or to a London auction-house!"

"London auction house?" said the Minister, unperturbed. "You must be mad. Affairs of this sort are done in private. Invitations sent out, announcing an event to be held at my hunting lodge north of here near Scotland. Discreet references to the nature of the event. That sort of thing. And about your misguided martyrdom—"

"I changed my mind," she said abruptly. "I'll do it."

The Minister looked surprised. He did not ask for an explanation, though. He was content just to have her agreement.

Jennifer did not volunteer an explanation, either. She did not tell him that the location of his lodge near the Scottish border was what made the difference. The *Liberty* was in a cove near the border. She would be close enough so that Lancelot and D'Arcy might still rescue her. If she were in London, rescue would be impossible.

It would take time to send out the invitations to the auction, she knew, and for the dignitaries to arrive. Time enough, maybe, for Savage and D'Arcy to learn of her whereabouts? So they could storm the lodge and carry her off to safety, before the day of the auction?

The Minister raised the top of the fur pelt back up to Jennifer's neck, then opened the cabin door and summoned the Redcoat officer inside.

"Lieutenant," he said to the man, "I've looked into the matter, in an unofficial capacity, of course. And it's my opinion that criminal proceedings are not warranted. I'll take care of the details with your superior." He narrowed his eyes challengingly. "You accept that?"

"Aye, Sir. Of course I do."

"You're a bright young man. Now do this: escort the young woman to my summer lodge near Sheladonly. Hold her there till my assistant arrives to take charge of her. She's to be my guest."

The lieutenant nodded, then stepped back outside to give instructions to his sergeant. The Minister went outside also, where he was accosted by the two trappers who pleaded with him for their reward. Jennifer heard him speaking angrily, but did not listen to what he was saying. She was too busy imagining her own fate. Images danced across her mind: dressed in veils and held captive in a Sultan's harem . . . or naked in the tower of a nobleman's castle on the Rhine.

She shut her eyes tightly. *Lancelot, please,* she thought. *Wherever you are save me!*

Chapter 25

Though the Minister cared not the slightest bit about his own personal dress and grooming, Jennifer discovered that he cared a great deal about having *her* coiffured and accoutered in the latest, most elegant fashions. No expense was spared to make her as stunning as possible. He arranged to have one of the most sought after tailors in London sent out to his hunting lodge at Sheladonly to create the gown she was to wear for the auction. Then, on the morning of the day the auction was to take place, a *coiffeur* of international repute arrived to create a masterpiece of Jennifer's long, honey brown locks.

As Jennifer stood before the full-length mirror now, viewing the result of the expert's handiwork, she was amazed. The stylist had fallen in love with the natural sheen and rich color of Jennifer's hair, and had flown in the face of convention by boldly declaring that he would leave it unpowdered. And instead of piling it high atop her head, he decided to brush it back from her forehead and from the sides, raising it only modestly, giving the effect of a lion's mane of silken honey brown.

"Oh, it's such a *daring* idea," the stylist exulted to her now as he pranced around her, touching her hair here and there very gingerly with his fingertips. "I truly was inspired! Darling, you bring out the *very* best in me, if only you could be my personal model. You don't suppose such an outrageous idea might be remotely possible?"

"It's very possible," Jennifer said somberly, inspecting herself in the mirror. "Just attend the auction tonight and outbid all the others. Then you'd own me for the period of my indenture, body and soul . . . and hair."

The stylist sighed and busied himself straightening the diamond tiara which adorned the front of the lion's mane of hair. "Alas, but I'm really only a poor working man."

The diamond tiara sparkled as it caught the light, as did the diamond earrings and the glittering opal necklace she was wearing. The jewelry had been borrowed by the Minister to enhance the image of elegance he wished her to convey.

Her gown also glittered softly in the late afternoon sunlight streaming through the tall bedroom window. It was made of a silverish velvet that began as a broad, many-folded scarf, which was draped low and wide across Jennifer's breasts. The ends of the scarf passed over her shoulders and joined together in a bow at the small of her back. Her entire back and most of her shoulders were bare, highlighting her fair skin. The main body of the gown descended from the horizontal scarf, caressing the contours of her waist, flaring out at her hips, then descending to the floor in overlapping billowing hoops of silverish velvet. The sleeves of the gown were slit in three places, so that they appeared as silver streamers encasing her thin arms, ending in broad cuffs.

Beneath the gown was a pannier superstructure of white bone, giving the gown its billowing, flared look. Beneath the pannier, there was nothing at all, and this distressed Jennifer. When she had come out of her bath and reentered the bedroom, her clothing for the night had been all in readiness, except for her petticoats and drawers. She had sent the girl who was attending her out to find them, but the girl came back with nothing but word from the Minister that they would arrive at any moment. They had not arrived by the time the Minister insisted she begin dressing. He would bring them later, he said.

Jennifer noticed the hairstylist standing behind her, as she looked in the mirror. The man put his fingertips and thumb together, raised them to his lips, kissed them, and spread his fingers apart quickly, in a final salute to Jennifer's beauty. Then he bowed formally and left the room.

Jennifer turned away from the mirror and went to the tall window. She looked out at the lushly landscaped grounds below and at the Recoat soldiers off in the distance, ringing the perimeter of the grounds at the edge of the woods. They had been posted there during two of the three weeks Jennifer had been held captive in the lodge. It was only one more testament to the Minister's immense influence that he was able to secure government troops for an affair which not only was private rather than governmental, but was also of very doubtful legality.

From the instant the guards had been posted at the lodge, during the second week of her captivity, Jennifer knew Savage and D'Arcy would be unable to rescue her, even if they did learn of her whereabouts.

The door opened without the courtesy of a preceding knock. She knew it was the Minister. He was the only one who would be so ill-mannered. He came into the room wearing sportsman's clothing, rumpled and ill-fitting as usual. He walked up to her, looked her over appraisingly. He put his hand to the scarf draped over her breasts and rubbed the material between two fingers. He grunted approvingly. He moved his head forward, very near her throat, and sniffed. "Lilacs" he said, gruffly. "Your oils and perfumes cost me a ridiculous sum, but at least the effect is worthwhile. And of course everything I spent on you is in the nature of an investment."

"You're so flattering," she said.

"Just practical. And about to be a good deal richer." He paused. "Well, let's go. The guests have begun arriving. And remember our agreement: you act like a woman of class . . . and you go to the gentleman who bids the highest. You try to cross me by acting any other way and it's off to the Bultaco with you. Even if it means embarrassing myself by having you dragged away right in front of my guests."

Jennifer knew she no longer had the option of pleading guilty to Matthew's death. The day after she arrived at the lodge, she had been visited by an investigating magistrate, who questioned her about the murder. She told him the lie about her having been kidnaped by the murderers, knowing that if she said she killed Matthew, she would have been spirited away to London right then and there, without Savage or D'Arcy ever having a chance to rescue her. In view of her statement, the investigation had been dropped. Jennifer knew the Minister's reputation was weighty enough so that, once closed, the investigation would not be reopened, no matter what she said.

The Minister grasped her arm and started her toward the door.

"Wait!" she said. "You forgot to give me something. An article of clothing . . . "

"No time for that now. Come down as you are."

"But—"

He tugged her along by the wrist, out the door, then along the corridor overlooking the wood-wainscotted mainroom below, the walls of which were adorned with trophy animal heads and skins. The Minister led her out onto the stairway landing, then released her wrist as guests began to look up and take notice. The conversation in the room died down. All eyes were on her.

Jennifer raised her chin and began descending the stairs in a stately manner, the Minister at her side looking gruff and unsociable. She felt completely out of place dressed as formally as she was in the floor-length evening gown. Everyone else in the hunting lodge was wearing sporting clothes—expensive, fashionable sporting clothes, true; but sporting clothes nonetheless.

When they reached the bottom of the stairs, a cluster of guests began to converge around them, all of them beginning to talk at once. The Minister introduced her to them one at a time and Jennifer nodded her head in acknowledgment of each introduction. "Baron Friedrich, Lady Armitage." "Rajah Pavlam, may I present Lady Armitage." "Count Marcovici . . ."

Jennifer watched some of the men incline their heads slightly when she was presented to them, but she noticed that none of them responded in the proper manner, with a deeper bow. And she saw from the smug way they looked at her that these men were very aware of the fact that she was an object to be purchased. They were willing to play along with the pretense that she was a woman of refinement, but were not at all willing to show more than just the merest token gesture of courtesy to her.

After she had been introduced to the guests near the stairs, Jennifer was led by the Minister to other parts of the room, so she could be shown off at close range to everyone present. A young, liveried servant boy followed them around everywhere they went. Jennifer wondered why. She asked the Minister about this, but he just ignored her question.

All the guests were male, Jennifer saw, and most of them were middle-aged, with lines about their eyes. There was a commonness of expression among them: a look of closed-minded, selfish superiority. The few younger men present had a common expression too: a haughty, gay, nasty look that spoke of generations-old titles and inherited wealth.

A servant with a tray of drinks passed near. The Minister took one, not bothering to offer a drink to Jennifer. "You're doing well," he said, during a moment when they were unattended by guests. "You're giving the impression you're a woman of quality and style, who isn't used to being treated shabbily. That's certain to drive the price up. Because the main reason they'll want to buy you, you see, is so they can treat you shabbily. Degrade you. The only true appeal of a woman of high station is that you can drag her down low and rub her face in the mud."

She looked at him with an expression of revulsion.

A swarthy man with a hooked nose and bulging eyes came up to them wearing traditional sporting britches and coat, but with strange headgear that seemed to be a white sheet covering the top of his head, hanging down to his neck in back. "Sharif Ali of the Arabias," said the Minister in his gruff voice, "may I present Lady Armitage."

The Sharif gazed at her leeringly, raising an eyebrow. "Exquisite," he said to the Minister. "How many years?"

The Minister poked Jennifer roughly in the side with his elbow.

"I'm nineteen," she said.

"And are you well practiced with lips when head is held low?"

Jennifer stared at him incredulously, more in shock at the uncouthness of the question than in embarrassment. The Minister poked her in the side again, but she still did not answer. She stared at the Sharif with undisguised disgust.

The Sharif sneered at her and said to the Minister, "Like a new desert stallion, she will need be broken before achieving full value."

"Pay the price and you can break her," said the Minister.

The Sharif backed away from them, bowing as he did so, then turned and left.

"He was awful!" Jennifer said. "And so were you."

"Worry about him, not me. Chances are good he's the one who'll own you by the end of the night."

Jennifer felt a hollowness in the pit of her stomach. She envisioned herself being dragged across parched desert sands on camelback, her fair skin blistering from the heat . . . held prisoner in a tent as one of a dozen

404

mistresses, guarded by an army of eunuchs. The hollowness in her stomach was from the fact that she knew this was not a fantasy scene she was imagining. It could really happen. And from what the Minister had just said, there was a good chance it *would* happen. She shuddered. If only there were some way to escape! But no, there was none.

New guests were arriving all the time. A bearded, brown haired young man whom the Minister did not recognize came up to them and introduced himself. He was one of those who had been invited second hand, learning of the event from an invited guest. All invited guests had been urged to bring friends who were of the same financial stature.

"I'm honored, Madam," said the bearded man.

"It's a pleasure, Sir," Jennifer replied.

The man stepped back a ways and looked her up and down, his hand on his chin, eyes narrowed. He addressed the Minister with complaint in his voice. "Are you expecting to sell your goods, Sir, without letting prospective buyers view them first?"

"Not at all," said the Minister.

"Well for all I can see of the young woman's body, she may as well not have one."

The Minister motioned to the servant boy who had been following them at a distance. The boy went down on one knee, grasped the hem of Jennifer's velvet dress and raised it all the way up to her waist. Jennifer gasped and moved her hand forward to push the boy away, but the Minister grasped her wrist and, leaning close, said just one word into her ear, in a menacing voice, "Bultaco."

What could she do? She closed her eyes tightly, her face a mask of helpless humiliation. When the Minister released her wrist, she held it suspended in the air where he had left it, her fingers spread apart. She heard the conversation die away around her. She stood with her long legs pressed tightly together, naked from her waist to her pale blue kneesocks, her body completely exposed within the crisscross cage of whalebone that was her pannier. She felt the draft on her bare skin.

She heard the bearded man say, "Have you been out today?" A moment passed with no one answering, then she heard the Minister say to her, "Open your eyes! Answer his question!"

She opened her eyes. Her arched and furled brow showed the torment she felt. The man was looking at her with a taunting smile on his face, expectantly.

"What?" she said. She couldn't believe it! He was actually asking her a question, trying to engage her in a calm discussion, while she was standing here bare-bottomed, so humiliatingly on display!

"I said, have you been out today?"

"No," she answered in a small voice, cringing with mortification.

"Well, let me inform you then," he said, looking around at the others who were watching, as if playing to an audience. "It's a lovely day."

Everyone began laughing. Jennifer wished she could fade into nothingness. But she also felt deep anger. This man was toying with her, trading on her misery. The Minister gave a signal and the boy holding up her dress released it. It fell back into place around the pannier.

The bearded man said, "Very gracious of you," to the Minister. "Goods openly displayed. The ethical way of conducting commerce." Then he walked away.

From that point on, the Minister had Jennifer's dress raised for every guest who requested it. Making her torment and degradation even more humiliating was the fact that, while her dress was properly in place, she was commanded to continue acting out her role as if nothing unusual were happening, while the guests continued pretending she was a refined woman who was to be respected. Then her dress was raised and she was subjected to their abusive, smirking, lecherous gazes.

And then—this was the worst of it!—she was expected to *continue* acting like a lady, while her dress was held up around her waist: answering their questions, participating in discussions. As if this sort of thing happened to her every day. As if she was *used* to going around with her loins and buttocks openly on display! She was the laughingstock of the party and there was nothing she could do about it. If she resisted, she would be dragged off to the Bultaco.

She was wallowing in helpless agony at the impossibility of her situation, when she heard a familiar voice behind her, "She looks a bit narrow in the shoulders, if you ask me."

"Oui, mon ami," answered a second voice, "but zat eez not what matters. When one eez *vis-à-vis* weeth a woman, eet eez what's *between* ze shoulders zat counts."

Jennifer swiveled around sharply, her mouth open with astonishment. The Minister turned also and she knew instantly that she must disguise her shock and joy at seeing Lancelot and D'Arcy standing here next to her. She looked at the expensive clothing they wore and smiled inwardly at the thought of two invited guests who almost certainly were laying naked by the roadside somewhere, either dead or securely bound.

Savage wore a leather vest over a blood red damask hunting shirt. He had a wide belt around his waist and a dapper, plumed hunting hat on his head. D'Arcy wore a knee-length, wide-lapelled, brown sportsman's coat with wide turned-back cuffs. He had a white scarf around his neck, tucked into the collar of the coat. His shiny black boots looked Hessian-made.

"Her lips are a bit too thick for my liking," said Savage merrily, forcing her chin up with his hand so he could inspect her more fully. "Women with thick, sensuous lips like this have a tendency to be too demanding, too physical." He grinned at her. "Why, I'll bet you're a regular tiger, eh woman?"

Jennifer jerked her chin to the side, away from his fingers.

The Minister grasped her arm sharply. "We'll have no rudeness," he scolded warningly.

"Zat eez right," intoned D'Arcy, indignantly. *"Les femmes*—ze women—zay must nevair be rude to ze men! Zay must know zair places at all times, eez zat not so?" He was looking at the Minister.

"Yes," the Minister said in his gruff voice, "I think that too."

How far were they going to carry this? Jennifer wondered, looking at D'Arcy. If he asked for her dress to be raised, she would *die*. And she would kill him, too, the first chance she had! The insensitive cad!

"Ah well," sighed D'Arcy, shrugging. "Ze women zeze days, zay are not like in ze olden times. But what can one expect when—"

"You just arrived?" interrupted the Minister. "Here at the lodge?"

"Yes," said Savage. "And I think the first thing we'd best do is get some liquid refreshment into my friend here. It's the only thing that keeps his mouth from running on endlessly with these boring anecdotes." He started to turn away.

"We have a mutual friend in common, I believe?" said the Minister. Jennifer tensed, recognizing danger. This was the question he had been asking all evening of people he did not know and of whom he was suspicious.

"You know Mr. Hawthorne, I believe," said Savage smoothly, "of Hawthorne Freight and Lading? It was he who invited us as his guests."

"Yes, of course," said the Minister, not quite smiling—he never smiled—but giving the closest approximation. "Old Henry has been a crony of mine for years."

So that's the name of one of the men lying naked by the roadside, Jennifer thought.

"By the way," said the Minister, "where is the old bugger anyhow?"

"He eez not here?" asked D'Arcy, looking surprised.

408

"He say zat he meet us here no later zan seven-thirty."

"Mmm," grunted the Minister. "That's not for a while yet."

"You know," said D'Arcy, raising a finger and grinning, "in my country, when eet eez near ze evening, everyone—"

"I told you," Savage said to the Minister, interrupting D'Arcy, putting his arm around him and beginning to lead him away. "If we don't get some whiskey down his gullet, he'll be spitting out these anecdotes all night."

Savage glanced at Jennifer briefly, as the Minister looked at D'Arcy, and for an instant their eyes connected with nerve-jangling intensity. Savage saw in her eyes a look of helplessness and gratitude. In Savage's eyes, Jennifer saw a look of hateful anger for every man in the room. Then his back was toward her and he was leading D'Arcy off toward the refreshment counter at the far end of the lodge.

During the next hour, every ounce of Jennifer's concentration was focused on finding some way to go talk with Savage and D'Arcy, without the Minister's constant presence. But the Minister did not let her away from his side for even a moment as the evening progressed, until it was time for dinner. Then, when the great platters of roast meats and fishes—and the giant bowls of steaming vegetables, breads and victuals—were brought out from the kitchen and set upon the buffet board, the Minister took Jennifer aside into one of the small, windowless guestrooms on the main floor.

His manner by this time had become extremely coarse, and his expression did not contain even the slightest trace of civility. Now that Jennifer had already met all the guests and given them the desired impression of her, the Minister no longer needed her cooperation. She had served her purpose. He could treat her any way he wished now, without concern for her reaction.

His grip on her arm tightened as he shut the door to the room, leaned toward her, and said, "There's another event I scheduled for tonight that I didn't tell you about. The auction starts in about three hours. Between now and then, you're going to be bedded by the men whom I figure will be the top five bidders."

Her eyes went wide and she drew back.

"I figure to whet their appetites. Once they have a taste of you, they'll want you all the more. It'll drive up the bidding. Now here's the thing: I can either have you tied to the bed and gagged . . . or you can do it of your own will. Either way, I don't care. I'm only giving you the choice 'cause I figure you may be such a harlot that you'll actually do it of your own will. That'll look better for the bidders' sake than if I have to rope you down."

Jennifer noticed the hint of movement on the other side of the bed from where she stood and she realized the Minister had not intended to be alone with her in the room. Someone was there, crouching in wait, probably with ropes already in his hands. Was there any way to escape this? she wondered desperately. She looked back at the Minister's grim, impatient expression and knew that there was not.

"Hurry it up, I haven't all day. What's your decision?"

"I'm not a harlot," she said softly. "But . . . " She lowered her chin and shook her head, her eyes cast downward. "No more tying. I can't take any more of being tied, and—" She swallowed hard, holding back tears. "It's torture, being tied and unable to move, while they—"

"Save the sob story, I'm not interested. Just give me a yea or nay. You'll lay with them of your own will?"

"Yes."

"All five of them?"

She nodded, her eyes closed.

"You're a bigger slut than I thought." He addressed the man who was hiding on the other side of the bed:

"Get out of here, Derek." Jennifer watched the man stand up. He was tall and husky, and yes, he carried several lengths of rope in his hands. She would not have stood a chance of fighting him off. "Now take off your clothes," the Minister said to her, after the husky man left.

She let out all her breath. Her shoulders sagged. She felt completely deflated, as if her energy and will had all drained away from her.

"I'll do it, then," said the Minister, grabbing for her.

"No," she said, backing away, holding up her hand. "I'll do it." She removed her slippers. She turned away from him, and raised up her skirt, then unfastened the stays of the whalebone pannier. She removed the bulky hemispherical cage from her body, and afterward took off her blue kneesocks. But then she found she needed the Minister's help after all. She could not undo the laces at the back of her dress, where they were hidden under the bow-tied ends of the broad draping scarf.

The Minister's hand went up to the laces and he tugged and jerked at them roughly, until they finally came undone. Then Jennifer slipped the draping scarf dresstop down her shoulders, and pushed it past her stomach and hips as the Minister watched. Finally, she stood before him naked, her head hung down.

The Minister gathered up her dress, kneesocks, and slippers from the rug, bunching the elegant, expensive garments roughly into a ball, and slipped them under his arm. Then, as a parting gesture, seemingly for no other reason than to show how vicious he could be, he clutched the rounded curvature of Jennifer's belly with his free hand and shoved her forcefully backwards, watching with glee as she stumbled backwards onto the bed, her legs flying up and apart in the air.

"Don't try to leave, either," he said. "I'll have Derek standing out here by the door." He left her lying on her back on the bed, not even able to summon the will to get in under the green, down cover.

When the Minister came out of the small guestroom,

he was watched from across the length of the main room by Savage and D'Arcy. Their eyes had not left Jennifer since they had arrived. They had watched as she was pulled into the guest room, and then as the husky man emerged a moment later carrying rope.

Now they saw the Minister speak a few abrupt words to the man, who remained standing outside the door. Then the Minister walked to the room next door, opened the door, tossed the bundle of clothing inside, and shut the door. Savage and D'Arcy watched him straighten the collar of his waistcoat before reentering the main room.

The Minister went over to a hook-nosed man wearing strange, white-sheeted headgear. When he said something into the man's ear, the man's bulging eyes lit up and he grinned from ear to ear. Then the man with the sheet on his head hurried over to the room Jennifer was in and went past the husky guard at the door into the room.

"I think we should go in zair and slay heem," D'Arcy said bitterly, sipping at a goblet of punch to make himself seem inconspicuous. "And zen we should slay ze Minister."

"That's not the answer. It'd make us feel better, but it wouldn't get her out of the room. It would only get us killed."

"Zat eez why you are ze Captain and I am only ze First Mate. You have a head for what works and what does not work. I have a head only for what makes me feel good." He and Savage both watched the Minister go up to four other men, one after another, and say something to each of them. The guests then looked at the door outside which the husky man stood guard.

"All right," said Savage, putting down the plate of food he had been idly holding. "Let's go see what we can do."

They walked across the room to the Minister. "Sir!" said Savage, forcing an unfelt look of good-humored cheerfulness over his features when the Minister looked at him. "My associate and I were noticing that the girl entered the room over there, that one over there, and didn't come out. Then a Mediterranean-looking gentleman entered the room after her."

"So?" said the Minister belligerently, looking as if he felt he were being challenged.

"So! Well, being red-blooded sorts ourselves, why we wondered if we too might have a stab at . . , uh . . . acquainting ourselves with the young lady. If you follow my meaning."

The Minister regarded them less antagonistically now. "It's only the top bidders who can sample the wares. Sorry. But you see the need to put a limit on how many get the privilege."

"Eef eet eez ze high bidders you weesh to honor, zen perhaps we should be included," said D'Arcy.

Savage saw the hook-nosed man leave the room, shutting the door after himself. The Minister saw it also. A slim, dark Italian, now standing near the buffet board, began moving off toward the room. Someone in the group he was passing recognized him, though, and called out his name. The Italian stopped momentarily to exchange greetings.

The Minister looked at D'Arcy. "You two have sizable fortunes to spend here tonight, is that it? You think you might top off the bidding?"

"Allow me to introduce my associate," Savage said, gesturing at D'Arcy with an open palm. He remembered the story Jennifer had told him as they were escaping toward the cove, about how excited everyone had become over the ruse involving D'Arcy's signet ring. "May I present the Marquis de Calhoun, patriarch of one of the great trading families of France."

D'Arcy snapped his boots together and bowed from the waist.

The Minister suddenly became alert. His stare was piercing. "You're the Marquis Calhoun?"

"At your service, *monsieur*."

"Then yes. Go. Go! Into the room, she's yours for the taking! Both of you, with my compliments!"

"*Merci bien.*"

The two of them started off toward the room at the other end of the long expanse of hall, not noticing the ominous expression on the Minister's face as he continued looking after them. They were almost at the door, when the Italian, who had disengaged himself from the conversation with his acquaintance, reached it first.

"Excuse me," said Savage, roughly shouldering the man aside."

The man's eyes lit up in indignation. He grasped Savage by the shirtfront as Savage was about to open the door. "*No* one insults Count Bernardo Marcovici!" raged the man. "I *keel* you before I allow such an offense to stand!"

"Kill me later," said Savage. "I'm busy now."

The man's mouth dropped open and he slapped Savage hard across the face.

Savage quickly put his hand out to restrain D'Arcy from reacting. Reluctantly, D'Arcy obeyed the command and did not respond. Instead, he turned to the husky man guarding the door, who seemed about to enter the fray himself and said calmingly, "Eet eez nothing. A leetle argument between friends." Since they were so far removed from the main body of guests, the fracas did not cause undue attention.

"Will you yield me the right of first entry *now?*" asked the irate Count Marcovici.

"No," said Savage, rubbing his hand across his lip where he had been hit. "But how's this instead: I'll offer you your satisfaction. I challenge you to a duel on the morrow. Your choice of weapons."

"I accept!" he declared, throwing his head back defiantly. "I go to alert my second."

"Do that," said Savage, watching as the man stormed off, his back rigidly straight, his head held high with great dignity.

Savage noticed the Minister still watching him and

D'Arcy with that same strangely alert look. He nodded and smiled at him. The Minister did not reciprocate. Savage opened the thick, heavy door to the room and he and D'Arcy entered. The instant they were out of sight, the Minister rushed toward the main doors of the lodge, then hurried outside.

Inside the small room, Jennifer lay on her stomach on the bed, her head buried in the crook of her arms. She felt a hand touch her shoulder gently. Another hand, she thought. She did not respond. Then she heard his voice: "Jennifer."

She whipped around instantly, her eyes enormous with wild excitement. "Oh, Lancelot!" she cried, wrapping her arms around him, hugging herself to him with all her might. She felt his arms encircle her tightly. "And D'Arcy," she said, looking at him gratefully with her still-wild eyes.

From the way D'Arcy was looking back at her, with the expression of a child caught in the midst of a guilty act, she remembered that she had no clothes on and that he was seeing her completely naked. She pulled away from Savage quickly, gathered up an edge of the down comforter and wrapped the green quilt around herself.

She looked from one man to the other. Suddenly all signs of helplessness and gratitude dropped away from her and she shouted in a demanding, angry voice that surprised her as much as it did them, "Where have you been! Why didn't you come for me when I was at the trapper's cabin!"

"We did not know you were captured," said D'Arcy apologetically. "Both of us thought zat you were with ze other. So until we met again at ze coast—"

"We don't have time for that," said Savage sharply.

Jennifer looked at him. "How are you going to get me out of here? Do you have a plan?" D'Arcy looked at him too.

Savage's expression was grim. Then a sardonic smile

415

crept across his face. "It's too crazy to be called a plan. But it's all we've got, so we might as well try it."

When the door opened a moment later, Count Marcovici was standing outside the room talking to the guard. He quickly turned to address the exiting pair, with the intention of slapping Savage once more. His attention was instantly diverted, though, by D'Arcy, who shouted at him, "As my associate's second, I warn you, Sir, zat you shall not live past ze morrow! Prepare to die on ze field of honor!"

"*I* die?" Count Marcovici shouted after them, becoming enraged at the fact that he was addressing only their retreating backs. "I am the most expert marksman in all Italy! We shall duel with pistols, and I will—turn back to face me, you cowards!"

When he continued to be met by only their backs, as they hurried away, he turned to the guard, who also was staring after the pair, and declared, "I will put my ball *right* between the coward's eyes! You come there on the morrow! You watch! *Never* has a Marcovici been so insulted without extracting the most horrible vengeance!" He said these last words with his index finger raised high in the air, waggling furiously from side to side. Then he sharply pulled down the hem of his belted coat, which had hiked up, swiveled about on his high heel, and burst into the guest room, slamming the door after him.

He stood by the bed, gazing down, breathing through flared nostrils, still furious at the affront. "Ah, my little chicken," he said to the curled-up form under the green comforter, "you do not know how *violent* I become at such insolent provocations. No, you live in a woman's world of flowers and lace. You do not know the way Bernardo Marcovici's blood *boils* when insulted.

"Ah well," he said, unfastening his sword belt, then starting to undress, "I must not speak of this now. I gazed upon you earlier, I know how lovely you are. A woman of your beauty must be un*bear*ably impas-

416

sioned. I know! Yes! I am a master at matters of passion and desire. As you shall soon discover, eh?" He removed the last stitch of his clothing, thrust his shoulders back grandly, and puffed out his chest. Then he grasped the edge of the comforter. "Now," he declared, "prepare for the thrill of all thrills! Let your budding femininity rejoice to receive Bernardo Marcovici!"

He jerked back the comforter.

The naked form his eyes fell upon was very much lacking in budding feminity. Marcovici's mouth dropped open as he gaped in disbelief.

"Now *you* rejoice," said Savage, "to receive *this*." He slugged the man hard in the jaw, then leapt up from the bed. As the Italian stood there tottering and weaving, staggered from the blow, Savage hit him twice more in the jaw with a left and right in rapid succession.

Count Marcovici crashed to the floor. Quickly Savage raised him up, under the arms, and dragged him onto the bed, covering him completely with the comforter. Then he began dressing in the man's clothing. He had barely gotten the too-tight britches on, when he heard the musket shot from beyond the door. Damnation! he thought. Something had gone wrong.

Beyond the door, all the way across the main room near the front entrance, D'Arcy was retreating backward, pulling Jennifer with him by the hand.

"Don't shoot in here, you fools!" the Minister screamed at the Redcoat soldiers he had just led into the lodge. "You'll touch off an international incident! Use blades if you must. But catch them! Stop them! Don't let them escape!"

D'Arcy and Jennifer ran away from the Redcoats, past the Spanish nobleman who had received the shot which had been meant for D'Arcy. The Spaniard lay on the floor clutching his bleeding chest, his face contorted in agony. As they ran, Jennifer stumbled, unaccustomed to Savage's heavy boots which she was wearing. She fell and D'Arcy lost her hand. He turned and went back for her, but by now three Redcoats were on top of her with more coming. Other Redcoats were charging at D'Arcy, bayonets bared.

There was no choice. He turned and ran. The plumed hunting hat Jennifer had been wearing, with all her hair tucked up under it, had come off in the fracas, and as D'Arcy leaped over a bannister and rushed up the stairs, he heard a Redcoat declare in surprise, "Bloody bloomin' Mother o' Mary, e' ain't no man! It's a girl wearin' man's duds!"

Half a dozen Redcoats were chasing D'Arcy up the stairs now. He reached the top and grasped an iron-stand candelabra just as one Redcoat came charging forward. He sidestepped the bayonet and swiped the man across the head with the candelabra, dropping him to the carpet. Then he threw the heavy iron piece down the stairs at the others charging after him, knocking one down, making the others fall back to avoid stumbling over their fellow.

D'Arcy looked down at the main room below to see how Jennifer was faring. She was being held fast by two of the soldiers. As D'Arcy watched, Savage bolted out of the guest room, wearing only britches and boots, a sword in his hand. A Redcoat nearby swiveled toward him with his bayoneted musket. Savage leapt to the side of the flashing bayonet and ran the man through with his sword. He did not see a second Redcoat, though, who was coming up behind him.

D'Arcy grabbed the musket from the hand of the Redcoat he had smashed with the candelabra, swiveled with it and fired. He had not taken time to aim carefully, but the ball struck the man nonetheless—barely. It hit him in the ankle, making him scream in pain.

Savage turned and kicked the man backwards. He looked in the direction where the shot had come from, raised his sword in salute to D'Arcy on the stair landing, then rushed away toward the kitchen of the lodge.

D'Arcy turned to see another Redcoat on the stair landing with him. He parried the man's bayonet too late, receiving a stinging slice in the skin of his left flank. He ran the man through, then shoved him backwards into the other soldiers rushing up the stairway. Then he ran into the nearest room, slammed the door, and tripped the bolt.

He heard the pounding at the door and the shots that were fired into its latch, shattering the wood. The latch would hold for only a minute at best. He opened the window, looked to see that the roof sloped down low enough to provide the possibility of escape, then climbed outside.

He rushed along the sloping roof to the very edge, moving in a crouch so as not to fall forward at the steepness of the angle. Even before he reached the edge he saw a horse and rider galloping around the corner of the house. The night was too dark now to recognize the rider's face, but not so dark as to prevent D'Arcy seeing that the rider was bare-chested.

"Lancelot!" he yelled.

Savage reined in his steed and looked up. D'Arcy threw his captured musket to the ground below, gripped the edge of the roof, and swung down off of it. He was dangling now by his hands. Savage moved the horse under him. D'Arcy dropped onto it, behind Savage. Savage kneed the horse sharply.

"The musket!" yelled D'Arcy.

"No time!"

They raced off toward the woods amidst a flurry of bullets. Redcoats were coming around the corner of the lodge now and others were firing down from the windows in the building's second story. When they reached the woods, they rode deep enough in until it became too dense for horseback. Then they continued fleeing forward on foot.

"Zay steel have Jennyfair!" D'Arcy declared, out of breath.

"You're bleeding in your side," Savage panted. "How bad is it?"

"Not so bad. Zay steel have Jennyfair, I say."

419

"We'll clean it out," Savage said as they crashed forward into the woods. "Then we'll wrap it in cloth for a bandage. As soon as—"

"Are you deaf?" D'Arcy shouted, his face ferocious. "*Zay have her!*"

"*Goddam it, shut up!* I know they have her, you think I'm blind! Now shut up and *run!*"

Chapter 26

The auction went ahead as planned, despite the violent interruption that had caused the death of one guest and several soldiers. The Minister was not about to be cheated out of the large sum he expected to get for Jennifer just because of a bit of mayhem and murder. The only concession he made was to delay the event an extra hour, so security could be beefed up and guests calmed down.

The rescue attempt had not dampened the Minister's spirits in the least. In fact, he seemed in unusually fine fettle as he led Jennifer into the main room to a special podium he had had brought in for just this occasion. He was speaking to her in a gloating, exultant voice as he marched her forward through the crowd, his grip on her arm very tight. "Almost made it, didn't you? You would have succeeded, if I hadn't called in the troops as early as I did. Like to know what made me aware something was amiss? How I knew enough to be suspicious?"

She said nothing, just kept her eyes directed straight ahead as he pulled her along toward the podium. Her expression was grim.

"It was that signet ring bearing the House of Calhoun seal. I found it in your room when I was going through Armitage's belongings after his murder." He sneered gloatingly. "That's how I knew the Frenchman was an impostor, claiming to be the Marquis Calhoun. There *is* no Marquis Calhoun. The House of Calhoun is nothing but a fabrication based on a signet seal you or Armitage affixed to the documents I received."

She was at the podium now. It was waist high, with steps leading up from the side. Next to it, at floor level, was a lectern, which was to be used by the auctioneer. The Minister released her arm and nodded up at the podium. Jennifer offered no resistance. There was no hope of rescue now. All she could do was passively cooperate. If she resisted, she would end up back at the Bultaco.

She climbed the podium and turned to face the guests. All eyes were looking up at her, most of them filled with lecherous excitement. She was wearing her silver velvet gown again, though this time without the hooped pannier cage. Her skirt was mercifully down in place. Even if the Minister ordered it raised, though, Jennifer would not react strongly. At this point, she was numb to feelings of shame or embarrassment.

The Minister went to the auctioneer's stand and, after a brief introductory talk, began the auction. Bidding was frenzied and tension ran high during the first few minutes, with at least a dozen guests participating. Soon, though, the price rose high enough to weed out all but the most serious two or three bidders.

Jennifer was astonished by the figures being bandied about. The Minister seemed not at all surprised. He had expected that her looks, bearing, and temperament would fetch a high price, and he now took it in stride as his expectations proved justified. "Five thousand pounds is bid," he said, banging a gavel. "Who will offer six?"

Perhaps that was how he had risen so far in government, Jennifer thought. By having a sure sense for spotting opportunities that others missed. Pauly Garrett would never have believed such a price could be paid for her or he would have attempted an auction himself. And even Matthew, whose sense of greed was unsurpassed, had not considered the idea.

"I offer a half thousand more than five!" declared

Count Marcovici fiercely, standing at the front of the crowd, wearing a blue smoking robe. "I *must* have her!" he exclaimed, glaring with hate and rage directly at Jennifer. "It is *she* who caused me such ignominious insult! Cooperating with those barbarians to rob me of my clothes, to . . . to *humiliate* me in this way! I will make her pay! I swear to you, gentlemen, I—"

"Do I hear six?" said the Minister.

Sharif Ali put a finger to the bridge of his hooked nose in thoughtful reflection, then raised the finger in the air.

"Six," said the Minister, banging his gavel. "Do I hear seven?"

For a long moment, no one spoke or gestured. Had the bidding finally reached its conclusion? Jennifer wondered. Would the leering, hooked-nose Arab be her new owner?

"Do I hear seven?" the Minister asked again.

Count Marcovici looked as if he were dying of anguish, his thin Italian face trembling, the whites of his eyes showing. "I cannot pay more than I have already offered! But you must give me a chance to—"

"My apologies, Count, but this is strictly a business transaction. Six is offered. Do I hear seven?"

"Wait, wait!" exclaimed Marcovici excitedly. "I have an alternate proposition! Let me have her for only a day—just twenty-four hours!—and *then* you can sell her for—"

"I'm sorry," said the Minister stone-faced. "Six is bid, do I hear—"

"But I will offer a quarter of the entire sum! To have her for only—"

The Minister gave a signal with an inclination of his head and Derek walked over to the excited Count. When Marcovici saw the husky man come up to him from the sidelines and stand discreetly at his side, he understood the hint. He flung his head back with great dignity, pulled the smoking robe tighter around him, and stalked out of the room toward the guest suites.

The Minister seemed unhappy about this, Jennifer saw. She knew his unhappiness was not caused by the Count's having taken offense. It was caused by the fact that the Minister had very much wanted to accept the Count's offer, but could not do so without having Sharif Ali withdraw his bid.

"Six is the bid," said the Minister. "Hearing no others? . . ."

The hook-nosed Arab smiled with leering, menacing eyes at Jennifer. Vulgarly, he stuck out his tongue and licked both his lips.

"Six once. Six twice . . . "

"Six and half-a-thousand more," said a nervous, hesitant voice.

Everyone in the room looked off to the side at the previously unheard from bidder. They saw a bent-over old man with a lined, goateed face. He had the deep coloring and features of an Arab street beggar.

Sharif Ali suddenly became angry and shouted across the room at the man. "*You*, Elizar? You come here as my guest! Not to partake of the auction, but to discuss the purchase of arms! And now you *bid* against me?"

"A thousand pardons, Sire!" exclaimed the old man guiltily, bowing his head repeatedly. "What you say is so. As Allah is my witness. But still . . . " he stopped bobbing his head up and down and looked at the man unflinchingly from under a lowered brow, " . . . the bid stands."

Sharif Ali turned to the Minister at the lectern. "I insist this man be excluded from the bidding. It was I who received your invitation. I allowed him to join me only because we had business to discuss."

"Who are you, Sir?" the Minister asked the old man.

"He is a nobody!" declared Sharif Ali. "The lackey of a band of rebel dogs!"

"I am a nobody, as he says," admitted the old man. "But I am a nobody who has funds at hand to support my bid. They are with my entourage, a mile down the road."

"The rules are clear," the Minister said to Sharif Ali. "Anyone can bid, if they have the money."

Sharif Ali threw up his hands and cursed at the Minister in Arabic, then turned to curse at the old man. Then he stormed out of the room, as had Count Marcovici before him.

The Minister asked for more bids, and when none came, he declared Jennifer to now be the property of the Arab named Elizar. Elizar came up to the front as the guests began to disperse. When asked when he would like Jennifer delivered, he declared "Now, this instant. Bring her to my entourage. I will render payment the moment we arrive."

The Minister seemed pleased. Jennifer was too emotionally numb to feel anything other than amazement that this was really happening. She kept looking at the bent-over old man as the three of them were transported by carriage to Elizar's encampment beyond the grounds of the Minister's lodge. They were escorted by a contingent of mounted troops. What did the old man want of her, Jennifer wondered.

The old man's eyes never left her. They were kind eyes and were bright with a look of awe-struck fascination. He gazed at her as though he were astonished that she really existed.

When they reached the encampment, the Minister disembarked first. The old man put his hand on the back of Jennifer's hand, as she was about to leave the carriage, and asked with keen interest, "Have you a sister?"

"No," she said. "Why?"

"Get down here!" the Minister ordered Jennifer curtly from outside the carriage. "We've business to transact."

There were six men in Elizar's entourage. They wore English clothing, but even in the darkness of the night Jennifer could see that they were Arabs, not English.

A square tent had been raised along the road and it was illuminated inside by torches. The Minister went inside with Elizar and the two came out again a moment later. "There's a trunk full of gold in there," the Minister said to one of the Redcoats. "Put it in the carriage."

When that was done, the Minister shook hands with the old man. "Pleasure doing business with you," he said. He handed over the rolled-up contract of indenture.

"I no longer belong to you?" Jennifer asked the Minister, as he turned to go.

"Not any more."

"Then here," said Jennifer. She spit in his face, a thick gob of saliva that spattered across his mouth and nose.

The Minister went beet red with rage. He raised a fist to strike her, but Elizar stepped between the two of them quickly, raising his palms in front of him and exclaiming, "Please! Please! My property! Do not molest my property!"

The Minister jerked his sleeve to his face and wiped away the spit. He glared at Jennifer with fierce hatred. She raised her chin and stared back coldly. The Minister turned on his heel, entered the carriage, and screamed at the driver to take him back to the lodge. The carriage sped off down the road, followed by the Redcoat troopers.

"You are truly a fiery one," said Elizar, turning to Jennifer.

"What do you want me for?" Jennifer asked. The man was too ancient to have bought her for any lustful purpose. "What do you intend to do with me?"

"All in good time," he said. "Though this much I shall tell you now: I have spent money for you that was meant to buy arms to free my people. If my decision proves unwise, I shall lose my head over it." He showed her that he was speaking literally rather than

426

figuratively by putting his thumb to his throat and drawing it sharply from left to right.

The men in the encampment were standing around them, staring at Jennifer.

"For now," Elizar said to her, "be content to know that we will not harm you. What we do, we do only to insure your safe arrival in our country. We cannot risk your escaping during the journey."

"What do you mean 'what we do'?" she asked apprehensively. "What is it you're going to do?"

Elizar reached into his pocket and withdrew a twig with small yellow flower buds on it, speckled with black dots. He held it out for Jennifer to see. She leaned forward curiously and looked at it. When Elizar crushed the speckled buds in his hand, a strange, very pleasant aroma wafted into Jennifer's nostrils.

Blackness descended and she sank into a murky swampland of deep opiated sleep.

She awakened fully only twice during the journey. The first time, she opened her eyes and saw that she was being fed some sort of mutton stew by Elizar. She was chewing and swallowing and it seemed as if she had been doing so for several minutes, even though she had been asleep. She was in a chair on the deck of a ship at sea, a blanket covering her to protect her from the biting wind. The sea was brilliant blue, the clouds above were fluffy and incredibly white. She looked at Elizar and saw him smile warmly at her and say, "Ah, so you have awakened for a brief min—"

Blackness.

The second time, she awoke in a small ship's cabin. It was nighttime. Moonlight streamed in through the porthole window. She was wearing a warm fluffy nightgown. She went to the window, opened it, and took a breath of fresh cold air. There was the salty smell of the sea outside. Elizar was sitting in a chair, fully dressed. He looked at her groggily, having just come awake, and said "You had best sit down, fiery one, before you f—"

427

Blackness.

When she came awake the next time, the voyage was over. She did not know how long it had lasted. Two days? Two weeks? Several months? She was wearing her silver velvet gown again. The vessel was in a harbor. She saw a hand in front of her face, holding what looked like a sprig of dry parsley, which had a curious musty scent.

"You will not fall back asleep this time," Elizar said, waving the parsley before her nostrils, then putting it into his pocket. "You feel healthful and rested now, yes?"

She blinked hard. "I feel like I've been asleep a hundred years." She rubbed her eyes. They seemed very sensitive to the light. After a moment, she looked out, tentatively, at the world around her.

They were sitting on chairs on the deck of the vessel again. It was a warm, sunny day. The ship was tied to a wharf, but no people were visible since the ship was at the very end of the wharf. Jennifer stood up, and in the instant before Elizar grabbed her hand and jerked her back down, she saw a cluster of strangely garbed people at the other end of the wharf and on the land.

"Do not show yourself so recklessly," Elizar said.

"Recklessly?"

"Your life is in danger here. You must always remember that." He handed her a flask of water. Though she was very thirsty, she hesitated to drink from the flask or even to put it near her mouth and nose.

Elizar smiled gently. "Do not be afraid, it is just as it seems. Water. Nothing more."

She took a long, soothing drink.

"Now I tell you more of our situation. Not all. But what you need to know for the moment." He bent forward, his lined face serious. "We must transport you onto the island. There is an inspection point we must pass through manned by very barbarous militiamen. If they discover you . . ." He made the gesture again with his thumb drawn across his throat.

"I'm not at all fond of that gesture," she said.

"You will be even less fond of the actuality, I assure you. So listen. We will put you in a rug and roll you up, and there should be no problem. Hold your silence and all will go well."

"Why are you telling me this?" she asked suspiciously. "Why don't you just keep me drugged and not risk my refusing to go along with your plan?"

"The buds of the lucille plant have their limitations. When one is jostled or shaken, the effects do not hold. You will be both jostled and shaken during your transport in the rolled rug. It is unavoidable."

She regarded him warily. "Elizar, you tell me my life is in danger, but don't say why or from whom. How am I to know whether to keep silent, like you say, to avoid being beheaded . . . or to shout at the top of my lungs so someone can rescue me from *you,* who might be the one planning the beheading for all I know?"

"Do you not trust me?"

She laughed at him openly. "You drugged me! You tricked me into sniffing that plant!"

He smiled at her. "Do I not have a trustworthy smile?"

She looked at him and said nothing.

He patted her hand. "I do. And you must trust me because of it. For if you do not, then—"

"Don't make that gesture again!" She paused, then said, "I'll do as you say."

Elizar lost no time in putting his plan into operation. He took Jennifer below deck and, with the assistance of two of the crew, rolled her up in a giant intricately decorated rug. "Can you breathe?" he asked.

"Barely." It was hot and dark inside the rolled-up rug. She began to perspire uncomfortably.

"It will be only a moment. We load the other rugs first. You will be last, so you can be placed on top of the others in the cart, rather than the others on top of you. And remember. Silence at all times."

It was not "only a moment." It seemed like an eternity before she felt herself finally being lifted up at the two ends and then carried bouncingly off the ship onto the wharf. Harsh words were exchanged at what Jennifer assumed was the inspection point. Some words were in English, but most were in a strange foreign tongue. Soon she was jarringly dropped—rather than gently placed—onto the cart, which began rumbling forward.

After several minutes of traveling, she wanted to ask what was happening, but dared not risk speaking. Even though they were away from the inspection point, she might still be in danger. After a few moments more, she heard Elizar's voice. "We're away from the harbor. You can relax now."

"I'd rather breathe," she said. "Can you let me out of here?"

"Not yet. Too many people along the road. Soon, though."

"But—"

"Silence!" he said. She heard the clopping of a horse and then other voices speaking in the foreign tongue. After a moment, the sounds died away.

There was an opening at one end of the carpet which allowed in light, but it was not large enough for her to see anything through it. After a long period of time, the cart stopped. "We've arrived at last!" Elizar said in a happy voice.

"Then get me out of here!"

"Elizar, you scoundrel!" said a welcoming masculine voice from off to the side. "So you returned after all. And here I thought you'd surely taken our money to the gaming tables and were fearful of ever showing your face again!" The voice had a lilt of joyousness to it and an accent that was different from Elizar's. Jennifer wondered what land they were in.

She heard the sound of other carts rolling up alongside the one she was in. There were the happy exchanges of greeting and welcome. Then the man with the strong masculine voice said, "And now, Elizar, the muskets. Show them to me. Where are they, wrapped in these rugs?" Jennifer felt a slap on her shoulder through the rug. "I can't feel them. Here, you men, unroll these."

"Wait, wait, wait, Sahib Kaheeli!" shouted Elizar fearfully. "I must tell you of something first! It is of the utmost urgency. You see—"

"Go ahead, men. Elizar, you tell me while they're unrolling the weapons. I don't want to lose a minute in seeing these beauties. You know how long we've waited."

"But wait! Sahib—!"

Jennifer felt herself being raised up and carried bouncingly forward several feet.

"How much did that weasel Sharif Ali milk us for, the whole amount?"

"I did not purchase the weapons, Sahib Kaheeli!" Elizar declared, with great fear and anxiety in his voice. "Instead I spent the money for—Wait! Do not unroll that carpet!"

"*Didn't buy the muskets?*" roared the man named Kaheeli, with the violent thunder of impending doom in his voice. Jennifer suddenly felt herself dropping down sharply and then being rolled over and over with dizzying, mind-reeling rapidness. "What could you *possibly* spend the money on that's more important than muskets?" roared Kaheeli.

"Aaaiiiiiii," moaned Elizar.

Jennifer spun out of the carpet into the sunlight, rolling over and over and over, until she came to a rest on her stomach on the dirt ground. She was so dizzy and light-headed and nauseous she could not even move. Her dress had hiked up during her twirling ejection from the carpet, so that it now was bunched up above her waist, nakedly exposing the lower part of her body.

431

For a moment there was dumbfounded silence. The calm before the storm. Then: *"Elizar,"* thundered Kaheeli in a withering rage, *"I'll have you chopped into horse fodder! I'll have your wretched hide staked out for the ants! I'll—Elizar, this? This is what you bring me in place of muskets?"*

Jennifer tried to raise herself up off her stomach, but was so nauseous and weakened from the dizziness, she could barely move. She managed to put her hands to where the dress was bunched up above her hips, but could not command the strength to raise herself up so she could pull the dress down. Brightly exploding stars danced before her eyes.

Kaheeli's voice was quieter now, but just as furious. "I mean, Elizar, what am I to *think?* And at your age! You old satyr! You rake! You profligate goat!"

Elizar seemed on the verge of crying. "Aaiii, Sahib!" he moaned. "You do not let me explain! There is such a wondrous reason why I have spent our weapons money on—"

Jennifer felt a rough hand rubbing appraisingly up her leg and over her behind. She moved her arm behind her and shoved the man's hand away.

"And Elizar," said Kaheeli in wonderment, "seven thousand pounds? I mean, it's nice . . . in fact, it's quite nice, but, Elizar, *seven thousand pounds! Cleopatra herself wouldn't have gone for seven thousand pounds!* I refuse to believe that you spent so much money for this girl. I absolutely *refuse* to believe that you—"

Jennifer finally managed to push herself onto her side. She looked at the man.

"I believe it," Kaheeli said quietly, staring at her face.

She tugged her dress down. She tried to sit up, but was too dizzy. Her hair was in her face, her skin and silver dress were filthy from being rolled about in the dirt. She stared at Kaheeli, bleary-eyed.

He was tall and broad-shouldered and had a thick, black full beard with mustache. He seemed to be in his mid-thirties. He had a turban on his head, a ring in one ear, and he wore what appeared to be a white ankle-length robe rather than blouse and britches. The collarless robe had a slit extending from the neck to the man's navel, showing his powerful, curly-haired chest. He was very handsome, but overshadowing his handsomeness was a look of incredible masculinity. Virile, potent maleness practically radiated from him.

He squatted down in front of Jennifer and regarded her scrutinizingly. His eyes were black like olives, his skin very darkly tanned. He turned his eyes to Elizar. "Can it be?" he asked in a whisper. Elizar rolled his eyes heavenward in gratitude and relief at the change in the man's response.

Kaheeli turned back to Jennifer and put his hand on her chin, roughly tilting her head backward as he stared at her. She grasped his thick wrist and tried to shove his arm away, but he slapped her hands aside, almost absently, and continued looking at her face. His gaze was impersonal, like that of a man inspecting merchandise. When he looked into her eyes, the nature of his gaze changed. He recognized her as a person, capable of speech. "Do you have a sister?" he said.

Now Jennifer really did slap his hand away from her chin with all her might. "He asked me that, too!" she raged. "What is this all *about?*"

He stood up and backed away from her toward Elizar. "Touchy, isn't she?" he remarked quietly, not turning his eyes away from Jennifer. He put his hand on Elizar's shoulder. "You did good, old one. It was a wise choice. Worth a thousand times as many muskets, if all works well."

Jennifer stood up and dusted herself off. She brushed her hair out of her face. She looked at the group of men who were now unloading various provisions from the three carts. They were Arabs like Elizar. Many wore long white robes, though, like Kaheeli, rather than blouses and britches. The area

433

they were in seemed to be a mining encampment of some sort. An open mineshaft gaped at her from the side of a cliff a few yards away, its entrance braced with beams.

· Jennifer went up to Elizar and Kaheeli as they stood talking, and stopped directly in front of them. "I want you to tell me why you brought me here," she said, looking from man to man, "and I want to know right now. I'm tired of being drugged and wrapped in a rug and scared to death by threats that my life's in danger."

She put her hands on her hips and tossed back her head to get her hair out of her face. "Just because you own me doesn't give you the right to——"

"A hellcat," Kaheeli chuckled to old Elizar. "She'll surely——"

"And stop talking about me as if I wasn't here!" The *arrogance* of the man! She breathed through flared nostrils, feeling fury race through her.

Kaheeli looked at her, intrigued. He clasped his hands on her shoulders. She tried to shove them away, but he was far too strong for her. He did not even seem to notice her efforts. He smiled at her and said, "Welcome to Jazirat." Then he pulled her forward and embraced her in a formal hug of greeting. When he released her, she stumbled backward a few paces and glared at him.

"I am Kaheeli Avram Omar," he said, still smiling, making light of her rage. "I am baron of the bandits, prince of the potters—only as a disguise to hide my real calling, however—and leader of this noble rebel band you see here before you . . . in its most decimated state, I might add."

He gestured sweepingly. "These men here and this old dog Elizar are the last of our guerilla band. Most are rotting in the dungeons of the royal palace." He paused. "Would you not prefer a meal and drink before hearing more?"

"No!"

"Then you shall hear all of it now, the answers to your questions. Or *see* all of it, to be more precise." He turned to Elizar. "I must go into the city now, to see my spy. I will take her with me."

"But Kaheeli! The danger!"

"We will disguise her to minimize the danger." He went to Jennifer. "Come," he said, putting his arm across her shoulders tightly, walking her forward toward the mineshaft entrance. She tried to push his arm away, with no success. He did not even notice her efforts to resist him. He seemed to take it for granted that he had the right to do anything he pleased and could not conceive of any woman wishing to prevent him from doing so.

"You will change into the clothes of my country now, so as not to be conspicuous. As Elizar has told you, your life is in danger if you are viewed without disguise."

"From whom? Who am I in danger from?"

"The Kurds. Mercenary warriors brought in by the Monarch to serve as the militia. It's they who make life on the island a nightmare. They would snuff you out like a candle if they saw you, and with as little concern."

As they entered the dim mine, Jennifer was surprised to find several women inside, along with a variety of provisions. The front portion of the mine, just beyond the entrance, was very wide and high-ceilinged. Kaheeli took her to a chestnut-haired beauty who was in the midst of chopping food for a meal, and said, "Katia. Dress her for the city."

"Yes, Sahib Kaheeli," the girl said, blandly looking at his arm across Jennifer's shoulders. When Kaheeli left, the girl's bland face turned hateful. She went to a pile of garments stacked haphazardly next to a pile of pottery-making tools. She picked out several items, bunched them into a ball, and flung them at Jennifer's chest, uttering a foreign phrase with spiteful venom.

When Jennifer came back outside, she was wearing

a green halter top and shortened britches of a heavy, coarse-knit material. The sleeves of the top and the legs of the britches were dark smoky veils. Her hair was covered by a low, close-to-the-skull turban of the same green material. Her stomach and lower back were bare.

"You look wonderful!" Kaheeli said, when she approached him.

"I feel ridiculous. And these clothes don't hide my light skin. If I'm in danger, shouldn't I—"

"Cover yourself fully? Not at all. It's not your obvious Norseman ancestry that causes you peril. There are many light-skinned ones in Jazirat. Though most are Arabs, such as Elizar, and a few are of East Indian origin such as myself."

He reached down and took the extra smoky veil Jennifer held in her hand, which she had not known what to do with. "This you definitely must wear," he said, fastening it over her lower face, connecting it to the turban. Only her blue eyes were visible now.

"And one thing more," Kaheeli said sternly, in the manner of a teacher imparting valuable advice. He tapped his finger on the bridge of her nose, through the veil, to emphasize the point. "Hold your tongue when we are in the city. Jazirat women do not speak in public."

He led her to one of the carts. When she began climbing into the front seat, he stopped her and motioned for her to ride in the back. There was no seat in the back. She sat on the wooden floorboards among a multitude of ceramic vases and jugs and boxes of pottery-decorating materials.

"We'll arrive in time for the royal ride through the bazaar," Kaheeli said to Elizar, as the two of them climbed into the front seat. "It should prove instructive, eh old one?"

"What is it you're taking me to see?" Jennifer asked, as they started forward down the dirt road, rocky foothills looming up on either side of them.

"You shall see what you shall see," Kaheeli said.

"There you go with these childish mysteries! Why can't either of you ever answer me straightforwardly?" She was so frustrated she wanted to scream.

"I will tell you a story," said Kaheeli.

"I don't want to hear a story!"

"Once there was a peaceful island called Jazirat. Its principal export was . . . nothing. Its principal import was more of the same. The people lived happily in undisturbed poverty, amusing themselves with the exotic drugs that grew in abundance on the island, in the roots, shrubs, flowers. One day English traders came and uprooted many of these wondrous roots and shrubs, thinking to make a fortune selling the drugs to other nations. Alas, they soon discovered that when removed from the soil of Jazirat, all the drugs quickly lost potency, save only the lowly black-speckled blossoms."

They were nearing the city. Jennifer could see it below them as they rounded a curve. It was sprawling, desolate, uncivilized-looking, with unpaved streets and whitewashed mortar buildings.

"The English traders never returned, but an adventurer who learned of their exploits did, bringing along an army of Kurdish mercenaries." Kaheeli's voice became bitter. "This adventurer became ruler of Jazirat, through murder and intimidation. A tyranny was begun to force the natives to reveal the secret of how to alter the drugs so they could be exported without losing their effect."

"The sadness," said Elizar, "is that no such secret exists."

"The sadness," said Kaheeli, "is that the tyrant is a barbarian who killed most who resisted and threw the others into the dungeon to rot."

They arrived at the main street of the city, which was the avenue of the bazaar. Merchants lined both sides of the street, displaying their wares in ramshackle booths or simply on the dirt ground before them. Most

437

were Arabs, dressed in white garb. The women were dressed much the same as Jennifer, which seemed seneless to her. To wear colorful garments in a place as dusty and dirty as this? The ground was like white powder. Dust rose thickly into the air as they traveled down the street.

Merchants called out to them in strange tongues, hawking their wares. Beggars came up to their cart, seeing Elizar's English dress and thinking he might be a rich Englishman. Elizar cursed them in Arabic, shoving them away. They now passed a stall where Jennifer heard strange music. She saw a man sitting cross-legged on the ground, playing a wooden flute. Next to him was a young boy whose blind eyes were open, showing only whiteness, no pupils. In front of the boy, a thick snake was rising into the air from a woven basket. There was the smell of food being cooked nearby, but it was not a pleasant smell. Jennifer made a mental note to be very cautious about any food she was given on this island.

"Kaheeli," said Elizar urgently, pointing down the road. "There!"

Kaheeli pulled the cart hurriedly over to the side of the road, almost knocking over a table containing carved wooden pipes and hookas. The man behind the table cursed furiously in Arabic. Jennifer looked in the direction where Elizar had pointed. A group of riders were trotting down the street, wearing black, hooded, sheetlike clothing and carrying giant scimitars in scabbards on their wide red belts. They were all exceptionally tall, as if they had been chosen for this trait, and they looked fearsome and sinister on their black steeds.

In the lead, on a magnificent white Arabian, Jennifer was astonished to see a woman. From the distance and due to the great cloud of dust that arose before the riders, Jennifer could not make out the woman's features. She could see the flaming red hair though, long and wild, and the woman's rigid, disdainful posture. She wore golden riding breeches tucked into brown hipboots and a golden sleeveless vest with no blouse or slip beneath it.

"There you see the answer to all your questions," Kaheeli said to Jennifer in a low, bitter voice. "This woman you stare at so disbelievingly, she is the most ruthless tyrant in the Arabias. She is Queen Isabella, ruler of Jazirat."

People on the road fled for their lives out of the path of the oncoming riders, who did not bother to slow their pace. An old man hobbled out of the way too slowly and was trampled by several of the horses. The riders were very near the cart now, about to pass by. Jennifer could see the woman's features clearly.

She gasped. It was like looking in a mirror.

Queen Isabella's head was held high as she looked to the left and right, casting contemptuous glances at her subjects as she rode forward. Her skin was fair, her lips thick, her eyes large under shapely brows. A mirror image.

"I can't believe it," Jennifer said to Kaheeli.

Kaheeli reacted to her words with only a slight twitch that came to the lips of his stony face. Next to him, though, Elizar winced painfully.

The Queen reined to an abrupt halt only a few feet past them, raising her arm to stop the riders behind her. She jerked the white Arabian around and trotted back to the cart. She looked at Jennifer with biting disdain. "Did I hear *speech?* In a public bazaar?"

Jennifer kept silent. She lowered her eyes to appear humbled and contrite. Her heart pounded so loudly with fear, she could hear it in her ears.

"A thousand pardons, Your Highness!" declared Elizar, with abject pleading in his voice. "Forgive me, forgive me, I beg your forgiveness!" He joined his hands as if in prayer and held them out beseechingly toward the Queen.

Forgive *him?* Jennifer thought. She glanced up and saw that Elizar had succeeded in shifting the Queen's attention onto himself.

Elizar began blubbering—crying, though no tears came to his eyes. "I only recently bought this one to help me prepare my potions. She's not yet trained in our ways! She does not realize the great offense of breaking Your Highness's wise and just mandates. Oh, have mercy on my wretched soul, your noble Highness!"

The Queen glared at him sternly. "I recognize you, Elizar the chemist. I demanded a potion from you to spare me from aging. That was months ago! You've yet to deliver!"

"Oh, be merciful with my pitiable self, your kind, generous Highness," Elizar whined and blubbered, though still showing no tears. He bowed up and down repeatedly in his seat. "The concoction is extremely resistant. Some say impossible! It fights me at every turn. Soon I will have it, though, I stake my life on it!"

"Yes," said the Queen, "that's exactly what you stake." She glanced again at Jennifer, who quickly lowered her eyes. She felt the queen's gaze burning into her. She wished the dark smoky veil she wore over her face was a thousand times darker.

Suddenly she felt a sharp sting on her shoulder as the Queen's riding crop came slashing down. She bit her lower lip to keep from crying out. "For unseemliness," declared Queen Isabella. Jennifer felt another sharp blow of the riding crop on her opposite arm. "For the vulgar beauty of your eyes." Then there were four more stinging slashes of the crop, making her cry out in pain, her eyes tearing.

She heard one more slash and this time Elizar screamed in agony, as the crop smashed him across the forehead. "Bring me that potion!" shouted the Queen. She kneed her horse and bolted away. The black-clad riders galloped off after her.

Now that they were alone again, Elizar sighed a loud, long exaggerated sigh. He pressed his hand up against his bleeding forehead.

"You were quite good," Kaheeli said to Elizar.

" 'Oh, forgive me, forgive me, your gracious noble Highness'," he mimicked, pantomiming the old man's cringing, begging posture and expression. " 'I am only a worthless, humble, lowly—"

"Enough, enough," said Elizar.

"—wretched, miserable beggar, who—"

"Yes, yes," said Elizar wearily. "But you know, I must learn tears. I would have been so much more pitiful if I could only have shed a few small drops."

"Be content with your skill such as it is. Shakespeare would have been proud."

Kaheeli turned and looked back at Jennifer. She stared up at him with eyes that were vivid with violent emotions—rage, hate, fear—but she said nothing. Kaheeli grinned tautly. "I see you can learn a lesson, at least. Good. Remain this way till we leave the city." He turned in his seat, facing forward again. "You can make your abject apologies later."

She picked up a ceramic jug and heaved it at him, as the cart started forward. It hit him between the shoulder blades and rebounded back into the cart, shattering on the wooden floor.

Kaheeli turned back to her very slowly. His features were hard as he stared at her. "You feel you should be asked after, is that it? I should say to you, 'How are you, poor girl?', and give you sympathy?"

Her eyes raged at him.

"You nearly cost all of us our lives," he said. "The danger to you, and to us while we're with you, lies in your face. Surely you can see that now. Had Isabella become curious at the familiarity of your eyes and pulled away your veil, she would have instantly realized our plan. And that would have been the end of all of us."

Jennifer could hold her silence no longer. She looked around to make sure no one was within hearing distance, then said quietly but furiously, "And just what *is* your plan?"

"Why, to substitute you for Isabella, of course. You are about to become our Queen."

441

Chapter 27

A short distance past the bazaar, they arrived at the island's single harbor and pulled to a stop in front of a waterfront tavern with an Arabic name. Kaheeli jumped down and went inside to meet his spy. Jennifer remained in the back of the cart, subjected to the rude stares of seamen of various nationalities who passed nearby as they left the tavern.

Jennifer had been eyeing the boxes of pottery-decorating tools in the back of the cart for some time. Now she took a slab of black chalk from one of the boxes, picked up a large piece of the jug that had shattered after she'd thrown it at Kaheeli's back, and began writing on the remnant. She was almost finished, when Elizar in the front seat turned around to see what the scratching noise was.

"What is that you are writing?" he asked.

"It's a . . . a . . . a description of the Queen! So I won't forget."

Elizar held out his hand for the piece of broken pottery. Reluctantly she gave it to him, scowling. He looked at it closely.

> Deliver this to ships' chandler Drumsky
> in London. You'll be rewarded.

He turned it over to the other side:

> Lancelot—Jazirat Island. Jennif—

"What does it say?" Elizar asked, turning the writing upside down and then sideways.

"It says red hair, open golden vest, white Arabian stallion."

Elizar handed it back to her, slumped down in the front seat, and began idly playing with the many colorful rings on his fingers.

Jennifer watched the exit doors of the tavern. Two blond Nordic seamen exited. A moment later, a sailor—who appeared to be either a Greek or a Turk—left, walking not very steadily. Then several minutes after that, a young seaman left wearing raggedy merchantman's clothing that appeared to be English. She watched him keenly.

The man staggered rather than walked. His eyes were thin, squinty slits. When he opened his mouth, Jennifer knew instantly that the man was indeed English. He began talking to himself drunkenly, playfully imitating a pirate's throaty diction. "Aye, me hearties," he mumbled, stumbling forward a few paces and then back. "Yo ho ho and a bottle of . . . what's that yer say? Keelhaul the smarmy bugger! Lash the scalawag to the yardarm . . ."

The seaman stopped in his tracks when he saw Jennifer waving him forward and making urgent, pleading expressions at him. He craned his head forward and gawked at her. Then he looked around to his left and to his right. He looked back at her and pointed a thumb at his chest, silently mouthing: Me? Jennifer nodded spiritedly. The man staggered over to the cart. He raised his eyebrows quizzically at her. She turned to make sure Elizar was not looking, then pulled out the man's turtleneck collar and stuck the piece of broken pottery inside. Then she pushed him away. He looked at her very strangely. "Well, blow me down," he mumbled. He shook his head in bewilderment and stood there staring at her, despite her urgent motions for him to leave.

Kaheeli came out of the tavern and saw Jennifer

desperately waving the man away. He climbed into the cart without a word, apparently viewing her actions as nothing more or less than he would expect. Elizar started the cart forward and they slowly rumbled off.

"Bad news," said Kaheeli grimly. "The British Proconsul arrives in a month."

"So soon?" asked Elizar, looking at him.

"That's the word from my spy. Negotiations will start and end the very day he arrives. Isabella will end up with riches enough to keep her Kurds for decades to come."

"And the British will have the explosive. Aiieee, this is bad. This is very bad indeed."

"What explosive?" Jennifer said.

Kaheeli turned in his seat to glance at her, then turned back to Elizar. "Start the girl's instruction right away. Thirty days from now, she'll have to walk, talk, eat, ride . . . even think as Isabella."

Now that they were on the open road again, away from public view, Jennifer leaned forward and put her arms on the back of the seat, between the two men. "Aren't you neglecting something?" she said.

"Kaheeli neglects nothing," said Kaheeli.

Her voice became sharp, infuriated by the man's incredible conceit.

"You've given some thought, then, as to how you plan to get *me* to go along with your scheme? Not that a minor detail like that should concern the great Kaheeli."

"Of course I've given it thought."

"Oh, of course!" Jennifer was not sarcastic by nature, but this tall, handsome Indian was incensing her with his haughty arrogance. "Well I don't think I *will* go along with your little impersonation scheme, thank you very much," she declared, driven by a desire to challenge him, to show him up. She folded her arms across her chest and raised her chin petulantly.

Kaheeli held his hand out to Elizar, nonchalantly. Elizar reached inside his coat, withdrew the rolled-up contract of indenture, handed it to him. "You will impersonate Isabella for me," Kaheeli said, unrolling the document and reading her name, ". . . Jennifer VanDerLind. And in return I will destroy this devilish slavechain of parchment for you." He looked at her. "One day's impersonation, for three years' freedom."

She was burning with exasperation. Kaheeli knew she would love to turn down any proposal he offered, to make him lose face. So he had offered one she could not possibly turn down. The impudence of the man!

"Yes?" Kaheeli said in a self-satisfied voice.

"Yes, damn you!"

"Do not be so displeased, Jennifer VanDerLind. Aside from gaining your freedom, your impersonation will benefit you in another way also."

"What way?"

"Your indenture paper shows you are from the Colony of Massachusetts. I know of the American Colonies' moves for independence. It is directly because of these moves that the English Proconsul comes to Jazirat. England wants to negotiate for a powerful new explosive that's been developed here, to use it against your Colonies in the coming rebellion."

"It is a combustible of amazing strength," said Elizar, "with power five times that of common gunpowder."

"They'll use it to quash your rebellion the instant it begins. The increased range made possible by the explosive will let English cannons fire at your troops, ships, cities, gun emplacements—without ever being exposed to answering fire. Redcoats can attack your Colonial soldiers from beyond the range of your soldiers' guns."

Jennifer was stunned. "There really is such an explosive?"

"The Queen's chemists came upon it accidentally," Kaheeli said. "They were seeking the way to alter drugs so they could be removed from the island, when they discovered that certain elements found only in

445

Jazirat soil, when blended with flashpowder, create the explosive."

"I have to get some of this new explosive!" Jennifer said excitedly. "Why, if General Washington could have—"

"Impossible. Thirty score kegs have been produced and no more can be made. The soil elements, from the base of the hotsprings, were completely used up in the manufacture of these kegs. The Queen's been driving our people mercilessly in her search for new soil of this rare nature—digging beneath the earth, in the sides of mountains, even under the hotsprings themselves. But no more of it exists."

They were nearing the encampment now. Jennifer saw the mineshaft opening to the left and Kaheeli's squared-off tent a distance off to the right. The chestnut-haired girl named Katia passed along the road near them, carrying a woven basket on her head. She glared at Jennifer hatefully.

"So you see, Jennifer VanDerLind?" Kaheeli said, as the cart halted. "Your aid in denying England the explosive, by impersonating Isabella, will benefit both of us."

"I don't see. How does it benefit *you?*" She climbed out of the cart.

"Isabella needs the money England will pay for the explosive. Without it, she won't be able to maintain her army of Kurds. She can't keep looting the populace to pay them, because she's done it for so long already there's little left to loot."

"Without money for her mercenaries," Elizar said, "her tyranny will topple."

Kaheeli waved his hand, as if dismissing the matter. "Now!" he said enthusiastically, slapping his arm across Jennifer's shouders. "We begin your instruction." He started walking her forward. She tried to shove his arm away, again, and again met with no success.

"Later we tell you the details of our plan. Now, though, you must concentrate on nothing but your

446

transformation into Isabella. For once you are in the palace in the midst of the barbarous Kurds .·. . if you err even *slightly* and are revealed as an imposter . . . "

"Yes?" she said, as his words faded out.

He shook his head ominously. "Better not to think of it."

The next few weeks were spent training Jennifer in all aspects of Queen Isabella's behavior. It was not difficult for her to learn to act like Isabella, she discovered. The streak of sadistic cruelness had to be faked, but as for the other traits, it was mostly just a matter of letting the worst aspects of her own character take over, so that she behaved in a shrewish, demanding, insufferable way. This was easy, actually, she discovered, since Kaheeli brought out the worst in her by his very presence. To develop a swaggering walk when around him, or a snide way of speaking, seemed like a natural response to the man's arrogance.

Jennifer was the only girl in the camp who reacted to him this way. Among the few single women present, all seemed to be deathlessly enraptured of the Indian. When Kaheeli would choose out one of the girls to lay with him in his tent at night, the others all looked on her with great envy.

During the weeks she had been here, Jennifer was the only girl Kaheeli had not chosen. Probably, she thought, because he knew she'd tell him what to do with his invitation, in no uncertain terms. But deep inside her there was an irritating stab of curiosity. Why hadn't he picked her?

She would have liked to be chosen by him, so she could coldly turn him down. She knew he would not force himself on her. His conceit was too great for him to feel he would need to resort to force in order to have a woman.

If things went well, Jennifer thought, she would not be taken by force ever again, by any man. She would finally be free of that damnable indenture. That is, if

447

she managed to carry off her impersonation without being killed.

And it wouldn't be long now, she thought, as she walked across the rock-strewn landscape toward the campfire, before she'd find out whether that was to be the case. Tomorrow was the day she was to be substituted for Isabella. She raised the hem of her white toga as she walked, to save herself from tripping. The toga was standard wear for women when in the campsite, but it was damnably difficult to walk in.

Kaheeli and his men had just returned from one of their nighttime raids on the richer merchants from the island's far side, who continued to pay the Queen's taxes despite Kaheeli's prohibitions. Tonight's raid had netted a sizable treasure for the guerilla's warchest, Jennifer had heard, which would go to help finance the rebellion.

Now Kaheeli was changing out of his raiding clothes and facemask and preparing to join her at the campfire. Tonight he was finally going to tell her the details of the plan they would enact in the morning.

Elizar was already at the campfire when she arrived, sitting on one of the large surrounding rocks. "Some brew?" he asked her, offering Kaheeli's pot that was warming near the fire. She shook her head. The thick syrupy mixture of fermented beans, grains, and herbs turned her stomach. She had not yet lost her amazement at the fact that Kaheeli could stand the stuff, much less actually enjoy it. But enjoy it he did.

Jennifer sat down on a rock near the fire and waited. A few moments later, Kaheeli appeared from his tent and came over. "So, Jennifer VanDerLind, are you ready to abandon us peasants and take your rightful place as one of the royal, magisterial caste?" His tone was light and amused as he poured a mug full of the brew and sat down on a rock near her. He was wearing his white robe again, though without the turban this time. His hair was cropped short and brushed forward, emphasizing the manly fullness of his face.

"I'm ready," she said.

"Excellent. And here is what you are ready for: to-morrow morning, you and I go with Elizar to the royal palace. Elizar has been granted an audience to present the 'anti-aging' potion the Queen has requested. You and I will be posing as his assistants."

"The potion is really no more than a base of black-speckled blossoms," Elizar said, "with other ingredients added only for show."

"Isabella will sniff it, taste of it, and—" he snapped his fingers "—her consciousness will evaporate like the mist."

"If only I had a drug which could make *her* evapo-rate like the mist," lamented Elizar, playing with the rings on his fingers.

"A closet will have to suffice, old one." He sipped from his brew and smacked his lips. "Once she is asleep, you will change clothing with her, unwrap your hair, which Elizar will have colored in the morning, and prepare to greet the Proconsul. He's due only a short while after our own audience."

"Where will you be?" she asked.

"Elizar and I will remain with you in case anything goes wrong. Although, truth be told, if anything goes wrong, our being with you will not do any of us much good."

"Then why—"

"As a sign of good faith," Elizar said. "We could not put you in danger and then abandon you. If you fail, we shall suffer your failure together."

"What is this talk of failure!" said Kaheeli high-spir-itedly. "We are on the brink of a new era of freedom for Jazirat. Joyous thoughts, that's more what is called for." He turned to Jennifer. "When the Proconsul ar-rives, he will make you an extremely generous offer. You will turn it down, demanding half again more than he offers."

"What will he do then?"

"My spy tells me his instructions under such circumstances are to return to England for consultation. He will then come back a short while later and either meet your demand or seize the explosive by force."

Jennifer was confused. "I don't understand. If he's going to come back several weeks later and get the explosive anyway, then what good——"

"Very much good!" said Kaheeli. "By that time, the explosive will no longer exist. When the Proconsul leaves, you will order the main force of your Kurds to escort him back to the harbor, under the pretext that his life is in danger from me and my men. Then, when the majority of Kurds are away, my men will attack the palace! They will fight off the remaining Kurds and free those of our brothers who rot in the dungeons. Then, with our renewed and enlarged force, we will launch a surprise attack against the main body of Kurds when they return to the palace."

"This diversion of the Kurds is necessary," Elizar explained, "because even though they will look to you as their ruler, if you were simply to give an order to release the prisoners, it would cause them to cast a very suspicious eye on you."

"This way," said Kaheeli, "we avoid the problem. And once the island is back in our hands, we destroy the explosive. I know, I know, you'd prefer to have it for your Colonies. But remember, the English will return. And if it exists, they will take it. So it must not exist."

Kaheeli flung the contents of his mug into the fire. The brew made the fire spit and crackle. "That concludes your briefing on the plan," Kaheeli said. "And as for your instruction in the ways of Isabella, you lack only one last pattern of behavior."

"I do? I thought you'd told me everything and drilled me on it?"

"Everything but one thing. I delayed mention of it till now because I expect it may cause friction between us."

Jennifer looked at him with curiousness and anxiety.

"What is this last area of her behavior you didn't mention to me?"

"The Queen is a wanton. A very libidinous, passionate woman. You noticed the way she dressed? Are you familiar with the Latin word *nympha*? It means—"

"I know what it means," she said quickly, cutting him off.

"Well, Jennifer VanDerLind, you must be as wanton and obsessed and starved for it in your impersonation, as is the Queen in reality. Or the scheme will fail. Chances are excellent you will not have an opportunity to demonstrate this area of behavior during the short period of your impersonation. But if the situation does arise, you must be prepared to meet it."

"I can act . . . that way," she said, "if I have to."

"Good," said Kaheeli. "It is just as I thought. You are conscientious about your task and willing to do all that is necessary." He stood up and took her hand. "Come, we go to my tent. You will show me your appetite and how well you perform."

"Now wait!" she said, pulling her hand away. "I'm not going to . . . to do that with you."

He looked puzzled. "But it is the only way of seeing that you can indeed simulate the great excesses of hunger and consuming desire. It is a drill, just as we have drilled you on all other aspects of Isabella's behavior. You have walked swaggeringly for us, you have spoken with great arrogance, you have—"

"Yes, well this is one thing I will *not* give you a demonstration of. You'll have to take my word on it. *If* the occasion arises, which it better not, then I'll act like . . . like a bitch in heat!" She remembered the phrase from the painful days at the Bultaco. Yes, she knew, she would have no trouble acting out such a role. She had *lived* the role for several weeks. But she'd be damned if she would give this arrogant Kaheeli the satisfaction of having her fling herself at him hungeringly, just to prove the point.

So that was why he had made no attempt to bed her

451

earlier. Why risk making the overture and being reject-
ed, when he expected all along that she would be his in
the end anyway? And with *her* being the one to act
desperately in need of *him*.

Kaheeli looked upon her fiery refusal with even-tem-
peredness. "Buddha tells us," he said, "that in the end,
that which must be, is." He bowed slightly from the
waist. "Good night to you, Jennifer VanDerLind." He
nodded briefly at Elizar, then walked off toward his
tent, stretching widely and yawning.

Jennifer did not understand the meaning of his last
remark, but she was not interested enough to ask about
it. All she wanted now was to just take her bath and
get to sleep. She wanted to be well rested for tomorrow. "Good night, Elizar," she said to the old man.
"See you in the morning."

The old Arab nodded and smiled at her, but then
turned his eyes back to stare abstractedly into the
campfire. He sipped at his mug of brew.

Jennifer went to the hotspring pool, undressed, and
waded in. It felt warm and wonderful as it always did,
becoming hotter the closer she came to the hotspring
itself, so that the warmth gently surrounded her and
seemed to flow all through her. The night air was mild
now too, rather than chilly as it had been last night. In
fact, tonight was such a wonderful night for bathing,
she wondered why none of the other girls were in the
pool? Usually there were at least one or two others
here when she came to swim. Maybe it was the
lateness of the hour.

As she floated peacefully on her back, letting herself
relax, she did not notice the hand with many rings on
its fingers, which pushed out through the bushes at the
edge of the pool and tossed a palmful of gray-white
crystals into the water.

Jennifer floated for several more minutes, then
turned over and swam back to the shore. She got out
and began drying herself on the towel she had brought.
It was then that she felt the strange feeling creeping

452

over her. Her skin began to tingle all over. She shrugged. Maybe she had been in the water too long, she thought. But then the feeling seemed to centralize, so that while her skin continued to tingle all over her, there was a growing intensity of the feeling in her breasts and loins. Then her tongue and mouth began to tingle strongly too.

What is this strange feeling? she wondered, becoming worried. She had never felt anything like it before. It was as if the electric power of lightning had begun slowly surging through her, jangling her nerves with the electricity. She began to jerk slightly and to twitch. She couldn't stop herself. The feeling in her loins and breasts and mouth was no longer an intense tingling, it was a wild, throbbing sensation. It was as if she had an itch that would not go away, that begged to be satisfied . . . the "itch" was a feeling of raw sensuality.

She sank down to the ground, feeling weak. She was breathing in quick, shallow gasps. Her body begged to be touched. She felt strangely doing it, but it's what the feeling seemed to demand. She put her hands to her breasts to try to stop the electrifying pulsating sensation.

She nearly swooned with the feeling. Her breasts begged to be squeezed, not merely touched gently as she was doing. Her loins had the same desperate ache. Even her lips . . . she compressed them tightly, opened them, ran her tongue across them. The itch of raw sensuality was driving her mad!

She began rolling about on the ground, hugging herself, shuddering and twitching, trying to make the feeling stop. It would not stop, it became more and more intense. The *craving* . . . she knew what it was . . . it throbbed all through her, demandingly.

She could not stop herself. She wrapped the towel around her, grabbed her toga, and fled toward Kaheeli's tent.

She raised the flap and went inside. An oil wick lamp spread a yellow glow through the inside of the high squared-off tent. Kaheeli lay on a thin mattress, on his side, still wearing his white gown. He looked up at her as she came in. "Ah, you are here," he said matter-of-factly. "I expected you earlier."

Now she knew. "You!" she exclaimed. "You had me dru . . . it was one of your drugs, wasn't it . . . you somehow put it . . ." She could not speak or even think. The wicked nerve-jangling sensation flooded through her. She rolled her head languorously on her shoulders. She licked her lips with her tongue. She heard herself whimpering and could not stop.

And *he,* Kaheeli, the *bastard,* he did not make a move toward her! He wanted her groveling at his feet. He lay there on his side smiling smugly, waiting.

She turned and fled out of the tent. She'd die first! But then . . . No. No, I don't want to. No, I can't go back there, I can't give him the satisfaction of seeing me . . .

She went back into the tent. He was still smiling at her smugly. She released the towel and let it fall away from her. She lay down on the mattress beside him. She put her face next to his, her eyelids half closed, and she breathed "Take me."

"I?" he said, amused. "Take you? You are the one who is the wanton *nympha,* your Highness. If you have any desires you wish satisfied, do not ask me to take the initiative. I am but a humble Indian potter." He turned onto his back, put his hands behind his neck and looked up at the sagging cloth roof of the tent. He sighed with boredom.

She made a resolve to stay rooted to the spot where she was now, not to make any movement toward him at all. Her mouth was quivering with sensuality. She bit her lips. She rubbed her wrist hard over them. She rubbed her tongue along the edges of her teeth. She couldn't stand it!

She flung herself half on top of him and pressed her mouth against his. She pressed hard, feeling the pressure of his lips against hers. She forced his lips apart and her tongue darted into his mouth. His tongue answered her. Yes, she found, here was the answer, here was the satisfaction her sensuality craved. She felt his black beard and mustache against her face like a coarse blanket.

Her breasts throbbed achingly. She climbed more fully on top of him and pressed herself tightly against his chest. Yes, this felt good, this was what she needed. She pressed more tightly, but still it was not enough. No, she needed *squeezing,* violent pressure. She took his hands away from behind his neck where they were clasped and put them on her shoulders. And he, oh, the dog! The blackguard! He left them there!

She grasped his hands again and clamped them firmly over her breasts. He grinned at her and obligingly began squeezing with mounting pressure. She started mumbling, but the words were not clear.

"What is it you say?" Kaheeli asked.

She shook her head and did not answer, just continued rolling her head from side to side. Kaheeli let his hands relax. "No!" she moaned at him, putting her hands to the backs of his, pressing.

"What were the words you were saying?" he asked. He began to squeeze again, slowly, then with more and greater pressure, easing the jangling high-charged sensation, turning the "itch" to a satisfying surge of pleasure.

She began mumbling again. When her words became louder, she almost made herself become quiet again, but she stopped herself from doing so for fear Kaheeli would cease his fondling and kneading. The mumbled words grew louder, until finally they were a clearly audible whisper, embarrassing her: "Yes . . . oh, yes . . . ohhh *yessss* . . ." Kaheeli pinched her nipples between thumbs and forefingers and just held them like that tightly. She moaned with pleasure.

Now that her mouth and breasts were achieving satisfaction, the nerve-dazzling sensual ache in her loins became more demanding and unbearable than ever.

She looked down the length of Kaheeli's body. Yes, there it was, straining up long and tall against the fabric of his gown, as curved and hard as his scimitar itself. But first, she wanted something else. If she was to be a wanton, then at least she would be a *sat*isfied wanton! She took his hand by the wrist and moved it down her body, pressing it between her thighs. And now, not just leaving his hand to its own wandering, she directed it further, putting the fingertips there, just where she needed them, there, yes *there, there!*, at the core of her, the very kernel of her being.

She moaned loudly like a banshee at the streaks of dazzling, searing pleasure that flashed all through her. She knew the others in the camp would hear. The girls had been notified of what would take place tonight, that was why she had had the hotspring all to herself. They knew it would be drugged, and now they were listening with pricked ears to hear the sounds she would make. She ordered herself to hold her silence—she'd be damned if she would put on a show for them!

But her willpower evaporated like dew under a baking sun, as Kaheeli rubbed and squeezed and flicked at her essence with his fingers. She moaned, and whimpered loudly. Now the hunger in her was a yearning to be *filled,* to feel the fullness inside of her. She pulled his robe up to his neck, exposing his big, brawny, dark-skinned body. He was covered with softly curling hairs. His legs and chest rippled with muscles, his stomach was flat and hard. His rigid maleness was a beauty to behold.

She lay down on the mattress on her back and pulled at him to make him move on top over her. He did not budge. She tugged at his arm. Still he did not budge. She sat up and glared at him in ferocious puzzlement. Kaheeli merely put his hands behind his neck again, and grinned at her smugly. The quivering ache was still in her loins, growing in fierceness. She mounted him. She suspended herself above him on all fours, her face near his throat, her long brown hair dangling down into his face. Slowly she lowered her hips down until his proud mast pressed against her. Then she eased herself down all the way so that she was sitting astraddle of him. The sensation was exquisite! She leaned back and put her palms on her knees, then began moving her hips up and down on him, piercing herself with ecstasy.

Now Kaheeli abandoned his passivity. The grin on his face turned to a look of sensual torment. His face tensed and began to sweat. His breathing quickened and his chest heaved. He began moving with her, rhythmically. Jennifer felt herself being driven closer to it, closer to it . . . then it exploded within her, a burst of pleasure, and then more bursts—a wild rapid-fire chain reaction of eruptions of ecstasy. A guttural moan came suddenly from deep in Kaheeli's throat and his body stopped its motion, his hips frozen in a highly arched-up position. Then, slowly, he let out his breath and lowered himself back to the ground. Jennifer collapsed forward on top of him, her cheek against his shoulder. The energy she spent had drained her completely. She drifted off into a hazy, satisfied, fulfilled sleep.

She awoke before he did in the morning. She was still on top of him. She got up, wrapped the towel around her waist, and dressed in her toga. Then she went outside the tent to where last night's campfire had been. The pot of brew was still resting on one of the rocks ringing the dead campfire. The brew had congealed into a thick, cold, gray porridge. She picked up the pot and marched with it back toward Kaheeli's tent, paying no attention to the glances of the few early risers. The male eyes watching her were mocking; the female eyes were envious.

She marched into the tent, gazed down at the long naked body, and in a sweeping motion of her arm, splashed the congealed porridge along Kaheeli's length from his sex to his neck. He jerked awake instantly at the feel of the coldness on his body. Looking down at himself, he saw the source of the coldness, and looking up he saw Jennifer standing there with the empty pot dangling in her hand, smiling in a self-satisfied way at him. He grasped at her ankle angrily to pull her down, but she stepped away quickly and then kicked him in the chin with her bare foot as he tried to rise. "Swine! she cursed. "Devil dog! Indian weasel!"

He stared at her, then slowly nodded his head with a look of acceptance. "You will make a wonderful Queen, Jennifer VanDerLind. Not only do you pass all tests well, but your vindictive wrath and spite are of the most royal, magisterial order. Now hand me my towel."

She walked out of the tent, her nose in the air.

It took most of the morning for Elizar to stain her hair the proper shade of redness with his powdered clays, oils, and mashed berries. When he was finished, Jennifer dressed in the green veiled halter top and pants, and hid her hair from sight under a woman's low turban. She fastened the thick smoky veil over the bottom of her face and let Elizar paint around her eyes and shape her brows so they would look less like Isabella's.

Then the three of them entered the front seat of a cart and began the journey to the palace.

"By the end of this day," Kaheeli said to her, "you will be a free woman and I will be the liberator of my people." He looked away. "Or, the three of us will be dead, having died in a most agonizing way."

Chapter 28

She saw Lancelot and D'Arcy as the cart passed through the bazaar on the way to the palace.

They were going from booth to booth, asking a question of each merchant, then moving along to the next man when the merchant shook his head no, or shrugged uncomprehendingly. Jennifer knew they had only recently come into port from the fact that both were still wearing their heavy, cold weather sea-coats, though the weather on the island was warm and balmy.

Excitement surged through her. She prepared to call out to them, but just as the cart came near where they stood, a contingent of the Queen's fearsome, black-clad Kurds marched past on the other side of the road. She could not call out without the Kurds hearing. They would halt at the sound of a female voice in the public square and investigate. And if they lowered her veil . . .

As the cart went past, D'Arcy looked up and she caught his eye. She made an urgent, beseeching expression with her eyes and forehead and jerked her hands about desperately. D'Arcy grinned. He winked at her playfully, kissed his fingertips and blew the kiss at her. Then he turned back to the discussion Savage was having with the merchant. *Oh, she could kill him!* And he was supposed to be in love with her? Surely a man should be able to recognize the woman he loves, disguise or no disguise!

"Why did you wave your hands like that?" Kaheeli asked sharply. "We're lucky the militia didn't stop us to ask about the suspiciousness of it."

Should she tell him? Or was it best to not let him know she had allies present, in case he went back on his promise to release her after the impersonation? "My arms fell asleep," she said. "I wanted to revive them."

"Next time, sit on them." His voice was angry, his expression agitated. "We've come too close to freeing my people from tyranny to have our attempt *blasted* apart at the last moment by a stupid error."

"Calm yourself," said Elizar, putting a hand on Kaheeli's wrist. "You are an ignorant peasant who assists me in chopping roots and blending oils. Ignorant peasants do not loosen their tongues in the presence of their masters."

"Yes, master," said Kaheeli. "A thousand pardons, master, I am but a worthless wretch, a lowly vagabond, a—"

"Yes, yes, yes. See how much humor you have left when we're in the bastion of the palace, surrounded by a score of Kurds."

The palace loomed up before them a few minutes later, appearing to Jennifer very sinister and foreboding. It was a dark, medieval stone castle built upon a high hill, with crumbling towers jaggedly piercing the sky.

"Impressive, is it not?" said Kaheeli to Jennifer. "At one time many centuries ago there were archers behind those battlements, cauldrons of boiling oil in the turrets and towers, and water in the surrounding moat. Now it's only a rotting hulk. Aside from the royal residence and militia headquarters, the only thing still in use is the dungeon. And the torture chambers therein."

They rode up the winding path to the castle and stopped at the drawbridge, where they were halted by black-garbed Kurds.

"I am Elizar the apothecary. These are my assistants. I have been granted an audience with Her Majesty."

460

Two of the Kurds jabbered at each other in their strange, warbling tongue. Then one of them motioned the cart forward with a sharp jerk of his musket. The drawbridge creaked when they rolled over it. It seemed in such great disrepair, Jennifer thought it would probably fall apart if anyone ever tried to actually raise it.

They rode across the interior courtyard, which was filled with Kurds, then left the cart and entered the main building, where they were again stopped. Elizar repeated his words to three more Kurds at the entrance to the interior stairs. One of them, whose wide belt was golden rather than red like those worn by the others, hit Kaheeli's scimitar with the butt of his musket and shouted, "Off! Off, off, leave!"

Kaheeli unfastened the weapon and lay it on the wooden table. Then they were escorted up the stairs by the Kurd with the golden belt.

The Kurd knocked on the broad wooden door at the top of the stairs and shouted, "An ancient apothecary, Majesty, and two who assist."

A moment later the door opened and Queen Isabella stood framed in the stone doorway, her wealth of red hair untamed and blazing, her blue eyes scornful, a pistol held in her hand. She wore a long side-slit skirt of purple satin with a rectangle of the same material serving—inadequately—as a covering for her upper body. There was a slit in the rectangle for her head, with the flaps hanging loosely down her torso, one in front, one in back. There were no sleeves or sides to the garment. The flaps were joined together at their bottoms by a single connecting loop on each side.

"In," she said, jerking her head. The three of them entered. "Good, Randisan," she said to the Kurd, then slammed the door shut. She swiveled to face the three of them.

"Your Highness," said Elizar, bowing deeply, "I have—"

"On your knees, dog!"

461

Elizar dropped to his knees and bowed deeply, his forehead touching the floor. Jennifer and Kaheeli followed his example. Isabella grasped Kaheeli by the front of his gown and pulled him back up to his feet. Kaheeli stood straight and tall, looking directly ahead of him, rather than cause an affront by returning the Queen's gaze.

Isabella narrowed an eye at him and cocked her head. She put her hand to his chest and moved it down his torso, squeezing and pressing him as she did so. The pistol in her other hand was held level, loosely aimed at his midsection. The Queen's roving hand stopped at his lower stomach and remained motionless. When she saw Kaheeli's white robe elevate away from his body below where her hand rested, as if the robe were being pushed away by a lance, she snickered disdainfully, and stepped back.

She looked down at the old Arab. "Now, Elizar. My potion! You've finally found the way to spare me from aging?"

"Indeed I have, Highness. The elixir need be freshly prepared, however, just moments before consumption. That is why I have brought my assistants."

"Well get up off the ground then, you goat!" she ordered, kicking him in the shoulder. "Go, go! Get to it! Prepare it for me now!"

Elizar and Jennifer stood. The Arab motioned Jennifer and Kaheeli over to a long wooden table near the wall. They went to it and began laying out an impressive array of herbs, roots, vials, and other ingredients from the case Elizar had brought. Kaheeli began mashing several beans and seeds in a cup, while Jennifer stirred together two different colored liquids.

Elizar said, "What is transpiring now, Highness, is that the pink liquid is—"

"Shut up, fool."

Elizar bowed his head.

The Queen was watching Jennifer curiously. Jennifer

462

did not look up from the oils she was mixing. The Queen still held the pistol level in her hand. She leaned forward toward Jennifer and looked closely at her eyes, scrutinizingly. "Yes," she said, intrigued, "you have changed them. In the bazaar I slashed you for their insolent beauty. So now you alter them to afford me no cause of slashing further." She sneered and prodded Jennifer in the belly with the muzzle of the pistol. "You think Isabella needs *cause* to strike you?"

Jennifer shook her head.

Isabella stared at her. Kaheeli took the opportunity to fetch the hidden twig of black-speckled blossoms from the case and drop them into his mashing cup. The Queen's expression as she stared at Jennifer's eyes suddenly became intensely alert. She stared a moment longer, frowning in concentration, then stepped away from Jennifer. "Elizar," she said, "you underestimate me."

Elizar's eyes showed his fright. "How so, Majesty?"

Kaheeli hesitated for an instant in his mashing.

The Queen grinned tautly and looked at Elizar. "You think I do not have foresight enough to provide tools for your preparations. You think I lack that estimable trait."

"Oh no, Your Highness! Truly! I merely—"

"But you are wrong. Come. Look at my tools." She walked to a door in the opposite wall and opened it. "You with the mashing cup," she said. "You look too."

Kaheeli put his cup down on the table, then followed Elizar over to the open door of the storage room. Elizar looked inside, hesitated, and said guardedly, "There appears to be nothing inside but an empty cabinet of shelves, Majesty."

"Look closer."

Elizar hesitated to enter the room. Instead, he craned his head forward. Isabella kicked him hard in the behind, shoving him inside. She swiveled, her pistol aimed at Kaheeli's face. "In," she said.

Kaheeli's eyes were on Isabella's, steely and unswerving.

"In!" She cocked the pistol.

Kaheeli moved into the room with Elizar. Isabella shut the door and locked it. "I told you, you dilapidated antique!" she shouted at Elizar through the door. "You underestimate me!"

Jennifer had been moving stealthily forward ever since Isabella had turned her back on her. Now she was almost close enough. She raised the jar in her hand to smash it over Isabella's head. The Queen turned sharply to face her, forcing her to bring the jar down an instant sooner than she planned. Isabella stepped back adroitly and watched the jar pass harmlessly in front of her and shatter on the floor.

She laughed at Jennifer, a merry, unforced laugh. "What a joke you are," she said. She walked over to a high-backed chair and slouched down in it, holding the pistol loosely in her lap. There was no trace of concern in her manner about Jennifer's presence. She seemed to feel that there could not possibly be any threat to her from someone like Jennifer. She refused to take her seriously.

Thumping sounds came from the storage room, as Kaheeli tried in vain to force open the heavy, locked door by throwing his weight against it.

Isabella continued to stare at Jennifer's eyes. "You thought I would not notice?" she said, ignoring the thumping sounds. "Even after looking closely at your eyes? Here, take down the veil. This I must see."

Jennifer removed the veil from her face and the turban from her hair.

Isabella smiled in fascinated appreciation. "Amazing. Truly. A relative of some sort are you?"

Jennifer was interested too in learning if they were related. "My name is VanDerLind," she said. "My father's father, Silas, was from—"

"The Northlands," said Isabella. "Yes, so was my grandfather, Hogan. Until he left for Spain to marry my grandmother." She was still smiling. Except for the hard, razor edge of ruthlessness in her eyes, it seemed to Jennifer that she was looking at herself, only with red hair. "A second cousin you must be then. And a VanDerLind like myself. How novel."

The thumping sound from the storage room grew louder.

Jennifer took advantage of the Queen's temporary lowering of her guard to inch slowly forward. Isabella made no move to stop her until Jennifer was almost on top of her. Then the Queen raised the pistol nonchalantly so it pointed at Jennifer's belly and said, "How would you like to die, cousin? Gut-shot now, or of old age later, in the dungeons. I'm willing to let it be the latter. It will amuse me to have you around."

"I'm in no hurry to die," Jennifer said, stopping her advance.

"Then march over to the door and open it, so I can yell down to Randisan to lock you in irons." Her expression turned cruel. "You'll love our dungeons. Rat infested. Dank. Slimy. I hear the sun hasn't shined down there in half a millenium."

Jennifer still had the veil and the turban cloth in her hand. As she turned, she snapped the turban over the muzzle of the pistol, knocking it aside. Then instantly she leapt upon the Queen, forcing her over backward in her chair.

The pistol discharged, sending the ball slamming into the stone wall and ricochetting zingingly about the room. The thumping at the storage room door became more violent than ever. Jennifer scratched and kicked and hit the Queen furiously. She was being scratched and kicked in return and felt hard blows landing all over her body. She was too fiercely energized, though, to feel any pain.

She smashed furiously at the Queen with her elbows and knees and fists, thinking of nothing but hurting her *quickly*, before she could gain the advantage. And she surely would have the advantage, for Jennifer was not

465

a fighter, while the Queen seemed as though she were raised by a pack of wolves.

Jennifer felt her hair being yanked hard, forcing her head back, and then saw Isabella's furious face, enraged but still fully in control of herself. The Queen managed to jab her knee into Jennifer's throat and suddenly Jennifer was falling backward, choking and gasping helplessly. Isabella looked at her with a confident, taunting grin.

Jennifer rose to her feet and backed away. She clutched her throat. Isabella rose also. She found her empty pistol and grasped it about the muzzle. She started coming forward now, brandishing the pistol as though it were a club, walking in a swaggering, haughty way, a disdainful smile crossing her lips. "You are a joke, cousin," she sneered. "But, pity for you, you've ceased to amuse me."

Jennifer backed away, clutching her throat, until she felt the table at her back. She could breathe freely now and did not have to hold her hands to her throat. She had a plan, though. She wanted to bring Isabella in close, without making the Queen feel threatened and possibly stopping. She made choking noises as Isabella moved closer . . . and closer . . .

Isabella raised the pistol butt high, ready to strike.

Jennifer swiveled, grasped Kaheeli's mashing cup from the table behind her, turned back and flung the concoction of beans and speckled blossoms into Isabella's face.

The pistol came smashing down, but the glop of liquid splashed partly in Isabella's eyes, offsetting her aim. Jennifer jerked aside and avoided the blow. She raised the mashing cup in her hand, ready to smash Isabella with it. But it was not necessary, she saw.

The Queen was staggering back and forth, straining to keep her eyes open. Her posture was slumped, her stomach arched forward, shoulders and arms back, knees slightly bent. What force of will the woman had! Jennifer marveled. Almost unconscious on her feet, yet still struggling to resist the drug's effect. The Queen weaved about, her eyelids open by only the slightest sliver.

Jennifer went to the storage room and unlocked the door, then jumped back quickly as it burst open and Kaheeli came charging out. He glanced at Jennifer fiercely, pulled back his fist to smash her in the face. "It's me!" she shouted, backing away.

"Kaheeli!" yelled Elizar, grabbing the man's arm.

Kaheeli looked at Isabella as she staggered back and forth. He looked at Jennifer who was the same distance away from the storage room door. The fierceness was still in his eyes. He shook off Elizar, his fist still cocked back powerfully, ready to smash forward.

"Do you need more cold brew between your legs and over your chest before you treat me civilly!" Jennifer declared.

His face relaxed. He lowered his arm.

Now she came close to him and stared up at him, her eyes fierce. "You animal!" she screamed, reacting to the fact that after all she had just been through, she almost had to suffer being beaten by him too. "Can't you *see?*"

Elizar came up to her and tried to calm her. "Do not be hard on him," he said. "You both were near the door, it was impossible to tell who unlocked it. Your clothing is different, true, but fiery one, please to consider: We see one standing victorious and one weaving about barely able to stand. As for which of you we would expect to come out victorious after a confrontation . . ."

Jennifer was still angry and wanted to protest further, but suddenly a loud knock came to the door. "The Proconsul, Majesty, from England."

She tensed. She looked around at the upturned chair, the shattered jar on the floor, the weaving, zigzagging Isabella. She went to the door. "Make the dog wait!" she shouted through it. "I'll see him at my pleasure."

467

Elizar took a cloth from his case, wet it with oil from a vial, and hurriedly began wiping around Jennifer's eyes, removing the preparations he had used to alter her eyes and brows.

Kaheeli straightened up the room, then went to the Queen's desk to search for powder and ball to reload Isabella's pistol. He began slamming the drawers in frustration. "I can't find it!" He discovered a hard-leather swagger stick and brought it over to Jennifer. "Hold this in your hand instead. The effect will be the same."

Kaheeli turned toward Isabella. "I will strip her of her clothing and you can change into them."

"Oh no you don't," said Jennifer, stopping him. It was crazy, but she felt protective of the barely conscious Queen. At least in the sense that she felt reluctant to have Kaheeli removing her clothing. She guided the Queen into the storage room and shut the door after the two of them.

After she changed clothing, she opened the door again. Kaheeli and Elizar both looked at her in awe. "Allah," said Elizar. Jennifer felt very strange wearing the Queen's scanty top and deeply slit skirt. Part of the feeling was embarrassment, but another part was a subdued thrill of excitement.

Elizar came close and began inspecting her. "You have visible scratches on your body," he said, "but it is not of major concern. Your Kurds will simply assume you have been in another impassioned tryst. They are used to such from you."

Kaheeli was in the storage room looking at the Queen. She continued to weave about, refusing to fall down unconscious. "Such strength of will!" he marveled. "Look how she resists the drug's effects."

Elizar took another twig of speckled blossoms from his case, went to the Queen, and crushed it under her nostrils. The second dose was too much for her. Kaheeli grasped her from behind as she collapsed like a sack of sand. He looked about. There was no place to hide her.

"Behind the shelves," Jennifer said. She and Elizar pulled the waist-high cabinet of shelves a few feet away from the wall. Kaheeli dragged Isabella behind it and lay her down on the floor. She was motionless now, except for her peaceful breathing.

Elizar turned to Jennifer. "From this moment on, you are Isabella, Queen of Jazirat. Do not allow even a *specter* of Jennifer VanDerLind to remain. Your life, and ours, depends on the faithfulness of your masquerade."

Jennifer straightened herself, throwing back her shoulders, raising her head defiantly. She turned and went back into the main room. Elizar and Kaheeli followed, shutting the storage room door behind them.

She opened the door to the tower stairway. "Randisan!" she called down.

The Kurd came up the stairs.

"The Proconsul."

The Kurd shouted in his native tongue to others downstairs and Jennifer heard footsteps begin their ascent toward them. Randisan turned to Jennifer and spoke in an urgent, rumbling voice. "He comes not alone. Troops he brings. Outside the gates."

The Proconsul arrived at the top of the stairs, escorted by two Kurds. He looked more like a ruffian than a diplomat, despite his white wig and formal attire. A red sash cut across his gray vest, beneath his long-tailed black coat. His face was thin, seamy, and intimidating. He bowed from the waist deferentially, but his expression belied the gesture; it was devoid of respect or courtesy.

"You've brought troops onto my soil?" Jennifer said in haughty outrage. "How dare you!"

"They're merely for my protection," said the Proconsul. "It's no secret that a masked guerilla is still at large on your island, leading his men in looting raids."

Jennifer motioned him inside with a jerk of her

469

head, went in after him, and shut the door. The Proconsul seemed almost as arrogant as Isabella herself. Rather than wait for an invitation to be seated, he went over to the Queen's desk and sat down behind it, putting his folio case on the desktop before him.

Jennifer grinned in disdainful amusement. "Did they choose one as ill-mannered as you deliberately? Figuring to fight fire with fire?"

"Let's get down to business," he said coldly. He looked at Elizar and Kaheeli, who stood off to the side. "Who are they?"

"A chemist and his assistant. To advise me on the value of the explosive and its rarity."

"You need no advice on value. I have in my case two items. One will establish the value of the explosive. The other will insure a satisfactory culmination of our negotiations." He unlocked his rectangular black case, opened it, and pulled out a slip of paper with writing on it. "Item one," he said, handing it to her.

She looked at it. It was a financial figure.

"That is what we are prepared to pay. It is the value of the explosive."

Jennifer crumpled it up slowly in her hand, laid it on her palm, and flicked it into his face with the back of her other hand. "That amount, and half again more," she said.

The Proconsul did not flinch. "The second item I would like to enter into the negotiations is more direct." He reached into his case with both hands, and withdrew two pistols, one in each hand. One was pointed at Isabella, the other at Kaheeli.

"Get out of here, you slimy British worm!" She started for the door to call in Randisan. She heard the metallic click of the pistols being cocked, and stopped.

"To answer your question," said the Proconsul, coming over to her, "yes, I was specially chosen for this mission. Difficult situations are my specialty." He went past her to the door and lowered the horizontal bolt into its catches at both sides of the doorway. Then he went to the high window, looked out, and fired a pistol into the air.

Immediately Jennifer heard the sound of running feet and firing muskets. There were shouted British commands, furious scuffling noises, and a moment later, the answering sound of Kurdish voices raised in their high-pitched war cry. A loud banging came to the door. "Majesty!" shouted Randisan's rumbling voice. "Majesty!" More banging on the door.

Jennifer exchanged a secret look of fright with Elizar. This was not in their plan. How would this new turn of events affect them?

"We really had intended to negotiate further," said the Proconsul, "in the case of your refusal. But events have made this impossible. War has finally broken out in the Colonies. British troops have been attacked at Lexington and again at Concord. General Howe requires the explosive immediately, to quash the rebellion in its infancy."

Jennifer glared at him fiercely. He leaned back in his chair and put his booted feet up on the desk, holding the pistol leveled at her. "Oh, don't take it so hard, Your Highness. You'll still be paid the sum I showed you. It's more than a fair price."

"I refuse it! I will not honor this act of outright thievery by pretending an agreement has been reached!"

The sounds of firing and shouting and screaming were coming not only from beyond the window now, but from inside the tower as well. She could hear them through the thick door. The battle was becoming more furious.

"Tell me this," she said demandingly. "What do you intend to do with me?"

He shrugged. "Leave you to go about your business. We've no desire to interfere with your sovereign rule."

She laughed contemptuously.

"Oh, you'll have to be held hostage in your tower here," he said, "but only for the night. And only to in-

471

sure you don't have the explosive sabotaged. A contingent of our troops is ringing the warehouse to protect it. Still, if you were to order your Kurds into action—those of them not being rounded up downstairs—it could cause problems. So we'll just simplify matters by saying that if anything happens to the explosive, you'll be killed. Other than that, you're free to conduct business as usual. Your minions can come and go unmolested. The civilian ones, that is."

"I'll have your head chopped off and dragged through the streets for this," Jennifer said acidly.

"I think not. I think what will happen is that you'll suffer the minor inconvenience of being held hostage for a few hours, until His Majesty's vessel the *Serpentine* arrives tonight. The explosive will be loaded aboard, and she'll sail off with escort to the Colonies, to make delivery to Howe. I'll sail back to England, you'll receive the sum of money we agreed on—"

"I never agreed!"

"And that will be the end of it."

There was a banging at the door again, but this time it was followed by a British voice. "Mission accomplished, Sir!"

The Proconsul got up and opened the door. "Bring them in," he said to the Redcoat officer standing outside.

Jennifer watched in horror as the Kurds were herded into the room by armed Redcoats. Many were bloody and wounded. They came through the door in a flood, at least two score of them, falling down wearily upon the floor, or standing about raging. They brought with them the smell of sweat and blood.

Jennifer went to the Proconsul. "You're holding them up *here*? With *me*?"

"Only until the *Serpentine* arrives and is loaded." He looked at her with a lecherous expression. "I've heard of your reputation, Majesty. All of you in the same room for most of the night. Should be very cozy."

She slapped him hard. He slapped her back. Ran-

472

disan, just now being escorted through the doorway, charged at the Proconsul, but was stopped short by the butt of a Redcoat's musket in his stomach.

The last of the Kurds came through the doorway. Some were so badly wounded they had to be carried. Once they were all inside, the Proconsul put his pistols into his case, bowed to Jennifer, and left the room. The Redcoats left after him, then the door was shut.

Jennifer looked out at the menagerie of black-robed and hooded warriors. Many were leaning against the walls or lying on the floor. Some were standing. A few were groaning loudly. One of them pulled at the hem of her skirt in his delirium. She stepped away from him.

She looked across the room at Elizar. "You!" she shouted above the din. "I want you!"

Elizar hurried over with Kaheeli behind him. He bowed repeatedly before her.

She grasped his arm and pulled him roughly over to the high window, stepping over the bodies of men on the floor as if maneuvering through an obstacle course. The window looked down on the harbor.

"There," she said, pointing to the *Liberty* berthed next to the British warship. "That three-master. Ignore the name on it—it changes with each port. I want you to summon the captain of the ship and bring him to me. You might find him in the bazaar. He's tall with black curly hair and a scar on his cheek. He—"

"I know the one of whom you speak, Majesty," said Elizar.

Jennifer looked at him, surprised.

"I was once at an auction where the gentleman with the scar made an unexpected appearance."

"Get him. Bring him to me." She wanted to add that Elizar should tell Savage what her situation was, but she knew the Arab would not obey such an order, even if she could say it to him without arousing suspicion. He would hesitate to let anyone know she was not Isabella for fear word might somehow get back to the Kurds here in the room.

Jennifer turned to Kaheeli. "You may leave also, if you wish. To accompany him."

"I'll remain with Your Majesty," said Kaheeli, bowing slightly.

Jennifer watched Elizar cross over to the door. Would they really let him leave? Or was the Proconsul's promise that she could conduct "business as usual" no more than empty words?

He knocked on the door. It opened, disclosing two Redcoat guards holding bayoneted muskets aimed at his throat. Jennifer held her breath.

Elizar said something to the guards in a humble, craven voice. One of them nodded and raised his bayonet. Elizar passed on through. The door slammed shut behind him.

Jennifer turned her eyes back to the sea of Kurds, whom she would be brushing against and cooped up with for the rest of the day and into the night.

A chill of fear swept over her. The impersonation had been dangerous enough when the only Kurd she had to deal with was Randisan, and even then for only a minute at a time. Now she had to carry off her masquerade before scores of Kurd warriors, at close quarters, under constant observation. Many of them were in pain. All were in the foulest of moods. If they discovered her to be an impostor . . .

She shuddered violently.

Chapter 29

Savage was standing outside the waterfront tavern with an Arabic name, asking a young seaman if he had seen a girl of Jennifer's description, when Elizar came up to him. The old Arab stood off to the side patiently. Savage glanced at him while continuing to talk to the seaman. When the seaman told him no, he hadn't seeen any beautiful brown-haired girl since arriving on the island, Savage let him go. Then he turned to Elizar to see what he wanted.

"Captain Savage of the *Liberty?*" asked Elizar.

Savage tensed. He looked around. English sailors from the warship that had docked only a few hours earlier were passing by. Others were present in great numbers up and down the road. "No," Savage said. "I'm Captain Smithers of the *Bonny Lynne*. What can I do for you?"

"You were a sportsman when last I saw you, with even a third name. Wearing a most elegant plumed hunting hat."

Savage looked at the old man closely. He saw that D'Arcy, from several feet away where he was questioning a merchant, was looking at the Arab too.

"Do not be alarmed, Captain," said Elizar. "I am a friend."

"You're not a friend of mine if you were at that hunting lodge the day of the auction."

"If I were other than a friend, would I not be speaking with an English officer at this very instant, divulging your identity? But rather, I am here, bringing you a message from her Highness the Queen of Jazirat. She commands your presence and that of your blond friend at the royal palace immediately."

"For what?"

"I'm sorry, I am not privy to the working of the royal mind. I know only that it is of the utmost urgency." When Savage looked reluctant to come, Elizar added, with an air of mystery, "You may be aided in your quest for this girl you seek after."

Savage nodded for D'Arcy to come over. Then the three of them rode in Elizar's cart to the palace. The situation that greeted them when they arrived was frantic and filled with danger. First they approached the drawbridge of an old castle and Savage saw that it was guarded by a contingent of Redcoats. He and D'Arcy sweated tensely as the cart was stopped and they were asked their business. Savage silently cursed himself as a fool for falling into this trap. But then the old Arab explained to the guards that they were on official business and that their safe passage had been promised by the Proconsul. They were allowed on through without incident.

Inside the courtyard there were more Redcoats rushing about, and more still at the base of the stairs inside the main tower. A seamy-faced man in formal diplomatic attire, including a coat with tails, was rushing about yelling, "Tonight! It must be loaded tonight!" Savage felt like a rabbit who had walked into a lion's den. He was certain many of these troops knew of his reputation and would spring on him instantly if they heard his name. Fortunately, none of them seemed to know him by his face alone. He and D'Arcy were ordered to remove their weapons and then were allowed up the stairs.

It was at the top of the stairs that the scene became even more like a frantic madhouse. The heavy wooden door was opened by Redcoat guards standing outside. Inside they saw giant black-robed figures pacing about the room in furious agitation, gesturing with their hands, filling the air with loud warbling noises as they chattered to one another. Many lay against the wall, wounded and bleeding.

Standing at a window looking out, with her right side facing toward them, was a raven-haired woman wearing a purple garment that clearly revealed the contours of her beautifully shaped breasts. Next to her stood a tall, full-bearded man wearing a turban, who was watching the black-robed figures with an expression of unease.

"No wonder I nevair hear of Jazirat," D'Arcy said to Savage, gazing in amazement at the situation. "Thees island, eet eez full of crazy people."

They entered and the door was shut behind them. The warbling noises ceased, as the black-clad warriors looked at the new arrivals. The old Arab at Savage's side gestured toward the raven-haired woman standing at the window across the room, "I present to you Her Majesty Isabella," he said, "the Queen of Jazirat."

The woman turned to face them.

The shock hit Savage like a fist. Next to him, D'Arcy gasped. Instinctively, Savage started to say her name. "Jen—"

"Hold your tongue, knave!" she shouted, cutting him short. She looked down her nose at him, her expression cruel. "What impudence! Speaking to me before you're spoken to!" She came across the room toward him in a swaggering, strutting walk.

Savage could not believe his eyes. This *was* Jennifer, wasn't it? If it was, then she must be in immediate danger to make her put on such an act. The best thing he could do, if this was the case, was to play along with her act until he understood what the situation was and could figure out how best to help her. Yet, as he looked at her haughty, arrogant expression when she stopped in front of him, he could not help wondering: *was* it her?

Her eyes showed no sign of recognition. They glared

at him challengingly as she said "On your knees! Lackeys bow before Isabella."

The old Arab immediately fell down to the floor and bowed completely forward, touching his forehead on the floor. "Salaam," he said, "Salaam, Salaam."

"Thees eez so crazy," said D'Arcy.

A strong blow knocked his head to the side, sending him reeling into Savage. "Get down on your knees!" shouted the rumbling voice of the Kurd who had hit him, the man's finger pointing imperiously down at the ground. Savage grabbed D'Arcy about the shoulders to hold him back when he started moving murderously forward.

"Down," Savage said to him quietly.

Without taking his fierce eyes off the Kurd, D'Arcy lowered himself to his knees, as did Savage.

"Good, Randisan," said Jennifer. "They'll learn their manners."

Other Kurds came forward next to Randisan to look down threateningly at the two foreigners.

Savage was watching Jennifer's expression. There was not a single crack in the shell of arrogant impersonality. The question tore at him: *Was this Jennifer?* If it was, she was acting out her role flawlessly. The girl came a step forward, put the end of her swagger stick to Savage's chin and raised his head up. She gazed at him critically, and then sneered, "Too thin-lipped for my liking. Men with firm, thin lips are unphysical. I'd say you're probably atrocious in bed. Isn't that right, Captain?"

"You'd know better than I, Your Majesty," he said. When he saw Randisan start fiercely toward him, he added quickly, "My judgment could never be as superb as Your Highness's."

"True," she said. She moved over to D'Arcy. D'Arcy was staring up at her with bafflement, anger, curiosity, resentment. He did not know what to make of her and it showed in his eyes. Jennifer's hands went to his long blond hair and she ran her fingers through it in a possessive manner. She held his hair out at the sides and looked at his ears. "And this one," she said, "too thick headed between the ears." She bent forward and looked him straight in the eyes. "Of course, when you're *vis-à-vis* with a man, it's not what's between the *ears* that counts."

Randisan laughed rumblingly. He spoke in his warbling native tongue to the other Kurds and they all laughed too. Savage was struck by the eeriness of it: malevolent, black-garbed warriors, their eyes deathly serious, making trilling, warbling sounds that was supposed to be laughter.

"May I ask why Your Majesty wished to see us?" Savage said.

"You have a ship in our harbor with men and weapons. I'm being held prisoner here. I may command use of your services." She motioned for them to stand. "We will not discuss this now, though. I want something else first."

"And what might that be, Your Majesty?"

She came up close to him and put her hands on his chest. She looked him in the eyes smirkingly as she lowered her hands along his torso, touching him at his sex and then squeezing tightly as she felt it swelling in her hand. The Kurds did not react with surprise at her behavior. They seemed to take such behavior from her for granted.

"Over there," she said, nodding in the direction of the storage room. "I'd prefer my chambers, but as a prisoner, I suffer inconveniences." She turned her eyes to D'Arcy and looked him up and down. "You too," she said. She swaggered over to the storage room, followed by the two of them. She stopped at the door just as she was about to enter and gazed at Kaheeli evaluatingly. "And you," she said.

One of the Kurds snickered. Randisan kicked him in the groin, making him groan in excruciating pain.

Jennifer let the three men precede her into the room, then she entered and closed the door.

479

"Jennyfair," shouted D'Arcy furiously, "I'm going to spank you so badly zat—"

"Wait," she said, holding up a palm. She put her ear to the thick door and listened. She could hear nothing. She opened it a crack. The sound of the warbling voices came through clearly. She closed the door again and heard nothing. Good, they would not be overheard.

She turned to Savage and D'Arcy and flung herself at them an arm over each, hugging herself to them. "Oh, Lancelot," she cried. "Oh, D'Arcy. I'm so glad you're here." She moved over so that she was fully against Savage now, though one hand remained on D'Arcy's shoulder. She buried her face against Savage's chest. He hugged her tightly.

"Are you all right?" he asked.

She did not answer. She pressed herself against him as she began to shudder. The role she had been playing had taken every ounce of her concentration and energy. She had had to become obsessed with the role, so that no part of herself showed through. For the past several hours she had lived and breathed and *been* Queen Isabella. It had taken its toll. She continued shuddering, knowing now what it was to be possessed, to be inhabited by the soul of another.

Savage was embracing her tightly. Finally the trembling stopped. She pulled back her head and looked at him. Then she looked at D'Arcy, who was deeply wounded and hurt by her embracing Savage and not him. He was looking at Savage resentfully. Jennifer squeezed the back of his neck, where her hand now rested under his blond hair. It was not enough. The bitterness was still in his eyes. The problem was still with them, she saw, as turbulent and frustrating as it had been at the dry lakebed: two men in love with the same woman . . . a woman in love with two men.

"Jennifer," Savage said, "You've got an army of warbling baboons out there and then another army of

Redcoats just beyond. It's time to tell us what's going on."

"*Oui*," said D'Arcy, "and ze first thing we must talk of is zis: who is *he*?" He stared with cold fury at Kaheeli, who stood looking about innocently, occasionally gazing up at the ceiling. Most of the time that Jennifer had been in Savage's arms, with one hand caressing D'Arcy's neck, D'Arcy had been glaring at the handsome bearded stranger, as if at a new rival.

"I am Kaheeli Avram Omar," Kaheeli said, turning to him. He inclined his head formally.

"I do not like heem," D'Arcy said to Jennifer. "I theenk I may hit heem."

"Oh, D'Arcy, stop! He's a . . ." She hesitated. What *could* she call him, really? "He's a friend. And he's going to help me get free of that horrible indenture contract I told you about, which has been ruining my life ever since I signed it."

"How eez he in a position to help you do zat?"

"Well, he . . . you see, he . . ."

"I am her owner," said Kaheeli proudly. "She is my property."

"I *am* going to hit heem."

"Don't you dare!" she said, grasping his wrists, not sure if he really might. When D'Arcy made no violent movements, merely glared fiercely at Kaheeli, Jennifer cautiously removed her hands from his wrists. "It's complicated," she said, looking at D'Arcy, and then at Savage who now also was staring at the Indian with a look of hostility. "What it comes down to is that by buying my indenture papers, Kaheeli saved—"

"Kaheeli?" repeated D'Arcy. "Not Mister Omar? Or *Monsieur* Omar? Or—"

"Oh, stop it! You're like a child! Now listen to me. By buying my papers, he saved me from being sold to someone else at the auction who would have kept me in indenture for the whole three years. Kaheeli isn't going to do that. He's going to tear up the papers."

"That's generous of him," said Savage, his voice heavy with suspicion and distrust.

"Not you too?" she said. "Lancelot, you can't be at odds with this man. And neither can you, D'Arcy. Because we all have to work together if you plan to get me out of here alive." Her voice became sharp. "There are Kurd warriors out there, in case you haven't noticed. And they happen to be very fond of their Queen. And they happen to be very *un*fond of people who harm their Queen."

"So who weeshes to harm zair Queen?"

She took him by the arm and tugged him over to the storage case near the far wall. D'Arcy looked behind the case and saw Isabella, curled on her side on the floor, her red hair hiding her face from view. Scratches and bruises and teeth marks appeared in various places on her skin. Savage came over and looked also.

"Zair Queen?" D'Arcy said.

Jennifer nodded.

Savage bent forward and brushed the hair back from the girl's face. He stared. "A sister?" he said to Jennifer.

"She's a second cousin, whom I never knew I even had." She paused. "The Kurds haven't found out I'm not their real Queen—not yet. The longer I'm up here with them, though, the better the chances they will find out. And if that happens . . . it'll be a bloodbath."

Savage looked at Kaheeli coldly. "I'm glad your indenture was bought by this one," he said to Jennifer. "If you were sold to anyone else, they might have put you in situations where you could get hurt. Where you might be exposed to danger." He looked at her. "All right, how do we get you out of here."

"That will not be so easy," Kaheeli said. "The British are holding her prisoner here to insure the safety of a stockpile of explosives, which they are in the process of thieving."

"If anything happens to the explosives," Jennifer explained, "they say they'll kill me."

"Captain," Kaheeli said. "I know this is all confusing to you. If you will permit me, may I suggest a course of action?"

"What is it?"

"Take your ship to the far side of the island, where the explosive is warehoused, come in close to the shore and blast the warehouse with your cannons. The explosive will detonate instantly."

D'Arcy stared at him in disbelief. He pointed a finger and said, "Lancelot, zis man—I do not like heem, Lancelot."

"He's right, D'Arcy," Jennifer said. "You have to do it. There's more to this explosive than you know about. It has to be destroyed so the English don't get it. Then in the confusion after the blast—"

"Yes," said Kaheeli, "in the confusion, we fight through the guards and escape, rescuing Jennifer Van-DerLind to safety."

Savage and D'Arcy both looked skeptical. "You've got an army of Kurds in the room out there," Savage said to Kaheeli angrily, "and then half a regiment of British troops just beyond the door. When you say 'in the confusion we make our escape,' you're talking nonsense."

"Like ze crazy man," said D'Arcy.

"No one is going to be that confused, in the aftermath of a blast, to let us walk right through their ranks."

"In the aftermath of *this* blast," said Kaheeli, "they are likely to be on their hands and knees trembling like children, fearful the sky has erupted and is crashing upon their heads." He paused. "Let me explain to you about this new explosive . . . "

"Hurry," Jennifer said, eyeing the door nervously. "There isn't much time."

Savage and D'Arcy listened with keen interest as Kaheeli told them about the thirty score kegs of amazingly potent powder stockpiled in the warehouse on the island's far side. They made the same comment Jennifer had made earlier: they had to have this new explosive for General Washington. When Kaheeli explained that no more of it could be created and that a second English warship was at this very moment sailing to Jazirat to take possession of the stockpile that did exist, the desperation of the situation became clear. Savage could not take the stockpile for himself, since the warehouse was ringed by too many Redcoats. It was either destroy it or leave it to the British.

"We don't have a choice," Savage said. "We have to destroy the stockpile. What I don't like is having to depend on just the commotion after the blast to get Jennifer free from these Kurds, and then away from the Redcoats. I want more of an edge than that."

He thought a minute. "Here's what we'll do. The instant we hear the blast, we attack the British."

"Attack?" said Kaheeli, dumbfounded. "The three of us?"

"We trick the Kurds into doing it. Jennifer, when we go back into the room, you tell the Kurds you've forced me to support you with my men and ship. Say you told me I'd never get out of here alive if I didn't agree to it."

She nodded.

"Tell them my men will be stationed outside the castle gates in full force, ready to attack. When they hear the blast, that'll be their signal. That's when the Kurds are to rush out of here and attack the British in the tower here, and fight their way down to the courtyard. To join up with my men who'll already be there."

"A wonderful plan!" said Kaheeli. "You pit the despicable Kurds against the despicable British, and let them destroy each other. And since the Kurds will think they are being reinforced by your men downstairs, they *will* attack. They never would undertake such a mission otherwise, being unarmed as they are."

"When zay hear the blast from ze warehouse explosion," said D'Arcy, "zay weel have proof of our support, even if zay doubted eet before."

Savage nodded. He looked at all of them. "It's risky. We're still at a major disadvantage. This place is crawling with Redcoats. And aside from that, when the Kurds fight their way down to the courtyard and find they've been lied to and *aren't* being reinforced . . . "

"Zay weel not be happy," said D'Arcy.

"We'll have to be out of here by then." Savage turned to D'Arcy and began talking about the steps necessary to get the plan underway. "Before you pull the *Liberty* out of the harbor, you're going to have to blast that warship at anchor there. So they don't give chase once you—"

"*Me* blast ze sheep?" said D'Arcy. "You are ze Captain. You blast ze sheep. I stay here to help Jennyfair escape."

Savage looked at him sternly. "I have to stay here as hostage, to make Jennifer's story about threatening to have me killed if I don't help her sound believable."

"*I* stay as hostage," D'Arcy said, pointing to his chest. "You go to ze sheep."

"I'm the Captain," Savage said angrily. "You're my mate. And I'm telling you to take the blasted ship out of the harbor and—"

"No, *you* take ze blasted sheep out of ze harbor," exclaimed D'Arcy. "You are ze Captain! I am only ze mate! You are ze one who—"

"Stop it!" Jennifer said. "This isn't the time to—"

"I'm going to be here making sure she's safe until it's time to escape!" Savage raged. "You think I'm going to leave her in a situation like this?"

"You theenk zat *I* am going to leave her in ze seetuation?"

Kaheeli said to Jennifer, "If the rest of your Colonial forces are so well organized and harmonious, I fear for your revolution, Jennifer VanDerLind."

"Stop it!" she shouted at them. "Don't start fighting each other now. We have to go back outside, this is taking too long. It'll seem suspicious if—"

Without a further word, Savage spun around, jerked

open the door, and stalked out. He went to the Queen's writing table and began scribbling a hasty note. The others came out of the storage room after him. Jennifer resumed her role, becoming haughty, defiant, swaggering. D'Arcy and Kaheeli made a point of looking humbled and worn.

Savage finished the message, went over to the old Arab who had brought him and D'Arcy here originally, and slapped the note into his hand. "Take this to the three-master in the harbor, the one displaying the name *Bonny Lynne*. Hand it personally to Second Mate Harlan. Understand?"

The Arab looked at Kaheeli. When he saw Kaheeli nod with an almost imperceptible movement, he turned back to Savage and said, "It will be done."

Savage watched Elizar tuck the note out of sight in his clothing, then open the door and leave, passing the British guards unmolested. Savage went up to D'Arcy and said angrily, under his breath, "Harlan will take her out. I told him to leave a boat for us on the north beach, near the ridge."

Then he folded his arms across his chest and watched as Jennifer began addressing the Kurds, informing them of the surprise attack they were soon to mount, and of the full contingent of reinforcements from Savage's ship that would be waiting to aid them.

Chapter 30

They waited tensely, standing at the high, arched window aperture, looking down at the harbor off in the distance. Elizar should have reached the ship by now and given the note to Harlan. Harlan should have had time enough to position his guns and make ready for the surprise barrage. *Any second now,* thought Jennifer, as she stood between Savage and D'arcy, with Kaheeli to Savage's right. She breathed shallowly in excited anticipation. Behind her, the Kurds had gathered around in a semicircle, pressing up against the four of them in their eagerness to see out the window.

Suddenly it happened: a flash of yellow light from the *Liberty's* portside cannons, followed by a thunderous roar, and the splintering of the hull of the British warship that lay anchored parallel in the harbor. A yell of excitement rose up from the Kurds. A moment later, a second fiery barrage thundered forth, and the starboard-side hull of the British warship seemed to explode into splintering wood. There was no answering fire. Most of the ship's crew were in port. No one had expected an attack while berthed in a safe harbor.

A third barrage from the *Liberty* was all it took, directed low at the warship's waterline. The vessel keeled over to its side, its masts dipping down into the briny sea. A feverish cheer rose up from the Kurds and they began dancing about and hugging each other. The *Liberty* moved proudly out from the harbor now, under full billowing sail, into the open sea. British sailors and troops had rushed out from the taverns and inland establishments, and now stood about on the dock staring in awe-struck amazement at their devastated, fatally crippled warship.

"The doors," Savage said to Jennifer. "They'll be up any second now."

"Randisan!" Jennifer shouted to the Kurd leader standing off to the side. "The doors!"

The Kurd rushed over and threw the heavy bolt of wood across the width of the door, dropping it into its catches at either side. It was not a moment too soon. A knock came to the door, and then a fierce banging. "Open up in there!" came the voice of the Proconsul. "I want to talk! You hear me, Isabella! I want to talk to you!"

Jennifer swaggered over to the door. "Talk then, British pig," she called through the door. "Say what you wish, I listen."

"The captain of that ship called the *Bonny Lynne*. I know he's in there. I want him!"

She said nothing.

"I said I want him, do you hear! I'll slay the lot of you if I have to, open this blasted door!" A moment later, a banging sound came from beyond the door, as a battering ram of some sort was brought up and put into action. Musket shots were fired into the door also, but they did not penetrate the thick heavy wood.

"Move the tables and the desk against it," Savage said. Jennifer nodded to Randisan. Within seconds, Kurds were carrying over the massive wooden tables and desk and shoving them against the doorway. One Kurd started to go toward the storage room to see if anything else of substantial weight might be inside, but Jennifer shouted at him, "This is enough! Do you dare leave your Queen's side in the midst of danger?" The Kurd came rushing back.

Jennifer went back to the window, where Savage stood looking out. The *Liberty* was sailing out of view as it moved along the coast toward the far side of the island. "How long?" she asked Savage.

"Ten minutes for them to leave us a boat at the north side ridge. Another five to reach the warehouse and begin shelling."

They waited tensely, no one speaking, for the whole of the next fifteen minutes. The Kurds stood near the doorway listening to the pounding of the battering ram and the blasting of the muskets. When the door began to splinter, they shoved the tables tighter against it.

Jennifer's ears were pricked in anticipation as she listened for the sound of cannon fire. Then she heard it: a single cannon shot, muffled in the distance.

"Harlan eez finding hees range," D'Arcy said. "Any second now . . ."

"Order the barricades away," Savage told her.

"Randisan! The tables and desk, move them off! Then prepare to attack on the given signal."

The barricades were removed. Another single cannon shot was fired, off in the distance.

"Down!" Savage shouted to everyone in the room. "Onto the floor!" He put his arm around Jennifer's shoulders and lowered her to the ground. D'Arcy and Kaheeli got down on their stomachs and faces too, as did all the Kurds, imitating the examples.

Now that the barricades were gone, the door burst open and the British Proconsul stepped through, followed by a swarm of armed Redcoats. "What's this?" he said, looking down at the prostrate figures on the floor. "A trick of some sort?" He scanned the floor and saw Savage by the window. "There he is! Grab him, Lieutenant, and that blond one too, his Mate."

Several of the Redcoats crossed quickly over to Savage and D'Arcy and grasped them by the backs of their collars and by their hair. "On your feet, ya blighters!" Off in the distance, there was the muffled sound of a cannon shot from beyond the window, and then suddenly, following instantly upon it, came an enormous thundering blast that seemed to shake the castle at its very foundations. The room began to quake and heave violently and powdered mortar from the ceiling began dusting down upon them. The British troops staggered about trying to maintain their footing in the quivering, shaking tower. Most of them fell to the floor.

"Now," Savage said into Jennifer's ear, as the room settled back into steadiness.

She stood up quickly. "Attack!" she yelled. "Attack! Attack!"

The Kurds leapt to their feet and charged the unsuspecting British. The British who were already on the floor found themselves being stomped and kicked violently and their weapons jerked out of their hands. The troops who were still standing were charged at furiously, then kicked or beaten to death, or run through with their own blades.

The Proconsul, still on his feet, bolted for the door. Kaheeli grabbed him by the front of his coat and pulled him at a fast pace across the room, making the man run with him toward the window, where Kaheeli aimed him carefully and then released him. The Proconsul's momentum carried him screaming right through the opening and into the empty air.

"Attack!" Jennifer screamed again to the Kurds standing in the middle of the room. "Attack! Attack!"

The Kurds raised their voices in a warbling, deafening war cry, and surged on through the doorway to meet the Redcoats beyond, fighting with the weapons they had taken from the troopers now dead or dying on the floor.

Savage reached down and grasped a saber from one of the dead Redcoats. D'Arcy picked up a foil. Then the two of them followed the vanguard of the charging Kurds out the doorway, with Kaheeli and Jennifer behind them. On the stairway going down to the base of the tower there were many dead and wounded Kurds and British. Kaheeli grabbed a scimitar from a screaming Kurd whose arm was half severed, then moved up to join Savage and D'Arcy in the forefront. The three

490

of them formed a wall protecting Jennifer, who was behind.

The fighting was violent and furious, the air filled with shrill screams and warbling cries. Everywhere Jennifer turned, she saw wildly swinging arms and sabers and scimitars, fierce faces, blood-stained bodies and heads. Despite the efforts of the three men to protect her, bodies kept crashing against her from the sides, though almost always they were dead or nearly so by the time they reached her.

They were down at the base of the tower now. The Kurds were fighting in the foyer and pushing out through the front doors into the courtyard. Many had already reached the courtyard where they were fiercely engaging the British.

The element of surprise had done wonders. The British had not expected an attack from the Kurds, nor had they expected the earth-shaking thundrous blast that had engulfed them out of the blue. The Kurds were making great headway, slaying large numbers of Redcoats as the British retreated back in shocked disorganization. Soon, though, the weight of the Redcoats' greater numbers would inevitably come into play and they would grasp the advantage in a vicious, slaughtering advance.

"This way!" Kaheeli shouted to Jennifer above the din, grasping Savage and D'Arcy by the shoulders and pointing with his head. "The side passage!" He moved off to the side, away from the main exit where the fighting was the fiercest. The three of them followed him.

A Redcoat loomed up in front of Kaheeli, aiming a pistol at his chest. Kaheeli slashed his scimitar across the man's torso, almost slicing him diagonally in half. Jennifer grabbed the pistol from the fallen soldier's hand and stepped over him as she followed Kaheeli. Savage and D'Arcy were behind her.

Other Kurds and Redcoats blocked their path, but they were fewer in number in this side foyer and

Kaheeli, Savage, and D'Arcy managed to slice or smash their way through them. The side foyer ended in a cul-de-sac, fronted by a wooden door. Kaheeli jerked it open with a groaning creak and the four of them rushed through.

They ran down a narrow, dark passageway now, which curved in a wide arc. The cold stone walls were dank and moist, and it was very chilly. The floor of the passageway inclined downward as they ran along it. It seemed to Jennifer that they were beneath the ground, circling around part of the main tower. No one was ahead of them now and the sound of the fighting was growing dimmer at their backs.

Soon the passageway straightened out and inclined upward. They rushed along it for several minutes, their frantic breathing echoing loudly within the narrow walls. Then an arched doorway loomed up far ahead of them at the end of the passageway, its top and sides and base framed in bright light, showing that beyond the door lay the outside world. They ran forward, getting closer and closer.

Soon they arrived at the wooden doorway and Kaheeli, in the lead, stopped. The others stopped behind him. "Through this door," he panted, gasping for breath, "lies freedom for you. We are at the base of the castle gates on the northward side." He breathed gaspingly and pointed to the left, where the corridor took a sharp turn and continued on for several yards on a down incline to another door. This door was not framed in light.

"Through this door," he panted, "lies the dungeon, where a hundred of my men lie dying from lack of food, air, and sunlight. The dungeon was guarded by half a dozen Kurds before the British came. Now it is undoubtedly guarded by half a dozen of the Redcoats." He looked at Savage and D'Arcy piercingly. "Will you help me free my men?"

"We have to get Jennifer out of here," Savage said, panting and gasping for breath.

"Een only minutes," said D'Arcy, "ze fighting weel be over, and zay weel all be after us. Eef she eez not beyond ze walls by zen . . . "

"I understand," said Kaheeli. He raised his scimitar up in both his hands, above his head. He turned toward the door, leading to the dungeon and started forward.

Savage grasped him by the back of his gown, stopping him. "You crazy? Six Redcoats you say?"

"My people lie dying in the dungeon. I cannot leave them."

"Six Redcoats!" Savage declared.

"If I take three of them with me, I shall die proudly."

"Damn you, you blasted martyr!" shouted Savage.

"You are ze stupeed fool!" cursed D'Arcy. "Eef only zair was time, I would fight you right heer and beat you into ze ground! Weeth so much pleasure!"

Both of them raised up their weapons. Savage said to Jennifer, "Stay here." Then he and D'Arcy rushed forward down the side passageway, Kaheeli between them with his scimitar high above his head.

When they reached the doorway, Savage looked at the other two, who nodded. He threw open the door. Jennifer could see at least half a dozen Redcoats inside, turning in surprise toward the open doorway. Kaheeli let out a terrifying, blood-curdling yell and the three of them rushed forward into the room.

Jennifer heard the clash of sabers and saw the fierce, rapid movements of close-quarters combat. She rushed forward down the passageway and stopped several inches back from the open door. Savage was fighting off two Redcoats at once, she saw. D'Arcy ran a man through as she watched, then swiveled sharply to engage another.

Kaheeli was swinging his scimitar in a broad circle, holding several Redcoats at bay, slashing one who did not retreat quickly enough as Kaheeli advanced. A Redcoat behind D'Arcy raised a musket to D'Arcy's head. Jennifer aimed her pistol and fired, watching the bright dot of red blood spurt from the man's forehead, as he tumbled over backward.

From the side of the doorway, out of her view, someone grasped her out-thrust arm at the wrist and pulled her forward. Then the man leapt upon her, knocking her to the ground. He was a bulging-eyed, pink-faced Redcoat, whose teeth were bared as he clasped his hands around Jennifer's throat, strangling her. She squirmed and kicked and arched her body to no avail. She scratched at the man's face with her nails, as faintness descended upon her.

She was slowly losing her vision when she saw a boot catch the man square in the mouth and he tumbled backward away from her, clutching at his bloody face.

She looked. Kaheeli had kicked the man. He could not follow through with his attack, though, for he was engaged in a violent, swinging swordfight with another Redcoat. Jennifer grasped hold of the fallen musket of the Redcoat she had shot, not raising it up from the ground, just holding it. When the bulging-eyed man rushed toward her, she raised up the muzzle end with abrupt suddenness, impaling him in the chest with the bayonet. He screamed and blood oozed out of his mouth.

She looked up quickly. D'Arcy was fighting only one man now and, as she watched, Savage ran one man through and turned to fight another. These were the last of the Redcoats who remained standing and unbloodied. Kaheeli was free from his foe, who lay dead at his feet. He rushed to the wall and grabbed a ring with a massive, heavy key on it, from the peg where it was suspended. He inserted the key into the dungeon door, turned it, and shoved the door open. Then he turned to the Redcoat D'Arcy was fighting and kicked the man hard in the small of his back. The man's arms jerked up in the air. D'Arcy lunged low on one knee and ran him through the midsection.

Savage found an opening in the guard of the Redcoat he was fighting and stepped in quickly, smashing the man's jaw with the hilt of his heavy saber. The man crumpled to the ground.

The four of them looked at each other. They were alone. They were victorious. Kaheeli smiled triumphantly at D'Arcy and Savage, his eyes appearing wild. Then he burst through the dungeon door. Jennifer and the others followed him.

They were on a small stairway landing. Stone steps built against the stone wall descended down to the dungeon below. It was dark and dank and musty smelling. Straw covered the floor. Lighting came from several torches in holders on the walls. At least a hundred ragged, starvation-thin men looked up from the dungeon floor.

It appeared as if they could not believe their eyes. "Kaheeli?" said a hesitant voice. "Kaheeli?" said another. A chorus of tentative voices arose, all asking the same question. Kaheeli beamed with a wild-eyed, full-faced grin at them and thrust his arms out to the sides, over his head.

"Kaheeli!" came a shout. "Kaheeli!" cried another. Other voices joined the chorus, and soon the walls of the dungeon echoed resoundingly with the joyous, exultant cry. "Kaheeli!" they screamed. "Kaheeli!" they exulted, the sounds reverberating ceaselessly throughout the dungeon.

Kaheeli descended the stone steps. "You are free!" he shouted at the men, his words echoing back at him from the stone walls. "Do not rejoice yet, though, for you may die before the day is through. Fighting rages beyond these dank walls. The Kurds are being engaged by the British! Both are our enemies. Now the fighting dies down to its lowest ebb, so now we attack! *We can win!* Both sides are weakened from fighting, but we? We are strengthened! We are invigorated by freedom!" He shouted at the men: "Now you are free men, and now we free Jazirat from the foreigners who wish to enslave us!"

A wild rousing cheer went up from the men below.

"These are our saviors," Kaheeli declared, waving an arm toward Savage and D'Arcy and Jennifer.

"Isabella!" declared a hateful voice from within the throng of Arabs. The cheers died away.

"No!" shouted Kaheeli. "She has only posed as Isabella to aid us! She is an impostor. Now you have the chance to strike at the *real* Isabella, and at the Kurds and the British. Now—into the breach!"

Savage grabbed Jennifer's hand and pulled her down the steps with him as he and D'Arcy descended. Jennifer understood. If they were caught on the stair landing as these rabidly excited men surged forward, or in the corridor on their way to the door leading outside the castle walls, they would be crushed in the excitement and trampled to death.

They reached the dungeon floor and moved quickly off to the side, just as Kaheeli shouted, "To the battle! Arm yourselves with weapons from those you slay! Onward! Onward! To free Jazirat!" The horde of screaming, wild-eyed men rushed forward, surging up the stairs in an endless wave. Jennifer and D'Arcy flattened themselves against the wall to avoid being swept along in the tide of bodies. Savage flattened himself over Jennifer, pressing her tight against the wall.

Then the wave of bodies was past them, up the stairs, and out the doorway. Savage grasped Jennifer's hand and prepared to rush up the stairs immediately too, to waste not another second in making their escape. But Kaheeli moved away from the wall where he had flattened himself and held up a hand, stopping Savage.

"If you wait a few moments more, your chances will be better," he said. "My men will burst upon the battle with the fierceness of lions, attacking Kurds and British alike. The attention of those you wish to escape will be diverted by the attack. They will be less likely to notice as you rush off."

Savage was keyed with excitement. He did not want to wait. But he could see the wisdom of the advice and he nodded sharply, frowning in frustration.

Kaheeli clasped his hands on Savage's shoulders and embraced him tightly. He went to D'Arcy and did the same, while D'Arcy scowled. "The two of you have saved my country from the curse of tyranny," he declared.

He went to Jennifer. "But especially you," he said. "You are the heroine of our rebellion, the savior and redeemer of my people." He clasped his hands on her shoulders and looked her in the eyes intensely. She looked back at him, her eyes wide and uncertain, her lips slightly parted.

"You kees her and I run you through," D'Arcy said.

Kaheeli drew Jennifer forward and embraced her tightly. Then he stepped back and raised his scimitar. "I go now to lead my people to victory." He started up the steps.

Just then a weaving, unsteady figure came into the doorway at the top of the stairs. It was Isabella, wearing the green, veiled halter and britches Jennifer had originally come in. She had a pistol in her hand, which she waved about jerkily. Her eyes were barely opened slits and she was staggering about as if in a stupor. "There you are, impostor," she screamed. "*One* Isabella is all there's room for on this island!" She pointed the pistol at Jennifer.

Savage leapt forward in front of Jennifer just as Isabella pulled the trigger. He caught the ball high in his chest, just below his left collarbone. It ricochetted up and came out through the top of his shoulder. Jennifer screamed.

The Queen turned to leave, but then suddenly there was someone else on the stairs with her. It was Randisan in his black robe with the wide golden belt. "Traitor!" he yelled. "Armed reinforcements from the ship, you say! Not there! Not there! Slaughtered we are!" He slashed her across the side with his scimitar, slicing deeply into her, making her stagger off the landing and crash down to the dungeon floor below.

Randisan looked down now and saw Savage and D'Arcy—and Jennifer. He looked aghast. At the last moment, he turned his attention down to Kaheeli, who was charging up the stairs at him. But it was too late. Kaheeli's blade sliced into him, withdrew, and sliced into him again. Then Kaheeli kicked the man over the side, down to the dungeon floor to join Isabella. He rushed back down the stairs and went to Savage, who was being held up by D'Arcy. "How is he?"

"Not good," said D'Arcy. "Ze bullet eez not zair, but ze blood, he loses eet quickly."

"I'm all right," said Savage, forcing himself to straighten up and stand under his own power. Jennifer could see the effort it took. He winced against the pain, his face sheathed in dripping wet sweat.

"If only Elizar were here," lamented Kaheeli. "The old Arab has potions to stem the flow of blood as well as—"

"I'm fine!" Savage shouted. "Now stop this chattering and let's get the hell out of here!"

Kaheeli tore a strip of cloth from his robe and wrapped it tightly around Savage's torso, diagonally so that it covered the wound in his chest and shoulder. The bandage greatly lessened the flow of blood. "The placement of the wound," said Kaheeli, "it is not a fatal one—if he reaches a physician in time. The blood can flow at this rate for two hours maybe, without killing him. But after that. . . ."

They started up the stairs, Kaheeli and D'Arcy aiding Savage, supporting much of his weight. Jennifer came up behind. Her eyes were wide and she was trembling. There was a voice in her head. She realized she was praying. *Don't let him die, please, dear God, don't let him die!*

They moved down the passageway toward the door

leading to the outside. They went through the door. They were in the sunlight and open air now, standing in a rocky field. The stone castle wall was directly behind them. Shouts and screams and musket blasts came from within the walls.

They moved along the wall toward the nearest corner, where D'Arcy stuck his head forward and peered around the corner to see the front of the castle. Then he drew his head back. "Only three Redcoats," he said to Kaheeli, "guarding many horses."

"They must have moved the horses out from the courtyard," Kaheeli said, "to prevent the Kurds from mounting and escaping."

Savage had slumped down slightly, his back leaning against the stone wall. Now he straightened up and said, "Let's go. Three of them, three of us."

D'Arcy put a hand gently against his chest to stop him from moving forward. He grinned an awkward, sheepish grin at Savage. "Stay weeth heem," he said to Jennifer. Then he and Kaheeli bent over low and rushed around the corner.

Savage was gazing at her steadily. His grin was tender. He put a hand to her cheek and brushed away a streaming tear. Then he pulled her to him and kissed her, a long, gentle, loving kiss. She felt his lips pressing against hers, while hearing the sounds of gunfire and agonized screams. "This is hardly the appropriate place for it," Savage said, "but I'll tell it to you anyway. In case you haven't remembered. I love you." She pressed against him, clasping her hands tightly behind him, her cheek against his neck. "The time I spent away from you, doubting you. What a fool I was."

She hugged herself to him, crying silently. "The wound isn't so bad," she said. "If we can only get you to a surgeon . . ."

He made no reply.

She was hugging him tightly, her cheek against his chest, when D'Arcy and Kaheeli came back from around the corner. They were leading three horses, each of the men carrying an armload of muskets. Kaheeli walked with a pronounced limp. His right leg below the knee was sheathed in blood.

D'Arcy saw Jennifer's unguarded expression as she stood with her cheek against Savage's neck. It made him stop short and stare at the expression on her face. His jaw dropped slightly open and a look of agonizing realization came to his eyes. Jennifer turned her head away so that she would not have to see the pain he was suffering. She knew that now, for certain, he knew. If there had been doubt in his mind about which of them she loved more dearly, with the fullness of her heart, there could be doubt no longer.

D'Arcy slowly regained his composure. He came up to them and said to Savage, "Come, we get you up." He put down his muskets and, with Kaheeli's help, hoisted Savage onto the steed. D'Arcy picked up one of the muskets he had brought and held it out to Savage. "Can you carry thees?"

"Of course I can carry it. You think I'm a bloody invalid?" He grasped the musket and laid it across the saddle before him. Then, when a bolt of pain hit him, he lurched forward in the saddle, his head down near the horse's neck.

Jennifer mounted up and took two of the muskets Kaheeli gave her, holding them across the saddle in front of her. D'Arcy mounted up and also took two muskets. Then he grabbed the reins of Savage's steed. But Savage grabbed them back away from him. "It's not as bad as you think," Savage said, his voice low and strained. D'Arcy looked at him skeptically, but did not attempt to take back the reins.

"You are not coming?" D'Arcy said to Kaheeli.

"My fight is here with my people."

"Get a bandage on zat leg."

"Yes. I will do that." Kaheeli went to Jennifer and squeezed her hand. Then he took the last musket and limped over to the corner of the wall, trailing blood. "I think they will not see you as you ride onto the road. If

500

any attempt to follow, I will shoot the first of them. 'Tis a pity you must take this road that's so visible from the castle courtyard, but truly there is no other. The sides of this hillside are steep."

"*Au revoir*," D'Arcy said to Kaheeli. "I weesh you luck in ze fight against ze Breeteesh."

"Goodbye," Jennifer said to Kaheeli. He smiled up at her with all the arrogance and conceit at his command, making her remember that she had once foolishly disliked this man. He peered around the corner, waited a moment, then raised up his musket and yelled "Now!"

The three of them galloped forward, D'Arcy in the lead, Jennifer and Savage on a line behind him. They galloped onto the road. To the rear they heard someone yell, "Lieutenant! There he be, the one who captained the *Bonny Lynne!* The one who deep-sixed His Majesty's frigate in the harbor!"

"After them!" shouted another British voice.

Jennifer heard a shot fired and the voice that had spoken last suddenly screamed in pain. She did not turn back to look. She was riding hard, her eye on Savage riding at her side. His posture was slumped forward and his face pained, but his jaw was clenched in tense determination and his hands were steady as they gripped the reins. D'Arcy kept glancing back, too, to look at Savage.

When they reached the base of the hill, D'Arcy led them to the left, toward the north ridge, which was the beach nearest the castle, where the longboat had been left for them. As they moved off to the side, Jennifer could see the winding road they had just traveled down. A dozen mounted riders were rushing away from the castle at full gallop after them. Finally the short stretch of the ridge was in sight, no more than a ship's length from end to end, stretching between two high cliffs. Off in the distance, Jennifer could see the *Liberty,* cruising into view.

They raced toward the ridge, but then had to slow

their horses when they reached the stretch of sand just in front of it. They dismounted when they reached the ridge. D'Arcy started to assist Savage who shook him off, saying, "Turn your attention to the muskets, not to me!"

D'Arcy grabbed up three muskets in his arms, carried them over to the ridge, and dropped them down on the far side of it. He motioned for Jennifer to drop her muskets down there also. Then he shooed the horses away.

"Why leave the muskets on the ridge?" Jennifer asked.

Neither D'Arcy nor Savage answered, though they exchanged a hard knowing look with each other. D'Arcy helped Savage over the ridge, while Jennifer put Savage's arm around her shoulder from the other side and tried to support part of his weight. Savage's face was tensed and sweating with agony.

The longboat rested peacefully in the water only a few yards in front of them and off to the side. It rose and lowered with the tide, its bowline fastened to a long stake that had been pounded into the ground.

Jennifer looked back at the ridge. Beyond it, she could see the riders coming nearer, a cloud of dust trailing in their wake.

D'Arcy tried to walk Savage out to the longboat, but Savage pushed him away, almost falling down without the support, and said, "Oh no you don't."

D'Arcy looked at him steadily. "I do, Lancelot."

"You don't, I say!"

"What is this?" Jennifer asked frantically. What could they possibly be arguing about *now*, when each second was crucial?

"Get in ze boat," D'Arcy ordered her. She did as she was told. Then she watched Savage and D'Arcy facing each other down in an intense battle of wills. Savage had strained every muscle in his body to allow himself to stand fully upright and the agony of the effort showed in his white, drained-of-color face.

502

Jennifer looked with urgent desperation at the two of them, then looked beyond the ridge at the riders drawing nearer with each passing second. Then she looked back at the two of them and finally she understood: One of them would have to stay. If all three of them rowed away in the longboat, the Redcoats would reach this beach and begin firing at them within minutes. They would be easy targets, unable to row fast enough to get out of range of the Redcoats' withering barrage. They would be killed while floundering about in the sea.

Their only chance was for one of them to take up a position on the beach side of the high ridge and fire on the Redcoats to prevent them from reaching the beach . . . while the others rowed away out of range of the muskets. That was why they had left the weapons on the ridge.

"I'm the Captain," Savage said. "You're my Mate, and you do as I say. Get in the boat and return to the ship."

"You are ze Captain," D'Arcy said, grinning softly. "I am only ze Mate. So *you* must return to ze sheep. She eez your sheep." He spread his palms, as if in helplessness against the flawlessness of his own logic.

"Get in the blasted boat, damn you! There isn't time for this!" He started moving toward the muskets on the ridge.

D'Arcy swept him up in his arms, carried him over to the longboat, as he struggled against him, and laid him gently inside. Savage started to rise, but a bolt of pain shot through him and he lay back down breathlessly, knowing he would not be able to rise without aid. "You realize this is insubordination," he said to D'Arcy, looking at him with deep affection.

"So court martial me. Anyway, I always weeshed to be insubordinate. Eet eez een ze noblest tradition of ze Calhouns."

Their stares locked. Jennifer saw the intensity of deep feeling that passed between them. Then D'Arcy turned his head away and came over to where she sat in the boat. He touched her shoulder gently. "*Au revoir, cherie*," he said.

Jeniffer looked at Savage pleadingly. He was grimacing hard against the pain, but managed to nod his head in assent. She leaned forward and threw her arms around D'Arcy, hugging him tightly. "Oh, D'Arcy," she cried. He put his arms around her and squeezed her for a brief instant. Then, as if afraid to let himself continue holding her, he gently pushed her away.

The sound of the riders was very near now. D'Arcy stepped back and looked at her with a loving, tender, agonized expression. He tried—and failed—to make himself grin. Then he unlashed the bowline and shoved the boat into the sea.

Jennifer saw him rushing back toward the ridge and flinging himself down at the very crest of it, as she grasped the oars and began rowing away from shore, pulling with all her strength. The ridge was high enough so she could not see above it once the riders were very near. She saw D'Arcy aim one of the muskets, then saw his shoulder jerk as the weapon discharged, sending a puff of smoke out from the muzzle. He threw down the musket and grabbed the second one, aimed carefully and fired that too. Then he grabbed a third.

Jennifer rowed furiously, moving farther and farther out to sea. The Redcoats had not yet crested the hill. There were many of them and only one of D'Arcy, but none of them wanted to be the first to rush forward, to receive the ball from D'Arcy's musket. She saw D'Arcy's shoulder jerk and heard the discharge of the third musket. She rowed harder. She was almost far enough out to sea now so that she was beyond the range of the Redcoats' guns. D'Arcy was a tiny figure on the coastline, lying on the ridge on his stomach, his legs spread, holding the musket steady. She saw and heard the blast as the fourth musket discharged. He grabbed the single remaining musket.

Behind her, Jennifer heard the cannons from the *Liberty* roar and saw puffs of dust rise up many yards inland. The men aboard ship had seen what was happening and were trying to aid D'Arcy. It was a futile effort. The balls could not stop the individual Redcoats who were storming the ridge.

"Look at me," Savage said. She turned her eyes to him. His face was contorted in pain and was sweating, but he held his eyes on hers, steadily. One hand was pressed up against his shoulder where he was wounded. The other was grasping her ankle very tightly to turn her attention toward him.

She started to raise her eyes back toward the ridge, but Savage said, "Look at me!" His voice was commanding. "Look at me," he said more gently. She locked her eyes onto his. Jennifer's eyes were filled with pain and on the verge of tears. Savage's slate gray eyes were steady and strong.

"Don't take your eyes off mine," he said gently, preventing her from raising her eyes back to the ridge, where D'Arcy by now was probably . . .

"Talk to me," Savage ordered.

"I love you," she said.

"Keep talking."

"I love you, Lancelot." She was crying. Tears rolled down her cheeks onto her bare arms. Her muscles ached with each pull of the oars. She heard the barrage of musket fire from in front of her, one shot after another in rapid succession. The British had taken the ridge, she knew.

Jennifer did not raise her eyes. She kept them locked on the strong, handsome face of Lancelot Savage. And as she said the words, she remembered all the months of agony she had endured, and the tortures she had suffered through, to be able to say these words to him now and have him believe them. "I love you, Lancelot," she said. "You're all I live for. All I want."

His face was wracked with agony, yet his eyes remained locked on hers, steady and unwavering. "Don't

505

think of anything else," he said to her. "Think only of this. We're together now. And we'll be together always . . . my love."

She felt the jolt as the longboat hit the hull of the *Liberty*. The air and water were suddenly filled with diving bodies as men from the ship plunged into the sea to aid them. Jennifer heard musket fire still from the ridge and she almost raised her eyes up to look there. But instead, she rushed quickly forward in the boat, to Savage, and buried her face against his hard chest, sobbing wildly.

His arms closed around her. He held her tightly.